To Robyn

Also from Colleen Gleason and MIRA Books

THE VAMPIRE VOSS
THE VAMPIRE NARCISE

COLLEEN GLEASON

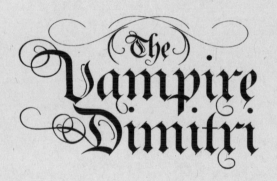

The Vampire Dimitri

MIRA

Recycling programs
for this product may
not exist in your area.

ISBN-13: 978-0-7783-1377-9

THE VAMPIRE DIMITRI

www.Harlequin.com

Printed in U.S.A.

ORROR

1691
A small village in the hills of England

Dimitri stared down at the blood. Everywhere. It was everywhere. On the bedcoverings. On the floor. On the table. On his hands. His arms.

The taste…still in his mouth. Rich, hot, full.

He swallowed the last vestiges on his tongue. *Ambrosia.*

He blinked, trying to focus, but his head pounded. When he tried to lift himself up, his sore muscles protested. Yet, life shimmered through him. His skin prickled, alive. Dimitri tried to breathe, but every breath he took in was laden with the scent. Bloodscent.

And then he remembered.

He remembered how it had happened.

Horror seized him.

And only then did he look over at the bundle of blankets and clothing, the lifeless form in a triangle of sunlight on the floor. One pale, plump arm hung out, marked and torn. Blood seeped everywhere: through thick quilts and the heavy layers of her dress. The mass of graying hair, loose and streaked with blood.

No. No. He held his temples, closed his eyes.

But he couldn't deny it.

And even as he sat there in a room half shadowed and half blazing with sun, Dimitri was filled with loathing and hatred.

No more.

I don't want this. I want out.

"Do you hear me, Lucifer?" he said, his voice hoarse and broken. "I want *out* of this. *Release me.*"

Silence.

Naturally.

For like all angels, fallen or no, Lucifer's preferred method of communication was via dreams. In the deepest of night. When one was the most vulnerable. The most suggestible.

The most easily lured and tricked.

"Release me, you damned bastard!"

But Dimitri already knew there was no way out. He'd already attempted it, tried to break the covenant in the last year since he'd left Vienna. He'd already denied himself what Lucifer had recreated him to need, twenty-five years ago: blood. Rich, warm, lifegiving.

The devil's Mark, depicting the insidious crack in his soul, was imprinted on his back and would never leave him. Thus it had been, for two decades.

And his attempt at self-denial, his attempt to thwart the devil and to break free?

The result was on the floor, a horrifying mess of limbs and tendons and mutilated flesh, destroyed. Dead.

Murdered.

Dimitri pinched the bridge of his nose, hard, a black ball of anger swelling inside him. His eyes stung.

Damn it all…he'd *tried.*

He'd left Vienna after the fire, left a world of opulence and hedonism that he'd never truly enjoyed, and refused it all. A year ago.

For a year, he refused to feed, to drink from anyone. He'd die first, damned or no. Surely if a vampire didn't drink of the lifeblood, he'd grow weak and die.

He'd *force* Lucifer to release him.

But it hadn't worked at all, and it was his very weakness that had caused this tragedy.

For when the old woman had found him, near death, weak after a year without sustenance, he'd been naught but a loose-limbed mass of bone and flesh. Ready to leave the life he'd been tricked into, back when he'd saved Meg twenty-five years ago. When he'd given up everything for her.

The old woman found him here, and tried to help him—for she couldn't have known. She was an innocent. She induced him to drink ale and broth, neither of which could save him.

And Dimitri: all through the night and into the day, day after day, he watched those solid blue veins. He lusted for the curve of her plump neck. He had to close his eyes to keep from taking what every humor in his body demanded.

And he was in control, despite the burning pain from

Lucifer's Mark—the agony that bespoke of the devil's displeasure with Dimitri. He resisted. He fought it.

Nothing was stronger than his resolve. Not even the devil.

Until she nicked her finger with a knife.

And he smelled the blood.

1

WHEREIN LORD CORVINDALE IS REDUCED TO ANALYZING HANDWRITING

One hundred thirteen years later
London

Who in Lucifer's bloody hell did Miss Maia Wood-more think she was, giving orders to an earl?

Dimitri, the Earl of Corvindale, glared down at the elegant script covering a piece of thick stationery. Feminine, perfectly formed, with only the occasional embellishment and not one ink splotch, the words marched across the page in ruler-straight lines. Even the descenders and ascenders were neat and properly aligned so that none of them overlapped. The stationery smelled like feminine spice and lily of the valley and some other intriguing note that he refused to expend the effort to define.

Naturally her demand was couched in the most proper of syntax, but Dimitri was obviously no innocent when it came to female machinations. Though he strictly avoided women—*all* of them, especially the mortal ones—he was well-schooled in the way they worked and in reading between the lines, so to speak.

And from what he read between the lines here, Miss Maia Woodmore was annoyed and filled with indignant self-righteousness, just as she had been during that incident in Haymarket three years ago. And she expected him to jump to her whim.

Lord Corvindale, it read, *forgive me for contacting you in this untoward manner, but it is only upon the specific direction of my brother, Mr. Charles Woodmore, that I am doing so.* (Here he could fairly feel her outrage at being ordered thus by her sibling.)

Mr. Woodmore (who I understand is a business associate of your lordship's) left word that, should I not receive correspondence or communication from him within a fortnight after leaving on his most recent trip to the Continent (which would be by yesterday's date, 18 July, 1804) that I must contact you in regards to the wardship of myself and my two sisters, Angelica and Sonia (the latter of whom is safely ensconced at St. Bridie's Convent School in Scotland).

Dimitri paused in this, his third perusal of the letter, to blink and frown at the precise, if not overlong, sentence. And then he went on to roundly curse Chas Woodmore for somehow convincing him to agree to this madness. It had been more than six years ago that Woodmore had culled such a vow from Dimitri, who'd hardly given it another thought since.

Naturally he never expected Woodmore to do anything as imbecilic as he'd done, running off with Narcise Moldavi instead of killing her brother, which was what he'd gone to Paris to do. Narcise's brother, Cezar, one must assume, would be livid.

But at least Woodmore had made arrangements for the safety of his own sisters, in the event Cezar Moldavi realized who was behind his sister's abduction—or perhaps it was an elopement, not an abduction. He would have no compunction about taking out his ire on three innocent young women.

Cezar certainly hadn't changed since Vienna. If anything, he'd become even more obsessed with power and control.

Dimitri returned to the letter, trying not to acknowledge the exotic perfume that permeated the paper. One of the many curses of being Dracule was his extraordinary sense of smell. Not terribly pleasant, when out and about on the streets of London, and even less so when trying to avoid scenting something he wished to ignore. Reluctantly he read on.

My brother impressed upon me the seriousness of this matter, and it is only because of his specific and unrelenting urgency that I dare send this letter.

I wish to assure you, Lord Corvindale, that the only reason I am contacting you is because of my brother's express wishes. There is truly no need for you to concern yourself with the guardianship of myself and my sisters, for Chas has often been away on business trips and we have fared just as well during his previous absences with the chaperonage of our cousin and her husband, Mr. and Mrs. Fernfeather.

He recalled that, based upon his single previous interaction with her, Miss Maia Woodmore was also this long-winded in person.

In addition, my upcoming wedding to Mr. Alexander Bradington will shortly put me in the position to act as chaperone for my younger sisters.

Dimitri realized he was crinkling the paper and he reminded himself that the written word, regardless of from whom it came, what language it was in, and what message it bore, was precious. Yes, he'd seen the engagement announcement in the *Times* some months ago. The news had been welcome to those who followed that sort of *on dit*—which certainly didn't include the reclusive Earl of Corvindale.

At that time (Miss Woodmore's perfect hand continued in its no-nonsense manner) *your services as guardian to my sisters and myself will no longer be necessary.*

*In fact, (*here her penmanship became the slightest bit thicker and perhaps even more precise) *I see no reason for you to bestir yourself in regards to my sisters and myself at all, Lord Corvindale. Despite my brother's concern, which I can't help but believe is overly cautious and more than a bit exaggerated, Angelica and I shall fare perfectly well in London on our own until Chas returns.*

I look forward to receiving a response at your earliest convenience.

Which meant, Dimitri knew, immediately upon receipt of the letter. Miss Woodmore was thus doomed to disappointment, for the message had arrived early this morning, when he was still asleep at his desk. Not that he would have jumped to respond to her anyway.

She signed her name simply, *Maia Woodmore.*

And there, for the first time, was a bit of feminine

embellishment, just on the lower curve of the *M* and on the upper swoop of the *W*.

Unfortunately for Miss Maia Woodmore, Dimitri had already been…what was the word? *Bestirred.*

Indeed, he'd been more than merely bestirred relative to their guardianship. And, he snarled to himself, it was only going to get worse. He was going to have to bring the chits into this very household if he meant to keep them safe from Moldavi and his private army of vampire goons. Damn Chas Woodmore's mortal arse.

Dimitri happened to know that Moldavi was in Paris with his nose permanently inserted in the crack of Napoleon Bonaparte's arse—or perhaps this fortnight he was licking the new emperor's bollocks—and it would take him some time to send his men after Woodmore and his sisters. But not very much time, despite the war between their two countries.

Which meant that Dimitri must move quickly.

He looked around his study, swathed in heavy curtains to keep out the sun. Books and papers were piled everywhere and shelves lined the walls, crammed full with even more tomes and manuscripts. An utter mess, Mrs. Hunburgh claimed, but she wasn't allowed into the chamber at all except for a weekly dust and sweep. No one else was allowed in but for the occasional visit by Dimitri's butler or valet.

And blast it, he'd intended to visit the antiquarian bookstore next to Lenning's Tannery again today. He meant to ask the blonde woman, who dressed as if she were a thirteenth-century chatelaine instead of a shopkeeper, about references—scrolls, papyruses, whatever—from Egypt in particular. He cursed under his breath. Now he wouldn't have the chance.

Napoleon Bonaparte had brought chests and crates of antiquities back from his travels through and conquest of Egypt, and the objects were being sold and distributed throughout Europe. Surely there was something in the ancient world of pharaohs and sun gods that would help Dimitri banish the demon of darkness who'd lured him into an unholy contract decades ago. Even though Vlad Tepes, the Count Dracula, had made his agreement with Lucifer in the fifteenth century, Dimitri suspected that his ancestor hadn't been the first mortal to sell his soul—and that of his progeny—to the devil. The legend of Johann Faust had become popular after Vlad's agreement, but there had to have been others since the beginning of time. He'd studied manuscripts and writings of the Greeks and Romans, even some from Aramea and other parts of the Holy Land.

Perhaps there would be something he could glean from the Egyptian antiquities and hieroglyphs that would give him direction. Not that anyone had been able to break the code of the Egyptian alphabet yet, but Dimitri was determined to try his hand at it.

After all, he had forever to do it.

And now the stele that had been found in Rosetta several years ago by the French, and was currently in the possession of the Antiquarian Society here in London, looked promising for translating the hieroglyphs. Thus, Dimitri was hopeful. He would love to get his hands on the stone himself, but that would mean having to be around *people* and playing politics and listening to gossip and jests and having to avoid the sun in public company…and all sorts of things he'd much rather avoid.

He'd considered stealing—rather, *borrowing* the so-called Rosetta Stone for a time in order to work on it himself, but in the end decided against it. Perhaps he might break into the British Museum, where it was kept, and make a rubbing of it one night—if he didn't have to spend his bloody time accompanying debutantes to masques and balls. His jaw hurt where his teeth ground together.

There was no way around it.

The two elder Woodmore sisters would soon be overrunning his solitude, upsetting his household and interrupting his studies. And, blast it all, so would Dimitri's own so-called sibling, Mirabella—for naturally, he'd have to bring her into Town, as well. He'd adopted the foundling as his sister years ago—and he supposed he'd put off her debut as long as he could. The very thought of three debutantes in his house made him grind his teeth sourly.

All of them would be disrupting his schedule and nattering on about parties and fetes and balls and whatever else they did. Squealing, laughing, atomizing perfume and spilling powder—and Luce's dark soul, Dimitri would have to ensure no one had any rubies with them.

Bloody black hell.

But Dimitri knew that the worst of it was going to be the very proper, very demanding presence of Miss Maia Woodmore.

Here. In this house. Under his very nose.

If Chas Woodmore was still alive when they found him, Dimitri was going to kill the bastard.

* * *

Maia Woodmore was fuming—which was something she rarely lowered herself to do.

In fact, unlike her younger sister Angelica, Maia had forced herself to become a paragon of poise and containment and propriety. Except, it seemed, in the case of contrary, arrogant, annoying *earls* named Corvindale.

It was as if all of the men in her life—whether she wanted them there or not—had decided to go off all shilly-shally and leave her to pick up the pieces and manage their leftovers. A task she was, thankfully, more than capable of doing, regardless of whether she wanted to or not. After all, it seemed as if she'd *always* been in charge, *forever* trying to make things right, trying to keep her younger sisters safe, well loved and well cared for.

At least, since their parents died.

Included in Maia's mental tirade, along with Corvindale, was her elder brother, Chas, who was always haring off somewhere and leaving her to manage things—not an easy task when one was an untitled, unmarried, somewhat-rich young woman of the *ton*. It was his great fortune that she was not only up to the task, but efficient and capable of doing so.

And also included in her annoyance was her fiancé, Alexander Bradington, who'd proposed on her eighteenth birthday, and then went off on a trip to the Continent three months later. He'd been gone for eighteen months.

But the Earl of Corvindale was the absolute worst of the bunch.

Alexander had been engaged in Rome and Vienna for

the past several months, delayed because of the war with France—which was hardly his fault, she allowed. But she *missed* him, and if he were here, they could just get married and chaperone Angelica and Sonia themselves.

Chas had once again gone off on some mysterious business trip, but this time, things were different. He'd left behind a note that made it sound as if the world was to end like it had in Pompeii, or France was to invade if he didn't return within a fortnight. To Maia's increasing concern, he hadn't. She'd be blazingly furious with Chas for foisting her and Angelica on the dratted Earl of Corvindale if she weren't so worried that something horrible had happened to their brother.

But Corvindale was here in London, and he had not only ignored her very polite missive—which had only been sent out of courtesy—but now, as she looked up at his dark, hawkish, arrogant face, he raised an eyebrow and eyed her as if she were some sort of crawly insect.

"Of course I received your letter," Corvindale said. His voice was flat with boredom. "I am the only Corvindale, am I not?"

"But you didn't deign to respond," Maia replied, attempting, rather admirably, she thought, to keep her voice level. Although, due to the fact that they were in the midst of a rather large crush at the Lundhames' annual summer ball, she did have to raise its volume to be heard over the conversation and music buffeting against them.

She and Angelica hadn't chosen to attend this event merely because they expected Corvindale to be here; in fact, she rather assumed he wouldn't bother to show at the Lundhames' any more than he had lowered himself to respond to her letter. Everyone knew the earl was a recluse who cared only for ancient manuscripts and scraps of parchment.

But here he was. Lifting that dark brow and looking down at her from his excessive height as if he couldn't spare the time to converse with her. Well, she fumed, the feeling was quite mutual.

"I consider the fact that we are conversing a fair response," Corvindale replied. "Particularly since, as I recall, we've never been properly introduced." His dark eyes gleamed.

Maia's face, blast her fair skin, went warm, and likely pinker than the roses on the shoulders of her cornflower-blue gown. No, indeed, they hadn't ever been *formally* introduced. But she certainly knew who he was—the tall, imposing man whose very presence at any social event was cause for the gossips to strain in their corsets to get a glimpse of him…let alone happen to speak with the rude, prideful earl.

And he certainly knew who she was…and not just because he and Chas had been business associates for years, and occasionally they'd attended the same events. She'd hoped that Corvindale hadn't realized it was she during that horrid night at Haymarket she'd come to think of as the Incident.

Maia held her breath so that the flush would dissipate and tried not to meet his eyes. Surely he wouldn't be rude enough to mention the Incident if he did realize it had been she. But he *couldn't* have recognized her. After all, she'd been dressed like a boy.

"Allow me to set your mind at ease, Miss Woodmore," he said, the boredom having returned as he glanced at the cluster of people behind her. "I will send instructions on the morrow with arrangements for you and your sister to move to Blackmont Hall until your brother returns."

He would send instructions? With arrangements? She folded her lips together in an effort to keep from telling him exactly how she felt about being told what she would do and how and when—without any consultation on her part—and by a man she had fairly detested on sight. Even three years ago.

How kind of you, Lord Corvindale, to at least apprise me of your intentions. Just like every other man in the world, including her brother, he had no regard for her opinion or feelings. It was as if she had the mind of a china doll. If they only realized how much she handled on a daily basis, how much she knew and comprehended about their world and its history.

She certainly had no intention of leaving her home at the drop of a pin to live at his, but Maia didn't have the time or the desire to discuss the "arrangements" with him further, for the prickling lifting the hair on her arms indicated that her headstrong sister Angelica was about to get herself into some sort of improper situation.

Unlike her two younger sisters, Maia hadn't been blessed with the Sight from their half-Gypsy grandmother. Yet, she possessed a keen intuition for brewing trouble that often manifested itself in a simple sort of *knowing*.

The Sight works in strange ways. Her Granny Grapes had said that, more than once when Maia expressed juvenile envy that her sisters seemed to have acquired the Sight, but she had not. That was when she was young and childish and didn't realize what a terrible burden it was for Angelica and Sonia.

So childish. But she'd long grown past that, realizing that her role was to protect and care for her more vulnerable sisters, particularly after the death of their parents. And she excelled at that, just as she did everything else. Except translating Greek, which she found a necessary evil, but the effort worthwhile.

And, she supposed, that sort of intuitive, prickling *knowing* when something was wrong, or odd, was perhaps her own version of the Sight.

"Very well, my lord," Maia said, making her voice sound rather like a queen agreeing to an audience with her subject. "I shall review your correspondence on the morrow."

She turned before he could respond, and immediately spotted Angelica in an intense, probably improper, conversation with Lord Dewhurst and his companion Lord Brickbank. Her sister was fresh and lovely in an Empire-waisted, butter-yellow gown, with her dark, almond eyes and gypsyish coloring. Not the usual peaches-and-cream coloring of every other female Londoner, like Maia herself.

And it took Maia only one good look to know that the Viscount Dewhurst was precisely the sort of man she had warned her sister about. A tawny-haired, golden god of a man with an insouciant smile, melting eyes and a neckcloth that had probably taken a dozen tries to fold properly, he was a rake of the first order, no doubt about it. The way he was eyeing Angelica as if he couldn't tear his gaze away was enough to make Maia herself feel all warm and tingly deep inside.

If Alexander ever looked at her like that, Maia would probably melt into a pool of skin and bones at once. She already felt warm and heart-rushed when he kissed her and slid his hand around the neckline of her bodice.

But, interestingly enough, Angelica wasn't speaking to Dewhurst. She seemed to be engaged in conversation with the red-nosed Lord Brickbank, who was staring at her in confusion.

"An*gel*ica," Maia snapped, moving toward her sister. It was beyond unseemly for her to be talking with two men that neither of them formally knew, and it was up to Maia to put a stop to it without causing an even greater scene. If she hadn't been distracted by the earl, this wouldn't even be a problem.

But before she could do so, Angelica gave a short little curtsy and took her leave of the gentlemen. Seeing Maia, the younger woman smiled saucily at her sister, then slipped off to dance with Mr. Tillingsworth for the new quadrille.

Well, at least the worst harm Mr. Tillingsworth would do to Angelica would be to put her into a catatonic state as he talked about his cats, ad nauseam. That was the benefit to dancing a country dance instead of walking through the garden or park with an uninteresting gentleman. At least during the dance, one was separated from one's partner often enough that it gave one a rest from an uninspiring conversation, whereas when one took a turn about the room or the patio, one could hardly hope for such a reprieve.

Angelica thus engaged, that left Maia exactly where she wished to be: unencumbered, and able to relax her vigilance long enough to enjoy a dance set herself. Despite the fact that Alexander wasn't even in England, there was no reason she couldn't participate in one of the box or line dances.

Casting a quick glance at Angelica, who was just setting up in the new set, Maia checked her dance card and noted that Ainsworth was her next partner. At least he wouldn't stomp on her feet, like Mr. Flewellington had done earlier.

As Maia bowed to Lord Ainsworth, she happened to notice Corvindale. He was standing in a secluded corner—a rarity in such a crush, but somehow he'd managed it—and was glowering. She couldn't tell at whom he was glaring; it was a general scowl, directed, it seemed, to the room at large.

There were women, she supposed, who would find the earl's dark, arrogant looks attractive—and would suffer his less-than-charming personality. He had a fine nose, long and not too broad, and a wide, square jaw. His cheekbones were high and sharp, giving his entire face the look of a stone bust finished with a large chisel rather than the finesse of a rasper or sandpaper. And since he tended toward dark colors in his clothing, his large shoulders and height were even more pronounced.

Maia lifted her nose and smiled at Ainsworth and tried very hard to push away the uncomfortable prickling of the fine hairs on her arms. The very last thing, the *last* thing, she wanted was to be living in that man's house—guardian or no.

The chit had no idea how much danger she and her sister were in. If she did, she wouldn't be lifting her pert little nose at Dimitri from across the room after telling him she would "review your correspondence on the morrow."

He willed the annoyance away, waiting for his fangs to retract into their sheaths. And the pounding to cease rushing through his veins.

The last time he'd been this discomfited by a woman had been the day Meg told him she was leaving. This was, of course, a completely different case. But the fact remained: Miss Woodmore made his blood boil and his veins bulge.

And not in a good way.

If the ever-proper miss had any concept how quickly he'd acted since he'd learned of Chas's disappearance, how thorough he had been in ensuring that the youngest of her sisters would remain safe at St. Bridie's (what a ridiculous name for a convent of nuns since none of them would ever become brides) in Scotland, and the fact that since three days ago and unbeknownst to them, she and her middle sister had been under his protection, her haughty look might be deflated into something more grateful.

But probably not. The more cornered and surprised she was, the more indignant she became. After all, he'd experienced her sharp tongue once before when she was cornered and surprised. She simply didn't remember it.

And aside of that, he saw no reason to inform Miss Woodmore of the danger lurking in the background. Chas Woodmore's secret life was just that—a secret, just as the existence of the Draculia was also undisclosed to the world at large.

Dimitri remained still, watchful for any sign that Moldavi had acted sooner than he had expected. His arms were folded across his middle as he scanned the room. Filled with colors too bright and bold, too many people, and, worst of all, a veritable mash of smells—most of them unpleasant or too strong—the ballroom represented everything he'd tried to avoid for…oh, the last century or more.

Emphasis on the *more*.

Most of his acquaintances assumed that Dimitri's avoidance of all things unrelated to his studies had to do with the fire in Vienna when Lerina died, but they would be wrong. Certainly, the event was a contributing factor, but his distaste for the life of a Dracule went much deeper than the loss of an investment and an accidental death. His discontent had started with Meg, twenty-four years earlier, when he'd saved her life and first become Dracule.

But the culmination of his journey to the life he lived now—the rigid, solitary, ironically Puritan one—had been That Day. That morning, when he'd awakened to find that even a year of denying himself had not released him from Lucifer. It had, in fact, bound him to the devil all the more tightly because of his murder of the old woman whose name he'd never known. An old woman who'd simply tried to help him.

He'd not made the same mistake since. He now consumed sustenance, never allowing himself to become so desperate as to maul a person to death—as most vampires were able to do.

He simply no longer took the blood from living bodies, thus denying himself the pleasure and satiation of the past. There was hope that, perhaps one day, the self-denial would be enough to grant him release from a demon who thrived on selfishness and self-centeredness. In the meantime, he studied every ancient document he could get his hands on, looking for another way.

Any way.

And the ever-present ache from his Mark, radiating down and behind his left shoulder, was a constant reminder of Lucifer's fury with him. The rootlike black marking extended from beneath the hair at the left side of his neck down over his shoulder and halfway down his back. It was a visible sign of his cracked and damaged soul, and the more annoyed Lucifer became, the more it throbbed and filled, rising up like twisting black veins.

The Mark twinged now as Dimitri edged against the wall to allow a promenade of three to mince past. They'd circled by thrice since he'd come to stand here, and he eyed them darkly. One of the women—the one in the center—met his eyes boldly as they brushed by in a wave of at least five different floral scents, along with powder and body heat, and Dimitri acknowledged her with a cold, uninterested look.

Women, especially mortal women, were the last thing on his mind.

Miss Woodmore was smiling as Ainsworth hooked her elbow and spun her in a neat circle before moving on to the next steps in the dance that separated them, and then brought them back, glove to glove. At least the dress she wore wasn't pink or yellow, but an unassuming blue with discreet pink roses on the shoulders. It clung and slid along her hips and thighs like damp silk as she moved through the paces, and Dimitri wondered darkly if Chas had seen and approved of that frock.

A sudden waver in his vision and a heaviness in his chest had Dimitri removing his gaze from the dancers and focusing on a couple strolling past. The female half was wearing ruby earbobs and a matching necklet, which was the reason for his flash of light-headedness. But she was far enough away, and she didn't pause, so the weakness passed almost immediately.

Yet another reason to avoid fetes and balls and dinner parties and Almack's and court. And even, as often as he could manage, Parliament. How he hated sitting in the House of Lords and listening to those mortals natter on about postage laws or minting coins or other inconsequential things like tea taxes. It had been the worst during that mess with the Colonies and the stamp tax imposed on them.

Yes, one never knew when one might be accosted by a ruby, and since Dimitri had been unfortunate enough to acquire that particular gemstone as his Asthenia, he must always be on guard from that danger.

Each of the Dracule, along with gifts of immortality, speed and extraordinary strength, also had a specific weakness endowed upon him by their partner in the dark covenant: Lucifer. Since the ruby festooning Meg's neck was the first thing Dimitri had seen when he woke from that fateful dream one hundred and thirty-eight years ago, his Asthenia was the bloodred gemstone.

Thus, other than a wooden stake to the heart or a decapitating sword, which would kill him, sunlight and rubies were the only things that would weaken or harm him. Despite that inconvenience, he could appreciate that his Asthenia wasn't something as commonplace as silver.

Suddenly Dimitri's eyes narrowed. By the damned bones of Satan, there was Voss again, sniffing around Angelica Woodmore.

Despite his reluctance for the guardianship, Dimitri took his responsibility seriously. Thus he was out from his alcove in a flash and making his way smoothly across the room. He would appear unhurried to anyone watching him, but in reality, he moved faster than a breath. He made his way from one side of the room to the other, through and around and between the crush of people, in an instant.

It wasn't so much anger as it was annoyance that burned through Dimitri as he approached the handsome, well-dressed man. Also a member of the Draculia, Voss, the Viscount Dewhurst, had just returned to London from somewhere in the New World—Boston, perhaps—after a decade of absence. Dimitri would have preferred him to stay away even longer than that, but one couldn't always have what one wished, as was evident by a variety of events in the past few days. This was the second time he'd found Voss accosting Angelica Woodmore tonight, however, and that fact did not sit well with Dimitri.

If he had to guess, he would surmise that Voss had heard the rumors that the middle Woodmore sister possessed the Sight. And Voss, being not only a rake of the highest order, but also a man who dealt with the buying, selling and otherwise hoarding of information, was likely intent on taking advantage of the absence of the chit's brother—and what he perceived as Dimitri's lack of interest in the girls—to see what Angelica could add to his inventory of knowledge.

As he drew closer, he heard Voss murmur something to Angelica about a waltz. And at the same time, Dimitri became excruciatingly aware that Miss Woodmore was approaching from the opposite direction. Her bronze-honey hair fluttered in wayward wisps about her temples as she bore down upon Angelica and her erstwhile suitor.

Dimitri turned his attention to Voss, and, coming up unnoticed behind the man, said, "Miss Woodmore will not be hastening anywhere with you, Voss. Most especially not to a waltz."

He heard the man's annoyed curse under his breath, but to his credit, he turned without hurry. "By Luce, Dimitri, have you not yet attended to that violinist's flat string I mentioned earlier? It's beyond annoying. I'm certain that a mere look from you would tighten it up perfectly."

"I don't know what you're after," Dimitri said, shifting between Voss and the spicy-floral-scented Miss Woodmore, who'd taken her younger sister by the arm and was towing her off in a different direction, "but I suggest that you remain far away from Angelica Woodmore unless you wish to find yourself in a most uncomfortable position. Neither Chas nor I will suffer your attentions to her or the other Miss Woodmore."

Voss gave him that lazy, hooded-eyed look that worked so well to seduce the ladies—even aside of the hypnotic thrall that the Dracule utilized to get what they wanted, when they wanted it. "Of course. The last thing a vampire hunter like Chas Woodmore would tolerate is one of the very creatures he hunts sniffing around his sisters. Never fear, Dimitri," he continued in that smooth, mocking tone, "there are plenty of other fish in the sea—or, as I like to think of it—lovely, narrow wrists, or slender, delicate shoulders to slide into. There's nothing like that pleasure, is there? The penetration…sleek and quick, and then the sudden flood of liquid heat, rich and full." His voice had dropped seductively.

Then Voss worked up an ironic smile. "But, of course, you wouldn't have any recollection of such a pleasure, limiting yourself as you do to bottles of cow's blood from your favorite butcher." He gave a sad shake of his head. "I cannot fathom for what purpose you've chosen the path of abstinence."

"I'm certain you cannot," Dimitri replied coolly. He didn't even bother to display the tips of his fangs. "Such discretion would be beyond your sensibilities."

"Discretion?" Voss's laugh rang out. "Let's call it what it is—self-flagellation, or even martyrdom. What a gray life you must lead, you emotionless bastard."

"Regardless," Dimitri said, "stay away from the Woodmore sisters. I'm fully aware of your penchant for taking whatever is offered—and seizing your desire when one is not forthcoming—and then leaving whatever remains as you saunter on to your next victim. Not to mention your carelessness and silly games."

At last, Voss's face darkened and his eyes burned with a dangerous red glow. "What happened in Vienna with Lerina was an accident, Dimitri, and well you know it."

"That may be the case," he replied, "but it's clear that

even tragedy hasn't caused you to change your manipulative ways in the century since."

Without deigning to wait for the other man's response, Dimitri turned and stalked off. Angelica Woodmore had been taken away by her capable sister and Voss wouldn't dare make another attempt to accost her. At least, not tonight.

Once the Woodmore sisters were safely home, Dimitri could return to his solace and uninterrupted studies for the last time in the foreseeable future.

Although…perhaps on the way home, he might walk through some dark, infamous street in St. Giles or along the river, just so he could be accosted by a gang of thieves or other blackhearts. He was in the mood for a good brawl.

Might as well enjoy as much of the night as he could, for tomorrow, his home would be invaded.

2

OF EGYPTIAN QUEENS

"We're nearly there now." Maia smiled at Corvindale's sister, who sat across from her and Angelica in the closed carriage. She glanced at their other companion and chaperone, Aunt Iliana, and included her in the smile. "The Midsummer Night's Masquerade Ball is one of the most exciting events of the Season."

Mirabella looked as if she were about to explode with anticipation for her first Society event, and Maia couldn't blame her a bit. The poor thing had been left in the country for the past seven years with hardly a visit or communiqué from her elder brother. At seventeen, she'd never been presented at court, and her wardrobe was horribly outdated.

It was really quite irresponsible of the earl—not to mention inconsiderate. How was the girl ever to make a match? She couldn't move about in Society until she was introduced at court, and until that happened, she couldn't even think of meeting a potential husband.

Maia was still seething over the way Corvindale had

fairly yanked the proverbial rug out from under her and Angelica's feet to get them moved to his London residence, with nary a thought to their preference or opinions. It had happened two days ago, so quickly and efficiently that she would have been in awe if she hadn't been so infuriated.

Certainly Maia was used to being the one in charge. And there had been times when she'd wished for a reprieve. But not this way, and not because of an ill-tempered earl.

The morning after the Lundhames' ball, as promised, Corvindale's note had arrived. It simply stated that they would remove to Blackmont Hall after receiving their normal afternoon callers, and they would stay under the earl's guardianship until Chas returned. Before Maia could fly to her study and snatch up stationery to respond in the negative, the earl's staff had arrived to pack their things, and the next thing she knew, the earl was there, as well.

Just as immovable and emotionless as a brick wall, he was, and nothing she said had any effect on him except to prompt that arrogant lifting of the eyebrow.

He'd arrived just in time to catch Viscount Dewhurst—who'd surprised them all by calling that afternoon—as he attempted to woo Angelica in a private corner of their library. Maia had to admit gratitude toward Corvindale for interfering in *that* matter, for Angelica had seemed more than a little starry-eyed when the viscount had arrived. And the more she saw of Dewhurst, the more certain Maia was that the man was of no good character—a rake and a rogue and the last sort of man with whom her beautiful sister should become enamoured. Someone like Lord Harrington would be a much better choice for Angelica.

Not only had Corvindale sent Dewhurst on his way, but Maia had also heard him say that the viscount had to leave immediately for Romania.

As for tonight, since Corvindale had considerately supplied them with a chaperone in the form of Aunt Iliana—who turned out to be a delightful matron, although no one was certain whose aunt she was—Maia really only needed to be concerned with herself. Aunt Iliana seemed like just the sort to watch them all like a hawk, but to have an enjoyable time herself.

Maia fully intended to do so, as well. The urge to relax a bit, to be anonymous and be not quite so on her guard for propriety's sake, stirred inside her. When was the last time she'd actually allowed herself to have fun?

Nevertheless… "Do try to behave with some decorum tonight, Angelica," she lectured her sister as they prepared to disembark from the long line of carriages. They'd arrived at the Sterlinghouse residence. "Put on a good example for Mirabella."

Angelica blasted her with a dark look as she gathered up her flowing Greek-style black gown. She was dressed as one of the Fates, complete with shears and a skein of thread.

"I don't believe you have cause for worry tonight," Angelica whispered back with an arch look. "No one will recognize me until we remove our masks, and so until then, all of my behaviors will be anonymous." She held up the black velvet mask trimmed with a gold and silver lace fall that would offer only teasing glimpses of her cheeks and mouth. "You shall have no scandal by association."

Hmmph. Maia barely held back a roll of the eyes. At least she didn't need to worry that Angelica would be coaxed into a dark corner by Dewhurst, as he was presumably long gone to Romania.

"Even you could do something scandalous, Cleopatra," Angelica murmured, "and no one would know!"

Maia drew herself up and the royal staff nearly rolled off her lap. If Angelica only knew how difficult it was to act stiff and proper all of the time. And why she seemed so unfailingly prim. "I certainly would not," she hissed back, her heart pounding. Having once nearly gone into the abyss of scandal, she would take care never to venture near its edge again. There was that lurking fear that if she relaxed even a trifle, she'd slide back into that black hole of impropriety...and this time, there would be no escape. "And how many times do I have to tell you, I'm Hatshepsut, not Cleopatra."

"Who cares about Hatshep-whoever? No one could tell the difference anyway," Angelica said dismissively.

"There's no asp on my staff," Maia pointed out.

"We're to don our masks before entering?" asked Mirabella, finally able to get a word in.

"Yes. We'll be announced as we arrive, but not with our real identities," Maia explained before Aunt Iliana could speak. "Only by our character or costumes."

She gestured with the gold mask in her hand and caught their chaperone's indulgent eye. At least the elder lady didn't seem to mind Maia's managing ways—which was more than she could say for her own sister. "Everyone is to be unmasked at midnight. Although last year, the unmasking was much later," she continued. "No one was ready until nearly one o'clock."

"It's our turn," Angelica said as the voices of the driver and footman reached them. She was out of the carriage before Maia could respond, followed by Aunt Iliana and Mirabella.

Taking a bit longer, ensuring that her long, whisper-thin glittery-gold gown didn't expose anything scandalous—like an ankle or a knee—Maia allowed the footman to help her alight.

When she stood still, the hem of her gown pooled on the ground in soft waves over her feet, which were encased in sandals with soles so thick that they made Maia as tall as her sister. Instead of hanging in one single-paneled skirt, the gown was actually six panels that overlapped, but that were only sewn together to just below the waist. This meant that there was ample opportunity for the long slits to show the sheer, lace shift she wore beneath it.

Not for the first time, Maia wondered if she'd made a mistake in selecting such a potentially scandalous costume. But she'd loved it the moment the dressmaker showed her the design, and that was the whole purpose of masquerade balls—anonymously walking the line of propriety. And, frankly, she'd hoped that Alexander would be back from Europe to accompany her to this ball so that it wouldn't have mattered whether it was on the line of scandalous or not.

Deep inside, worry gnawed at her. Would he ever return? Had he changed his mind? She pushed the unpleasant thoughts away. Despite his occasional letter, the doubts had been coming more often than not lately. For all of her exterior confidence, Maia felt the fear of rejection, of scandal, of humiliation looming in her future.

And unlike most other problems in her life, this was one she couldn't manage or control. She simply had to wait.

But here she was, without an escort, dressed in a column of cloudlike gold, with an underskirt as sheer and silver as a moonbeam…and completely anonymous. Between the several inches of added height, and the mask, along with the fact that dark horsehair curls had been interwoven with her chestnut hair, it was impossible that she would be recognized; especially since no one would expect prim Maia Woodmore to wear such a thing.

So she allowed herself to relax a bit more than she normally would.

The butler announced, "Her Majesty, Cleopatra, Queen of the Nile." Maia tried to correct him, but there was an angel and a Queen Elizabeth behind her, and the latter's farthingale skirts bumped Maia out of the way as she moved forward, so she gave up. She'd practiced walking in them, but there was no sense in getting herself unbalanced while on these high shoes.

Maia caught a glimpse of Angelica as she disappeared into the crowd. Aunt Iliana was on her heels, with Mirabella clinging to her arm, and Maia, for once, found herself not needing to be vigilant.

She'd hardly taken two more steps when she came face-to-face with a knight. She couldn't see his face, of course, but behind the mask, his eyes seemed familiar.

"Your majesty," he said with a little bow. "I see that you've been neglected by your swains. Would you care for a glass of sparkling champagne punch—or perhaps the effervescent lemonade?"

"A glass of the punch would be divine," Maia replied. She loved champagne, but very rarely had the opportunity to taste it.

"And when I return, perhaps you would care for a dance?" he added with another bow.

"But of course."

And thus the evening began, and soon slipped into a whirlwind of dancing and revelry. Once, as she spun carefully through the steps of a reel, Maia caught sight of a tall figure in a dark mask with a red and black waistcoat making its way quickly through the crowd. He seemed to move with great speed, despite the crush, and for some reason it put her in mind of Corvindale.

That had the effect of souring the evening, and Maia shouted to her current partner—a lanky court jester— a request for a cup of punch. The jester agreed, and led her away from the fracas that was the dance floor.

But her mood had been spoiled, for the very thought of the earl reminded her of their exchange in his study yesterday afternoon. It was the first chance she'd had to actually speak to him when he wasn't ordering her and Angelica about, and he'd been abominably rude, ensconced in his gloomy office with fascinating-looking books stacked hither and yon. He'd practically shouted at her when she tried to open the curtains to give him some light.

Even now, she flushed at the memory of his clipped voice as he looked up from his desk, clearly loath to be interrupted. "What. Do. You. Want. Miss Woodmore."

The periods between each word were clearly enunciated, along with the telling absence of a question mark.

She'd had to swallow a retort at his overt rudeness, and instead marshaled her manners. One really couldn't shout at an earl, especially when one was a guest in his home. She'd said placating things like, "My sister and I are very appreciative that you've agreed to our brother's request to take on our guardianship." And she'd actually managed to sound sincere, and to subdue the urge to lecture him on working in such dim light. "As I mentioned in my letter, I didn't realize he'd made such arrangements with you until he went missing. We've always had Mrs. Fernfeather and her husband when Chas has been gone. Regardless…I do not wish to impose upon you— your household any longer than is strictly necessary."

"That is one thing on which we are in agreement, Miss Woodmore."

By that point, her fingers had clutched her gown so tightly it would be horribly crumpled by the time she loosened it. "And so I wanted to make you aware of our plans to repair to Shropshire as soon as arrangements can be made for the house there to be opened. My fiancé will be arriving from the Continent in short order and once we're wed, you'll no longer be responsible for me, of course. My sisters, including the youngest, will come to live with me and—"

"An odd time to be planning a wedding, with your brother missing, Miss Woodmore. Or are you in such a hurry to marry that you intend to get the deed done before you even learn what has happened to him?"

The memory of those words even now sent anger flashing hotly through her. She'd been trying very hard *not* to worry constantly about Chas's mysterious absence—not to mention Alexander's continued non-appearance (for her claim that he was arriving shortly had been a bald-faced lie)—and the earl's implication that not only did she not care about her brother's disappearance, but that there might be a reason for rushed nuptials, infuriated her. *Pie-faced worm.*

Maia realized she was worrying and fuming again, and she happened to look up as the court jester handed her a cup of sparkling wine punch. It was remarkably cold and quite delicious, with its effervescent bubbles, and she drank it rather more quickly than she should have.

"Perhaps I should procure you another one, my lovely Cleopatra?" asked the jester. "Or would you prefer to get some air?"

Maia declined to correct him about her costume and, at the same time, decided she wasn't about to fall into his little trap and go out into the dark garden. She'd noticed the way the jester had been eyeing her jouncing bosom as they moved through the enthusiastic steps of the reel. He was just the sort to pretend to bump against her and slide his hand around to cup a breast. At least she wasn't wearing a gown with a low-cut bodice, but instead, a heavy Egyptian collar covered her shoulders and the front of her chest.

"Another cup of punch would be lovely," she replied, adjusting her mask.

At least she knew she had no chance of meeting up with Corvindale tonight, for when she'd mentioned the masquerade ball, he'd snorted his contempt for the whole concept and dismissed her from his study.

And she'd been more than happy to leave his arrogant presence, too, Maia thought as she drank a second…or perhaps it was a third…cup of sparkling wine punch. To her mortification, she had to muffle a tiny little burp from the bubbles.

"Madame?"

The jester had moved in rather close to her person, and she realized he'd asked her a question.

"Another dance?" she repeated. That would be the second in a row, which wasn't quite the thing if one wasn't dancing with one's fiancé, unless one wanted to be all over the *Times*'s *on dits*…but then, she was in a mask. And no one would need to know it was the proper Miss Maia Woodmore dancing two sets in a row—

And then she realized it was a waltz.

A thrill of excitement slipped through her. What a dangerous thought. To perform the waltz, the scandalous dance from Vienna that had caused the matrons at Almack's to lift their noses and tighten their jowls at the very thought of the debutantes participating…!

Chas hadn't even officially allowed Maia to waltz with Alexander…although she had managed to do so one time, briefly, in a secluded corridor, without her brother's knowledge until it was too late. And she'd loved it.

Loved being spun through the space in his strong arms, their bodies close together, their *thighs* brushing, the scent of his clothes and hair pomade close and fresh—

Maia realized the jester was waiting for a response, and also, at the same time, that her face was quite a bit warmer beneath her mask. And she was feeling quite a bit more relaxed and happier than previously...

"I should love to waltz, sir jester," she said boldly. And offered him her arm.

They'd taken two steps toward the floor when a large figure garbed in black and ruby appeared, blocking their path.

"How kind of you to fetch my partner for me," he said, speaking directly to the jester. "I was just about to collect her for our dance."

Maia was so surprised that she couldn't speak, and apparently the jester was similarly afflicted, for he merely stared at the man for a moment. She blinked hard, for it almost seemed as if the man's eyes had glowed red for an instant...but then the impression was gone. Then, without another word, the jester bowed, turned and walked away—almost as if he'd been hypnotized.

"Your majesty," said the new arrival, offering her an arm. "Shall we?"

She looked up at him, trying to see behind the mask and to read his eyes, to determine whether she recognized him. There was an aura of familiarity about the man, and for the flash of a moment when she took his arm and felt a little jolt of awareness, she wondered if it might be Alexander. It would be just like him to surprise her thus.

But she quickly revised that thought, tucking it away as wishful thinking. She'd forgotten for a moment her added height; this man was too tall to be her fiancé. His eyes were shadowed by the holes in his mask, which was unrelieved black and left only the very bottom of his face exposed. He wore a dark cloak, and beneath it a waistcoat of bloodred and black, with a brilliant red neckcloth that all but obscured his white shirt. A thumbnail-size ruby in the shape of a diamond studded the center of his neckcloth. She realized he was the tall figure who'd attracted her attention when she was dancing.

"Who are you?" she asked, looping up the extra length of the panels of her skirt into her hand.

He steadied her as they reached the floor and instead of turning her to face him, he shifted to come around to the front of her. "The Knave of Diamonds," he said, lifting her right hand in his gloved one and settling his other one lightly on her waist.

Although the country dances often required a touch at the hip or waist, and arms linking with arms, the position of the waltz was so different, so intimate, because it wasn't a passing position. And as she rested her gloved fingers on his shoulder, felt his fingers close around hers, and the burning weight of his hand at her waist, Maia felt warm, and a little dizzy.

He hesitated a moment before stepping into the dance, and she allowed him to direct her as they moved forward. The first few steps were stilted, as if he had to discover or learn the rhythm, and even then, they didn't spin and whirl with the same smooth alacrity as some of the other dancers. For some reason, she liked the fact that he wasn't so very practiced at the waltz.

Nevertheless, Maia felt as if she floated on a cloud, held steady by the firm grip on her hand and waist. Even with the tall shoes and the unfamiliar three-beat step, she hardly stumbled at all.

She glanced up at him to find her partner looking out

over her shoulder, as if scanning the room. This gave her the chance to examine what little of his countenance was exposed by the mask; namely, the shape of his chin and the formation of his mouth. Even his ears and hair were covered by a black tricorn, and the collar of his cloak came up to shadow his neck and the edge of his jaw.

"Hatshepsut, I presume," he said, glancing down at her as they began their second turn about the floor, still relatively slowly and carefully. "An exceedingly original choice of costume, despite the fact that she dressed as a man on many occasions." His voice was low, hardly more than discernible to her over the sounds of conversation and music.

"Baring my lower appendages would not have been appropriate, even in the spirit of accurate costuming. But you are correct," she said, keeping her own tones pitched low in hopes of disguising her identity. Although her partner definitely wasn't Alexander, she also sensed that he was someone she knew. "I am Hatshepsut. Everyone else thinks that I'm Cleopatra."

"Fools, all of them. Where is the asp if you are meant to be Cleopatra?"

His comment surprised a little laugh from her, and she saw his lips move, relaxing into fullness from their hard, serious line from a moment ago.

"But of course, no one truly knows what Hatshepsut looks like," she admitted. "Or if she was anything more than a queen regent."

"Indeed. But we expect to learn more if the stele from Rosetta is ever translated."

"One can only hope! Until we can read hieroglyphs, there will be holes and blank spots in our knowledge."

"I find it remarkable that you are even aware of Hatshepsut's existence, let alone such details about her questionable reign," he said after negotiating a particularly tight turn that made her a bit dizzy. "As well as the importance of the Rosetta Stone."

Emboldened by her continued anonymity…and perhaps by the champagne punch…Maia launched into a candid speech that she would never have imposed on a gentleman under different circumstances. They preferred to talk on their own topics, not that of their partners. "I've indulged my fascination with Egyptian history for many years now. It started when I read my brother's copy of *Biblioteca Historica* in order to help him with his Greek. Ask me about the Babylonians or the Indians, and I know little about them. But if one reads Herodotus or Diodorus, for example, there is much to be learned about the Egyptians. And now that more antiquities are being shipped back from Egypt, I can actually see them in the museum. That makes it all the more real."

"You assisted your brother with his Greek?" Was there a note of humor in the knave's voice?

"I didn't like it any better than he did, but I was determined…" Maia's voice trailed off as she realized how she'd been babbling. She bit her lower lip and swallowed. One of the things that had put off some of her early suitors had been her tendency to lecture and overexplain. Not that the knave was a suitor, of course, but she well knew that gentlemen did not like women who talked. Alexander was an exception, and he had indulged her interest in Egyptology by taking her to the British Museum on two different occasions.

Of course, he didn't have the foggiest idea who Hatshepsut or even Rameses III were, but that didn't bother Maia.

"Very interesting." The knave seemed to stop whatever else was about to come out of his mouth and clamped his lips together.

As she looked up at him, Maia realized suddenly that when one was confronted by a masked individual, one's attention tended to focus on the parts that were exposed—in this case, his mouth. And she found those lips to be more fascinating than they really should be, tracing their shape with her eyes, memorizing them. Wondering what it would be like to kiss them, for they seemed soft and full and very mobile.

"Careful," he said suddenly, his hands tightening on her, and Maia realized she'd become somewhat dizzy. The room had a bit more spin than the dance steps warranted, and she clutched the top of his arm, her face warm beneath her own mask, her heart suddenly slamming in her chest.

Oh. Maia blinked and focused on something over his shoulder—anything to turn her mind from the sudden, unexpected thoughts about his mouth. She couldn't remember feeling this odd before.

"How many glasses of champagne punch, Hatshepsut?"

Her attention flew back to him and his gaze fixed on hers, shadowed and dark behind small round eyeholes. His intense regard knocked the breath out of her as if she'd been punched. Or perhaps it *was* the champagne punch that made her feel breathless and warm and loose.

"I'm not tipsy," she retorted, forgetting to keep her voice low.

Those lips quirked into something that might have been an almost-smile, and he replied, "Naturally. Perhaps some air would be in order?"

She suspected that he didn't believe her; and in all fairness, she wasn't certain whether to believe herself. She was feeling rather odd, in a pleasant, tingly sort of way. "Perhaps it would be best, though I am loath to cut short my rare opportunity to waltz."

Without another word, he drew her from the dance floor, managing them through the other swirling partners. Oddly enough, once removed from the smooth rhythm of the waltz, Maia felt even warmer and lighter in the head, and she actually bumped against him in mortifying clumsiness. He tightened his arm and led her away from the crowd, where she was able to draw in cooler, cleaner air devoid of attar of roses—which seemed to once again be this Season's favored scent, as well as every other of the last years since she'd been out.

Maia's heart hadn't ceased its heavy pounding, and in fact seemed to increase as the Knave of Diamonds directed them away from the loud, close ballroom. Toward an alcove down one of the corridors, near which an open window offered a waft of breeze.

Perhaps it was because there was no other competition for her attention, for she was away from the music filling her ears, the mishmash of the smells associated with such a crush, and the need to concentrate on the unfamiliar dance steps…that Maia found herself overly aware of the strong arm to which she found herself clinging.

Literally clinging.

How many glasses of champagne punch *had* she had? There'd been one before the court jester…or perhaps two? And then another—

"I do hope you aren't about to cast up your accounts on my waistcoat, your majesty," he said, easing her away from him a bit, even as he steadied her step. Those high-soled shoes were rather an inconvenience.

"I beg your pardon?" she demanded, suddenly indignant. "Of course I shouldn't do such a thing."

No, indeed not. She simply would not allow it to happen, no matter how odd she felt. And she did feel a bit odd.

She blinked hard, realizing that she, the very proper Miss Maia Woodmore, was using the Knave of Diamonds to keep the floor from tilting and, quite possibly, her knees from buckling.

Pulling away from the knave, she found that she was able to stand on her own, even on the platformlike shoes that put her face just…a bit…below…his.

Maia looked up from the brocade waistcoat and the ruby-studded, bloodred neckcloth that was much too close to her face, willing herself to focus on the matter at hand—which was…well, she wasn't certain. They hadn't been conversing, exactly, had they?

Her eyes traveled over a stiff black collar that brushed his jaw, hiding the full shape of his face, then beyond a square chin…and to that same mouth that had fascinated her as they spun gently, if not smoothly, around the dance floor.

It was a mouth that, when relaxed, boasted a full lower lip and a slanted upper one—soft and smooth without being the least bit feminine when it wasn't flattened grimly.

"Hatshepsut?" Those lips moved, firming in something like exasperation. "Do you need to lie down?"

"Of course not," she retorted, annoyed again. "I am perfectly capable of holding my cups. I merely got a bit dizzy from the dancing. It was so very close in there."

"Very well. As long as you don't—"

"You might be much too tall, sir knave, and a bit overbearing—" she heard herself commenting, the words simply pouring from her "—but, despite what nonsense comes from it, you have been blessed with a well-formed mouth."

There was a pause for a moment, and then he replied, "Ah." The syllable sounded a bit strangled.

"I'm not an expert on mouths, you know," she continued, vaguely wondering why she was so fascinated by his lips. "One doesn't normally *examine* them quite as closely as one might think, unless the rest of the face is masked, and excepting if one is intending to kiss said mouth…and even then, one might not even have the chance to do so before the kiss commences."

"Ah," he said again after she paused.

"Of course, I've only been kissed by a limited number of pairs of lips," she said. Purely for clarification.

"And how many pairs would that be?" His voice rumbled deeply. Those lips were rather flat again.

She paused, pressing her own lips together in thought. Her mask shifted as she did so, and Maia was grateful for the reminder that she was still blissfully anonymous. "Perhaps three. No, four. Hmm. Perhaps…no, four." She wouldn't count Mr. Virgil. He didn't deserve to be counted, and the very thought of him made her feel ill. She looked up at her companion. "Four, my lord knave."

Their eyes locked, his so dark and shadowed behind those small holes that she could hardly fathom that they could have such a hold on her. But they did. Her stomach felt as if the bottom dropped out, leaving her warm and nervous in a very pleasant way.

Thanking God and all the angels in heaven for the fact that she was masked and completely anonymous, she whispered boldly, "But perhaps there might be a fifth."

And Maia held her breath.

3

IN WHICH THE KNAVE OF DIAMONDS HAS AN EXCEEDINGLY UNPLEASANT EXPERIENCE

Dimitri couldn't breathe.

The sudden surge of blood, pounding and insistent, filling his vision, stunned him.

The force of *need,* of a long-renounced instinct, suddenly burst free. His fingers trembled, his fangs threatened to shoot forth, bulging inside his swelling gums. He had to lower his eyelids to hide the hungry red glow lest Miss Woodmore see.

Foolish, damned, stupid, mad bastard.

What in Luce's hell had he been thinking, taking a woman like her away into a dark corner? Especially a woman who riled up his ire as easily as his frustration?

But he had no more thoughts; they scattered like a shattered goblet as her gloved hand rested against the ruby-colored glass pin adorning his neckcloth. Taller somehow, she lifted her face the fraction that she needed to, putting herself *there*. Right there. A breath away.

Saliva pooled in his mouth. His skin flushed beneath his mask. It had been so long since he'd wanted to kiss a woman. He tried to fight it away, but the Mark on his back raged and burned hotter, reminding him of how he'd denied himself unnecessarily. Her lips beckoned, plump and pink, and he wanted to see if they tasted as sweet and lush as they looked. The searing heat blazed even stronger now that Lucifer felt him wavering, and it radiated down Dimitri's back and through his limbs.

Embattled by pain, overwhelmed by desire and long-denied need, he couldn't keep himself from bending to her, covering her lips.

She surrounded him: her spicy, sweet scent, her confident demeanor, her small hands, the pool of her sparkling gown. Her mouth…that entity that alternately exasperated and teased him, with its top lip that was just a bit fuller than the bottom…softened beneath his, fit to his lips and gently brushed across his to one side. Her mouth was warm and lush, and she left a little wake of prickling, a dusting of pleasure on his sensitive mouth… and then she lifted away.

He went back for more, no longer fully master of himself. He found her lips again and took a longer, deeper drink from her taunting mouth. She made a soft, delicious moan that sent a new blaze of desire shuttling through his belly, her lips moving desperately against his. The world was red and hot, and the scent of her floral spice filled Dimitri's consciousness.

Perhaps it was this—the recognition of the tantalizing scent, its familiarity and corresponding forbiddance—that enabled him to grasp the last wisp of control and drag himself away. *God and the Fates, not* her.

Not anyone, but most of all, not her.

Fingers tightening into each other, gouging through the gloves into his palms, he stepped back, his heart pounding in his ears, his breathing much too loud. His fangs were out of control and fighting to be free, and he had to turn away, closing his eyes to hide the proof of the demon he was.

His ruthless control regained—albeit tenuously—he cleared his senses of the heat and sweetness he'd tasted, swallowed hard. Tried not to breathe too deeply, for fear that scenting her would make it begin all over.

And the crack that had begun to form in his ordered world he snapped viciously together.

Terrified by what she might see in his eyes when he opened them, Dimitri was weak with relief when he saw that she had turned slightly away. Looking down, he noticed her hand still somehow settled on his chest. She seemed to be wavering through her own battle for control.

Or, more likely, stability.

Dimitri wasn't certain whether he ought to curse the champagne punch that she'd indulged in, or to be grateful for its intoxicating properties.

"And so that makes five," he said, relieved that his voice was cool and steady. Emotionless. He barely remembered to keep it low, to a mere murmur, to further obscure his identity. *Fate protect me from that at least.* "I wonder if, at the next masque, you might attempt to make it an even half dozen pairs of lips to taste?"

At that, she looked up at him and he nearly went for her again. Her lips were swollen and glistening, half-parted with surprise beneath the curve of her mask. He blinked, drew in a breath and focused on the roaring pain blazing over the back of his shoulder. A satisfying reminder that he was, despite it all, still in control.

And still in defiance of the devil's will.

Then in an instant her lips allowed a smile to flicker over them and she surprised him yet again when she replied, "No, my lord knave. I think it might be prudent to stop at five."

"Indeed?" He had to offer her his arm in order to get her back to the dance, away from the temptation of this secluded alcove, and the mere thought of what had just transpired.

He had some blood whiskey in the coach. That would help steady him, dull the awakened need. Later, he could stir up some trouble in the depths of Vauxhall. He'd had a very satisfactory brawl in St. Giles the night after the Lundhames' ball, where he'd tossed five blackhearts into the river after they'd tried to stick him with a knife and relieve him of his purse. Never say he wasn't doing his part to clean up the thieves of London.

"Yes, I do believe I shall stop at five," she replied as they walked along. She wasn't weaving like she had been earlier. "'Tis a shame that my fi—my husband's kisses were never quite so…potent. Perhaps it's best if I keep this memory as my last random tasting."

Dimitri kept his mind blank, refusing to allow himself to absorb her words and the variety of implications therein. He didn't even need the reminder that she was betrothed. That fact simply didn't enter into the equation of his base stupidity; his actions had nothing to do with Miss Maia Woodmore in particular.

It could be any woman who tempted him thus, for he rarely indulged in the pleasures of the flesh. And even then, it was brief and impersonal. No kissing was ever involved.

"Very well, then," he replied, "Hatshepsut. And here we are, back to the party. I release you to your dances and your subjects, knowing that there is no longer a chance that you might be coerced into sampling the kiss of a highwayman or Romeo or some other character."

And then, suddenly eager to be far away from the shimmery golden gown and its well-kissed occupant, Dimitri released her arm and slipped into the edge of the crowd, already tasting the blood and alcohol to come, the energy bounding beneath his skin.

Maia watched the knave ease into the crowded ballroom, both relieved and disappointed by his flight. Her knees were shaking so badly she could hardly stand, and her lips felt as though they were twice their size.

They still tingled when she slipped the tip of her tongue over them, and she felt a shaft of tingling heat when she reimagined the kiss.

How could I have been so foolish? What is wrong with me?

But she already knew the answer, and once again, Maia was blessedly grateful for the mask that obliterated most of her features, and the other aspects of her disguise. The drink, along with the heady knowledge that no one could know who she was, had turned her into the same sort of capricious young woman who'd nearly gotten herself ruined three years ago.

Thank God that He, or Fate, or *something,* had intervened and brought Corvindale onto the scene before she'd made a foolish mistake with Mr. William Virgil.

Only, she wished even more fervently now that it had been anyone but her new guardian who'd saved her. The details of that night were so very vague and foggy, but one thing she did recall with absolute clarity was the earl's furious, dark eyes.

But that was three years ago…what was wrong with her tonight?

Hadn't she learned her lesson?

Yet, while she knew part of the reason for her capriciousness was due to perhaps too much champagne punch, there was the fact that she'd been so rigid, so perfectly proper and in control for these past years that it was no wonder it had fizzled behind her cloak of anonymity tonight. If Angelica had any idea what really went on in her thoughts… She hoped that Angelica had had enough sense not to sample the fizzy punch, as well.

Wishing she could take off her mask to relieve the warmth, Maia strolled along the edge of the room in the opposite direction of the knave. She didn't want to dance again—she wasn't certain she trusted herself—and did her best to stay out of sight of anyone who might accost her for his partner.

The only person she should want to dance with right now was Alexander—and he was far away. And he'd been gone for so long. She ought to focus on his kisses, and where his warm hands had gone, slipping along the bodice of her gown during one of their late-afternoon rides.

And so that was what she did. Centered her thoughts on that. She would not worry about whether he'd forgotten her—and their interludes in the closed carriage. Or whether he'd changed his mind.

And she certainly would *not* remember the way the knave's simple kiss had made her whole body hot and alive. Weak and trembly.

The sight of Angelica with a man wearing a curious square-shaped hat was a welcome distraction, for her sisterly annoyance sprang back to the forefront. Unlike most everyone else, the lower half of his face was masked and he looked like some sort of Far Eastern brigand, like one that might have attacked the Crusaders.

Angelica was waltzing, Maia noted, pressing her lips together and resisting the urge to stalk out there and drag her off the floor. That would just draw attention and recognition to both of them. Which, if Angelica was paying any attention to her elder sister's eagle eye, she would know—and would use to her advantage.

Maia would have a word with her later. Just because Chas wasn't around to ride herd on them didn't mean her sister could be so careless. Wondering where Aunt Iliana was, Maia scanned the room and noticed an angel across the way.

The angel looked as if she was having difficulty with her celestial wings, and a quick glance showed still no sign of their chaperone, so Maia *tsked* and started over to help Mirabella.

"Oh, thank goodness," the young girl said when she saw Maia. "I've lost one of my wings, and the back of my gown caught upon the staff of a shepherd I was dancing with, and I believe it's been torn."

Maia only needed a quick glance to see that repair was definitely needed. Delighted with an excuse to leave the ball, as well as yet another distraction from all of her other worries, she took Mirabella's arm and led her toward the sweeping staircase that led to the third floor of the Sterlinghouse residence. Up there, they would find a tiring room, or at least a private place to set Mirabella to rights.

As they reached the first landing of the stairs, Maia noticed a group of four men, dressed all in black, properly masked, entering through the front door. "The Four Horsemen of the Apocalypse," announced the butler as the quartet moved into the foyer.

She paused for a moment, that uncomfortable prickle of intuition lifting the hair on her arms, and looked down at them. There was something about the four she didn't like. Something *off*.

They walked into the foyer as if they knew where they were going—with purpose and speed, and without pausing to greet anyone. Suddenly nervous and not certain why—but she never ignored her instincts—she gripped Mirabella's arm, silently directing her to climb the stairs more quickly. They were already mostly out of sight from below due to a curve in the staircase, but for some reason, Maia felt compelled to get away before one of them chanced to look up.

Once at the third floor, she felt marginally less unsettled and wondered at her odd reaction to the men. Perhaps it had simply been the fact that their costumes had seemed so menacing. Mirabella hadn't noticed her haste, and Maia wasn't about to mention it. Instead she peeked inside one of the rooms, knowing from her previous visits that the Sterlinghouses had several parlors and a library on this stretch of the corridor, and that the ladies' tiring room was near the end.

The room was empty and a full moon shone through French doors, casting silvery light over several chairs and a table with a decidedly masculine feel. Not one of the ladies' parlors, but it would do for a moment for her to see to Mirabella's gown.

Maia didn't expend much energy trying to find a lamp, for there was one on the desk, turned to a bare glow. She turned it up and was just kneeling behind the angel to see to the back of her gown when the door behind them burst open.

Muffling a shriek of surprise, she bolted to her feet, tangled in the frothy fabric of her gown, and went down in a heap.

When she opened her eyes, a dark figure in a white shirt loomed over her and for a moment she thought it was one of the eerie men who'd caught her attention. But at the same time as she recognized her new guardian's features, Mirabella exclaimed, "Corvindale!"

"You," Maia muttered as the earl literally yanked her to her feet, disregarding the fragility of her gown. "What do you mean by—"

But she never finished, for the next thing she knew, strong arms swooped around her and he lifted her bodily from the ground.

Maia was so shocked and horrified that at first she couldn't speak. She struggled, trying to pull free, and heard Corvindale snap a command at his sister. "Outside. Now, Bella."

"Put me—" she started, but her own direction was cut off along with her breath when he did just that, fairly tossing her onto one of the chairs. She drew in a furious gasp to lash into him, but suddenly a heavy, dark cloth wafted down over her.

Confused, incensed and more than a little frightened at this sudden, un-earthly wildness, Maia kicked and struggled as he wrapped the covering closely around her. It had the effect of muffling her shouts and dulling her kicking and hitting, and when he tucked it tightly around her, *tying* it with something she could only imagine was a curtain cord, she began to lose her breath under the thick cloth.

He's mad! The Earl of Corvindale is mad!

He lifted her again and carried her somewhere... outside. She felt the subtle change in the air through the fabric, and remembered him ordering his sister outside. Through the French doors, onto the balcony, she guessed, based on the short distance. He deposited her none too gently onto some hard surface, and she heard more short, sharp commands to Mirabella.

"Keep her quiet. Stay here behind this planter until Iliana or I come for you. Both of you." This last was loud enough for her to hear clearly, and she understood that it was intended that way.

She strained her ears, and although she couldn't hear footsteps, she did distinguish the soft click of what had to be the French doors, closing behind him.

"Are you all right, Maia?"

The soft voice was close, and she felt a little nudge as Mirabella knelt next to her. "Get me out of here," she snarled, and then inhaled a bit of lint and began to cough inside what must be curtains. Providence knew when the fabric had last been beaten.

"Corvindale said to stay here," Mirabella said. "I think something's wrong in there, Maia."

Gritting her teeth to keep from coughing and launching into an obviously vain tirade, Maia closed her eyes. The chit was so cowed by her brother that not only did she not even call him by his Christian name, but she also blindly followed his every order. "I can't breathe," she managed to say, although it wasn't strictly true. Now that she wasn't struggling so much, she found that air did make its way through the fabric.

"I'll try to loosen it," Mirabella said, and Maia felt her beginning to tug at the fabric. But then she stopped abruptly. "Oh!" Her voice was a shocked whisper. "Someone—no, two men—just came into the— *Oh!*"

"What is it?"

"They're fighting. In the room. There are two of them attacking—"

"Who is?" Maia demanded, stilling for a moment, straining to hear.

"My heavens." Mirabella made an odd sound. "They have burning eyes. Red eyes. And they're attacking the earl!"

Red eyes?

A chill rushed over her. Red eyes? She'd heard about people with red eyes. Demons, and the *vampirs* of legend. But of course such creatures didn't exist, despite how real the stories might seem. "It must be part of the masquerade," she whispered back, trying not to think about the four men in black. "Somehow they have reflective pieces that make their eyes glow."

But even as she spoke, she remembered Granny Grapes spinning her tales of horror and suspense. She'd made it sound as if *vampirs* actually existed, and even that she'd encountered them. They were dark, powerful men who'd sold their soul to the devil in exchange for immortality and other superhuman abilities.

They could be killed by a wooden stake to the heart. She remembered that part of the legend because Chas had been unaccountably fascinated, as boys tended to be, by the possibility of blood and violence. He had pressed Granny Grapes over and over for stories about the hunting of the humanlike immortals, counting among his heroes a *vampir* slayer named Andreas.

The *vampirs* were sensitive to sunlight, too, and drank blood to live. Human blood.

Maia shivered, but it wasn't from the cold. It was because she remembered the last vestiges of a dream she'd had the night before. A dream that she'd tried to submerge, because it had been dark and hot and red. And there'd been a *vampir* in it, with his gleaming eyes that scored into her like fire…and his sleek fangs.

The dream had left her breathless and sweaty, her heart racing, and with a sort of expectant throbbing through her body. Even now, remembering the essence of it made her skin flush with heat.

"They're attacking him!" Mirabella said again, her voice still low. "Two of them. They're so…*fast*. Corvindale's thrown one across the room, but the other is on top of him—"

"Two of them? Do they have guns or weapons?"

"They're fighting with their hands and—kicking, and throwing things. It's…amazing," she whispered. "My brother…he's so fast, they're all so *fast*…but he's… I can hardly see him move. And…he just lifted that big *desk* and *threw* it at one of them," she said. Her voice was half shocked, half terrified. "Oh! He punched one, and *oh!* Oh, dear! *Oh.* There. He's back up and slammed the other one into the wall, and then he flipped over a sofa and landed on his feet—"

"*Who?*" Maia demanded again.

"The earl. He's fighting them off. Both of them. He's—but he's bleeding…and there goes a chair on the head and *oh!*"

The next thing Maia knew, the girl was dragging, or pushing and pulling, her somewhere. "We've got to hide. Behind this…potted tree," she managed, breathless with effort. "They might see us!"

But by then, Mirabella had ceased to pull and tug at her bound body, and Maia got the impression she was no longer near her. Where did she go? Surely she hadn't left her here alone, bound up like a loaf of bread?

And then…*Angelica!* Fear seized her, and with a flood of panic she remembered the Four Horsemen of the Apocalypse and the malevolent aura about them. Now she began to struggle anew, but Corvindale had been much too efficient with the curtain cord. She couldn't loosen it, and Mirabella didn't seem to be inclined to do much to assist.

"Mirabella?" she said, a bit more loudly now.

A shifting in the air, and then the presence of someone next to her indicated the younger woman's return. Maia felt her bump against her in haste. "It's Corvindale! A third man came in, and then something happened—he just stopped. Corvindale just…stopped. He's down on the ground, or dead, or something!"

"Did they shoot him?" Maia demanded. "Do you see a lot of blood?"

"I didn't see anything, and surely I would have heard a gunshot."

"Let me out of here," Maia said, struggling harder. She had to see. She had to find a way to take care of this. The earl couldn't be dead. "Do you see any blood?"

"He's looking around the room—there's only one man now," Mirabella hissed, her mouth close to the spot she must assume was Maia's head, but was really her shoulder. "Another one came in. He just kicked my brother…and he didn't move. Oh, dear God, I hope he isn't dead!"

"Unwrap me!" Maia said. Torn between disbelief that the implacable earl could actually be prone—not to mention that he'd allowed himself to be kicked—and the terror of what could be happening to Angelica, she found herself flopping about like a netted fish. Were there really *vampirs* here?

"No, I'd better not. Not until—oh, the man left. He's gone. I'm going to wait a minute to make sure he's gone for good. Then I'll sneak in and see to the earl."

Mirabella moved and Maia heard her shifting away, and then, after a long moment, the soft rattle of the French doors. And then a marginally louder rattle, and the gentle bump as Mirabella came back.

"Someone else came in! He nearly saw me. I don't know who he is, but I thought I should—"

"What about Corvindale? Did you see blood? Did you get in there?"

"He's not moving, but his eyes seem to be open. And his shirt is all torn, and there is a necklace of rubies across his neck that he wasn't wearing earlier. It's very peculiar. But I didn't get close enough because the door opened and I ran back outside."

Maia could hear the distress in her friend's voice, and she supposed she couldn't blame the girl for running after the door opened again. But how could she have left her brother there? Maia would never have—

Mirabella gasped. "The man is taking the necklace of rubies! Is he a thief—oh! Corvindale!"

And then the sound of the French doors crashing open and heavy footsteps had Maia tensing.

"Are you hurt?" Mirabella was asking, and then suddenly Maia was being scooped up and untangled from her bindings. Unfortunately she recognized the strong, efficient handling of Corvindale as he toted her away once more.

By the time the fabric fell away from her face, and she saw that the earl was, apparently, no worse for wear, he'd deposited her on the floor in the very same room she'd been in some time earlier. It was in shambles.

"Angelica!" was the first thing that came out of her mouth, just as she noticed Lord Dewhurst leaving the chamber. He was carrying a necklace of rubies.

The curtains had fallen in a thick heap around her feet, tangling with her high shoes and the multitude of folds from her gown. She tried to kick it away, frantic to get to her sister, but Corvindale stopped her with a strong grip around her arm. "Take your hands off me," she snapped. "I have to find Angelica."

Ignoring her, Corvindale lifted her from the pile of fabric as the door closed behind Dewhurst, and she noticed that his shirt was indeed torn, sagging over his uncovered shoulder, leaving his muscular arms bare. "Dewhurst will see to her," the earl said.

"Dewhurst?" Maia said, staring at the door. And wasn't the viscount supposed to be in Romania? "With my *sister?*"

"I'll deal with him later," Corvindale said grimly, grasping her by the arm and towing her toward the door. "Iliana's waiting in the carriage. You've got to get out of here," he said, and gestured sharply for Mirabella to follow.

"I'm not leaving without my sister," Maia said, digging in her heels.

The earl's response was simple, and it infuriated her further: he picked her up bodily and carried her out of the room and down the hall to the servants' stairs.

The next thing she knew, Maia was shoved into a carriage along with Mirabella and their chaperone. No fewer than three footmen were to accompany them, which gave her a modicum of security. The door closed and clicked locked before she could speak, and the coach started off with a violent lurch.

She could barely catch her breath, she was so incensed. But before she could gather her thoughts to speak, she looked over at her two companions. Mirabella's eyes were wide in her fair face, her fiery-red hair hanging in straggles around her cheekbones, red lips parted.

But Aunt Iliana had a more composed, but inten expression on her face. And for the first time, Maia n ticed that the woman was holding a sharp wooden stak

Maia had just finished opening the parlor drapes Blackmont Hall again—for someone kept closing ther and keeping the rooms so dark and dreary—when she heard the front entrance open. Her heart leaped, and she rushed to the parlor door to see if it was Angelica returning at last. But the low, sharp tones as the new arrival spoke to his butler indicated that it was the earl who had come home.

Determined to at least have some answers from him, she flew from the parlor and met him in the hall.

"Lord Corvindale," she said, positioning herself in the center of the passageway so that he couldn't walk to his study—where it appeared he was headed—without brushing past her.

"What is it, Miss Woodmore?" he demanded. His voice was flat and hard, and belied the disheveled, weary man in front of her. He'd either come home and changed into a new shirt (although she was certain he hadn't been in the house since she returned from the masquerade last night; for she'd been waiting to accost him), or had somehow acquired a different one, for this shirt, though wrinkled and loose, seemed relatively pristine as compared to the one in shreds last night.

But his features were etched even more sharply than usual. His heavy dark brows lowered in a scowl, his mouth in a flat line, his thick, dark hair springing in erratic waves from his head and around his neck. He was well overdue for a shave, as well, she noted with a sniff. His coat was smudged with dirt and his hands were ungloved and one had a line of dried blood on the back of it.

Although Maia had filled her sleepless night by attempting to rest, then read, and then later when neither served to ease her mind, to bathe away the lingering bit of lint and dust from the curtains in which she'd been wrapped, she felt very little sympathy for the man in front of her...despite the fact that he seemed exhausted. Tension emanated from him like heat radiating from a fire, but Maia didn't care. She needed answers, she needed to prepare, to take care of things and to address this situation—and she'd waited much too long for him. Aunt Iliana, who seemed to know much more than she let on, had merely assured her that they'd received word that Angelica was safe and that Dewhurst would be returning her shortly.

But the big question was: safe from *what?*

From the *vampirs?*

"It's nearly four o'clock, Corvindale. I would like you to tell me precisely where Angelica is," she demanded of him in return. "And when she is going to arrive here. But most of all, I require assurance that she is safe."

His eyes flashed darkly. "Your sister will arrive here at Blackmont Hall when I am convinced it is safe for her to do so." He made a clear gesture of dismissal. "Is that all?"

She drew in her breath and gave him an icy glare. "No, it is not. In fact, I wished to speak with you in regard to your conduct last evening."

"My conduct?" Ice fairly formed in the air around his words.

Perhaps he assumed that the very tone of his livid, affronted voice would make her turn tail and run, but he was very wrong. "Not only was it abhorrent and crude, but you didn't even take the moment to explain or apologize before shoving Mirabella and myself into a carriage and sending us off."

"Indeed."

"There was simply no reason for you to put your hands on me—" to her mortification, her voice dipped a bit with fury "—and toss me out onto the balcony like some sort of—"

Corvindale fixed her with icy black eyes. "In fact, I had sufficient reason for doing so. The least of which was the fact that you would not have obeyed me."

"If you had simply explained—"

"There was no time for explanations, even if I had believed you might have heeded them, Miss Woodmore. You would have ignored them just as you have everything else since arriving here, including keeping the windows in this house shrouded, my library in order and my preference *not to be bothered*."

Maia held her ground, despite the fact that his voice had risen enough that a nearby vase rattled on its glass tray. So he had noticed she'd been looking through his library…and doing a bit of organizing. Had he seen that she'd arranged his many copies of the Faustian legend by language and date?

"If you had simply explained that we were in danger and there was no time for discussion, I would have heeded your warning." She drew in a breath and managed to count to three before continuing. "In addition to an apology, I believe it isn't asking overly much to request an explanation for what happened last evening. I understand now that Angelica and I were in danger, but I would like to know why and from whom or what. And how it happened that you arrived in time to prevent whatever the outcome might have been…regardless of the clumsy manner in which you executed it."

"Clumsy manner?" he repeated.

She pinned him with her eyes and made an impatient gesture. Why would he not give her a straight answer? "You pushed me out onto the balcony, *wrapped up in curtains*. Can you not give me the courtesy of telling me *why?*"

"Because there were some very bad men who want to take you away and I needed to ensure that you didn't reveal yourself to them. That is why your blasted brother snared me into being your guardian. Because he knew there was no one else who could keep you safe."

Very bad men? It was all she could do not to roll her eyes in frustration. "Please, my lord, you sound like a character in one of those Gothic novels by Mrs. Radcliffe, making all sorts of Byzantine comments and cryptic warnings. If you would cease these ambiguous statements and simply tell me what is happening—"

"What then? You would accept my explanations and my orders without question?"

Was the man mad? "Certainly not. But at least you wouldn't feel the necessity to wrap me up and throw me onto the balcony."

Corvindale crossed his arms over his sagging, stained waistcoat and glared down at her. "The truth is, Miss Woodmore, your brother has gotten himself into serious danger with a society of ruthless men. By disappearing with the sister of one of them, he has not only put himself in a most injurious position, but also you and your sisters—for they would like nothing better than to use one or any of you to get to Chas."

Oh, Chas! Maia swallowed, trying to keep the panic away. "Then they are after us as hostages? Ransom?"

So the men weren't *vampirs*. Or were they? She shook her head. *She* was mad to even consider the possibility that *vampirs* could actually exist.

She spoke aloud, working through her thoughts as if he weren't even there. "But then that must mean Chas is still alive and hidden somewhere if they are trying to abduct us. He must still be alive. And safe." Relief bounded through her.

"Your brother is very cunning and able, and you are likely correct. I'm confident he can take care of himself. But you and your sister must not leave this house or see anyone without my permission. You are completely safe whilst in my custody, but Cezar Moldavi is not only ruthless but also reasonably intelligent. And your brother has betrayed him in a most egregious manner. He will not give up easily."

"Cezar Moldavi?" Maia froze. She'd heard that name. She was certain of it. But where? Perhaps Chas…

"You recognize that name, then?"

"I'm familiar with it but I have never met the man, like yourself. I mean to say, now that I've met you—"

Dimitri shifted, his impatience clear. "Yes, yes, Miss Woodmore. Please refrain from stating the obvious. Now, I am expecting Mr. Cale any moment now. What other items must you drag forth and force me to ponder?"

"You still have not tendered an apology," she said clearly, not about to be brushed off. *Really.* The man had some sort of nerve. "I have never been handled so—"

"Miss Woodmore," the blasted man interrupted again, "do you mean to say that should a man push you from the path of an oncoming carriage he should bow and scrape at your feet in apology for mussing your skirts? Or should he ask permission first, before doing so?"

It was all she could do to keep from stamping her foot. Was the man that obtuse? "Well, I do believe—" She stopped herself this time. He was *not* worth the effort of getting riled up. *One attracts more bees with honey than vinegar.* Although she didn't think either would appease the dratted individual in front of her. He simply disliked everyone.

Nevertheless, taking a deep breath, she spoke again, keeping her tones dulcet with effort, speaking to him as if he were a young child. "I did not realize we were in some sort of danger. You made no effort to impress that fact upon me—a fact which you obviously well knew. Perhaps in the future, Lord Corvindale, you might be a bit more forthcoming. Particularly about things that apply to me and my sisters."

"Perhaps."

Incensed by his insouciant remark, clearly meant only to shut her up, she stepped forward and was rewarded when he actually seemed to rear back a bit. *Good. The wrath of a woman is not to be underestimated.* "There is one more thing, my lord. I requir your assurances that my sister's reputation will be int when she is returned here to your custody—or that will take the appropriate steps to correct any pro' thereof." The last thing any of them needed was dal attached to Angelica. That would ruin an she had of making a match with Harringto other well-respected gentleman.

"You have my assurances that I will ¿

to protect your sister's reputation, Miss Woodmore," he replied stiffly. "No one—other than perhaps yourself and Chas—is more concerned about it than I am. But you haven't any reason to worry. She is safe from Moldavi and in unblemished company."

Maia's eyes narrowed. *He's not telling me something.* She was certain of it. He was obfuscating, drat the man. But before she could press him further, there were footsteps and voices in the foyer.

"My lord," said the butler as he appeared. "Mr. Giordan Cale has arrived."

Maia hardly glanced at Mr. Cale as he strode down the hall toward the earl. She had the impression of a well-dressed, handsome man with a haggard, taut expression.

"Dimitri," he said to the earl. And then he turned to Maia. "Miss Woodmore." He gave a quick bow as she curtsied, getting a better look at him. He was very handsome, with strong features like a Roman god and tight, curling chestnut hair. He looked just like Michelangelo's statue of *David,* except, of course, that she couldn't accurately compare the statue to this man's physique.

Corvindale frowned. "If you'll excuse us," he said dismissively to Maia. Then he looked at Cale and gestured down the corridor. "My study."

"There was no time to give the lengthy explanation would have required—let alone convince Miss more of its veracity. It was necessary to take matters my own hands," Dimitri said moments later

d himself more than a bit annoyed that he

felt compelled to explain, even to the man he considered his closest friend. Not to mention the fact that he was beyond furious that Belial's men had caught him by surprise with the rubies. The other two had been no match for him, and Dimitri had been about to use the stake he had beneath his waistcoat when Belial himself burst into the chamber carrying that ruby necklace.

He didn't know how they'd known of his Asthenia for rubies. No one had known except Cale—though he'd die before revealing it. Meg had known, but she was long dead by a stake to the heart. Although Voss had tried valiantly to find out that night in Vienna, he hadn't succeeded until last night when he'd discovered Dimitri with the necklace draped across his skin.

Dimitri's neck still burned where the gems had blazed into his skin, and although he was satisfied that he'd moved quickly enough to hide Mirabella and his ward, things had very nearly gone wrong. A fact which the latter seemed unwilling or unable to comprehend. "Miss Woodmore has been rather vocal in expressing her annoyance with my choice of tactics," he continued.

Cale wasn't completely successful in hiding the amusement in eyes that were nevertheless laced with tension. "She didn't sound terribly pleased with the event," he agreed. "I heard quite a bit of your exchange."

Damnable vampire hearing. "Miss Woodmore would argue with the devil if he claimed he were from hell," he said, pouring them each a healthy shot of his best brandy—this time, without blood.

His head was a bit soft from last night's overindulgence of blood whiskey between the interlude with Hatshepsut and the attack by Cezar Moldavi's men. N urally he'd only interfered to keep Miss Woodmore from waltzing with that court jester because it had been his duty as her guardian, but it had led to an unnecessary detour in that shadowy alcove—not to mention a distraction that had put him off guard. And just as naturally, Dimitri hadn't given their brief kiss more than a passing thought, but, still, that delay had caused him to be a bit too slow in realizing the vampires had arrived.

Which was another reason he was in no mood to placate Miss Woodmore.

He'd rushed through the house, looking for his wards and his sister so as to get them to safety, and had barely done so when Belial's associates had attacked him. Fortunately their absence made it appear that Dimitri was searching for the girls as well, thereby misleading the vampires before Belial flung the ruby necklace at him.

"They gained admittance to the party?" Cale asked.

"There were five of them, all makes, including Belial," Dimitri replied.

Makes were vampires who'd been "made" or sired by another Dracule. While enjoying the same characteristics as the original Draculia members—ones like Dimitri, Cale and Voss, who were invited into the brotherhood by Lucifer himself—these made vampires were less powerful and more susceptible to weakness.

Sired vampires could also make their own minions, but the further down the chain of evolution, so to speak, the less powerful and slower they were. Each of them quired not only their own Asthenia upon awakening r being made, but they also inherited any weakness eir sire, and his or her sire, and so on.

Moldavi acted more quickly in sending his men here

than I'd anticipated, but it could have been worse if Iliana and I hadn't been at the masquerade. She managed to alert me to their arrival, and staked one who apparently attempted to attack Angelica in the garden. And Dewhurst—er, Voss. He's taken to using his title again."

"And now Voss has absconded with the younger one? Angelica?"

Dimitri submerged the bubble of rage at the thought of Voss seducing his way beneath the skirts of Chas Woodmore's sister while she was on Dimitri's watch. Certainly Voss would have his own reasons for choosing her in particular, but knowing that it would infuriate Dimitri was just icing on the bastard's cake.

If he didn't get to Voss first, Woodmore would do it—and shove a stake into his heart without hesitation. Good riddance, but Dimitri would rather have the honor himself if Angelica was ruined while he was responsible for her. Even though he didn't hold Voss directly liable for Lerina's death in Vienna, the tangled web of the other man's games and manipulations had certainly set that path in motion. Since that night, Dimitri had been more than receptive to a reason for ridding the earth of the man's presence.

"Voss has sent word that he'll return her when he's certain I can assure him of her safety, but of course he has some other reason for abducting her."

"Of course he does. It's Voss we're speaking of. The man can't keep his cock or his fangs put away," Cale replied. "But he isn't about to let Moldavi get to her any more than we are. So she's safe—after a fashion."

Unfortunately Cale was correct. Voss would keep Angelica for his own purposes, and then drop her as if she were a hot coal when he was finished. Dimitri doubted even the threat of Chas Woodmore and his ash stake would cow Voss. "Which is precisely the reason I've told Miss Woodmore that all is under control."

"Three deaths last night at the hands—or should I say fangs—of Belial and his men?" Cale asked. "Or were there more?"

"Three in total. Iliana got one in the garden, and Voss witnessed two in the ballroom while I was attending to Miss Woodmore and Mirabella. He claims there would have been further carnage if he hadn't intervened." Dimitri was inclined to believe him, much as he hated to give the man credit for anything productive. "Although, of course, he didn't lift a stake to any of them."

"No, he wouldn't. They were after the Woodmore girls without a doubt?"

"Of course. Now that Chas has run off with Narcise." As he spoke, Dimitri watched Cale without appearing to do so. He wasn't surprised when his friend's face tightened almost imperceptibly, confirming his suspicion that Giordan Cale still had that unhealthy attachment to Narcise Moldavi.

The question that Cale was likely asking, just as Dimitri was, was whether Chas had abducted Narcise against her will, or whether they had eloped. Either was possible, although the irony of a vampire hunter eloping with a vampire made the latter choice rather fascinating.

"Naturally I spent the rest of the night doing the usual to hide the evidence of their visit," Dimitri explained.

"I'll give you some assistance today if you still need to close some holes," Giordan offered. Dimitri nodded in acceptance, for despite his initiatives since the tragedy, there was still more to do.

Last night's strategy had included a few stories told about masquerade skits gone awry, a selection of his own rumormongering, and a bit of memory altering at White's, Bridge & Stokes and other men's clubs afterward— all so that no one would know exactly what had happened to leave three people dead.

Their deaths were tragic enough—not to mention unnecessary—that the actual cause would only make the event even more horrific. That would only lead to the same sort of public outcry and uprising against the Dracule that had occurred in Cologne in 1755. Even more people would die if that happened—fools who thought they could actually hunt and kill the strong, fast immortals. There were few who could hope to take a vampire by surprise and best them in battle, and they had to be well-trained, thus Dimitri ensured that most members of his household staff were as well-equipped as mortals could be for an encounter with Dracule. And in addition, Dimitri had long made it a practice to hire made vampires whose sires were dead for a variety of tasks, including acting as guardians and protectors of the Woodmore sisters. There were, despite the link to Lucifer, quite a number of Dracule who weren't blindly driven by the need for violence and power and sought only pleasure and immortal life.

Dimitri's scowl deepened and the familiar burn of disgust billowed in him. Vampires like Moldavi and Belial who routinely left a trail of violence and dead mortals in their paths repulsed him. Voss might be a creature concerned only with himself, but he didn't have the lack of respect for mortals that Moldavi and his ilk did—leaving children bled dry and to die in the fields.

Moldavi particularly enjoyed the blood of young, virginal boys.

"Woodmore is here in England," Cale said, surprising Dimitri. "He contacted me. The assumption is that he knows where Narcise is, but he didn't say that in the correspondence I received. He was careful. No one else would even know it was from him."

"Moldavi wants his sister back and he'll do whatever he must to retrieve her—including coming out of his position licking the bollocks of Napoleon Bonaparte. Woodmore isn't about to take the chance of being found. He's too damn smart."

"We're meeting at the inn in Reither's Closewell."

Dimitri looked at his friend sharply, but Cale's face was carefully blank. Too blank.

Chas Woodmore couldn't know the history between Narcise and Cale if he was turning to the latter for assistance. *Satan's bloody bones.* If Woodmore would have been a bit more patient and waited for Dimitri's assistance on the mission to kill Moldavi, none of this mess would have happened.

"When you see him, tell Woodmore to get his arse back to London and see to his sisters. You can attend to Narcise," he suggested.

"Over my damned dead soul," Cale replied. "She's Woodmore's problem now."

4

AN INCIDENT IN VIENNA

Despite Dimitri's easy conversation with Giordan Cale, he was unable to dismiss the fact that somehow, someone knew of his Asthenia for rubies. That conundrum couldn't help but take him back to the night of the fire in Vienna, the night that had ultimately sent him back to England, and that had cemented his mistrust of Voss and the hatred between him and Cezar Moldavi.

He remembered the night as if it had happened yesterday, although it had been in 1690—more than a hundred years ago. He'd been celebrating the opening of the gentleman's club he'd had built in the city of Vienna, which was going through a great architectural renewal now that the Turkish siege had ended.

"If Cezar Moldavi attempts to enter," Dimitri had directed his manager, "inform me immediately." At that time, he held a glass of whiskey that he'd hardly yet sipped. It was an exceptional vintage, of course, for he would offer nothing less to the patrons, especially on the opening night.

There were other forms of libation, of the fresh-blooded sort, too, of course. Dimitri did not stint on luxury, at least in his investments. The Puritan days of Oliver Cromwell were long gone.

But the one sort of vintage he didn't offer was that which Cezar Moldavi preferred: that of young children. Boys in particular, but either gender would do. Dimitri's mouth flattened with repugnance.

Only yesterday, word had filtered through Vienna of yet another child's body found in the woods. The girl's blood had been drained nearly away, and she'd been left to die.

She'd been eight.

The blame had been visited upon a group of Jews, as they were regularly accused of such a horror, but Dimitri knew better. Over the centuries, the Jews had been often accused of such blood libel—of taking blood from Christian or even Muslim children and using it for their religious ceremonies. But, in fact, it was certain members of the Dracule who not only murdered the children, but also perpetuated that myth. Just one of those ways Lucifer created chaos among the mortals.

That was part of the reason Dimitri had dissolved his partnership with Cezar. There were many things about the life as a Dracule that were violent, unsavory and base, but child-bleeding was one thing he wouldn't look away from. Once he'd learned of Moldavi's blood-thirsty propensity for children, he'd released him as an investor in the gentleman's club.

"We are to disallow Moldavi entrance for any reason?" replied Yfreto, the club's manager.

"Precisely. He's not been invited" was Dimitri's

reply, referring to tonight's festivities. "Naturally that won't keep the dog-licker away, so 'tis best to be prepared."

"Of course, my lord. And, incidentally, we have more than half the private chests still available in the anteroom for the guests."

Dimitri nodded in approval. Everyone who entered must leave weapons—stakes and swords in particular, along with all valuables, including jewelry and gemstones—in a private chest. Each with its own key, which was then given to the patron. By placing such a wide moratorium on articles that entered the establishment, Dimitri would ensure that no rubies made it to his vicinity, while at the same time precluding any accidental stakings or other violence.

The Dracule were a particularly savage lot.

Aside of being savage, the Dracule were patrons of pleasure. Night after night, they drank and fed and fucked—in as many different ways as they could, for there was none to stop them or to say them nay. That was, Dimitri had come to realize, the reason Lucifer had offered immortality to his earthly minions. When one had nothing to fear, when one had any and all sort of pleasure easily at hand, one became even more self-serving, greedy and base. Just the sort of person Lucifer would appreciate, and the sort who would do his bidding when and if he required it. Rather like an army—or, perhaps more accurately, a society of agents—in waiting.

One could find such a superficial, hedonistic life unfulfilling, to be sure, so Dimitri had decided to combine business with pleasure. Thus, he'd thrown some energy and funds into a private pleasure house designed specifically for the Dracule.

It was either that, or return to England.

He'd been gone from that country more than twenty years. Ever since Meg—for whom he'd given everything—had left him.

During this, the opening night of his gentleman's club, nearly every chair was filled with Dracule and a select group of mortals who were allowed to associate with them. Men played draughts, backgammon or chess. Groups of candle stands clustered in corners and on tables, along with a few shallow bowls, covered and filled with glowing coals for lighting the opium pipes.

"You appear displeased, my lord. Is there something you lack?" A slender hand smoothed over the back of Dimitri's shoulders and tickled the ends of his hair, bringing with it Lerina's familiar scent.

He looked up at her and lifted his whiskey glass. "I have all I need right here." There might have been a flicker of affront in her eyes that she wasn't specifically included in his statement, but Dimitri wasn't certain. And he was sorry if it was the case. She was a beautiful woman, but she required more attention and care to maintain her happiness than he was able, or willing, to give.

Thanks to Meg.

The fresh bite marks on Lerina's shoulder were a testament to the attention and pleasure he'd given her—and, to be fair, she'd given him—earlier today. Lerina was one of those relatively rare mortals who craved the touch and bite of a vampire, particularly when such feeding was accompanied by coitus. And Dimitri was inclined to oblige since a man had to get his pleasure from somewhere.

Yet…she hung on too much, touched him too much, talked too much, and when she did talk, it was of things he had no interest in: fashion and gossip and picnic outings. He never wore a wig, and had no interest in hearing about her trials and tribulations in finding a fashionable one. He didn't know if she'd ever read a book. Like most women, her knowledge of history—except for the most recent events here in Vienna with the Turkish siege— was dismal. And once, early on, when he'd actually thought she might help him forget Meg, he'd expressed interest in obtaining a copy of Sir Isaac Newton's telescope to look at constellations, she'd suggested that he invest in real diamonds instead of the ones in the sky.

Lerina's laughter, becoming more high-pitched, had begun to grate on his nerves. She simply wasn't interesting or stimulating, and nor was she silent and forgettable.

Aside of that, she had been trying to convince him that he should turn her Dracule—so that they could live together forever.

Forever, Dimitri knew, was much too long to spend with any woman—including Lerina. And when he thought about it in that way, he was almost relieved that Meg had left him. Almost.

And so, tomorrow, when the sun came up and the last of the patrons left, Dimitri intended to bid farewell to Lerina. He'd send her off with a fat purse and three chests of fabrics, as well as the deed to a small house here in Vienna.

He looked up at that moment and saw Voss threading

his way toward him. Voss had never been a particularly close associate of Dimitri's, for he was much more interested in seeing how many women he could feed on and bed, smoking opium, and generally drinking himself into a stupor, but they'd played cards together more than a few times in London and Paris. He was charming enough, and didn't grate on Dimitri's nerves as much as unintelligent people did, but there was one problem with Voss. It was that, while Dimitri found him an amusing companion, he didn't trust him.

"Charming place, Dimitri," Voss said. He was holding a leather-wrapped parcel. "I've brought you a congratulatory gift."

"That's kind of you." He took the parcel and found a bottle of most excellent brandy wrapped up with a pewter goblet. The cup's craftsmanship was exquisite: detailed and yet masculine.

He would have set it aside, but Voss smiled. "Do taste it tonight. I've never had better. I thought perhaps you'd be able to tell me from whence it comes." His eyes glinted with mischief.

Always agreeable to a challenge that exercised his mind, Dimitri agreed to the test. Holding his large, wide coat sleeve out of the way, Voss poured him a generous dollop in the pewter goblet, then, with a lifted brow for permission, poured himself a drink of the same in another glass.

Dimitri sipped from the brandy. It was excellent, indeed, and he fully enjoyed the warmth as it burned its way to his belly. Even Lerina's constant toying with the ends of his hair didn't detract from the pleasure of the excellent libation.

Voss had noticed, and had been admiring Lerina, of course, for a man would have to be blind not to notice her. But Dimitri saw that his admiration was merely objective, not possessive.

Aside of that, with Dimitri's marks, as well as his scent, on Lerina, no one would dare make an overture. It was a point of honor among the Dracule that no one fed upon—let alone coupled or otherwise interacted with—one who was marked. Whether it be mistress, servant or other associate, a mark was a claim of possession not to be violated. Voss might be an arse, but he certainly wasn't stupid.

And the consideration that Voss might be interested in becoming Lerina's protector was rejected almost as instantly as Dimitri thought of it. The blond man wouldn't be interested in the obligation of maintaining one single woman. "Obligation" *and* "one" being the detrimental modifiers.

As Dimitri rolled a second sip of brandy around in his mouth, he realized with a start that it wasn't merely brandy. He swallowed, trying to place the additive. It wasn't blood, but it was nearly as pleasant.

"Have you decided on the location of its vintage?" Voss asked, watching him closely.

"Spain." *But there is something else.*

His companion's brows raised. "Indeed. You do not disappoint me, Dimitri. But precisely where?"

"I'll have to sample a bit more," he replied, moving now. Lerina's hands fell to his shoulder, but then she shifted onto the chair next to his and began to toy with the large, heavy buttons on his coat.

Dimitri was, thankfully, distracted for a moment by

the approach of Yfreto, who needed his attention in the card room. By the time he returned to his seat after addressing the issue, Dimitri noticed that Voss had just returned, as well.

"Have you had enough time to consider now?" the latter asked, handing him the refilled goblet.

Dimitri sipped again, once again noting the additive. *"Salvi,"* he said. "You've added *salvi.*" It was an herb mélange that caused a heightened sense of pleasure and relaxation in a Dracule. For a mortal, however, it would put them to sleep in moments.

Voss inclined his head. "Indeed. I thought a bit of additional enhancement might make it all that more difficult for you, expert as you are, to identify the genesis of the drink. But you've yet to tell me—where in Spain?"

They were interrupted three more times during the course of their conversation, and the enjoyment of the very excellent brandy. Dimitri was feeling the effects of the *salvi,* and recognized the same in Voss's eyes. Just then, Dimitri's front steward approached, carrying an unfamiliar wooden chest. As he looked up to greet him, Dimitri noticed Voss suddenly go very still.

And as the chest came closer, he felt it.

"My lord," said the steward, opening the chest to reveal a set of pewter goblets, identical to the one Voss had given him, that Dimitri had drunk from and still held in his hand. "I found these in the front alcove. Hidden behind the curtain."

With the coffer lying open, Dimitri was assaulted by the presence of a ruby. His chest became heavy, his breath thicker, his limbs slower. It took him only an instant to realize what Voss had intended. He'd been swapping the cups, refilling each new one with brandy, all in an effort to see which cup caused him to display some weakness. Fury rose inside Dimitri as he turned his attention to Voss.

The other man lifted his glass in salute. "A gift for my host. A collection of a dozen of the finest craftsmanship."

"So that's what you've done," Dimitri said. It took incredible effort for him to move and speak as if nothing was wrong, despite the fact that his companion was watching him closely. "I wondered. And you expected to trick me thus?"

It was just the sort of thing Voss did, purely for amusement.

Which was precisely why Dimitri had never fully trusted the man.

And why he would not, simply *would not* show any weakness. The ruby was far enough away, and obviously of an insignificant size, so that he wasn't completely paralyzed or weakened. Which implied, at least, that Voss meant him no real harm.

And then suddenly, Dimitri saw something else that drew his attention from the chagrined man in front of him.

Cezar Moldavi had just entered the chamber, surrounded by five of his companions.

Another problem to attend to, but one that much more delicate.

Silently Dimitri cursed Voss even more viciously. Not only was he impaired by a good portion of excellent brandy laced with *salvi,* but also by the presence of a ruby.

"I would throttle you but I'm afraid I have more imminent concerns to deal with. But you are no longer welcome here, Voss. See that he leaves," he added to the steward, forcing the words out as smoothly as he could.

Voss stood and gave a short little bow. But Dimitri no longer had any interest in him.

"Who allowed that child-bleeder entrance?" he growled, still in his seat. Even Lerina shifted away, seeing the warning in his face as he looked around for his manager. *Where the bloody hell was Yfreto?* "I gave strict instructions—"

"Dimitri," said Moldavi, sweeping toward them boldly. "Your place is quite accommodating."

The other man was slight of build, but neatly groomed. His unwigged and unpowdered dark hair was combed straight down over his forehead in the old style of a Crusader. He had a wide jaw and full lips, and he carried himself as if expecting to need to defend an attack at any moment. His shoulders hunched slightly, but his eyes never seemed to rest in one place for long.

Dimitri merely looked coolly at him. He made no move to rise, nor allowed any inflection into his voice. "I hardly expected to see you here, Moldavi." Especially since Dimitri had dissolved their business partnership over a year ago, buying out his would-be partner while the building was still in the early stages of construction. "There aren't any children about."

"More's the pity," said Moldavi. His voice had a bit of a sibilant hiss due to an accident wherein his jaw hadn't healed properly. Rumor had it he'd been beaten and left for dead by a band of his schoolmates. "Children have the sweetest, purest blood."

"I wouldn't know," Dimitri replied, still concentrating on his breathing. The chest with the goblets was still on the floor nearby, but he would not give Voss—who was taking his time leaving the chamber—the satisfaction of confirming the man's trick. Revealing one's Asthenia was akin to acknowledging a flaccid cock or any other private weakness. Not to mention dangerous. "I don't recall sending you an invitation, Cezar."

The other man smiled unpleasantly, and a tiny gold fleck glinted in his left fang. "I was certain it had been an oversight. You've always been so inclusive of all of us. Which is why I brought a gift for you." He stepped aside and revealed a cloaked figure behind him.

Dimitri had never met Cezar's sister before, but there was no mistaking her, for her beauty was legendary among the Dracule. Narcise Moldavi was easily one of the most striking women living—or immortal, as she happened to be. Her skin was smooth and ivory, and she had violet-blue eyes that were disconcertingly empty. Long, shiny black hair fell in lush waves over her shoulders. And her violet gown was made of some material that clung to her as if molded in the wind, revealing taut nipples, the jut of her hip bones, and even the swell of her *mons venus.* Other than a bracelet encircling her upper arm with a feather dangling from it, she wore no other adornment.

It wasn't because of Lerina—or even Meg—that Dimitri was unmoved, however. "I have no interest in your leavings, Moldavi," he said. Despite the lure and lull of the *salvi,* there were a variety of reasons Narcise's presence had no impact on him, including the emptiness in her face. Although he'd seen the brief flash of shame and anger in her eyes, Dimitri saw that it was clear she was under her brother's control. "Especially your sister. Although, she's not precisely your type, is she? You prefer to let others partake while you sniff out other amusements." *Such as hard cocks and little children.*

"You dare to insult my family?" Moldavi's eyes burned with fury. His companions closed ranks, showing their fangs.

"On the contrary. The insult was directed to you alone," he replied. "Now if you'll excuse me." He made it a statement, not a question, and turned away from the repugnant man. Dimitri didn't trust himself to stand, but he had no fear of putting his back to Cezar Moldavi.

At that moment, another of Dimitri's acquaintances, Lord Eddersley, approached, and took Voss's vacant seat.

"Is all well?" he asked Dimitri, eyeing Moldavi over his host's shoulder and then meeting his eyes.

Dimitri felt the shift in the air and the change in smell as Cezar Moldavi and his group moved on. He had no illusions that the man was actually going to leave the premises, but Dimitri wasn't inclined to make a scene. Not tonight.

He didn't need to prove anything, and Moldavi had obviously wished to make the point to his companions: that he could enter uninvited and disrupt Dimitri's evening. Engaging with the man would only fuel Moldavi's fire, and give him more attention than he deserved.

However, once Dimitri found out who'd allowed the bastard in, there would be hell to pay. "Just dealing with a nuisance," Dimitri replied to Eddersley as Lerina excused herself.

"He's walked away, but he's not leaving."

Dimitri nodded absently at Lerina as she turned to walk off, her hand sliding along his arm. "As I assumed." He picked up the bottle of brandy Voss had left, then set it back down. Perhaps it might be best if he stayed away from the *salvi*.

A short time later, Dimitri happened to look over just as two figures emerged from one of the shadowy alcoves that had been built to provide privacy.

His body went cold, then hot with anger, when he recognized them both. Cezar Moldavi and Lerina.

He was still watching when Moldavi looked over and met his eyes boldly, sending a message of smugness.

Dimitri tensed, his jaw setting. Now he understood.

And as the two strolled closer, he saw the marks on Lerina's left shoulder. The one that had been pristine and smooth earlier tonight. Confirmation of his suspicions.

Fury suffused him and his fingers curled around the arm of his chair. Such blatant disrespect couldn't go unchallenged—for everyone in the place knew Lerina was marked by him. Dimitri rose to his feet.

The room swayed much more than he'd expected, and he paused to bestow yet another curse on Voss for tampering with his mental faculties tonight. The chest with the ruby-studded goblet had been closed and taken away, but the *salvi* was quick, deep and strong…and, apparently, very long-lasting.

His knees nearly buckled, but Dimitri allowed no weakness to show. With great effort, he kept himself upright and steady and focused his attention on Moldavi. In another moment, he'd walk over to the man and confront him…

But as it turned out, that wasn't necessary. Moldavi certainly knew what he was doing, and he released Lerina as he drew near Dimitri. Sparing only a brief, cold glance at his mistress—as of now, former mistress—Dimitri focused on his past business partner. Now, he allowed his fangs to show and his eyes to burn.

Without either man saying a word, the room became hushed and tension stretched. Cards were laid on tables, drinks set down, chatter stopped. This was going to be a battle before witnesses.

"For one who arrived uninvited, you've gone even beyond that disregard," Dimitri said, his voice calm and cold. His fist clenched and the room tilted a bit, but he was steadied by fury. "Your insult is inexcusable."

Moldavi said nothing. He merely stepped closer, leaving his companions, including Narcise, to cluster behind him, watching. "Perhaps if you had placed more value on the lovely lady, it wouldn't have come to this."

Dimitri flickered a glance at Lerina, and saw the combination of horror and shame on her face. What had likely begun as a petulant bid for his attention had turned into a grave mistake on her part, as well as that of Moldavi's.

He would deal with Lerina later.

"Leave," Dimitri said to him. "Or I'll see that you do myself."

Moldavi flashed his gold-flecked fang. "I should have been invited tonight. This was my investment as well, and your ridiculous sensibilities cost me a great amount of money. It's you who have made a grave insult. I merely repay you in kind, Dimitri."

"I'll not do business with a child-bleeder." Dimitri stepped toward him, and the next thing he knew, Moldavi was lunging.

With a stake in hand.

Dimitri dodged, still unsteady and fighting the spinning of the room, and then dove at his attacker. They bumped into a chair and table, sending them tumbling, as Dimitri smashed a fist into Moldavi's face.

The stake arced toward him, and he caught the glimpse of a countenance tight with fury and desperation as a powerful arm brought it down toward Dimitri's torso.

A shift aside, and the weapon slammed into his rib cage, the point burying deep. Pain shot through him, but at least he was feeling it and not dead—which was what a stake to the heart would do to a Dracule. Instant death.

Enraged, Dimitri grabbed Moldavi's arm and yanked it, then whipped him across the room. The bone snapped as he released him and the other man tumbled into a heap.

Dimitri turned to see three of Moldavi's companions aligning themselves toward him, but before he needed to respond, Yfreto and four other footmen stepped in between them.

"Get out," Dimitri ordered, taking a menacing step toward Moldavi.

Somehow, the room had righted itself…but he saw through burning eyes that everything was coated in red. The scents of fear and smoke filled his nose, and he turned just as someone screamed.

"Fire!"

It was all over after that.

Even now, Dimitri remembered the sudden hot blaze, the smoke, the rage of the flames.

The fire had been started during the altercation with Cezar—someone had knocked over candles or an opium bowl and the rich fabric had shot up in flames.

There was, of course, nothing that could be done except watch the place burn to the ground.

Dimitri and Eddersley discovered Lerina's body the next day. She was burned so badly it was only a remnant of her gown that identified her.

Shortly after that, Dimitri left Vienna and returned to England. Glad for an excuse to leave, sickened by the loss of life and property, disgusted by the actions of his fellow Dracule, and by his own foolish acceptance of Lucifer's bargain, he decided he was through with it all.

He wanted out.

He wanted his mortal life back.

5

IN WHICH OUR HERO
MAKES A REVELATION

Maia awoke with a start.

She hadn't realized she'd finally fallen asleep, worried as she was about Angelica and Chas, but she must have done, for the world had become dark and silvered blue with moonlight.

Her heart was racing, and her skin warm and damp. Sitting bolt upright, she reached to touch her shoulder, the side of her neck, her throat. Her pulse pounded furiously as she looked at her reflection in the mirror across the room.

Nothing. There was nothing there.

Her shoulder and neck reflected back at her, pale and almost ghostly, shadowed where her clavicle rose, but unblemished. The long braid of her hair hung over one side, making a darker stripe down over her pale pink night rail. Maia's eyes looked like wide dark circles and her mouth a paler one.

It had seemed so real. The burn of his mouth, sliding over her lips, tasting and sucking on them…the heat had been intense, undulating through her so that the nightgown clung to her damp skin. His lips moved to her jaw, to her ear, down to the soft, hidden curve of her neck…and then the flash of pleasure-pain when his fangs penetrated her skin and released the blood pulsing in its channel. She remembered the dream, remembered arching, sighing, feeling the shimmering warmth draining from her veins as his hot mouth closed over her skin, and sipped. Licked. Nuzzled.

She touched the side of her neck again, and pulled away, looking at her hand for the blood that wasn't there. Her fingers brushed over her lips in an echo of the kiss. Her heart still pounded and her chest felt flushed and full. And down low, an insistent throbbing, a hot reminder of the intensity of her dream.

It put her in mind of that shocking interlude with the Knave of Diamonds…so warm and liquidlike. Intense.

Maia didn't need to throw back her covers; she must have kicked them off during the dream. She dropped her feet to the floor, relieved to feel the relative cool of polished wood beneath them. During the summer, she had no need of a rug to warm the floor. Her night rail fell in a light cloud to just over her feet, loosening and allowing a bit of air to relieve her heated skin.

She couldn't banish the dream; and in fact, Maia realized she clung to the memories that were now sliding into mere wisps. She'd never seen his face, the shadowy man who came to her, whose weight she'd sworn had been pressing her into the mattress only moments before. She still felt his imprint on her body. Heavy. Hot.

But she was clearly alone. Clearly the victim…or

perhaps *recipient* was a better term…of a mere dream. A most realistic one, but a dream nevertheless.

And why she was dreaming about phantom vampires visiting in her chamber when she'd received such happy news today, Maia couldn't understand. At last she'd gotten word that Alexander was coming home and should arrive within a week. Perhaps sooner.

Before she opened the letter from him, she'd been overcome by apprehension. She'd nearly put it aside to open later, at night, when, if the news was bad—if he'd changed his mind or wasn't coming back—she'd be able to stay in her chamber alone with it for a bit. The last thing she wanted was for Corvindale to see her humiliation or grief.

She'd held it, looked at the crinkled envelope, folded and a bit dusty and stained from its long journey, and considered how she would react if it wasn't good news. What she would do to hide her pain. And then Maia had to wonder why she was so worried about it. Alexander had never given her any indication that he didn't hold her in high esteem. Certainly there'd been the faintest whiff of scandal attached to her after the Incident with Mr. Virgil, but she'd been so careful and had acted the epitome of propriety since. Alexander had come on the scene more than a year later and if he'd heard whisperings about it, the incident hadn't seemed to bother him.

But if he were to call off the engagement… Maia's stomach twisted. She'd lost her parents, too, and although this would be nothing like the pain she'd experienced then, it would be devastating. The announcement had already been made. It would be a scandal if her engagement was broken, for whatever reason. A terrible scandal.

When she opened the letter and read his brief note, her fears had ebbed. *I shall be home within the week. At long last.*

That made it sound as if he'd missed her, didn't it?

Just then, she heard a new sound on the moonlit street below. It sounded like a carriage door opening, and Maia rushed to the open window when she heard voices. Had Angelica returned?

She looked down and saw a hooded and cloaked female figure climbing up the front steps as the carriage rumbled off. *Please let her be Angelica!*

Maia didn't hesitate. She slipped quietly out of her chamber, heedless of her bare feet and flowing nightgown, hurrying silently down the corridor to the stairs. But by the time she got halfway down the angular staircase, pausing on the landing at the second floor, she recognized the voices below.

Not Angelica.

A door closed on the lower level, and she heard the businesslike tread of solid footsteps coming from the corridor where the earl's study was located. The last person she wanted to encounter was Corvindale, so Maia turned and started to climb back up. Worry and disappointment replaced the momentary surge of hope, but then she heard something that made her pause.

"—from Dewhurst," wafted up an unfamiliar feminine voice.

"What is the message?" Corvindale replied, his words rising clearly.

Maia crept back across the landing and started down

the next flight, aware that her feet would be in view of whomever was in the foyer should they look up. *Don't look up.*

"He bids you come retrieve the girl," said the woman, who was obviously the messenger. "From Black Maude's."

Corvindale's curse was sharp and vulgar. "She's at Black Maude's?"

Maia saw the top of his head as he whirled and started off, presumably back down the corridor in preparation for leaving.

"Wait!" Maia said, surging faster down the steps.

He turned up his face and their eyes caught as she hurried down, and for a moment, Maia felt the breath knocked out of her. *Him.*

No, impossible. She forced herself to breathe, to pull her attention from his glittering dark eyes. He was dressed in a white shirt that sagged and a loose neck-cloth, as usual.

"Miss Woodmore," he said, but his voice wasn't nearly as cold as it usually was. "I presume you heard the conversation."

"I'm going with you," she said.

"No," he began, but she interrupted.

"Yes. She's my sister. She might need me. Who knows..." Her voice threatened to break, a combination of desperation and fear weakening it. "Who knows what he's done to her."

Corvindale held her gaze for much too long and then snapped, "You have three minutes to dress yourself appropriately." He turned away and stalked off.

Maia looked down, having momentarily forgotten

her state of dishabille, and realized that the moonlight streaming over her had highlighted the flimsy fabric of her summer gown and her bare feet.

Three minutes wasn't nearly enough time, but she would manage it. She had no doubt that Corvindale would leave without her.

Dimitri hadn't expected the ever-proper Miss Woodmore to meet his deadline, so he was surprised and annoyed when, precisely three minutes later, she came tearing down the stairs. That was the thing about her. She was constantly surprising him with her stubbornness and, much as he hated to admit it, her wit. Even when he became his most earlish, she didn't back down.

A quick glance told him that she actually *carried* her shoes, and that some loose cloaklike garment was draped over a frock that he suspected wasn't completely done up, for Luce's sake, and he had a moment of serious regret.

If he'd given her a bit more time, she might not have presented herself partially clothed. Although whatever she'd donned would be an improvement over the transparent pink thing she'd been wearing earlier.

Without a word, he gestured for her to precede him out the side door where his footman was waiting with the landau. He'd chosen to be driven in the closed carriage rather than to drive himself for a variety of reasons—the least of which was the benefit of having another set of male hands if assistance was needed to procure Angelica—but now as he climbed into the very small, close space with Miss Woodmore and they started off, he regretted that decision. He should have had Iliana join them, for she was nearly as welcome a set of hands as a man. As well, she wielded a stake rather well for a mortal woman.

His companion, a very different sort of mortal woman than Iliana, but no less stubborn or intent, was busy putting her shoes on. The cloak had slipped from her shoulders confirming that, yes indeed, her dress sagged because it wasn't properly done up in the back. From what he knew of current fashion, it was unlikely that she'd had the time or ability to even pull on a corset and *that* was not a comforting thought.

Dimitri settled into his seat across from her and focused his eyes anywhere but *there*.

The aversion of his gaze didn't help matters much, for in such an enclosed space the blasted woman's presence was not to be ignored. The essence of a spice like cardamom or perhaps something even more exotic mingled with some sweet floral like lily of the valley, along with female musk and the crisp clean cotton of her frock, creating that potency he found impossible to dismiss. How in the bloody hell could a woman smell like a damned spice cabinet and a garden and still be so enticing?

Either slumber or her hurried dressing had mussed up her hair so that flyaway strands sprung from the braid that hung over one shoulder.

One ivory-blue shoulder, bared and pristine.

Elegantly curved. Brushed with a swath of moon, and then shadow, and then streetlight with the motion of the carriage.

Dimitri jerked his gaze away. He swallowed hard, felt the throbbing of his gums as he tried to keep his fangs sheathed and the rest of him from stirring. Satan's black bones, he was as bad as a green boy with his first whore. Even with Meg he hadn't experienced such a lack of control.

Pressing himself back against the seat squab, he angled his left shoulder so that the hard edge of the cushion frame dug into the throbbing, painful Mark on his skin, adding to the constant agony with which he lived. The deep, sharp response was a welcome distraction.

Yet…his thoughts would not be suppressed so easily. It would be nothing to reach across and close his hands over smooth, fine skin. Lower his face to hers again, taste her lips again, fill his hands with soft, silky flesh. *Heaven.* His nostrils flared automatically as she moved, sending a renewed waft of her scent into him and her gown shifting tauntingly.

With great effort, he kept his eyes from burning red and hungry. His fangs were extended, but still hidden. *It's been too long.*

A hundred and thirteen years. Three months. Five days.

His Mark twinged sharp and hot.

It should have gotten easier. It shouldn't be this impossible to keep from *needing* something he hadn't had for so long—especially since he no longer made the mistake of starving himself. But the saliva pooled in his mouth and his heart thudded in his chest. His skin prickled and his muscles leaped beneath, as if coiling up and ready to spring.

It was her proximity. The fact that they were so close and intimate in this small vehicle. The fact that only last night he'd allowed her to taunt him into *kissing* those damned full, top-heavy *lips.*

His unease was also due to the fact that moments before Voss's messenger had arrived tonight, Dimitri had been dreaming. Slumped in a chair, in his study, dreaming that he was arching over a slender, ivory body, filling his hands with feminine curves, tasting the warmth of her mouth…sinking into a virginal white neck, drinking the rich lifeblood as she moaned and writhed, pressing herself against—

"Where are we going?"

Miss Woodmore's question yanked Dimitri from the dark vortex of his thoughts. He swallowed hard, grateful for the redirection. *Angelica. At Black Maude's.* "Billingsgate."

Pulling the cloak back up to her shoulders, she commenced with some odd contortions that he realized were her attempts to do up her dress.

Dimitri made a sharp disgusted sound. "Turn around, Miss Woodmore," he said. "Allow me."

Her gaze flew to his, her eyes rising in a lowered face that made her look even more shocked. "I don't think—"

"It would be best if you didn't. Think," he added for clarification as much for himself as for her. Because when she huffed and turned around to present him with her back, his newly ungloved hands trembled.

Perhaps not the most intelligent decision he'd ever made, but this entire farce had commenced with a foolish decision six years ago, when he agreed to act as guardian to Chas Woodmore's sisters. That had been before he'd ever seen or met any of them.

Not that he supposed he could have denied Chas's request anyway. Especially if he *had* seen them. For Dimitri always did what was right. He did what honor demanded, despite the searing reminder of the devil's Mark on his back.

Miss Woodmore's skin was warm.

He didn't exactly touch it, not directly, but he could feel it through the thin fabric. And perhaps a fingertip brushed over its smooth silkiness when he buttoned the first button at her nape. A finger might also have brushed the curve that swept down to her shoulder. Nothing like his own, roped with the rootlike Lucifer's Mark, scarred and dusted with erratic hair.

He was quick, his fingers nimble, his fangs thrust out so far his gums hurt, filling his mouth. Her scent, the light brush from the hair swept over the back of her neck, the heat from her skin and the confirmation that she wore no corset made his gaze tinge red.

He didn't need to remind himself who she was: his ward, whom he was bound to protect. A *mortal*. A chit who infuriated him for any number of reasons. A young woman preparing for her wedding to a fine gentleman. The sister of one of his friends.

No, it wasn't who she was, or who she *wasn't,* for if Dimitri wanted her—wanted anyone—he'd have her. He'd lull her and coax her and ease her in. Simple as that, and damn whoever or whatever got in his way.

But he didn't. Want. Anyone.

He'd given it all up decades ago. He was an island.

And he'd remain that way until he discovered a way to put himself back the way he was, or until he died.

As soon as Dimitri finished, he removed his hands and tucked himself into the deepest corner of his seat, cursing Voss anew for everything he could think of: for taking Angelica, for whatever he'd done to her in the interim and for choosing a place to hide so far from Blackmont Hall that the ride was interminable.

"Are you going to tell me what's happening?" Miss Woodmore demanded. Apparently, in her eyes, fully clothed was fully armed.

"I'm certain I don't know what you mean." Dimitri sounded bored even to himself, and was rewarded when his companion sat bolt upright in her seat and fairly quivered with indignation and fury. How her eyes snapped and snarled, and she wasn't even Dracule.

"You certainly do, my lord. You aren't a bit obtuse. Were those really *vampirs* at the masquerade ball last night?"

Damn and blast and Lucifer's head on a pike. Had the staff been talking? Of course they knew all about their master and his lifestyle, but they were well-paid to keep their mouths shut—particularly around Mirabella, who had no idea about her own history with the Dracule. She'd been too young to remember anything when Dimitri took her in. Or could Iliana have slipped some information?

Dimitri waved an impatient hand. "If you must know, yes. I suppose I'd best answer your question or you'll never leave me be."

Miss Woodmore's breath caught audibly and she sagged back against her seat. Apparently she hadn't expected such immediate confirmation. "*Vampirs?* They're real? They truly do exist? Why are we in danger from them?"

He wavered for a moment, then chose the path of least resistance—in this case, meaning the path of fewer questions. "Cezar Moldavi is a vampire and because he is angry with your brother, he's looking for you and your sisters." He used the English term for the Dracule despite the fact that Miss Woodmore was somehow aware of the Hungarian pronunciation of *vampir*.

"Sonia, too?" Maia gasped, eyes growing wide. She looked as if she were about to erupt from her seat and charge off to Scotland.

"Be still, Miss Woodmore. I've already ascertained that your youngest sister is safe, and I've made the necessary arrangements so that she will remain so. A convent school is an excellent sanctuary for one who wishes to hide from vampires. They can't cross such a holy threshold." He eyed her narrowly, forcing himself to ignore that increased pulsing on his shoulder. "Perhaps you might consider joining her."

"Indeed not!" she replied, her shocked, fearful expression dissolving. "I know you don't wish for Angelica and me to burden you any further—and you are not alone in this opinion, for it's my fondest wish as well—but I am not about to be shipped off to St. Bridie's. Alexander—Mr. Bradington—will be arriving within a week, for I just received a letter today and—"

"Ah, yes, the erstwhile groom is at last returning to our little island here." A flash of distaste soured his belly. The man was welcome to the termagant sitting across from him. "I suppose you'll be bringing dressmakers in and speaking to flower-sellers and cakemakers, and there will be all sorts of activity disrupting my household, now that you've continued to rearrange my library." He glared out the window, ignoring the way the moonlight seemed to turn her rich chestnut-bronze hair to silver.

She opened her mouth to speak, but Dimitri dared not let her. "We're nearly there," he said, shifting in his seat and turning his scowl on her. "You'll stay in the carriage, Miss Woodmore. Black Maude's is no place for a proper young lady."

Her pointed chin lifted as if pulled on a string, and her eyes narrowed. "My sister—"

"Miss Woodmore," he said, allowing his voice to go low and silky, "you of all people know what can happen to a woman if she is seen where she should not be seen." He fixed her with his gaze. "Do you not?"

Even in the faulty light he could see the range of emotions that flashed across her face: shock, first—the bald blanching of widening eyes and parted lips. Then mortification and chagrin as she struggled to keep her chin up and her eyes from skittering away, and at last, fury.

"So you do remember," she said through a stiff jaw. Ah, the woman put on a good face, especially when she was backed into a corner. He had to give her credit for that. "How kind of you to remind me of my unfortunate near-mishap. What was it, three years past?"

Dimitri spread his hands and fingers in a blasé motion. "I don't quite recall the details," he said. "Other than the fact that you were dressed in boy breeches with your hair tucked up under a cap, and were attempting to enter a very disreputable area of Haymarket."

And that the man who'd taken her there, the bollocks-sucking William Virgil, would have compromised her if they'd been seen—or worse if they hadn't. Much worse.

"I was never certain whether you had recognized me or not," Miss Woodmore was saying in a surprisingly cowed voice. "I had rather hoped that no one had."

But Dimitri had indeed recognized Miss Woodmore—by her scent when he passed by, which, he supposed, was why it was burned into the insides of his nostrils so that he couldn't dismiss it, devil take it. Especially when they were in such close quarters as this blasted carriage.

Miss Woodmore didn't recall much of that evening; Dimitri had made certain of it afterward by utilizing his thrall. She couldn't remember that she'd actually walked into an establishment not very different than Black Maude's. One that catered to the particular tastes of men who craved young, virginal women. Reluctant, young, virginal women.

The more reluctant, the better.

It was a residence that she would never have been able to leave if Dimitri hadn't intervened.

And Miss Woodmore certainly didn't remember how three men and the madam of the place had attempted to keep Dimitri from removing her from the premises. And how he'd scooped up Miss Woodmore whilst baring his fangs and blazing his eyes and applying his brute force to pummel those repugnant people.

And how he'd very nearly *used* his fangs, for the first time in a century. Not to feed, but to destroy. To tear them into shreds.

No, Miss Woodmore couldn't remember him carrying her breeches-clad body back safely with him, ignoring what would be a scandalous display of curves and a torn shirt if anyone were to see her. The only thing she would remember was him helping her into a hackney and escorting her back to Woodmore.

That journey was the first time he'd been subjected to Miss Woodmore's tart, insistent tongue.

As a result of his forethought and expediency, the entirety of her scandal was that she'd been seen in breeches and out at night without a chaperone, in the company of a disreputable male—and that, only by the Earl of Corvindale. And, naturally, he didn't lower himself to spread gossip.

Dimitri considered it a favor to Chas that he'd handled it thus, and a favor to Miss Woodmore that he'd never divulged the details to her brother. It was too bad that she wasn't aware of all he'd done, for perhaps she would be a bit more appreciative if she were, he thought as he examined her balefully.

No, on the other hand, he sincerely doubted that she would.

"I've always wondered what possessed you to do such a foolish thing, Miss Woodmore," he said in the tone of a schoolmaster speaking to a student. "You, who are known for your extreme adherence to Society's standards, and who wouldn't even consider dancing two dances with the same partner on a night. Or who would never be seen without her gloves, even if they were spotted due to an unfortunate accident with an inkwell. And wasn't there an occasion when you refused—albeit with extreme courtesy—to speak to Mr. Gilbertson because you hadn't been properly introduced?"

And then it all went to hell, because she looked at him suddenly. Sharply. Her eyelids at half-mast, and with an unpleasant gleam in them. "My goodness, Lord Corvindale. I had no idea how closely you followed my reputation."

He was saved from having to respond as the carriage stopped in the filthy alley behind Black Maude's. Dimitri wasted no time in making his exit.

Maia took no trouble to muffle her annoyed footsteps as she approached Corvindale's bedchamber door. It would serve him right if he heard them pounding along the corridor.

It was well past noon the morning after they'd retrieved Angelica from the horrible, dirty, scandalous place called Black Maude's, and Maia was tired of waiting for the earl to drag himself from slumber. She needed to talk to *someone* about her sister, about what had happened.

She could hardly fathom it. It was simply inconceivable that Angelica had not only been bitten by one of those *vampirs*…but that it was *Lord Dewhurst*. How could that be? How could a member of the *ton* be a *vampir?*

There were these creatures—who, impossibly, actually *existed*—and they were after her and her sister, no one would tell her anything of substance, and her brother was missing and Alexander was coming home, but his letter hadn't really said anything to make her feel certain that he still loved her…and she felt *so lonely.*

So alone.

Maia swallowed as the prickle of a frustrated tear burned the corner of her eye. She didn't want to be in charge anymore. She didn't want to have to handle this—whatever this was—on her own. She didn't know how. She didn't understand it.

And she was more than a bit frightened. *Vampirs* attacking and killing people at a masquerade, and one of them a member of the peerage. And then one of them abducting her sister! According to Angelica, Dewhurst—or Voss, as she'd called the viscount (which was a warning sign in itself)—wasn't one of the angry, evil *vampirs* who'd killed three people at the Sterlinghouses' ball. Through this, Maia realized that Angelica had come to care for the man, only to learn that he was not only a rake, but a *vampir,* as well.

Definitely not someone she ever wanted Angelica to encounter again.

Maia shook her head and swallowed again, blinking hard. She'd had to deal with the death of their parents when she and her sisters were still in short skirts, and to help them get on without Mama and Papa. Chas was so absent that it all fell to her, all the time.

All the time. All of the problems. She'd been in charge for as long as she could remember, and normally she *liked* it. Liked managing things, solving problems, taking care of people. It made her feel as if she had some sort of control over her life.

But this…this was simply too confusing for her to handle alone. Too confusing, and too *dangerous.*

For the first time she could remember, Maia was frightened.

And there was no one else for her to turn to except Corvindale. Much as she hated the thought.

She was not going to show the earl weakness, but she *was* going to get some answers. Could he *know* that Dewhurst was a *vampir?* Was that why he'd been so coldly furious about Angelica's disappearance with the viscount?

Incensed at the thought that he'd kept that information from her, she held on to that emotion and drew in a deep breath. "Corvindale!" she called, knocking firmly on his chamber door.

She waited, and heard nothing from within. But she knew he was there—Greevely, the earl's valet, had told her. But only after she'd stared him down. That expression of determination and haughtiness was a learned one that she'd had to adopt in order to handle their affairs while Chas was gone. It worked without fail.

Except, it seemed, with the earl.

"Corvindale! I must speak with you!" she said, knocking harder and more vehemently. She'd been more than patient, waiting for him to drag his lazy bones from his chamber. *"Corvindale!"* Her sister's well-being was at stake, not to mention Maia's own concerns.

"Go away." His bellow nearly shook the rafters, but Maia was not to be thwarted. She'd sat up all night, holding her sister so that Angelica could sleep without fear. And twice, the poor thing had awakened from nightmares.

Maia drew in a deep breath and turned the doorknob, cracking the door. She wasn't quite brave enough to look inside, although she could see that the room was swathed in darkness. "Corvindale, I must speak with you. It's nearly two o'clock and I've been waiting all morning—"

"Go away, Miss Woodmore. If you must speak with me, you can wait until this evening."

Maia gritted her teeth. It wasn't as if she hadn't had to roust her brother once or twice or several times in the past. It was one thing to sleep until noon after a late night at the theater or his club, but when he hadn't stirred by midafternoon, and there were pressing problems to be solved…

She opened the door a bit wider, and the bright spill of light from the day made a long, narrow wedge on the floor and over the foot of a heavy wooden bed. The chamber smelled a bit like tobacco, along with lemon or bergamot and something clean and spicy—possibly from his soap or hair pomade, although she couldn't be certain if Corvindale even used pomade. His hair never seemed to be shiny or stiff from such an application and it certainly didn't stay in place for very long and instead seemed to curl up and around at the edges and his ears.

"Corvindale! It's imperative that I speak with you. This is a matter that cannot wait, and if you do not come out then I will come in."

There. That ought to bring him forth. If Maia knew one thing about men, she knew that they didn't like to have their bedchambers invaded by the fairer sex.

Except for their wives and mistresses, she supposed. And for some reason, her face flushed hot. What if he had a woman in there with him? A mental image of tangled sheets and a bare-chested man next to an equally bare woman made her cheeks even hotter.

Did unmarried earls actually bring those sorts of women into their homes? Or did they visit them at outside establishments? Or did he have a regular mistress?

How could a woman even stand to spend any length of time with his rude, controlling self? She supposed that while they were engaging in such activities, perhaps he wasn't talking quite so much. Her cheeks burned hotter.

"I am abed, Miss Woodmore, and have no intention of leaving it. If you insist upon speaking with me at this time, then don't let something as ridiculous as propriety keep you out."

Well, that made it sound as if he was alone. She drew in a deep breath and inched the door open farther, curling her fingers around the edge as much to keep it in position as to force herself to move forward. "My lord, I must speak with you regarding Angelica."

"I'm afraid you'll have to come in. I can't hear what you are saying."

Her fingers tightened on the edge of the door. She could just picture the contrary smile on his arrogant face—at least, she would if she could even fathom the man smiling. Which seemed an impossibility. He was playing with her, pushing her. Hoping to run her off.

Vile man. I'll show you who's not afraid of you and your bedchamber.

Still holding the edge of the door, she stepped fully onto the threshold, the door opening into a wide angle. She glanced at him once, then swiftly looked away, and her cheeks burst into flame.

He was *naked,* and the image that she'd seen for only the briefest moment was burned into her brain.

And it was much more fascinating—no, no, *intimidating*—than her previous, mental one.

Try as she might, closing her eyes, blinking, looking into the depths of the shadowy room, she couldn't banish the image of him sitting up, lounging against the head of the bed. The sheets were *low,* down to his *waist,* and a broad, very hairy chest and muscular arms showed dark against the white sheets. Maia tried to swallow, and her throat made an odd creaking sound because it was so dry. She felt all sorts of fluttering, hot feelings inside.

At last she found her voice. "This is exceedingly untoward."

"What is it, Miss Woodmore?" He was taunting her. *Definitely* taunting her. "Surely the sight of a man's torso isn't all that upsetting to a woman who is due to be married in short order."

"You could cover yourself," she said from between unmoving jaws.

"I see no reason to do so. Now what is it you must speak with me about?"

He really is the vilest man. She refused to look at him. Absolutely refused to allow her peripheral vision to scan over the impossibly square angle of his shoulders, outlined so well by the pale bedcoverings.

Maia continued, turning her attention to the matter at hand. "It's Angelica. She's been bitten by a... by one of those creatures that came to the masquerade ball. *Vampirs.* And she had horrible nightmares last night, my lord. I held her all night long, and she cried and thrashed." Her voice turned rough and she had to swallow hard to keep it steady. Despite her own dream of being bitten—a dream, a memory, that hadn't fully left her and still wrapped itself slyly around her consciousness—she knew that Angelica's experience had not been the hot, sensual one of her dream. "She won't tell me precisely what happened, but I fear that the worst has been done." If Dewhurst had ravished and ruined her sister, Maia would go after him herself, *vampir* or no. If Aunt Iliana could do it somehow, carrying a stake and presumably using it, so could Maia. "Not to mention…"

He shuffled under the bedcoverings, and she heard the crisp shift of the starched sheets. "I'm aware of all that you've told me, Miss Woodmore. And if you find it reassuring, your sister has assured me that…er…there is no reason to demand satisfaction or that Dewhurst come up to snuff. She is intact."

"Up to snuff? I should hope not!" Maia exclaimed, forgetting herself and glancing at him. His face didn't seem to have the same arrogance she was used to. Was the man softening, or was it merely the result of being awakened? "Even if he did—well…I would *never*… Chas would *never*…allow him to come near her again." Angelica compromised and wed to a *vampir?* Never.

"You seem to have forgotten that *I* am Angelica's guardian at this time," Corvindale said. The arrogance was back.

And so was her fury with him. God rot Chas for sticking her and Angelica with this impossible man as a *temporary* guardian. "As I said, my lord, *I* would not allow it."

He shifted and the sheet *slipped farther*. Maia tore her gaze away, but not before she saw…oh, God, a hip? A flat, ridged belly…and the shadow of something lower? She'd felt Alexander's chest before, of course, through his shirt…and, once, under it…but she hadn't really *seen* it. And even if she had, she didn't think it looked quite so…dark. And imposing. And—

Maia swallowed hard, and focused on the heavy curtains obscuring his window. She needed some answers, and she was going to get them—even if the man strode naked from his bed to come over and close the door himself. "What is my brother doing? How long has he been involved with these creatures? And what is *your* involvement, my lord? Do you associate with them, as well? Did you know that Dewhurst was one of them?"

"Do not concern yourself with me, or the other details, Miss Woodmore. All you need know is that you and your sisters are safe under my care, here at Blackmont Hall and at St. Bridie's, too. As for your brother… when he returns, I'm certain that he will answer at least some of your questions. And I am hopeful that he will do so in short order. Now, is there anything else, Miss Woodmore? This conversation hardly seems worth interrupting my sleep and threatening your reputation. Or is your reputation no longer a concern for you, now that you are off the marriage mart?"

She snapped upright and once again turned to look at him, meeting his eyes head-on. "You are beyond vile, Lord Corvindale," she whispered in a purely heartfelt tone.

And the man actually had the nerve to *grin* at her. A cool, arrogant smirk.

Very well, then, my lord. You might be the gentleman, but I have my own ways of smirking right back at you.

"Corvindale, I insisted on speaking with you because I felt you should know all of the information. I had hoped you'd do the courtesy of telling me what is happening and why. But apparently you cannot be bothered to do even that."

She drew her shoulders back, and settled her hand on a hip, digging her fingers into her flesh in an effort to keep from curling them around his neck.

If he wasn't going to give her the information she wanted, she was going to make his life as difficult as she could, including opening the curtains in every window in the house. And putting vases with flowers on every table. And reordering *all* of the books in his library. And… "I also wanted to speak with you because it will be of the utmost importance that Angelica is seen out and in Society. This must happen as soon as possible so as to combat any rumors or *on dits* that might have begun since she disappeared after the masquerade. That is the only way to preserve her reputation."

"And this concerns me, how?" He sounded deeply bored.

Maia gave him her own version of an arrogant smile. "Because you must be seen out and about with us. Quite a lot. In the next few days. In order to ensure that Angelica's reputation isn't besmirched, we will need the presence of an earl." Not that she was going to enjoy being in his company that much, but if she'd learned one thing about the earl, it was that he *hated* being bothered by people.

Any people, for any reason.

Going out in Society for the next several nights, due to his duty—which he'd also demonstrated was something he would not shirk—was going to be a most unpleasant experience for him.

Thus, she would enjoy every minute of it.

She turned to go, and then paused to look over her shoulder. "I shall determine which invitations we will accept, my lord, and then advise your valet so that he can see you are properly dressed for the occasions."

And she would make certain that she would pick

the most crowded, flamboyant events to attend. Just because she could.

With that, she walked out of his chamber and closed the door with finality.

6

IN WHICH OUR HEROINE
MAKES A CONFESSION

"Angelica?" Maia rushed out of her bedchamber, hair swinging loosely, nightgown bunching around her feet. "What is it?"

She'd been in a half slumber, spiraling into that warm, red world of sensuality that seemed to lure her every night as of late. It was the first night since her return from Black Maude's that Angelica had slept in her own bed, and Maia had kept her ears attuned for any sounds of distress from her sister's chamber…until she slipped into her dreams.

There must have been something that woke her, for when she came out into the hall, she nearly collided with Angelica.

"Oh!" her sister said, obviously surprised to see Maia.

"I was coming to check on you," she said, looking at Angelica's wide eyes and pale face. Something had happened. Something more than a dream… Then she noticed something in her sister's hand. "What's that in your hand? A stick?"

But even as she said it, she understood. It wasn't merely a stick in Angelica's hand, held close to the folds of her nightgown, but a stake. Meant to stab a *vampir.* "Oh," she said. She looked at her sister and their eyes met. The poor darling! She'd had such a horrible experience.

"What are you doing awake?" Angelica asked.

"I came to check on you. What's happened?" Maia asked, grabbing Angelica's hand and allowing her to lead the way back to Maia's chamber.

"I had a dream," Angelica replied. But Maia noticed that she glanced covertly back toward her chamber, as if expecting to see something. Or some*one* coming out of the door. "That Vo—that Dewhurst came into my chamber at night."

Maia looked at her sharply, her attention captured. They settled on her bed and she closed the door most of the way behind them. She left it cracked in the event there was something to hear from the corridor without.

"Darling, I'm so sorry," Maia said, closing her fingers around Angelica's. Her hands were chilled, so unusual for the warm summer's night. "How terrifying it must be. I didn't hear you cry out, although I heard something that sounded like you mumbling in your sleep. Or talking to someone."

"It seemed so real," she whispered. Her eyes were far away. "He…"

Maia couldn't help but think of her own dreams. Certainly they'd awakened her…but never because she was frightened. Only because she wanted them to be real.

She squeezed her sister's hands and struggled for the words to comfort her. "Sometimes dreams can be more frightening than reality," Maia said. "And sometimes, they can be so much more...beautiful...than reality."

"What do you mean?"

"Well." Maia felt her face warm as she realized the direction in which their conversation was going. She sat up and pulled a pillow onto her lap, clutching it over her torso. Perhaps this wasn't an appropriate conversation to have after all. "I don't know if I should tell you about it. After all, you're still unwed and—"

"And so are you," Angelica shot back. "You aren't married yet, dear sister, and so you haven't any more experience than I have."

Maia couldn't hold back the little smile that came along with the warm bubbling in her belly. "But that isn't true, dear *younger* sister. Alexander and I have—" She stopped and decided that there were some things Angelica didn't need to know. The very thought of Alexander and his imminent return made her middle fill with nervousness. She collected her thoughts, trying to figure out just how much to confess. "Well, we *are* engaged, and Chas and the lady patrons haven't been as vigilant as they were before our engagement was announced."

Angelica's eyes bulged, and Maia read the bald shock there. Obviously she believed that her elder sister was just as prim and proper as did the rest of the world. Including Corvindale.

"You and Mr. Bradington have—"

"No, no," Maia said. "Not exactly. Not *precisely.* But...Angelica. It's quite nice. Erin and Beth are right.

It's very pleasant. And I think it gets nicer." She could do nothing to diffuse the blush warming her cheeks.

"And what does this have to do with dreams being better than the reality? Or did you mean they were more frightening than reality?"

"Well." Maia hesitated. Perhaps this wasn't something she should confess to her sister. After all, it was very…personal. She looked away, adjusting the pillow in her lap. Perhaps it would be best if she changed the subject. But before she could, Angelica pressed.

"What is it?"

Maia glanced around the room, noticing the soft golden light cast by the lamp and the rumpled bed-clothes. Somehow, in the dimness, in the middle of the night, it seemed almost permissible to talk about it—just as she and Angelica had shared confidences when they were younger, deep under the covers when they were supposed to be sleeping. It had been a long time since she'd wanted to share her deepest confidences…with anyone. But she needed to. Maia drew in a deep breath and spoke. "After your experience with Dewhurst, I had a dream. About…it."

"You dreamed about *Dewhurst?*"

"*Shh!*" Maia looked toward the ajar door. "You'll wake Mirabella! No, I didn't dream about *Dewhurst*." She looked at her sister, scrutinizing her closely. What would Angelica think of her if she knew she'd liked the bite of a *vampir?*

But perhaps…perhaps it would make her sister feel a little better, knowing that there was a different perspective. After all, even in Granny Grapes's stories, there had been *vampirs* who didn't mean to hurt people. And there were people who'd found the creatures fascinating. "It's going to sound horrible to you, Angelica. You'll think me mad."

"Not any more than I already do," Angelica replied with a small smile. "Tell me."

Maia realized her fingers were plucking energetically at the lace on the pillow in her lap. "I dreamed that a *vampir* visited me in my chamber. But it wasn't frightening. It was…like embracing Alexander, and kissing him…but it was different. Better. And when the vampire bit me—"

Angelica gasped. "What?"

"In my dream, he bit me. Right…here. It didn't hurt, in my dream. In fact, it was…it made me…" She clamped her lips shut, realizing her voice had become a little breathy. That was just too much information. The next thing she knew, Maia would be confessing the kiss she'd shared with the Knave of Diamonds. Something *real* that had happened…and that she'd forced herself to try and forget.

Perhaps that was why she'd been focusing on the dreams so much—they weren't real. They couldn't happen.

She couldn't feel guilty about them. Especially now that Alexander was coming back.

"You *liked* it?" Angelica exclaimed, causing Maia to glance toward the door for fear someone would hear them.

Her whole body froze, her belly dropping low and her heart stopping when she met a pair of glittering dark eyes in the dark corridor. *Corvindale.* Maia felt ill and hot and faint all at once and she clutched the pillow to her chest. "My *lord*."

How long had he been standing there? What had he heard? *Oh, heavens...* What if he'd heard her talking about her *dream?* Thank God she hadn't told Angelica about the Knave of Diamonds, too!

His face seemed stonier, even more tight and angry than usual, and she had to swallow hard to keep her heart from surging up into her throat. She couldn't remember a time she'd ever been so mortified.

"My apologies. I was just arriving home and heard voices," the earl said—or something like that. Maia couldn't hear a thing over the rushing sound in her ears and the pounding of her heart.

Of all people to hear her confess such a thing…it had to be Corvindale.

She wanted to crawl under the bed and hide. But she didn't. She managed to speak calmly, she supposed; but she couldn't remember exactly what she said. And soon he was gone to investigate some noises he'd heard below, leaving her and Angelica alone again.

With the door closed tightly behind him.

Her sister didn't seem to realize what had happened, and for that Maia was grateful. But her cheeks were still hot and it took a long time for her heart to stop pounding so erratically.

Part of the reason was that, for a moment there, she'd only seen part of the earl's face. The lower part, exposed by the wavering light from her lamp. And for a stunning, heart-stopping second, she'd focused on his mouth.

And she recognized it.

The Knave of Diamonds.

It was a good thing she was curled up on her bed, for her knees turned to water and she was literally unable to breathe.

But by the time the earl had spoken, and then taken his leave, Maia had realized her error. There were a multitude of reasons that the knave couldn't have been Corvindale—the most compelling of which was the fact that the masked man had not only conversed and flirted with her, but kissed her, as well. All without one insulting comment.

For Corvindale to have done something so out of character was an impossibility. Especially since it was clear that he despised Maia as much as she despised him.

Although "I do hope you aren't about to cast up your accounts on my waistcoat" might qualify as an insult....

"Angelica," Maia whispered, when she saw her sister with her ear pressed to the crack of the door. "What are you doing?" But it was obvious: she was listening to whatever Corvindale had gone to investigate.

Curious and willing to have a distraction, she joined her taller sibling, forced to half crouch next to her at the open door. They listened for a moment and heard nothing but the faint creaks and groans of the house.

"Did you really like it, in your dream? When he bit you?" Angelica whispered.

Maia froze. "I don't want to talk about it," she snapped softly. *I wish I'd kept my mouth closed.* She heard a dull thud below, then silence.

"I cannot imagine finding it anything but horrifying," Angelica whispered back.

Maia had to close her eyes as a warm shiver of remembrance trickled through her. "Even those stories

Granny used to tell us, about the vampires...even then there were some people who didn't find it...horrible." Apparently she was one of them. Of course, perhaps if it happened in reality she might change her mind.... "And it was just a *dream,* Angelica."

They both heard the footsteps ascending the stairs at the same time. They whipped around simultaneously, silently dashing back to the bed. They'd just tumbled onto it in a heap of nightgowns and pillows when someone rapped on the bedchamber door.

"At least he knocked this time," Maia muttered as the door eased open.

But then she saw who it was, and she was right behind Angelica as she flew off the bed. "Chas!" she and Angelica cried at the same time.

"Hush—no one can know I'm here," he said, embracing them both. "Come down to the study with me so we can converse privately."

Relief and annoyance rushed through Maia. She had plenty of questions for her brother, as well as a demand: to get her away from the Earl of Corvindale.

She was more than delighted to pull on a robe and follow him down to the parlor.

So these are Chas's sisters.

Narcise Moldavi watched as the two young women entered the parlor at Blackmont Hall. Wearing a wide-brimmed hat and men's clothing, Narcise leaned against the fireplace and waited, knowing that they wouldn't realize she was a woman. The brim shaded her face, and the faint brush of soot she'd applied beneath her cheekbones to give her not only the impression of gauntness, but a bit of stubble, made her look like a skinny old man.

The sisters were very different in appearance, as well as in demeanor. One of them was dark and gypsyish-looking like Chas, with lush brown hair, dusky-rose skin and exotic eyes. She took a seat and scanned the room, clearly observing and taking it all in. She was taller than the other, lighter-haired one, who strode in and immediately began to make adjustments: the lamp wicks, the pillows on the sofa, even Dimitri's stacks of books.

That one must be Maia, and the dark one was Angelica.

Both women were striking, but the elder one was a classic English beauty with her fair complexion. Petite and delicate, unlike Narcise, Maia had hair that defied description: it was neither blond nor chestnut nor auburn, but a mixture of the three shades, and then some. She had a heart-shaped face and a rosebud mouth that seemed to be pursed with annoyance. Her sharp green-brown eyes shot daggers at Chas when he was standing next to Dimitri, talking in a low voice as they sipped whiskey.

Chas had best keep her from Cezar's sight. Narcise shivered, thinking of what her brother would do to such a beautiful young woman as Maia Woodmore. Considering what he'd done to Narcise, his own sister…

Of course, the fact that she was Dracule and must live forever was added incentive for Cezar to do what he would. Or to have his friends do what they would, which was more to his taste anyway. Incest, at least, was not one of Cezar's many sins.

After all, no matter what sort of torment and pleasure they put her through, Narcise couldn't die without a wooden stake to the heart or ten minutes in the sun. Which was why Cezar had made certain all of the furnishings in her windowless chamber had been made of metal. He was taking no chances of losing his favorite bargaining chip.

At the thought, Narcise couldn't quite suppress the flutter of panic that swirled in her belly. Chas had helped her escape from that horror, but that didn't mean she'd never return to it. Cezar wouldn't stop searching for her until he was dead.

Or until she was.

Narcise remembered her fantasies of finding feathers and wrapping herself in them, then falling out of a window to lie in the sun. Eventually she'd have to die, weakened by the feathers and burned by the sun's rays. Some days, even now, she considered it. At least then Cezar couldn't get to her.

And Chas would be safe.

Her glance flickered to him as he greeted his sisters, who were both loose-haired and dressed in nightclothes, and they settled in their seats. At this moment, he looked more like an English gentleman—albeit an exotic one, with his Romanian coloring—than she was used to seeing him: in a white shirt done up to the throat, covered by a dark coat, along with pantaloons. He was holding a glass, his hair fairly tamed and pomaded smooth. Clean-shaven. All this in deference to his proper sisters, who, according to him, had no idea that he spent his days and nights hunting *vampirs*.

The irony that he was an enemy of her race only fueled Narcise's fascination with him. A Dracule involved with a vampire hunter. How absurd and dangerous.

And how surprising that she could actually find pleasure with a man, actually *trust* one, after all she'd been through.

Chas glanced over at her and she met his black gaze coolly. She'd learned long ago not to show weakness or truth in her face or eyes. It could be used against her. And it had.

Oh, it had.

Chas's eyes crinkled slightly at the corners as the ends of his mouth tipped slightly, and she knew he was measuring her response to meeting two of his sisters. Narcise tucked down the little unfurling of warmth in her belly. She felt safe with him. Safe and comfortable.

But he didn't need to know that.

Nevertheless, she didn't want to be here, but Chas had given her little choice. It was either come to London with him, or be foisted off on Giordan.

And that was not going to happen. The very thought of being in the same city, let alone the same room, as Giordan Cale made her ill. Knowing that Chas had met up with him at the inn in Reither's Closewell, where she and Chas had been staying, had been disturbing, to say the least. She'd remained upstairs in their chamber, out of sight.

Although, knowing Giordan, he'd probably scented her.

On Chas.

"You must be Narcise Moldavi. The vampire."

The words came from Angelica, who'd been looking closely at her. Maia hissed something at her sister, and then both of them focused their attention on Narcise. Neither appeared pleased, although while Angelica looked angry, Maia seemed merely surprised.

Annoyed at having her disguise expunged, Narcise directed her own gaze onto the little chit who'd spoken in such distasteful tones, allowing the flare of heat to blaze there for a moment. *You have no idea who you're dealing with, little mortal girl.* "I am." She drew off her hat and flung it onto Dimitri's desk. Her head and face immediately felt cooler as her hair sagged in its low knot.

"Are you here so that we can welcome you to the family?" Angelica responded just as coolly.

Narcise ignored Chas's slight movement, as if he were about to interfere. *I can handle this,* she said with a quick glare. "I'm here, in fact, endangering my person only because of *you,*" she told the girl.

Narcise moved deliberately, away from the fireplace and over to help herself to a glass of Corvindale's whiskey. "Your brother learned that Voss had abducted you and he insisted on coming to London, despite the danger to me."

"You know very well you didn't have to come to London with him," came a smooth voice from the doorway. "Don't blame your own cowardice on the girl, Narcise."

The glass slipped in her hand, but she held on to it. Just barely. Turning, she faced Giordan Cale for the first time in a decade.

Their eyes met for a moment and she felt the twin spears of loathing: hers for him, and the same emotion shining in his own burning gaze. He was baiting her, referring to her imprudent choice to accompany Chas to London rather than stay with Giordan at Reither's Closewell.

Narcise didn't bother to respond other than to add a warning flash of fangs to a brief sneer. Sipping her whiskey—trying not to gulp what she suddenly, desperately needed—she walked over to stand next to Chas.

But Giordan was no longer paying attention to her. He'd turned, presenting her mostly with his back as Dimitri grudgingly introduced him to the Woodmore girls. Narcise sipped from her glass again, focusing on the heat burning down to her belly and through her limbs and not the back of his head, or the way his coffee-colored coat stretched perfectly over broad shoulders. Giordan paid his tailor well.

He looked the same as he had the last time they'd seen each other, although then his face had been bitter and hard, and worn from nights of depravity and hedonism. Tonight, his handsome features were relaxed and his eyes bland, except for that brief flash of emotion when she first saw him. Giordan still wore his hair unfashionably short, in close, rich brown curls that left his Slavic forehead and temples exposed. She caught a glimpse of his hand, ungloved, curled into a fist against his thigh and realized he wasn't as unmoved as he appeared.

But whether it was anger or hate that tensed his fingers, she didn't know.

And she didn't care. She was hardly aware of the conversation going on around her until Dimitri made a joke that wasn't really a joke about Giordan taking over the responsibility of the Woodmore girls and their guardianship. It was quite clear to everyone in the room that he was deadly serious about it.

Giordan responded with easy humor, accepting a glass of whiskey that his friend had moved to pour for him. "I wouldn't dream of depriving you, Dimitri."

"But why can't we go with you, Chas?" asked Maia.

Narcise looked at her, noting the firm yet desperate note in her voice. Someone was either very attached to her brother, or exceedingly unhappy at Blackmont Hall. Pleased to have something to distract her from the presence of the man she loathed most in the world—or second most; that other honor belonged to Cezar—Narcise watched the elder Woodmore sister.

Upon closer observation, Narcise had to adjust her first impression of the young woman. Despite Maia's self-assurance and need to be in control, there was an underlying sort of heat exuding from her that made her softer and more sensual than at first glance. Perhaps something only another woman would notice.

Narcise glanced at the young Maia and amended her thought—perhaps only another woman who was very experienced in the ways of intimacy would notice the sense of unfulfilled sensuality smoldering beneath capable hands and brisk movements. It lingered in the eyes, Narcise decided. In the green-brown and gold eyes, in that full pout of an upper lip, and most of all, in the female, musky scent that her Draculian nose recognized.

This was a woman who was not experienced with men, but who was on the cusp of being so…who'd come to the edge and who hadn't gone over. Who was waiting.

Perhaps it was because Narcise herself recognized that feeling of unfulfilled expectancy. It had taken her decades to find it, to allow herself to truly feel on a plane deeper than the merely physical. To battle through the humiliation and pain at the hands of Cezar's friends and enemies alike, to finally make love with a man who truly awakened and aroused her. Whom she trusted and opened herself to.

Now she couldn't bear to look at him, even when they were in the same room.

Narcise turned her attention away from those dangerous thoughts and the man in question, and happened to glance at Dimitri. The man was a rock: hard, cold and emotionless.

Exactly the way Narcise wanted to be.

Dimitri noticed the contemplative way Narcise was looking at him, as if she meant to find some deep secret in his eyes. But she, intensely beautiful and deliciously scented as she was, was much easier to ignore than the daggerish looks Chas's sister continued to slip him.

He was trying not to think about the shock in Miss Woodmore's face when she'd seen him standing there, in the doorway of her chamber. Naturally he'd had a legitimate reason for being there, and it wasn't his fault that her voice carried so that he heard what she was saying regarding her dream about a vampire. The woman needed to learn restraint, blast it all.

But for a moment, his heart had stopped cold when he thought he saw recognition along with mortification in her eyes.

Then he talked himself out of it, for she simply couldn't have put the pieces together that he was the Knave of Diamonds. He'd even taken care to remove his costume with its glass ruby and red-and-black waistcoat immediately after their...interlude.

Apparently that interlude hadn't made as much of an impression on her as some dark, erotic dreams, which was a damn good thing. Although the fact that she seemed to be having the same sorts of dreams that had been plaguing him was another problem entirely.

He sincerely hoped that her dreams weren't nearly as explicit and erotic as his own.

Dimitri was half listening as Chas tried to explain to his sisters that he was a vampire hunter. The fact that he'd allied himself with a beautiful, if emotionally damaged, Dracule woman caused even more confusion for the Misses Woodmore. It simply wasn't logical, of course, and they had questions.

And even Dimitri could appreciate the position of the sisters.

Which meant, blast it all, that he'd be the recipient of more badgering by Miss Woodmore when her brother disappeared again with his paramour. For it had become abundantly clear that Chas and Narcise were not merely companions on an adventure, nor was she an unwilling partner in their journey. He could smell the intimacy between them.

That wasn't the only thing he could scent. Voss had been here, the bastard. Despite the fact that Angelica hadn't admitted it, Dimitri knew he'd been in the house—probably in the girl's chamber with her—tonight. For all he knew, she could have let him in herself, enthralled and helpless under his influence.

Dimitri's teeth ground together. He and Woodmore were going to take care of Voss as soon as they found him. And then Chas would have one of his problems taken care of…leaving him with a more sensitive one.

He scanned Narcise with objective eyes. Definitely a beautiful woman. But certainly not one who had ever interested him—even that night in Vienna when Moldavi had offered her to Dimitri as a bribe of sorts. When he had a woman, however occasional that event might be, he wanted her willing and without cold, dead eyes. Not that they were cold and dead now when she looked at Chas. Cool. But not dead.

Dimitri shifted impatiently and glowered at the trio of Woodmores, who had overrun his life, his home and now even his private office.

Would they never stop talking? He just bloody damn wished everyone would get out of his study so that he could get back to his work. His research and studies had been disrupted so much that he was certain what little he'd managed in the last week was worthless.

The stack of books that Miss Woodmore had taken it upon herself to neaten as soon as she entered this little meeting reminded him that he hadn't been to the antiquarian bookstore yet. He flattened his lips. He would go tomorrow, or the next day at the very latest. He was through having his work *completely* disrupted.

"Corvindale is your guardian for the foreseeable future," Chas was saying flatly, looking at Maia with an implacable expression, "but I wasn't going to stand aside and let Voss compromise my sister."

"I'm not compromised," Angelica said stubbornly.

"It doesn't matter," Woodmore replied, glancing around the room. "We know he was here tonight, Angelica. Whether you invited him or welcomed him or—"

"I certainly didn't invite him," Angelica shot back in outrage. "I wouldn't invite a terrifying creature like him anywhere!"

"It doesn't matter," Chas continued. "Corvindale and Cale are going to help me find him. And then I'm going to kill him."

And then Dimitri would be able to get back to his studies, and forget about the upheaval brought by a houseful of mortal women.

And perhaps then he'd stop dreaming about one in particular.

WHEREIN A CHOICE OF ACCESSORIES
PROVES DISASTROUS

The carriage rolled to a stop at the rear entrance of the establishment Dimitri sought. Tren, the footman, had aligned the vehicle near enough the back entrance that his master was able to step out from the open door—which had been fitted with a fanlike cover that expanded as the door drew wide, blocking any sunshine—directly into the little shop.

The smell of age and wisdom, littered with dust, worn leather and fabrics…and yet something fresh, curled into his sensitive nose. The door closed behind Dimitri and he found himself amid tall, close shelves lined with books. Walls of wide, shallow drawers like those found in the British Museum were interspersed with the bookshelves.

The soft glow of lamps came from strategic places on the walls, but Dimitri didn't need their illumination. He was well at home in dim light, and felt the familiar wave of peacefulness that always hovered in these surroundings. Merely stepping into the place eased his tension. Even the constant, screaming pain from his Mark seemed to ebb.

"Ah, you've returned."

He looked up to see the shop's proprietress emerging from between two stacks. A woman of indeterminate age, she blinked owlishly from behind square spectacles as if she'd just been awakened—or, more likely, pulled from whatever she had been reading. Yet her gray-blue eyes turned bright and she seemed pleased to see him. She wore a long bliaut that, along with the points of her wide sleeves, skimmed the ground. Around her waist hung a loose leather cord, to which a collection of keys to the many chests, cases and drawers was attached.

In one long-fingered hand was an open book that she appeared to have been perusing before his presence interrupted her. Her long pale hair was separated into two thick tails that fell behind her shoulders. A pair of finger-thick braids began at her temples and curved around to the back of her head. The fact that she neither showed the deference due an earl nor made use of the proper address he hardly noticed.

"No other customers again, I see," he commented, reaching idly for a dusty book. "I find it a wonder that you remain in business, this little shop tucked away in the back mews of Haymarket."

She smiled, replying, "'Tis a happy thing, then, that I have the patronage of an earl to keep my interests afloat."

"I gave your direction to an acquaintance of mine some weeks past," Dimitri said, glancing down at the excellent French translation of *The Iliad*, "but he couldn't seem to find you. I told him you were next door to the old tannery, but he didn't see the shop."

She didn't seem concerned about the loss of a potential customer. "Perhaps that was a day the shop was closed. Have you given any more thought to breaking into the museum and examining the stele from Rosetta?"

Dimitri didn't recall speaking such a fantasy aloud, let alone to this woman, but he was never able to summon his customary abrasiveness whilst here. Thus, he responded, "I'm certain I could arrange to see the stone privately if I thought it would be help in my quest. I am Corvindale, of course."

"That is, I'm certain, quite true. Are you in search of anything in particular today?" she asked. "There are some new scrolls I've received—perhaps you might take a look at them." She gestured toward one of the corners of the dingy little shop.

"Nothing in particular. However, it's rare that I leave without finding something to add to my library." Dimitri had never told her of his quest. How could one explain to an ageless, absentminded woman about his desire to break a covenant with the devil?

She'd think him mad and close up the shop to him, as well.

The proprietress merely nodded, then absently returned her attention to the book she held. "If there is aught I can do to help…" And she wandered off.

Dimitri normally would have done the same, but today things prickled at him. Uncomfortable things. He didn't want to be alone with his thoughts. "Have you," he began, following her. "Have you any old, very old, perhaps original, chapbooks of the Faust legend?"

She turned from where she'd paused at a table and looked up from her book. Satisfaction gleamed in her eyes. "Faust. And why would you be looking for a story you know so well?"

Dimitri couldn't keep the jolt of surprise from blasting through him at—not so much her exact words, but the sharp, suddenly knowing look in her fathomless eyes. "What precisely do you mean by that, madame?" he asked, placing all of the chill and inflection of an earl's power behind it.

"I think, Dimitri of Corvindale, that you know all of what I mean."

He glowered in all of his earlness, and thought even for a moment of allowing some of his vampire glow to burn in his eyes. Yet, he said nothing, simply waiting for her to explain.

The woman closed her book without marking the page. And it was a very thick tome. "You and Johann Faust have much in common, do you not? Your pacts with the devil are quite different, and yet the same. That is what I mean."

Instead of the thunderous rage that might have—perhaps should have—flooded him, Dimitri felt only a wave of shock. "How do you know this?"

She merely looked at him. "It matters not. However, might I remind you that your selections from here have ranged from *Lemegeton Clavicula Salomonis* to *Malleus Maleficarum,* as well as a wide variety of Bibles and kabbalistic literature. Even some from the Hindis. And you've even asked about *moksha.* All of them have had aught to do with recognizing demons or calling to them, or of the word and teachings of our God. And so," she said, still holding him with her gaze, "one draws conclusions."

Dimitri wasn't precisely clear on how she'd drawn such a conclusion—albeit a correct one—based on his purchases, but earls didn't lower themselves to arguing with shopkeepers.

Instead, he said stiffly, "There is one large difference between myself and Herr Doktor Faust."

She nodded, as if she already knew and was waiting for him to speak it.

"Faust called Lucifer to him. I did not."

She nodded again. "But he came to you when you were at your most vulnerable. That is how he works."

"Who are you?" Dimitri demanded, suddenly flooded with the memory of that dark, hot night when Lucifer visited him in his dream. A night of fitful sleep, filled with smoke and ash and the heat of London's Great Fire.

"My name is Wayren. This is my shop." She spread an elegant hand around the space. Then she looked at him. "What do you seek, Dimitri?"

"I've been searching," he said in a subdued voice he hardly recognized as his own, "for a way out. A way to break his hold on me."

"You're certain there is a way?" she asked, her eyes steady on him.

"No." Despair washed over him. "I'm certain there isn't. For if there were, I swear I'd have found it by now."

Without waiting for her response, he spun on his feet, confused and unaccountably furious, and left.

Dimitri snarled at his footman as he opened the door to the carriage waiting in the moonlight.

Nearly four days since the invasion of his study, and he, Woodmore and Cale had been unable to locate Voss in London. He'd been there that night, the cocky bastard, in Angelica's chamber…but somehow, he'd gotten away before Chas arrived. And since then, he seemed to have evaporated into darkness.

Probably with the blessing of Lucifer.

Dimitri would have suspected Voss had made his escape from London if he hadn't received a terse message from him today. Voss's message said that Belial was intending to attack the Woodmore sisters again tonight, and warned him to be on his guard.

As if Dimitri ever let his guard down. Voss knew better than that.

Chas was off tending to Narcise somewhere in London, keeping out of sight of anyone who might notice his presence while trying to find Voss. Dimitri didn't know where he was, nor did he have any safe way to get the word to Woodmore that his sisters were in particular danger, although he did leave a message at White's and Rubey's, as well as the Gray Stag and a few other locations Chas might visit. Using blood pigeons—ones that the Dracule specially trained to fly by following a particular scent of blood to deliver the message—wasn't secure enough, for Cezar had been known to intercept them.

Cale was spending the evening with the woman named Rubey. She was a mortal who operated an establishment catering to the pleasure needs of the Dracule, and she was also a friend of Voss, who could be contacting her—which was Cale's official excuse for the visit.

But Dimitri was required to attend to the ladies tonight at some party for some lord or viscount or earl named Harrington, where, according to Iliana, who'd heard it from Mirabella who'd presumably heard it from the sisters, rumor had it that the guest of honor was going to make a proposal of marriage to Angelica Woodmore.

If Iliana hadn't come down with some sort of sniffle and headache, complete with red, dripping nose and hacking cough, *she* could have ridden in the carriage with the young ladies and left Dimitri to follow in his own vehicle or even on horseback to ensure their safety along the dark streets.

But he dared not chance leaving them unattended in the carriage, and so he climbed into the blasted thing.

Assaulted immediately by perfumes and powders and acres of skirts and wraps and trailing-off giggles, Dimitri settled onto his seat with nary a word and hardly a glance at his companions. Silence had fallen, in fact, as soon as the door opened and he ducked in, as if his mere presence put a cork in their conversation.

One thing to be grateful for.

But as he adjusted his coattails and the carriage lurched off, Dimitri was assaulted by something else entirely. Something heavy and dark and crushing, over his chest and onto his lungs.

Rubies.

He looked up and around, already feeling slow and weak, already hardly able to breathe, trying to maintain an empty expression even as he felt his strength draining away. *Where in the dark hell are they?*

Then he saw them, dangling from Angelica's ears. Ruby earbobs. Large ones, too. She was watching him, as if she noticed his sluggishness, and he pressed his lips together to hide the affliction. The gems were strong, but they weren't enough to kill him or even to burn him…unless they touched his flesh.

But they made him feel as if he were deep in a pool of hot, red water…slow and murky, his limbs heavy. Before they came to Blackmont Hall, he'd made certain none of the women had rubies; all of his staff understood that no gems were to enter his home without approval from him.

How had Angelica come by these, then?

Miss Woodmore shifted at that moment and Dimitri saw that she, too, was wearing them. Ruby earbobs.

And then he knew precisely how they'd come about getting the stones, for his brain worked just fine even if his body was leeching into bonelessness.

Damn Voss to his dark hell.

He'd done it. Probably when he visited Angelica's chamber that night. It would be just like the man to leave them for the sisters, mainly as a jest to Dimitri— to let him know that Voss had breached his residence and found a way inside. He wouldn't have expected them to all be confined in a carriage together, where the proximity made the potency of the jewels even worse.

"Lord Corvindale!" Angelica said, as Dimitri tried to fight back the fury at his realization, strangled and weak. "Are you ill?"

All three women suddenly fluttered about him as if he were an injured child, and everything became a flurry of pastel skirts and perfumes and wide eyes. Which of course made the whole situation worse, as the rubies swung closer, and Dimitri angrier, resulting in an even more heavy strangling and crushing of his torso.

"A...way..." he tried to say, trying to push the girls and the four robins'-egg-size jewels away.

Then all of a sudden, there was a huge thump and a crash and the landau lurched to a halt. They all tumbled every which way, dislodged by the great force. Dimitri, still pinned in the corner, struggled to pull to his feet, getting a bit of a reprieve as the girls with the ruby earrings jolted away from him.

But before he could gather up his immense strength and master control of his ribbony limbs, the carriage door whipped open and he saw the flash of glowing red eyes. The next thing he knew, screams and scuffling and flying skirts filled the air and in the midst of the melee, Angelica was gone.

Taking, thank the Fates, half the paralyzing rubies with her.

Miss Woodmore was shouting orders and thrashing about on the floor of the carriage, tangled with Mirabella and Dimitri's legs and shoes, and he barely managed to grab on to her ankle or she would have lunged out the ajar door after her sister.

He yanked her awkwardly back into the carriage in an effort to get away from her, the rubies and the mess inside, and to fumble his way out and after Belial. But by the time he managed to get free of the rubies' hold and into the night air, it was too late. They were out of sight, out of scent, and any sounds from their flight were mingled with every other sound of London at night.

Damnation.

Tren, Dimitri's groom, was lying on the ground,

his face bloodied and his limbs unmoving. The horses had been cut free and were gone, leaving all of them stranded with the landau and no way to give chase. A small group of street urchins stood in the shadowy gap between two brick buildings, likely up to their ankles in the mucky waste that Dimitri smelled. They watched with wide white eyes. And behind him, standing in the doorway of the carriage, was Miss Woodmore, looking decidedly less fresh and smooth than she had moments earlier. And her mouth was moving.

Oh, was it moving.

Cursing, furious, still trying to shake off the last of his weakness, Dimitri blocked out his ward's recriminations and questions and demands and checked on Tren—who was alive and likely to remain so, as evidenced by his eyes opening and the curse words spilling from his lips—and then looked over to the children watching in the dark.

None of them were able to give him a clear answer on where the vampires had gone, and despite the fact that Dimitri was relieved that Belial had only seen fit to take one of the carriage's occupants, he was incensed that he'd been caught by surprise.

Yet another unfortunate event caused by Voss and his games and jests.

Frustrated by the fact that he couldn't leave the women and go off after Belial immediately, Dimitri sent Tren off to find a hackney or some horses so he could get them home. Then he could start combing the city for Angelica and Belial. While the groom limped off, Dimitri circled the area around the accident, sniffing, observing, listening intently in the distance for any clue that would lead him after the younger Woodmore sister.

We have time. His mind was clear and calm. Belial would keep Angelica safe and protected until he got her to Moldavi, and getting a young woman across the Channel during wartime would be some challenge, even for the Dracule—but it could be done. If Dimitri could find them before they left London it would be best, but he knew exactly where Moldavi stayed in Paris and where they'd be taking her. So if he had to go to Paris and face down the damned child-bleeder, he'd do it.

With relish.

Cool and intent, his brain clicked through the steps to hunt down Belial and his victim, running through the possibilities—would they leave tonight, would they keep her somewhere until a boat was arranged, would they leave from the docks here or go by land to Dover—even as his eyes observed and he lifted his face to scent over and under the smells weaving in the world, searching for the one that belonged to Angelica.

When he realized she hadn't stopped talking, trying to get his attention, and her insistence was *interrupting his concentration,* Dimitri turned and snarled at Miss Woodmore. To his surprise, she actually closed her mouth for a moment, looking up at him with wide, shocked eyes.

He drew in a deep breath, fighting to keep his eyes from burning red and from his fangs being exposed. And, staying his distance from the lethal rubies, as he met her gaze, he felt something inside him soften. She looked terrified and rumpled and, impossibly, as if she were about to cry.

"Surely you aren't about to cry, are you, Miss Wood-more?"

His words had the desired effect, for she straightened her shoulders, which had begun to bow inside her silvery-blue gown, causing it to gap at the bodice. Her gaze flashed almost as hotly as Belial's, except that it glistened with tears.

"Of course I am," she said in affronted tones. One of the tears spilled over and ran down her cheek and she wiped it away angrily.

Dimitri clamped his mouth shut on the automatic response he'd intended to make after her denial and looked at her again. And then realized he really shouldn't have done so.

That softening inside him started to twist and unfurl more quickly, like a sail gaining wind, and he couldn't help but notice how lovely she was in her dishevelment…particularly now that her mouth wasn't moving in demands and recriminations. The curve of her cheeks, soft and high, the point of her chin with its subtle dimple, and even in the faulty light, he could see dark lashes and brows enhancing the shape of her eyes.

And that mouth…his blood surged and he stopped himself cold from remembering the soft heat of it against his. And the cardamom-vanilla and sweet lily that wafted from her skin. Her hair looked silver-black in the moon, all of the nuances of color washed out and reduced to a simple chiaroscuro. Her coiffure was a bloody mess, but he found it much more interesting all tumbled about her temples and jaw and sagging along her neck around those earbobs than the way it had been forced into submission moments earlier.

"I should think that I'm entitled to a few tears," she said in a voice that seemed…less hard. More bumpy, unsteady in its cadence. Firm, still, but with feeling. "I am a bit frightened and confused. After all, we've just been in a carriage accident, attacked by horrible, bloodthirsty *vampir,* and my sister has been abducted by them." Now her voice began to rise. "And our very fierce guardian could do nothing to stop them. What was Chas thinking?"

The sail inside him lost its wind and Dimitri scowled. Damn her, she was bloody well right. Not that it was his fault that Voss had done something so foolish, presumably unaware of the potential consequences (which was always his excuse), but in all fairness, it *had* been Dimitri who allowed Angelica to be abducted.

And Dimitri wasn't used to being at fault.

He opened his mouth to say something—likely something snarly and rude that would send her huffing off into the closed carriage, which was exactly what he wanted: her away from him—but he realized he had a mouthful of fangs, thrusting long and sharp and in no mood to be sheathed. It just didn't seem to be the right moment for her to learn that he was one of those—what had she called them? Horrible, bloodthirsty *vampirs.*

At least she hadn't said "murderous." Although in the case of Belial and Moldavi, that would be more accurate.

Just then, Mirabella, who also looked as if she'd been tumbled down a hill and then dragged herself to her feet at the bottom, spoke. "Maia, where did you get those rubies?" She didn't spare Dimitri a glance, but hurried over to Miss Woodmore. Tension oozed from her. "Corvindale *despises* rubies," she said to her companion, under her breath presumably so that Dimitri couldn't hear—but of course he could hear everything, including Miss Woodmore's response.

"Rubies? The earl despises rubies? Why in the world should I care? *He* doesn't have to wear them." Her furious whisper broke at the end. "I want to find Angelica. We have to find *my* brother—at least *he'll* be able to save her. He can kill those *vampirs*—"

"But you don't understand," Mirabella was saying, still in a low hiss, glancing covertly at Dimitri from over her shoulder. "The very sight of them make him furious. You must get rid of the earbobs, for he hates them."

"What?" Miss Woodmore's voice rose incredulously, matching Dimitri's own surprise that Mirabella should know so much about his affliction. He'd taken great care to hide it from her, along with the fact that she wasn't truly his sister but a mere foundling he'd brought into his home years ago. "Get rid of my rubies?"

Naturally the staff knew, but they were also exceedingly well-paid to keep their master's secrets from everyone. Aside of that, none of them wished to risk the wrath of a Dracule, and, unlike Cezar Moldavi, Dimitri didn't make it a point of turning every one of his servants Dracule anyway. Iliana didn't have a loose tongue, either. She had her own reasons for keeping the secret.

"I'll do no such thing," his ward was saying, fingering her earbobs. She cast a sidelong glance at Dimitri, then leaned closer to Mirabella. "Why should mere jewels make him so angry? Was that why he seemed so odd in the carriage?"

By that time, Dimitri had turned away, annoyance and fury prickling over his shoulders. He refocused his attention on the scene of the kidnapping instead of wondering just exactly how much Mirabella knew about him, and where she had learned it. And the fact that Miss Woodmore seemed to have latched on to the concept of his dislike for rubies with her characteristic tenacity.

Just then, praise the Fates, Tren arrived with a hackney.

Dimitri wanted nothing more than to send the women back to Blackmont Hall and to get on his way, but he dared not relieve himself of their presence until he knew they were safe. So while they climbed into the hack, rubies and all, he settled onto the back of the conveyance, where the footman might perch, and allowed Tren to ride with the driver.

The ride to Blackmont Hall was without incident, and Dimitri went inside to ascertain whether he'd received any responding messages from Chas or Giordan Cale in regards to Voss's warning—which had, in fact, been pertinent. He found word that they were waiting at White's for news from *him,* causing renewed annoyance that the message had arrived too late to prevent Angelica's abduction, not to mention the fact that the presence of the rubies in his household—let alone in the confines of a carriage—had endangered the safety of both Woodmore sisters. Voss's irresponsibility was inexcusable. Dimitri armed himself with an ash stake and his thick walking stick. The bottom half of said cane was actually a saber that could come in handy if he encountered Belial.

Or Voss.

And then he shoved a pistol into his pocket and

slipped out of the house before Miss Woodmore could accost him again. The intense relief that he'd managed to do so was beyond annoying.

Moments later, he arrived at White's, the well-known gentleman's club where the Dracule had private, subterranean apartments hidden in the back. Ironically the club, which catered to the most powerful and rich members of the *ton,* had been influenced by Dimitri's own establishment in Vienna; however, the Dracule who frequented it rarely visited the main chambers—except to enter a bet in the books.

Famously there'd been an incident when Beau Brummel and Lord Eddersley—a mortal and a Dracule, respectively—had sat in the front, bowed window of the club and bet three thousand pounds on which of two raindrops would reach the bottom of the glass first.

Since Dimitri's similar property in Vienna had gone up (or down, depending upon how one looked at it) in flames, he had lost his taste for such investments, although he had helped fund moving White's from Chesterfield to St. James. Dimitri found it morbidly amusing that the *de facto* headquarters for the Whig Party was being financed by a Dracule, who had absolutely no regard for political parties, politics, or even patriotism.

His world was unaffected, for the most part, by the government or legal systems of his mortal counterparts. And, as one who'd lived through the Cromwell years and the return of Charles II to the throne before he even became Dracule, Dimitri had no qualms about his apathetic attitude. Government machinations meant nothing to him.

When Dimitri arrived, he found Chas and Giordan

Cale in the private apartments at White's. Other than the three of them and the two attending footmen, the chambers were empty. There weren't many other Dracule in London at the time—not that there ever were, for Lucifer was selective in his choices for soul induction. Dimitri thought sourly that he wished the devil had been even more selective, and passed him by almost a hundred and forty years ago. He certainly wasn't the sort of man Lucifer tended to gravitate toward.

At least, he hadn't been before becoming Dracule. He'd been a quiet, studious young man who grew up in a Puritan household where books and God were revered and clothing was black, brown, gray or dun.

He'd been perfectly content with his studies, for, as the youngest son of five and thus unlikely to inherit the Corvindale title, he was attempting a professorship in physics at Cambridge. And even after Cromwell died and Charles II was restored to the throne, Dimitri continued in his simple life of studies. Until he met Meg.

"At last," Chas said, looking up from the table. Tension had settled in his face.

"A drink, Corvindale?" Giordan asked as Dimitri strolled across the chamber. His neckcloth had been loosened and he was in his shirtsleeves. It appeared that he and Chas had been in the midst of a chess game.

Interesting, and hardly comprehensible, particularly since surely by now Chas was aware of the history between Giordan and Narcise. But then, if nothing else, Giordan was a gentleman, and well in control of himself.

Dimitri glanced at the board to see who seemed to be winning. It took him only a glance to confirm what he would have suspected: Chas was for the bold, brazen moves and Giordan more subtle and covert. Well-matched, but two different styles.

Interestingly enough, the queens had both been captured already.

Even more interesting than that was the absence of Narcise herself. The presumption was that Chas had settled her safely somewhere while he saw to the situation at hand. Perhaps with Rubey.

"Angelica has been abducted," Dimitri said without preamble. Accepting the drink, he sat at the table with them.

"Voss?" Chas spat, rising to his feet. If he were a Dracule, his eyes would be blazing red and orange. "If he caused it—"

"No," Dimitri said, taking a healthy swallow of whiskey, and then tersely explained what had happened. "We're going to have to search the city and then to Dover if we don't catch them."

Chas settled back into his chair and nodded. His eyes were fierce and his jaw moved slightly as if being clenched. "We'll have to split up."

They'd just finished determining the most likely places Belial would have taken Angelica, and the best routes, dividing up the locations, when the door opened.

Voss stood there on the threshold, gripping the arm of a cloaked and hooded figure.

Dimitri started up, reaching for the stake in his inside pocket just as Chas whirled in his seat to look.

"Don't be a fool," Voss said sharply, flipping open his coat to expose a large ruby in the center of his neckcloth. "Did you think I would be so foolish as to come unprepared?"

Dimitri remained standing, settling his hand onto the table in a pool of spilled whiskey as he fixed Voss with a dark glare. The ruby was far enough away that its potency was weak, but certainly he couldn't get much closer. *Bastard. A smart, sneaky bastard.*

Reluctantly he glanced at the figure next to Voss. It was obviously a woman, and Dimitri had a sudden, ugly feeling he knew who it was.

Impossible. Even she wouldn't be so foolish.

But he couldn't talk himself out of the certainty, and when she yanked off her hood and he saw Miss Woodmore's accusing eyes and mussed golden-chestnut hair, he couldn't hold back his exclamation of annoyance. *"You."* He turned his glare onto her.

"Of course I wouldn't come unprotected, knowing just how you feel about me," Voss was saying to Chas, who had withdrawn his stake and had it ready in his hand. "Keep your distance, and no one will get hurt."

"Maia," Chas said, "are you all right?"

"Other than worried to illness for the safety of my sister, while the rest of you sit about and play games at your club? Yes, I am fine. If it weren't for Lord Dewhurst, I would still be standing at the door, arguing with the butler. It was he who helped me gain entrance."

"How convenient," Dimitri replied from between his teeth. He sank back into his seat, but he couldn't control the blaze in his eyes as he returned his gaze to Voss. *Meddling arse.*

And then, out of the corner of his eye, he saw Miss Woodmore stiffen. She was looking right at him and he saw sudden shock and recognition in her eyes when she noticed the glow in his gaze.

She'd figured it out. At least he wouldn't have to hide his fangs from her any longer, but that was small comfort. Naturally she'd rush off to tell Mirabella at the first opportunity.

He snarled under his breath. Damnation. He'd have to enthrall her and clear her mind of the knowledge if he was to have any peace.

"I cannot believe your incompetence, Dimitri. I sent you the warning," Voss said flatly, drawing Dimitri's attention from his misery. "And you, Woodmore. Another disappearing and then reappearing act? Are you here to take care of your sisters or not?"

Fury propelled Dimitri to his feet again, his eyes fairly burning with the heat of anger. "Oh, aye, I got your message—along with the pair of bloody ruby earbobs, you sneaky bastard." He would have lunged across the room if Chas hadn't thrust an arm out in front of him.

"Easy," Woodmore said under his breath, holding his stake at a lethal angle. "He's mine."

Voss flashed his fangs, holding Dimitri's glare. "It was a jest, nothing more. I warned her not to wear them in your presence."

Like hell you did, you bastard.

"Damn your soul to Lucifer, it's your bloody fault Angelica's been taken," Chas interrupted. Dimitri could feel the man gathering up next to him like a spring, even though his expression didn't change and nary a muscle moved. "You and your cursed jests and games, Voss."

Before Voss could respond, Chas leaped, tossing a chair out of his way and bounding up and over a table to slam the man into the wall. He was fast, but Dimitri was faster, fairly flying across the room to grab Miss Woodmore, snatching her out of the way just as the two men tumbled to the floor.

She weighed no more than a pin, just as she had three years ago and of course a few nights ago, as well. And, unlike the other night at the masquerade, she didn't have yards of skirts and fabric bunching up and around them as he scooped her up out of the way, slamming her quickly against his torso to avoid being smashed by a flying chair.

It was probably best if she didn't see what was about to happen to Voss Dewhurst.

"Release me, you idiot man!" She slammed an elbow that was as sharp as her tongue into his gut and Dimitri grunted, shifting her so that she didn't have another chance at him. But she tried to kick at him and to yank away, even as chairs flew and tables upended. Chess pieces scattered. The bottle of whiskey crashed to the floor.

Addled woman. Do you want to get yourself killed? He whipped her out of the way just in time to keep from being crashed into by Chas and Voss, who were putting on a damned good show. If Dimitri weren't so furious with the latter, he'd be watching the fight with interest. For being mortal, and not as strong or fast as a Dracule, Chas Woodmore was brilliant. One would never know that he was overmatched.

And perhaps he wasn't overmatched with the vampires. Perhaps he was made that way—to hunt them. After all, God would have some sort of defense against the malignance of Lucifer's makes.

Chas whipped Voss into the wall, following him

with his stake raised. They crashed against the brick, and Dimitri stuck out his foot and sent Voss staggering away. Chas leaped, the stake in hand, ready to deliver the death blow as Miss Woodmore screamed.

"Don't! *Chas!*" she shrieked, burying her face in Dimitri's shirt.

Naturally Woodmore ignored her as he plunged the stake toward Voss's heart. The powerful blow fell, and Dimitri watched as the stake fairly bounced off Voss's torso. *What in the bloody hell...?*

Some sort of armor, blast him.

Everything fell silent for a moment, except for the sounds of labored breathing from the two fighting men. And then, with a muttered curse, Chas pulled up and away from where he'd landed on his target, a splintered stake in his hand.

As the action waned, Dimitri was no longer able to ignore the bundle of femininity clutching his shirt with two fists, and her warm breath burning through the linen to his skin. Not to mention the very evident press of breasts against his belly. A rush of heat swarmed through him and he made the mistake of drawing in a breath, getting a good sniff of her hair. Lemon and jasmine, and an undernote of cardamom-vanilla. Flowers and spice.

He forced himself to release her slender arms and made his own fall to his sides. "I do hope you aren't wiping your nose on my shirt, Miss Woodmore." He had to work hard to make certain his tones were laden with disdain.

Miss Woodmore jerked back as if she'd been stung, and he saw very pink cheeks just before she spun away.

"Armor?" Chas was saying to Voss as he brushed off his shirt. He looked bloody annoyed.

"After a fashion. I warned you I'd come prepared— for all of you." He glanced pointedly at Dimitri and Giordan, as well. "Now, if you would cease attacking me, I would appreciate the opportunity to assist you in retrieving Angelica."

"Your assistance is neither wanted nor needed," Chas told him. "Aside of that, I want you in no vicinity to any of my sisters. A different country would be preferable. Just because you were prepared this time doesn't always mean that you'll escape my stake."

Voss's laugh was short and sharp. "I didn't believe you were that foolish, Woodmore. In fact, I'm the only one who can assist you in saving Angelica."

Dimitri smothered a snort of disbelief and walked over to pour a new glass of whiskey. "Not bloody likely."

Voss shrugged, and glanced at Miss Woodmore. "Very well, then," he said coolly. "Best of luck to all of you." He turned toward the door.

"Wait!" Miss Woodmore stomped her foot.

Dimitri resisted the urge to roll his eyes. *Always the dramatics.*

"Are you just going to allow him to leave?" She glared at her brother. "Without hearing what he has to say? Angelica's in *danger* and all you care about is… is whatever insults you've given to each other in the past. I vow, the three of you are like little boys fighting over a ball."

Dimitri opened his mouth to tell her precisely how addled she was when Woodmore beat him to it. "I don't need his help." His tones dripped with brotherly disdain.

"Perhaps the lady is right." Giordan had remained out of the fray due to the fact, Dimitri presumed, that somewhere on Voss's person was some essence of Giordan's Asthenia, since he didn't appear to be in possession of an actual cat. And since Giordan obviously didn't feel compelled to manage the annoying Miss Woodmore, he'd been in the enviable position of observer. "At least hear what the bastard—pardon me, Miss Woodmore—has to say. Then turn him out."

"It's because of me that you even knew they were to attack this evening," Voss said, with a flinty look at Dimitri. Then he turned to Maia. "I was fortunate enough to cross paths with Belial, who is the *vampir* Moldavi sent to find your brother—or one of his sisters, who could be used as a hostage."

Dimitri watched him as he explained to Maia how he came to overhear Belial's plans. The man seemed truly overset, especially for Voss. Was it possible that he was sincerely concerned for Angelica? That it wasn't just another bid for attention, or a jest? He narrowed his eyes and watched, even as disdain crawled into his belly.

Voss didn't truly care for women.

He simply used them. Coaxed them and took what he could. While he meant no real harm to anyone, neither did Voss care about anyone else aside of himself and his pleasure.

Angelica Woodmore, a young mortal woman, would hardly be any different from the hundreds or thousands of others over the years. Willing and otherwise.

"When I arrived here to find her arguing with the butler," Voss was explaining about Maia coolly, "rather than leaving her on the doorstep where she might have been otherwise noticed, I thought it best to bring her within."

"They had ample opportunity to abduct her, as well as Mirabella, this evening," Dimitri reminded him between clenched teeth. He was still enraged over the debacle. "They chose not to. It was Angelica they were after." Moldavi could find any number of uses for the younger Woodmore sister's Sight.

"Because they'd already identified her. I'm certain, for by now, Moldavi has heard of her unusual ability. Angelica wasn't very secretive about it, at least among her friends. Not only does Moldavi want to use her to bring Chas into submission, but also to put her to work. He can force her to tell him what she knows about the person who owns any item he brings to her."

"You're wasting our time," Woodmore said. "We've finished our plan to search the city and now you've set us back."

"And where exactly were you going to search in the city?" Voss asked, lifting an arrogant brow. He removed a handkerchief and wiped his hands of a streak of blood as he glanced up at Dimitri. "Because she's no longer in the city. They're taking her to Paris. They're already well ahead of you on a boat going down the Thames."

Satan's bloody stones.

Chas and Dimitri exchanged glances. They hadn't expected them to use a riverboat to get out of Town. A ship or a stage, but not one of the small river vehicles.

Giordan nodded thoughtfully, and Voss continued, for he had their attention now.

"You didn't think Cezar would risk himself to come here, did you? Belial is bringing Angelica to him. The good news is that she'll arrive unharmed—for Belial won't dare allow anything to happen to her. She's going to be very valuable to Cezar. The bad news is…not one of you could expect to gain entrance to Moldavi's residence in Paris, to get to Angelica. Except for me."

Dimitri didn't bother to correct him. Moldavi would see him, if only for the chance to slam a stake into his heart. In fact, he'd relish it just as much as Dimitri would to do the same.

"You forget about me. Moldavi will see *me*," Giordan said. His voice was flat and his eyes empty. "I'll go."

"No, Giordan," Dimitri snapped, looking at his friend in concern. Cale didn't need to put himself through that again. There were other ways.

"I'll go," Voss said firmly. "Moldavi will see me. I've acquired some information he wants about Bonaparte. And I'll be able to get her back."

"How are you going to get to Paris? We're at war!" Miss Woodmore interjected. "Mrs. Siddington-Graves has been trapped there for a year!"

Dimitri didn't know who Mrs. Siddington-Graves was, and he certainly didn't care, but he forbore to say anything. Let Woodmore take care of his sister while he was present, blast him.

"Why should I trust you?" Woodmore was saying.

"I returned her once before, didn't I?" Voss pointed out.

"Complete with nightmares, frightening memories, not to mention marks on her skin. Not quite unharmed."

Dimitri saw a flash of emotion in Voss's expression that he would have described as chagrin, or even guilt, if he hadn't suspected that those feelings were as foreign to Voss as sunlight. "As you well know, I've spent my life collecting information and learning the weaknesses of my associates and enemies alike. I know how to influence Moldavi," he said steadily.

Glancing over at Miss Woodmore, Dimitri saw that she was following the conversation with interest. Hope and terror warred in her expression, and he thought it must have to do with worry for her brother. For, after all, if Chas never came back, she'd be under Dimitri's wardship forever—or at least until she wed.

The very thought struck terror in Dimitri's own heart and he focused in on the conversation, willing to offer up Voss first in the effort to retrieve Angelica. The man's arguments, much as he hated to admit it, were logical.

Chas seemed to come to the same conclusion. "Very well, then. I'll accompany you to Paris."

"No! Chas! What if Moldavi captures you, too?" Miss Woodmore interjected in an unnecessarily shrill tone, confirming Dimitri's suspicions. He winced, his ears ringing.

Her brother gave her an affronted look. "I am quite able to take care of myself, Maia. I've already evaded him once, and now I know exactly what I'd be walking into." He glanced at Dimitri, then Giordan. "Narcise will have to stay here, of course."

Damnation. Dimitri was *not* going to be responsible for another woman. Especially a Dracule who'd destroyed his best friend, and by all accounts seemed to be working on doing the same to his closest associate. Both of them were fools of the highest order.

Meg had nearly done the same to him.

"But, Chas...I still don't understand. Why are you working *with vampires* if you *kill* them?" Miss Woodmore asked, glancing briefly at Dimitri. She looked exhausted and confused, and he felt an unwilling softening in his belly again.

He ruthlessly hardened his thoughts and lifted his chin so he could look down at her from an even higher level. If she'd stayed home like any reasonable woman, instead of bartering her way into the most private apartments of an exclusive gentleman's club, she'd be sleeping restfully by now.

And dreaming.

Dimitri yanked his thoughts away from *that* avenue and drilled his attention steadfastly onto Chas Woodmore, who was trying to explain to his sister why he worked for Dimitri when he was bound to kill those of his race.

It really wasn't all that complicated, when one thought about it logically. Just as there were good and moral men, there were also members of the Dracule who were less inclined to live uneventfully alongside their mortal counterparts. People like Moldavi, who fed from children and left them to die. Or, when they wanted something, they'd burn a house down and watch people perish.

Or they'd feed on injured soldiers on a field, prolonging their agony just for pleasure.

Just as there were mortals who hunted game, killed it neatly and quickly and used it for nourishment, and there were others who tortured the animals just to watch them twist and cry and squeal...there were also Dracule, who fed expediently and took just what they needed from mortals, and quite often from willing ones, and there were Dracule who fed until the mortal was bled nearly dry. And left for dead.

As there were mortal men who hungered for power until it became all consuming, there were Dracule who did the same.

There were Dracule who merely lived lavish lives, filled with luxuries and pleasure, but who were content to simply enjoy the sensuality of it, without desiring to control everyone around them.

And then there was Dimitri, who no longer did any of those things. Whose Mark blazed with constant pain for precisely that reason: because he denied the pleasure, the very covenant that Lucifer had given him.

And searched for a way to renounce it.

Thus, instead, he lived in solitude and darkness, seeking an escape from an eternity of hell.

"At any rate," Chas was saying, "I'm going to Paris with Voss and we'll bring back Angelica. That's all you need to know at this time, Maia."

Voss interrupted, shaking his head sharply. "If you want to jeopardize my chances, then you may come. Otherwise…follow if you will, but some days behind me. There can be no hint to Moldavi that we're working together."

Dimitri snorted in agreement. "Even if he saw the two of you shaking hands, he wouldn't believe it."

Voss shot him a look of pure dislike. "Precisely."

8

OF FEROCIOUS DOGS, HISSING KITTENS
AND PROPER SYNTAX

Maia had so many questions she could hardly quiet her mind to select one for consideration.

But when she climbed into Corvindale's landau—for he'd absolutely forbidden her to hire a hack to take her home from White's, and she was simply too tired to argue about propriety—and settled into her seat across from him, suddenly her wild musings and whirling thoughts scattered, leaving her mind blank and focused on one thing: *him*.

The door closed, and as had happened little more than a week ago, they were alone in the vehicle. Corvindale seemed to take up the entire expanse of his seat, sprawling his long legs to one side and the flaps of his sable coat open wide like a bird fluffing its feathers to make it appear larger. Settled across the top of the squabs behind him were his arms, hands dangling casually. His dark hair, always a bit out of sorts, flipped up and around his ears and temples.

He looked none too pleased with the current situation; but that was nothing new. He'd never looked pleased with anything, ever since Maia had met him. But there was also something else about him that struck her. Something different.

A sort of wariness, like a large, ferocious dog who'd been cornered by a kitten.

Maia considered herself the kitten in this situation, and even through her weariness and confusion, she decided she rather liked the metaphor. And because she was the kitten, Maia thought she'd bare her claws—as small and insignificant as they might be.

"And so you are a *vampir*," she said, primly arranging her skirt so that not even the tops of her slippers showed. She would not think right now about what sort of mess her hem and shoes were in. Or what her hair looked like. She was hissing and spitting in her own quiet way, all the while trying not to be completely overset by the fact that *her brother had put her into the wardship of a* vampir.

"The proper term is Dracule. Or, if you insist upon using the archaic word *vampir,* I would appreciate if you would use the Anglican pronunciation—'vampire'—rather than attempting to speak Hungarian. Your accent isn't quite spot-on." He sounded supremely bored, and looked as if he hadn't a care in the world but her diction and whatever was so fascinating out the half-curtained window of the carriage.

But despite his interest out on the streets, he was watching her. Particularly when she wasn't looking directly at him. She felt the weight of his regard as if it were a thick blanket, shuttling down over her shoulders. Warm and heavy. And not altogether unwelcome.

"Very well," she replied, clearly enunciating her words so that there would be no mistake. "You are a *vampire,* then, Lord Corvindale, and I have a variety of questions—"

"Only a variety? I was expecting a plethora of them. Or perhaps a score?"

It was all Maia could do to keep back the little gust of a chuckle at this unexpected, wholly uncharacteristic show of levity. Or, perhaps he wasn't jesting and was being quite serious. She eyed him from the corner of her eyes and noticed his ungloved hand with its exposed wrist resting on the top of his seat. It vibrated and jounced a bit with the rumbling movement of the carriage.

As it happened, the moon or a streetlamp chose that moment to shine directly on it, and Maia found her attention attracted to the shape of that wide, dark appendage. Long, sturdy fingers, the ridges of slightly flexed tendons, the curve of a broad thumb and neat fingernails. It wasn't often she'd seen a man's hand uncovered—certainly Chas's, and her father's when she was young, and of course Alexander's—but Lord Corvindale's hand seemed particularly wide and well-shaped. Even there, settled, fingers bowed gently, a latent power seemed to emanate from it.

They reminded her…Maia caught her breath, her belly suddenly fluttering, and her mouth dry…they reminded her of the smooth, dark hands from her dreams. She could imagine them, sliding over her pale skin, large and strong—

"Well?"

Maia's eyes bolted back to Corvindale and she swallowed, frantically trying to catch up to the conversation. Then she remembered. She had a *variety* of questions for him.

But she would start with the most pressing one. "Do you truly think that Lord Dewhurst will be able to save Angelica?" She wasn't fully able to keep the pitch of concern from rising in her voice.

He seemed to relax a bit, his fingers shifting into a looser curve. "Voss—er, Dewhurst—isn't one of my favorite people," he said, clearly understating the facts, "but his arguments were sound and I believe that he'll succeed, if only because the man is very manipulative and sneaky. And, one must confess it, intelligent and resourceful, too. If not burdened with a lack of responsibility. Aside of that, Moldavi has no reason to suspect Dewhurst of any threat, so if he doesn't find them before they get to Paris, he certainly has the best chance of gaining access to Moldavi. And further, your brother is close on Dewhurst's heels. In the event he fails, Chas wouldn't hesitate to do whatever it takes to retrieve Angelica."

Maia blinked. She could hardly believe it, but not only had he given her information that she'd actually requested, he'd spoken in normal tones. "Your opinion means a good deal to me," she managed to say.

He didn't respond except to lift his brows and look down his straight nose at her.

So she continued. "Chas seems to think that Angelica isn't in any danger of being hurt, at least until that vampire delivers her to Moldavi. Do you agree?"

"I do."

Maia couldn't hold back a smile, partly borne of relief. "I can scarcely believe we are having a normal conversation, my lord." She realized that her own gloveless hands had ceased adjusting the folds of the cloak and gown in her lap.

"That," he said, shifting in his seat, moving his long legs so that they brushed briefly against her skirt, "is because you are asking reasonable questions. In a reasonable tone. Although, I might point out that if you had stayed home like any reasonable woman would have done, we wouldn't even be having this conversation. Civil or not."

She bristled a bit, then recalled that she wanted more information from him—and now that she was as assured as she could be that Angelica would soon be safe, she thought it prudent not to annoy him. Although whatever she'd done to annoy him in the past, she couldn't know, and therefore how could she keep from irritating him now?

"And so you are a vampire, and my brother is a vampire *hunter?* And you are friends? He works for you?"

"A rather irregular circumstance indeed, but true, nonetheless."

"But how can that be? Aren't you—well, mortal enemies?"

The corners of his eyes crinkled a bit, which Maia took to mean that he'd had a flash of humor. Astounding. Twice in one night; in less than one hour?

"Now who is sounding sensational, like one of Mrs. Radcliffe's Gothic novels, Miss Woodmore?" he asked, almost lazily.

Something fluttered inside her, for his voice had dropped low. She could barely hear it, mixing as it did with the constant rumble of carriage wheels. There were no other sounds outside, and she realized with a jolt that it must be very late. Near dawn.

"Well?" she prodded tartly. And then realized that, for all of her irritation with the situation, he was still an *earl,* a peer of the realm. And a vampiric—was that even a word? She dared not ask him, but he would certainly have an opinion—one at that. And her manner had become quite familiar with him.

He shifted, adjusting his coat lapels and running a hand briefly through his hair in a surprisingly endearing gesture. "I shall make a very complicated situation as simple as I can, Miss Woodmore," he said.

"Oh, you need not condescend to me, Lord Corvindale." The kitten had unsheathed her little claws again. "I'm quite capable of comprehending any situation you might describe. It was I who had to tutor Chas in geometry *and* Greek." And what a task that had been, especially since Greek was just as difficult for her. But she would never have admitted that to Chas.

"Indeed? Very well, then," the earl said. And his eyes crinkled a bit more, and perhaps even the corners of his lips shifted. "I have a variety of business interests throughout the Continent, the Far East and even some limited ones in the New World. As the wealthy and powerful often do, I have more than my share of enemies—"

"I can scarcely imagine that," Maia murmured.

"—who would take any chance to see my investments fail, or to damage them, or any variety of things," he continued as if she hadn't spoken. But his eyes had sharpened a bit and she knew he'd heard her. "Many of those are members of the Draculia, and there are some who are mortals, as well. Your brother acts as my agent and, if necessary, will—er—remove any problematic individuals from—er—causing any further disruptions. He also assists me in managing some of my other associates, who are also of the Draculian race."

"What you mean to say is that my brother is your paid assassin?" Maia said, her eyes wide. "He *kills* people?" She thought she might faint. Her heart was pounding in her chest in an ugly beat, thrumming through her stomach, which had suddenly become queasy.

Mama and Father...what would you think if you knew? Oh, Chas, what are you doing?

"Not people, Miss Woodmore. Your brother has never, to my knowledge, ended the life of a mortal person. But he has removed or otherwise dissuaded more than a few vampires—and he was doing so for quite some time before I met him. Which, by the way, was when he attempted to do the same to me." Corvindale fixed her with his eyes, and Maia felt a little wavering tug deep inside her. "You see, Miss Woodmore, the simple way to look at it is that there are good vampires, and there are bad vampires. Your brother kills the bad vampires."

"And presumably you don't count yourself among the 'bad' vampires?"

Maia didn't know how or why she had the courage to say such a thing—for once again, it dawned on her that not only was she in a carriage with an *earl,* one of the most powerful men of the *ton* and in England, but that he was a vampire. A bloodthirsty vampire.

And, ward or not, she was alone with him.

He made a deep sound that at first she didn't recognize as laughter, but when the light fell on his face, outlining harsh cheekbones and the straight line of his nose, she saw that his lips were curved. His laughter was brief and as sharp as he was, and then it subsided. "As I highly doubt that Attila the Hun or Judas Iscariot or even Oliver Cromwell considered themselves 'bad' or 'evil,' I suggest that your question is moot."

But then he fixed her with his eyes again. "Naturally, you could pose the question to your brother if you aren't certain which side of the battle lines I'm on, Miss Woodmore. But I suspect you already know what his answer would be."

Maia kept her lips compressed together. Indeed. Chas loved her and Angelica and Sonia, and he would never expose them to any danger if he could help it. And he was a good and moral man himself. "Indeed," she replied. "And so I am to assume that Cezar Moldavi is on the other side of the good-versus-bad-vampire battle lines."

"Your logic is astonishing." His words were bored, but she swore she saw a bit of light in his eyes.

It occurred to her at that moment that perhaps he enjoyed the verbal sparring as much as she—well, she didn't really *like* the exchanges of insults and banter between them, for Maia found it outside of infuriating. But perhaps he found it difficult being both vampire and an earl. After all, earls were intimidating all on their own, but to add the fact that he was a vampire into the composite…perhaps no one was willing to stand up to him.

Perhaps they were afraid he'd bite them—or worse— if they did.

Perhaps—now here was a fanciful thought—he

didn't mind being treated like a normal person. Occasionally.

"Do you truly drink blood?" she blurted out. "From people?"

He became very still. Even his eyes didn't shift, nor his fingers. And the carriage all at once seemed to shrink, becoming very close and dark, and her heart began to pound again in that ugly way. She wished fiercely that she could take the question back.

"It's the common means of survival and obtaining sustenance," he replied after a moment. "But I do not."

Maia opened her mouth to ask more, but something stopped her. She sensed that their tenuous connection might be strained, or even broken, if she did. Instead she said, "Is it true that vampires cannot go about in the sunlight?"

"Direct rays from the sun cause excruciating pain, so one must take care if one ventures out during the day. Surely you haven't heard this information from your brother," he said. "I was under the impression you and your sisters were blissfully ignorant of his…occupation. But you seem to have some…reasonable…knowledge."

"We grew up listening to stories from our Granny Grapes, who was part-Gypsy. She had many tales about the vampires in Romania. Of course, at the time, I had no idea that not only were they true, but that I would actually meet some of them."

"Granny Grapes?"

Maia felt her face soften into a fond smile. "She was our grandmother, and for some reason when I was very young, I got it all mixed up and thought she was our *great*-grandmother. So I got it into my head that her name was *Grape*-Grandmother. And so the name remained fixed."

Silence settled between them then, causing Maia to silently muse that she couldn't ever recall being alone with the earl and not fumbling or grasping for something to say. Or being skewered by his wit.

It wasn't an uncomfortable quiet. In fact, with the rhythmic rumbling of the carriage wheels on the cobblestones and bricks, the moment was rather pleasant.

Without being obvious, she glanced at him sidewise. He was staring out the window, and it occurred to her with a start that he might be watching for another attack.

But, she reminded herself, that was unlikely, as the attack had already occurred. And so perhaps he was simply fascinated by a world that was beginning to brighten with dawn. A world that he must never experience fully illuminated, and warm.

What a terrible thing, never to bask in the sun or to walk through the rows of flowers when they were in full bloom. Not that she actually pictured the rigid earl walking through flower gardens, brushing his strong fingers lightly over rose blossoms…

He turned and the broad light of a streetlamp played over his mouth and jaw.

Maia looked at him, her gaze suddenly fully fastened on the lower half of his face. On his mouth. Her breath stopped.

A mouth utterly, horribly, impossibly recognizable to her. A mouth that she'd remarked on, a mouth that she'd scrutinized and thought about the fact that she was doing so because the upper half of his face had been masked. A chill washed over her, followed by a rush of heat. *No.* It was impossible.

She'd almost made the same mistake before.

But the image was eerily familiar: his eyes in shadow, his mouth and jaw exposed.

Maia must have gasped or otherwise indicated her shock, for he turned to look directly at her. Their eyes met, suddenly clashing and holding, and she could no longer deny it.

"Is something amiss, Miss Woodmore?" he asked coolly.

It *was* he. There was no question.

I do hope you aren't about to cast up your accounts on my waistcoat, your majesty, the Knave of Diamonds had said that night.

While on this night, Lord Corvindale had said, *I do hope you aren't wiping your nose on my shirt, Miss Woodmore.*

She'd been kissed by the Earl of Corvindale? She'd waltzed with him? Flirted with him?

Maia felt faint. And queasy.

And…warm. Suddenly very, very warm. She needed to swallow, to lick her dry lips. That kiss had been… well, she'd tried not to think about it. Because of Alexander.

Because if she was going to marry a man, she shouldn't be thinking about the kisses of another one—especially a bad-tempered, vampiric earl. She shouldn't even have been *having* kisses from another man.

Something awful churned inside her. Guilt and shame, and yet…the tug of memory, of need, overrode it.

She raised her eyes and looked at Corvindale directly.

He must know it had been she, even if he hadn't at the time—for after their interlude, when he'd accosted her and thrown her onto the balcony, he would have recognized her from her costume.

Never one to shirk responsibility, nor to ignore the elephant in the room, Maia said, "Did you know it was me, my lord knave of diamonds?"

His eyes widened just a bit, then quickly shuttered. There was a beat of silence, then, "I meant to prevent you from doing damage to your reputation by dancing twice with a man not your fiancé. I am, after all, your guardian." Even though his words were flat, she sensed an underlying defensiveness there. She looked at him more closely.

Good heavens. Maia realized, suddenly, that she'd *kissed a vampire.*

Her lips parted in renewed shock, but at the same time, a rush of heat billowed up inside her, fluttering in her belly and disrupting her breath.

He turned his face away, suddenly and sharply, and she was reminded of him doing precisely the same thing as he ended their masked kiss that night.

Oh, yes. Every detail of that interlude had been burned upon her memory.

Corvindale's fingers curled tightly now, and his wrists no longer rested loosely on the top of the seat. He'd pulled them closer to his body, as if to arm himself.

She became aware of the sound of roughened breathing, and noticed the way his lips had pressed flat and hard. And deep inside Maia, her heart pounded madly. Her hands were clammy. Something was churning inside her.

"My lord," she said. She needed his attention, she needed him to look at her. But he didn't move. "Corvindale," she said more sharply.

At last he turned. She didn't know what she'd expected—burning red eyes, bared fangs, hissing and furious—but he appeared the same as he always did. Ah, except for the eyes.

There was, still, a faint glow there, as if he hadn't quite been able to subdue it.

And as their eyes met, she felt a little shimmy of warmth wriggling through, expanding and filling her.

"I have been thinking about the kiss," she said, once again addressing the elephant in the room.

"*The* kiss?" Corvindale replied. "An interesting choice of article." His voice had changed; the timbre was richer. Deeper. And there was something in his eyes. Something…different.

"I can't help but wonder," she continued, "if it was so memorable simply because of the environment. The mysteriousness of anonymity." Maia heard her voice, but her attention was focused on the man across from her. The tug, the connection between them was as real as if a string—no, a rope—bound them together. "A bit of freedom allowed due to the masks. One can only assume you felt the same way, my lord."

"One could assume," he replied mildly. But his eyes burned a bit brighter. He'd become so very still. This, even as his regard remained steady and strong.

"I suspect there is a way to find out." She swallowed hard, and felt even warmer and more filled with expectancy. Something twisting and fluttering moved in her. Her heart banged in her chest.

"Are you suggesting that you wish to be kissed?" His voice was emotionless.

Maia licked her lips, suddenly nervous. Yet, determined. Surely the experience had been overblown in her mind and would turn out to be little more than an awkward experience. "Yes."

"In order to determine whether the previous kiss was…memorable? Is that it?"

"Yes."

"I suppose it won't matter on the morrow anyway," he murmured, his eyes still on her. "And at least it will stop you from talking, Miss Woodmore."

One moment she was sitting, hardly daring to breathe, on her side of the carriage…and the next, those strong hands that she'd admired closed over her arms. He loomed over her, his eyes glinting white and normal in the low light, his body settling on the seat next to her. Warm and solid against her side.

Maia turned toward him, lifting her face, her heart beating so strongly she thought she might faint. When their mouths met, it was as if a blaze of fire exploded in her, suddenly released from some pent-up place.

She heard a deep sigh that shifted the solid torso beneath her hands, a low groan vibrating from him as his fingers tightened on her arms. But Maia was hardly aware of the pressure, for his mouth was hot and hard and demanded her full attention.

His lips molded to hers, soft and warm, yet insistent, opening against hers as he moved to cup the back of her head. He held her as his tongue slipped along her parted lips, sleek and warm, then thrust inside in a sudden, strong sweep.

Maia closed her eyes, overwhelmed by the rush of pleasure bursting inside her. Their tongues tangled and slipped together, lips sucked and nibbled, his mouth crushing down on hers as if he couldn't get enough. She bit back, slipped her tongue deeply into the warmth of his mouth and he gave a little shudder against her.

Her body had blossomed awake, now swollen and ready, hot and loose, and she found herself pressing wantonly against him, needing to feel all of his strength and heat. One of her knees somehow nudged against his leg, and the entire side of his torso and hip pressed into her curves. Beneath the smooth linen of his shirt, she felt the rise and fall of his chest. Its image, already burned in her memory, rose in her mind to match the swell of muscle that she felt beneath each palm. She wanted to feel the skin, the hair, the solid slabs of muscle she already knew were there.

Corvindale shifted away, and she opened her eyes to catch a glimpse of his face before he slid his arms around her, pulling her up against a solid chest. His wicked lips closed over the soft lobe of her ear, where hours earlier a ruby had hung, and Maia gasped at the shivery sensation of heat and slick, his breath warm against her skin, burning into her ear. She arched and shuddered, unable to keep a soft moan quiet as tickly pleasure rushed down to her belly, and lower.

When his hands moved, one to cup the side of her jaw as he buried his face into her neck, kissing, nuzzling, and the other to curl behind her hips and pull her close, Maia felt herself slide into a puddle of bonelessness. Pleasure made her weak and hot and she sagged to the side, leaning into the corner of the bench seat, dragging him with her.

Finding her lips again, he made her gasp into his breath when he roughed her mouth open with a demanding kiss. She took him, hot and long, sweeping deep and meeting him with her own nibbling teeth and molding lips. The heat of his body, the smell of him, close and male, she couldn't remember how to breathe...

His body eased her down along the length of the seat, their legs mixed in with skirts, her head jammed against the side of the carriage and shoulder against the back of the seat. He lifted away just enough for her to see a faint red glow in his eyes, and the flash of too-long teeth—*fangs*—and to yank off his coat and thrust it sharply across the vehicle.

And then he was back, and she pulled him close, down on top of her, one of his legs sliding between hers, hooking into her skirts. When his thigh came up between hers, pressing into her, Maia found herself agonizingly aware of the heat and swelling there at that juncture. She felt as if she were going to explode, that she couldn't catch her breath, and she shifted, moving closer, trying to find a way to ease the pressure there.

"My...oh..." she breathed, and then nearly arched up off the seat when he closed his hand over her breast, strong and sure. Through the layers of silk and her corset and shift, he located the sharp rise of nipple, giving a little sigh of discovery as he stroked over it with his thumb. The fabric shifted and sensitized her flesh, and Maia's whole focus went to that place where all of the pleasure gathered and spread, radiating down and through her, hot and sharp.

He pulled at the neckline of her bodice, drawing it down to expose the top of her breast. The fabric cut into her flesh at the back as the swell was revealed, and Maia saw her skin shuddering and heaving from her uncontrolled breaths, her breast a lovely ivory dome highlighted in the moonlight just before he lowered his dark head.

She nearly shrieked when his lips molded over her upthrust nipple. It was so hard and tight that the barest touch set her to gasping and trembling, but he gave no mercy. His mouth was hot and wet, and his tongue strong as it swirled around the peak of her breast. He drew her deeply into his mouth, sucking and licking in a hard, fast rhythm, then slowing and teasing as if he wanted to explore every little wrinkle. Maia's world became dark and red and liquid, and she clutched at him, her hands curling into his hair and wide shoulders, pressing herself against his thigh.

The sharp rise of pleasure pulsed through her body, centering there between her legs, filling and throbbing as she tried to find the top, the end. Something.

His skin was so hot, his hair brushing her chin, his hands grasping her shoulders as if holding on for dear life. She felt a sharp edge, something on her skin, and then the flush of release roared through her. Maia lost control of her thoughts as she trembled and exploded inside, and then slid into the warm pleasure of *after*.

He lifted his face, and when their eyes met, Maia felt her whole world still. It was too dark to read his expression, but the heat there, and the dark need, made her mouth go dry. The tips of his fangs showed just beneath his upper lip, changing the shape of his mouth, making it full and soft and she wanted to kiss it. Again.

She became aware, as the pleasure sifted away and reality sneaked back in, that he hadn't moved. That his hands gripped her with a death grip, and then he turned away, his eyes closing. His breathing was harsh and deep, as if he'd been running or struggling.

Maia reached up to touch his face, something she'd never thought to do before now. Touch the Earl of Corvindale? Still harsh and dark and taut as stone, nevertheless his skin was warm and rough with stubble. He flinched when she brushed against him, her fingers light on his cheekbone.

His eyes opened and now they blazed fiery red, suddenly and openly, and the fangs seemed to show even longer. Maia swallowed, a zing of fear shooting through her, but she didn't remove her hand right away. She let it slide into his hair and brushed it over an ear. Soft, warm, thick.

He looked down, his nostrils widening, his breathing changing and she felt his muscles stiffen suddenly. She realized he saw her bare breast, and suddenly aware of her dishabille, looked down to see what he did.

There was a dark streak, a slender line across the mound of white flesh. As if she'd been scraped. Blood.

Maia's gaze jerked back up to him, and she saw the struggle in his face. His eyes, blank and focused somewhere distant, his mouth flat and compressed, his jaw so tight that his cheeks were hollow.

Blood.

She scarcely dared breathe, waiting. Would he bite her?

Would it be just as it was in her dreams…or would it be terrifying, as Angelica described?

Why wasn't she frightened?

His face was a mask of darkness, of concentration and control. All at once, he shoved her away—or perhaps himself—and the next thing Maia knew, the heavy weight and heat of him was gone, and there she lay, sprawled in the carriage, one breast bare and her body still vibrating from…whatever had happened.

And she realized, too, that the rumbling of the carriage wheels below them had ceased.

The space was quiet and still, but for the distant sounds of voices calling and the low rasp of his breathing.

Maia jerked herself upright, shoving her breast back into place, tugging up her bodice, wondering precisely what this all meant, and why he'd pulled away and was looking at her as if…as if he *loathed* her.

"What is it, my lord?" she asked, hiding her trembling fingers in the vast wrinkles of her skirt. "Is something wrong?"

Oh, God, everything is wrong.

"My lord?" He gave a short, bitter laugh. "Always the proper miss. Or at least, nearly always." The inflection in his tones made it sound like an insult.

She looked at him sharply. "Certainly you can't blame me for *this*," she said, gesturing to encompass the carriage and all that had occurred there that evening.

Instead of responding, he merely looked at her. Watched her. His eyes glowed faintly still, but there was no sign of the tips of his fangs. His mouth seemed more full than usual, lush and soft.

"Blast it," he muttered, still looking at her. "Miss Woodmore."

She glanced back up at his gaze and felt a little tug of connection between them, his eyes luring and compelling her. And then suddenly, she gasped, realized what was happening.

"Am I enthralled?" she demanded. "Have you enthralled me with your vampire gaze?"

A rush of anger followed by confusion came over her, and then ebbed, leaving her to realize that if that was the case then she'd had no control over anything that had occurred. It wasn't her fault for kissing another man, and allowing him to…well, whatever. She closed her eyes and felt the memory tingle through her. Her lips curved softly as a little flutter of pleasure tickled the inside of her belly. It wasn't so bad after all.

It was even better than her dreams.

When she opened her eyes, he was still staring at her. But now his mouth was flatter and his eyes darker and the tension emanated from him in heavy waves.

Maia looked away, surprised that the earl had nothing to say, and noticed again that the carriage had stopped. They were returned to Blackmont Hall, and the dawn had come.

She rose, tired of waiting, awash with confusion and attempting to appear as if nothing was amiss when everything was, in fact, a frightening vortex of problems. "Good morning, Lord Corvindale," she said when he made no move to assist.

Instead he sat there, his flat gaze fixed on her, no longer burning, but now black with loathing. The white of his shirt blazed bright against the dark velvet seat and

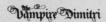

below the swarthy skin of his neck and jaw. His eyes like black jet beads.

She flung open the carriage door with no little finesse, her knees shaking, her own mouth compressed in a worried line and her face hot and flaming, and she helped herself down from the vehicle and stalked into the house.

IN WHICH MISS WOODMORE
GOES SHOPPING AND
DEMANDS AN APOLOGY

"You aren't truly going," Narcise said, eyeing Chas from across the room. She stood near the table, trying to appear nonchalant by plucking the petals from a bouquet of daisies he'd brought for her.

He looked at her, his powerful, swarthy hands filled with stakes and a clean shirt. Normally the sight of a wooden pike in his capable grip sent a shiver of excitement mingled with fear rushing through her. But she was too upset right now to feel anything but anger and apprehension.

"Of course I'm going," he replied sharply, shoving the items into a leather satchel. "She's my *sister,* Narcise. Do you think I would leave her safety up to chance? Especially with Voss?"

She shrugged, trying to make the movement nonchalant, while at the same time, her insides turned unsettled and her body numb. "Voss is smart enough, and Cezar likes him because he always has information he wants. He won't be suspicious of him, so Voss will have no problem getting in. And with those smoke-bomb packets you gave him, he'll have an easy way to escape."

Chas stopped and fixed her with a steady look. "I don't want him anywhere near my sister. Not only do I not trust him, not only have I heard legend upon legend of him ruining women, but he is also a Dracule."

Narcise was surprised at the pang of hurt his words produced. She'd thought she was well beyond such sensitivities. Damn it…after all she'd been through, she *should* be stronger than that. "And so you can commingle with we Dracule, we damned and damaged demons…but not your sister."

"Blast it, no, Narcise." He jammed a hand into his shiny dark hair. His muscles shifted beneath the rolled-up sleeves of his untied shirt and she noted the sleek movement with a warm shiver of appreciation. "It's different for her than for me. I understand what I— I understand what it's like."

"Well, Chas, I suggest you begin to help her understand. Because from the way she was acting that night in Dimitri's study, I wouldn't be surprised if Angelica was in love with Voss. And she doesn't know what to do about it. She probably doesn't even realize it."

"Never," he snapped. "And even if she fancies herself in love with him, I won't permit it. I'll kill him first." Chas had shoved his weapons and shirt, along with a pouch of coins and bills, into the satchel, and now he slung it over his shoulder. He was leaving her here. Alone.

A moment of panic chilled her and she dropped the daisy she'd been torturing. Cezar could find her. Or worse, Giordan. "I'll come with you, Chas."

"Don't be a fool," he said, his tone softening. "You

can't allow yourself anywhere near Cezar. Paris might be a big city, but you know as well as I do that he has spies and makes everywhere. I won't risk you, Narcise."

"It was almost impossible for us to leave Paris safely *last* time. He still has makes and mortal soldiers watching for you everywhere…you know it. You'll never get out of the city again, with or without Angelica. Let alone into Cezar's place."

"You know better than that. Last time *you* were with me and he was searching for you—"

"But he didn't know I was with you—at least at first. Chas…" Her voice trailed off. She knew she was being awful and selfish—wasn't that part of her Dracule nature?—but if she lost Chas, she didn't know what she'd do. He was the only one she trusted to keep her safe.

The *only* one, she told herself firmly when her resolve wavered.

"Oh, Cezar would see me. You know that for certain. He'd be delighted to welcome me back into his lair."

Dark fear seized her. He was right. Chas would have no problem getting in to see her brother. It was the getting out that would be impossible. "Chas, please." She hated that she begged; she'd given that up long ago.

"Don't insult me by implying your brother is more than a match for me," he said, his voice a little flat. "You know what I'm capable of. And if we knew what his Asthenia was, I'd have brought it to him long ago."

Narcise tried to believe Chas. She wanted to believe him; and much of what he said rang true. After all, it had been her fault Cezar captured Chas before they made their escape. But as was the case for anyone who had been at the mercy of or tortured by another, it was hard to dismiss the sense of omnipotence that the captor inflicted upon the victim. And Cezar had done a good job of it over the course of decades.

"You'll be safe here, Narcise," Chas said, gesturing to the stone walls. "He won't find you, and then when I get back we'll go to Wales."

They were in the cellar beneath the ruins of a former monastery in London, accessible through an old wall in a cemetery. All of the religious articles except around the building's perimeter had been taken away, and those that remained were partly covered by moss and lichen. That made it uncomfortable and more than a little painful for her to come into the space, and Chas had to nearly carry her in, but that was only until she crossed the threshold and closed the lead-filled door behind her. Then the pain was gone and she could be comfortable.

In fact, the chamber was rather luxurious, with a large bed, trunks, a table and chairs, and even a row of small venting windows to allow fresh air and filtered light into the space. Boxwood grew up and around the windows, which were at ground level, keeping the dangerous sun from streaming through directly. A thick rug covered the concrete floor, and a tapestry hung on one wall.

Chas had discovered the place as a haven for a group of made vampires when he was hunting some years ago, and chased them all away. Those who escaped the point of his stake didn't dare return, for he was fast and fierce. Aside of the physical attributes, he somehow had the innate ability to sense the presence of a Dracule. Even those of the Draculia couldn't recognize the mere presence of another, and they certainly couldn't identify the arrival of a vampire hunter like Chas. In combination with his speed and strength, which was nearly a match for any vampire, this ability made Chas Woodmore both feared and respected among the Dracule.

"Very well," she said, knowing she sounded a bit petulant. It was just that she'd hoped and planned and attempted to escape from her brother for more than a hundred years, and now that she'd finally done so, with Chas's assistance, she was terrified that her freedom would be taken away from her.

That Cezar would somehow find them. Or her. Or Chas.

Damned or no, she would never allow herself back with Cezar. She'd wrap herself in those painful brown sparrow feathers and jump from a tower into the sunshine before allowing him to touch her again.

Or his friends.

Freedom was glorious.

Chas looked at her from across the chamber, hesitated, as if trying to make up his mind, and then strode over to her. The next thing Narcise knew, she was flattened up against the cool stone wall, his hands on her face, his mouth crashing onto hers.

She closed her eyes and kissed him back, their mouths molding and smashing together, tongues fighting and sliding. Her hands curled around his skull, fingers digging up into his thick, black hair as he pressed her into the wall as if to leave the imprint of his body on hers.

"Be safe," she managed to say as he pulled away to catch a breath. "Come back to me."

"I'm in love with you, Narcise," he said, looking down at her with glittering green-brown eyes. He bent to brush a softer, farewell kiss against her throbbing mouth. "Make no mistake…I'll return. But," he said, stepping away, his face settling into something firm and serious. "While I'm gone, you have other things to attend to."

Narcise blinked, trying to pull herself out of the gentle, warm haze he'd caused to rise in her, to focus on him.

"Do what you must do," he said steadily, "to get beyond the past. Otherwise…" He shook his head, his mouth hard. "I love you, but I won't wait for you to come to love me."

But I do love you. The words didn't come, though she wanted them to. She knew they would be a lie. Dracule didn't—couldn't—love anyone but themselves. She'd made that mistake once before. "I can't lose you, Chas."

But he'd turned and swept from the room.

"Mr. Alexander Bradington has sent a message for you."

Maia froze, her hand holding the teacup halfway to her mouth. Her insides dropped, her face warmed, and she felt a rush of nausea replace the confusion that had been churning through her since returning early this morning. In the carriage with Corvindale.

She looked over to see the earl's butler in the entrance to the breakfast room, holding a small tray with a card on it.

Maia forced herself to wait until he brought it over to her, calmly replacing the teacup in its saucer. Then, as no one else was present at the table or in the room, she broke the seal and unfolded the card.

Darling Maia (if I may), it read, *I returned last night from my travels. I should like to call on you at two o'clock this afternoon. Please advise if you will receive me then. Alexander.*

Relief exploded in her belly. Surely he wouldn't call her "darling" if he were going to break the engagement or had otherwise changed his mind. Would he?

Maia read the note again, concentrating on the words written therein and trying to glean any other sense or emotion from them. The phrasing was correct and polite, which was nothing more or different than she'd expect from him. Alexander was the consummate gentleman. It was the proper thing to do—to ensure that she was dressed and at home and prepared to see him. Even after his eighteen-month absence, he was so very considerate. Instead of rushing to see her at the earliest opportunity and interrupting her breakfast, he gave her notice of his intention. A proper gentleman.

Her hands felt clammy and her stomach unsettled.

She would not think about what *she* had been doing last night when Alexander was arriving home. She would not ever think about that again, now that her fiancé had returned.

"Will there be a reply, Miss Woodmore?"

"Oh," she said. "Of course. I'll return in one moment." She rose from her chair and hurried out of the breakfast room and up to her chamber, where she kept her personal writing implements and stationery.

Except that she wasn't able to find a good ink pen in her drawer, and so she had to resort to rummaging through Angelica's desk drawer for one. While she was doing so, she pulled out a sealed letter that had been tucked away beneath a box of note cards. Obviously something Angelica had meant to keep, but for some reason, hadn't opened.

Was there bad news in it? Something she didn't want to know?

Maia considered for a moment, looking at the strong masculine writing on the outside. It said merely *Angelica.* Sensitivity prickled over her arm. All at once, she knew: this was important.

She had to read it, she reasoned. Angelica was gone. There was the chance she might not return…only for a time; for Maia wouldn't allow herself to consider the worst, and Corvindale's relative ease with the situation had given her confidence that Angelica would soon be safe.

She smoothed her fingers over the envelope, wishing she had more than her intuition to direct her.

Without further thought, she took the letter to a candle used for melting the wax for the seals and lit it. Holding the message just-so above the flame, she waited for it to soften just enough to be pried away, but without damaging or distorting the seal. Moments later, her steady hand rewarded her by lifting the black blob of wax so that she could read the note.

Angelica,

I am very grateful for the information you provided me, and because of that, I plan to fulfill my end of the bargain and leave London. I bid you farewell, then, and offer you a warning: do not wear the rubies in the presence of Corvindale, or even at all while you are under his care. I intended the earbobs to be a jest that only he would comprehend, but in retrospect, I've reconsidered. Wearing them could only cause you hurt and, whether

or not you believe it, that is the last thing I should
ever wish upon you.

Your servant, Voss.

Dewhurst. She'd known it. Maia stared down at the
message. A variety of emotions rushed through her,
ranging from anger to shock to confusion.

Where did one begin to make sense of this?

Not to mention all of the other things she had to
make sense of.

What to do with the letter?

Corvindale.

The very thought of facing him after last night made
her knees weak and her belly flutter. *No.* She absolutely
could not. Her cheeks flamed.

But he should see the letter. At the very least, he
should read the reference to the earbobs—which had to
be the rubies that had suddenly appeared in Angelica's
chamber. She'd told Maia a ridiculous story that they'd
been part of Granny Grapes's collection, but Maia was
no fool.

She hadn't believed that story any more than she believed Angelica when she denied wearing Maia's cro-
cheted pink gloves on a picnic. They'd been stained with
blueberry juice and had never come clean.

According to the letter, Dewhurst—Voss—had intended to leave London. Apparently he'd changed his
mind; perhaps because he learned that the vampire Belial meant to attack Angelica.

Maia shook her head, bit her lower lip and drew in a
deep breath. It had to be done.

Blast it.

Slowly Maia replaced the writing implements in her
sister's drawer and then her gaze fell on the note from
Alexander. She'd forgotten about it, and that someone
was waiting below for her response.

Dashing off a quick reply that she would of course be
pleased to see him anytime he wished to call, she started
out of Angelica's room. But then she caught a glimpse
of her reflection in the mirror and paused.

Her eyes went immediately to the simple lace edg-
ing of her bodice…and the thin red scratch peeking up
from behind it. Such a tiny wound; no worse than if
she'd scraped herself with the edge of her fingernail.
The bleeding had stopped last night and it was hardly
noticeable, except when one was looking for it.

Maia bit her lip again and tried to pull up the neckline to further hide it. It wasn't so much that it was ugly,
but what it represented.

Ignoring the fluttering in her stomach, she looked
away and took in the rest of her image.

Her brown hair was smooth, pulled back in a simple twist for morning. Neat, if unexceptional. The hol-
lows under her hazel eyes were darker than usual. Her
cheeks were still pink from the mortifying thoughts of
moments ago. And her mouth, with its fuller upper lip.
She tried to press it flatter, so that both lips seemed to
match…but she couldn't keep the top one from appearing swollen and off balance. Messy.

With a snort of disgust—for usually it was Angelica
who spent time fawning in front of the mirror—Maia
stalked out of the chamber. She was neat and well-
groomed this morning, if a little plain in her simple
coiffure and muslin day dress. She didn't look any dif-

ferent than she did any other day—which was to say, well. Rather pretty, in fact.

But it didn't matter one whit how she looked. She simply didn't want to appear that she was overset by what had happened last night…or, alternatively, that she was trying to—what was the word?—*appeal* to him.

Of course not.

Corvindale was no more than an arrogant, rude, stormy earl who thought he controlled everyone. Glowering at her from across the seat in the carriage, he'd looked at her as if it were her fault that they were in there together. But then…he'd moved.

Maia's throat went dry as she remembered him, looming over her, gathering her up and crushing her to him. His hands, his mouth, the strength of his body against hers. Her knees felt weak, and she actually had to grip the railing of the staircase.

It was his enthralling of me. His hypnotism.

He made me want to touch him.

Maia couldn't banish the stark image of his head bent over her bared bodice, the dark splay of his fingers against the pale color of her gown and lighter skin. And with it, even now, came the jolts of hot pleasure, panging in her belly and lower. Definitely lower.

Biting her lip, Maia shook her head in an attempt to clear her mind and to dislodge the memories. She felt no guilt.

Why should she?

She remembered when he looked at her so intently, catching her eyes and holding her gaze. He'd lured her in, just like Galtier the *vampir* had done to countless women in Granny Grapes's stories. Although… Maia frowned. In the stories, the women never realized what had happened to them. They didn't remember.

Then another thought struck her. Had he done it previously, at the masquerade ball? Was that why she'd been so bold?

The last vestige of guilt that might have lingered fled, leaving her much relieved. Certainly one little kiss after a few champagne drinks when her fiancé had been gone for eighteen months wasn't the worst sin in the world, but Maia had had no little pang of remorse for it.

Especially since she hadn't been able to completely forget it. But now it had all become clear to her. She wasn't complicit in anything. It hadn't really been her fault.

Lifting her head high, she squared her shoulders and continued down the stairs to the foyer. The butler, Crewston, was still waiting patiently and she handed him the note for Alexander.

"Where is the earl?" she asked.

"In his study, of course, miss," he replied.

Relief flooded her. At least he wasn't in his bedchamber. Her face heated again at the thought…which was now accompanied by a tactile memory from when her hands had settled against his linen-covered chest last night…and she shoved the accompanying images away.

Thus, her knock on the door to his study was bold and loud. If she had a squiggle of nervousness, Maia quickly squashed it and drew in a deep breath.

When he bade her enter, in the same annoyed voice as he always had, she opened the door with confidence and strode inside. Immediately she smelled the age and must of old paper and worn leather, and a hint of pine mingling with woodsmoke and cedar. Masculine smells that reminded her of her father's library…and yet, not precisely.

As always, the curtains were drawn nearly completely together over each of the three windows that studded the exterior wall. And as before, she felt compelled to walk to the other end of the long chamber to open them. But this time she resisted the urge, understanding now why he blocked the sun. Nevertheless, the room was well-lit with lamps and candles so that it was as bright as day. And there was the barest crack of sunlight triangling through one set of drapes at the far end.

Books lined the walls, many of the shelves appearing to be two and three rows deep. Piles of other tomes, messy and awkward, littered the floor, his desk, the table, even the cupboard where he kept whiskey and brandy. Papers joined them, scrolls, sheafs of parchment bound together, along with pens and ink. Maia had noticed on previous occasions that the majority of the works he studied weren't written in English, but in a variety of languages—from Greek to Latin to Aramaic to others she didn't recognize.

He was writing when she came in, and even from her stance, she could see the splotches of ink on the paper. His penmanship was dark and bold, and rushed. He wrote with his left hand, and when he lifted it to dip the pen to refill its ink, she caught a glimpse of the smudge along the side of his palm. One of the perils of being left-handed, which was why she used blotting paper.

She doubted he would take kindly to the suggestion.

"What—" He looked up from beneath ferocious black brows. "Miss Woodmore." He sounded exceedingly displeased.

She tried not to look at him, but it was difficult not

to notice the strong, bare forearms resting on the desk. The color of well-tanned leather, they were covered with dark hair and surprisingly muscular. His wrists were solid and his square hands capable and ink-stained, dusted with more hair on the backs of them. His coat was nowhere to be seen; nor was a waistcoat or neck-cloth. Although, perhaps that rumpled pile in the corner chair was the coat. The white shirt he wore fit over broad shoulders and the string that tied it at the neck was loose, and it sagged, showing the hollow of his throat. And—Maia's knees went weak again—a little bit of dark hair springing up from beneath.

"I have something I believe you should see." she said, ignoring the squirming in her gut and the flush rising once again in her cheeks. Stepping closer, she offered him the letter from Dewhurst.

Corvindale hesitated, then, muttering something under his breath, fairly snatched the missive from her hand. He barely glanced at her, and Maia found that no small relief. He seemed even more ill-tempered than usual.

Unable to stand still while he read the note, she walked to the far window and pulled the curtains open. Wide. With a good, hard, sweep of the heavy fabric.

Corvindale flinched, but she wasn't certain if it was from the letter or from her bold disregard for his preferences.

It occurred to her, then, that she should be furious with the man for luring her into such improper situations. Why wasn't she?

Why, instead of being angry, or feeling violated— which she *should* feel—was she merely overwhelmed by the sensations…the eroticism…of the interludes?

Recalling them with the same sort of wonder as she did those hot, red dreams?

Why—

"Where did you get this?" he said, breaking the silence.

Maia turned. "It doesn't matter. It's obviously to Angelica from Lord Dewhurst. She hadn't read it."

He glanced down at the letter, his lips twisting, then back up at her. "So you count lifting seals as another of your talents, Miss Woodmore?"

"Another of my talents?"

The lips she'd kissed last night flattened into a mere line. "There are too many to enumerate, but I would count your aptitude for arguing excessively about the most minor of details and your uncanny sense for disrupting the most pleasant of days as two of your most well-honed abilities."

Maia lifted her chin and walked over to the middle window, which sat at the halfway point of the chamber. Casting him an arch glance, she grasped each curtain panel, one of which overlapped the other, and yanked them apart with a flourish. A blast of sunlight cascaded into the room, bringing a soft, yellow glow to the piles of books and papers…and just brushing the edge of his desk. Still, the part of the room where his desk and the doorway were located was still swathed in shadow.

"Do go on, my lord," she said. "You flatter me so."

His scowl grew darker. "Miss Woodmore, you are impossible."

"More flattery, Lord Corvindale? Incidentally," she continued, "the most important part of lifting a seal is not the lifting itself, but how one replaces it. It's important to ensure that the edges of the wax line up perfectly to its original outline."

"Thank you, Miss Woodmore. I shall sleep much better this afternoon, knowing that trick." Was it her imagination, or did his lips move slightly up at the corners?

No. Absurd.

"I suppose you will expect Mrs. Hunburgh to prepare something special for your tea with Mr. Bradington today," Corvindale said, looking back down at his curling paper as he dipped his pen into the inkwell.

Maia opened her mouth to ask the obvious, then closed it. Of course Corvindale would know everything that occurred in his house. "No, indeed," she replied. "I'm certain that Alexander and I won't confine our visit to the parlor. A walk in the garden would be most lovely, don't you agree, my lord?"

"It would certainly be my preference." He looked back down at his work, and Maia was struck by how heartfelt his response was. She felt momentarily ashamed for her sly comment. But then he continued, thus absolving her from any guilt. "That way I won't be obligated to listen to your giggles and his waxing poetic over your beauty, and whatever other inane conversation you must be compelled to have."

Maia gritted her teeth but didn't reply. She supposed she had rather asked for it, at least this time. She considered whether she wanted to raise his ire further by opening the last set of curtains, and, unaccountably annoyed by the businesslike scratch of his pen over paper, she was nearly ready to do so when he looked up.

"Still here, Miss Woodmore?"

It was, she realized later, the studiously blank, emotionless expression on his face that did it. There was not a hint of shame, nor sympathy, nor consideration therein. Only boredom showed there, and barely that at all. The man was less emotional than a brick walkway.

And that was what set her off.

"Yes, Lord Corvindale, I am still here, although heaven knows why I remain in the presence of such a vile beast of a man. You took advantage of me—of our situation last night—and I demand an apology. You might be a vampire, but that doesn't give you the freedom to enthrall women to—to get them to…" Here she couldn't help but trail off, because the last thing Maia wanted to do was to put into words what had actually happened. And if she did that, she'd be forced to recall all of the details.

Which wasn't a prudent thing.

"I might have been ruined, Lord Corvindale," she finished.

His brows drove together and his mouth became a hard line. "Miss Woodmore, you overstep. I've allowed you to flaunt your regard for my hospitality and my wishes by leaving your vases of flowers in every corner of my house—including this room—and the curtains wide in the parlors, your gloves and wraps and shoes on tables, and listening to you and your sister and my sister giggling at all hours of the day. I've even disregarded your invasion of my private chambers and this study. But you will receive no apology from me for the events of early this morning."

"My brother has always spoken so well of you, my lord," Maia said, trying to keep her voice from shaking. "He made me believe you were a man of honor and that was why he entrusted us to you. And I've been willing to overlook your rudeness and arrogance, and, now, even the fact that you are a vampire. But your violation of my trust last night is in no way acceptable."

His laugh was short and sharp and bitter. "On the contrary, Miss Woodmore. It is with deep regret that I inform you that, despite my endeavors to remove your knowledge of my Draculian afflication from your mind, all effort on my part to do so failed. In short, Miss Woodmore, you appear to somehow have become immune to Draculian thrall."

"What—" Maia froze, staring at him. "That's nonsense."

He lifted a brow. "In fact, I wish it were, Miss Woodmore. Indeed, despite three attempts last evening, as I have done hundreds of times to others in the past, I could not hypnotize you. You were never enthralled. Which means that you were fully aware of and participatory in everything that occurred in the carriage."

10

Of Weddings and Kisses

Narcise heard a noise.

Her first reaction was relief: Had Chas forgotten something and returned?

He'd only been gone a few hours—perhaps he'd been in London, still putting things in order and making preparations, and had come back. Or realized that he didn't need to go after all. Perhaps they'd already rescued Angelica.

But that was a brief, initial reaction that soon fled.

She listened intently, the hair prickling at the base of her neck. Likely it had been a mouse or squirrel, knocking a little bit of rubble across the concrete floor. Or maybe it was the guard that Chas had arranged, or even Dimitri bringing her—

The slight scuff of a foot, so faint a mortal would never hear it, had Narcise slipping off the bed and reaching for her saber. That was one good thing Cezar had done: taught her to fight with a blade. He'd allowed her to learn, likely as much for his own entertainment purposes—watching her duel with men who wanted to fuck her—as to give her a false sense of hope that it might be a useful skill in gaining her freedom someday.

In the end, it hadn't. It had been Chas who'd freed her, not her own abilities—a fact which made her alternately furious and grateful.

Slipping the sword from its leather sheath, she turned on light feet and moved into the shadows.

The slender but lethal blade comforting in her hand, Narcise stood in a corner behind the doorway and wondered if she would be better served waiting for whoever it was to come in, or if she should rush through the door and meet them on her own terms. But she didn't have the chance to make such a decision.

Just as the door opened, she scented him and whipped out from behind it.

"What are you doing here?" she demanded, shoving the point of her blade up against Giordan's chest. Just below the hollow of his throat.

"I have no bloody idea," he replied. Eyes flashing, he grabbed the blade with his bare hand, yanking it away from his skin. It sliced along the inside of his palm and fingers, and immediately, his bloodscent permeated the air.

Narcise stepped back, allowing the sword to fall away, her heart pounding. Rich and warm and familiar, the essence of him filled her nose. Despite the loathing that settled like a stone in her belly, she couldn't dismiss her body's instant reaction: the blood in her own veins surged, her gums swelled, threatening to eject her incisors, and her mouth watered. Awareness prickled her. She swallowed hard.

"You did that purposely," Narcise snapped, backing away.

Giordan's expression was no less hostile. "As did you, my dear."

She used a cloth to wipe his blood from her blade and shoved it back into its sheath. "I ask yet again—what are you doing here?" Then she shook her head. "Forget that. Just leave."

"Nothing would please me more," he replied. His eyes raked over her, making Narcise feel, for the first time in a long time, as if she were dirty and used. "But Woodmore sent me. He indicated there was something I was to retrieve. Now that I've arrived, I can only presume he meant you."

"Certainly not," she replied. "I'm to stay here—perfectly safe—until his return with Angelica."

"And if he doesn't return?" Giordan asked mildly. He'd walked over and picked up one of the blankets to wipe the cut on his hand.

"I'll go to Dimitri. He'll protect me."

"I never thought of you as one who needs protection, Narcise. You take very good care of yourself."

"Except when I'm locked away by my brother."

Giordan looked at her. "Even then, you were formidable. In your own way."

She turned away, dwelling on how much she hated him and not the waves of memory, familiarity and emotion that threatened to soften her. "I don't know why Chas sent you here, but I'm not leaving. Especially with you. Just go."

"You don't know why he sent me here?" He gave a sharp laugh. "I certainly do. Here, where I could smell him all over you. Where I could scent both of you on the bed and against the wall and everywhere else. The entire place reeks of you two, together. That, my dear, is why he sent me here."

Narcise turned back, all casualness. "Then why prolong the agony, Giordan? There's no reason for you to stay and stew in your jealousy." Her heart thumped hard and her knees felt weak.

His eyes flared red and the next thing she knew, he was there in front of her. His bloodied hand curved around her throat, bringing the scent of temptation much too close. "Jealousy? You believe that's what I feel? You're a fool, Narcise." He shifted his fingers to cup her jaw no less gently. "If I still wanted you, a bloody damned vampire hunter wouldn't keep me away."

His fingers were strong, and she couldn't keep from inhaling him: the fresh blood, the masculine scent of him, the heat emanating from his body.

"I think we've always known what you really wanted," she managed to say, managed to keep the bitterness from roiling in her. Blocked the horrible images still burned into her memory. "And it wasn't me, was it, Giordan? My brother is a much bigger prize."

"Obviously you haven't told Woodmore that. Or he wouldn't have bothered to send me here." Giordan moved closer, his legs brushing against hers. Though he was broader, they were nearly the same height, and his eyes bored into hers.

She couldn't help it. She stepped back, twisting her face away, and his grip loosened. Her heart was in her throat now and another move closer could make her knees buckle. She wanted to shove him back but she didn't dare touch him. Instead she wiped his blood from her chin and onto her trousers.

"Why do *you* think he sent me here?" Giordan insisted. Moving closer again. His fangs gleamed now, showing just a bit beneath his lips. "Why, Narcise?"

She could see the pulse pounding in his throat, the vulnerable golden skin in the V of his loosened shirt. Now his hand whipped out, curling into the front of her man's shirt. He shoved her back, into the wall.

Her sword…damn, she'd left it in its sheath. In the corner. But she was strong, as strong as he was. He didn't frighten her.

"Just can't keep from touching me, can you, Giordan?" she taunted, though her mouth was dry. Her heart choked her, pounding hard in her chest. "Isn't that why he sent you?"

His eyes blazed, steady and yet somehow cold, and his fingers tightened around the linen of her shirt. He yanked her toward him, her body slamming into his as he released her shirt. His arms whipped around her, one at the back of her neck, pinning her thick hair in place, and the other grabbing her hip and pulling her up against his body.

He'd knocked the breath out of her, and for a moment Narcise could only look up into his eyes, ringed with the glow of red fire. Her knees trembled. Her insides swirled. His bloodscent filled her nose, still oozing from his cut, still printed on her fingers, tempting and rich.

She hated him, hated how he'd humiliated her and used her…but her body knew his too well. Craved it still.

Giordan tightened his grip at the back of her skull to border on pain, holding her head from moving, wrapping her hair around his wrist. His face came closer, his mouth full and ready, his fangs teasing beneath his upper lip, and Narcise closed her eyes. Her own lips softened, her heart raced. She braced herself, feeling the shudder of pleasure already building inside her.

He brushed his lips over hers. So lightly, it was like a breeze. A lush, familiar breeze. She held back a sigh. Then he came back, his parted mouth fitting over hers, a little tease of his hot, sleek tongue swirling around her lips. Warmth shuttled through her in a forceful blast and she followed him, tasting, wanting more.

He released her. Shoved her away so that she bumped against the wall, her eyes flying open.

The smug satisfaction on his face had her leaping for her sword.

"Bastard," she said, somersaulting over the bed to get to her sheath. She whipped out the blade and faced him. "Get out, Giordan. Or I will use it."

"As I said," he repeated, his eyes cold again, his fangs retracted, "if I wanted you, no one would keep me away. Not even you."

Furious, she lunged, blade out and swiping lethally through the air. He jumped nimbly aside, his eyes filled with arrogant humor. She came at him again, slicing and swirling, but he avoided her much too easily, infuriating her even further.

"You're too overset, my dear. You're acting out in haste and—" he twisted and vaulted gracefully over the bed "—anger. You're sloppy."

The chamber was red in her vision, colored red and hot with her fury, and Narcise drew in a deep breath as she spun around. Away from him. He was right, Luce

damn him. She had to gather her control. Breathing
heavily, she paused, then turned, holding the saber at
the ready.

He stood there, across the room, his breathing a bit
heavier but by no means was he out of breath, the bastard. He wasn't even in a readied fighting position. His
short, rich brown curls clustered over his head like that
of a Greek god and she knew that the rest of him was
as golden and muscular as one, as well. Blood streaked
his shirt and stained his hand, where it had slowed to
an ooze, and his trousers.

Narcise met his eyes and lifted her chin. Holding
his gaze, she took the point of her sword and opened
the palm of her other hand to it. She saw the flare in
his eyes, the widening of his nostrils, and she waited.

"Don't be a fool," he said, his voice taut.

She raised her brow. "What is it, Giordan? Don't trust
yourself to stay in control?"

"I haven't fed. In two weeks."

A little shiver raced over her. That was a long time.
Particularly for him.

"If you cut yourself, you know exactly what will
happen."

She did indeed, and the very thought had her trembling inside. Hot and trembly and frightened. And
needy. She swallowed hard. "Get out," she said, stepping back so that he could get to the door. "I'll not say
it again, Giordan."

He cast her one last inscrutable look, then strode past
her to the door. His fingers on the handle, he yanked it
open and turned back. "I never figured you for a coward, Narcise."

She slammed the door behind him, wishing for a lock.

It was a long time before she stopped trembling. And even longer until she managed to dry her tears.

He couldn't get her scent off his hands. It was as if he'd dipped his fingers into the inkwell of Miss Maia Woodmore, and now they were stained for good.

Dimitri closed his eyes. He had, in fact, dipped his fingers, his mouth, himself into her inkwell—so to speak. He couldn't slip any more deeply into that inky abyss where he would lose himself, lose control, lose the great walls he'd constructed. Where he'd *feel*.

His disgusted snort was loud enough to pull himself out of the mental miasma. *Satan's bloody bones, the woman's got me thinking in metaphors.*

He focused his attention on the scenery of London passing by the window of his carriage. The same carriage in which the incident with Miss Woodmore had occurred early this morning, and the reason he didn't seem able to dismiss it from his mind. Aside from the fact that her very self permeated the cushions.

Braving the sun and getting out of Blackmont Hall early this afternoon—after a fitful attempt to gain a few hours' sleep—had been the lesser of two evils. He hadn't been jesting when he enthusiastically agreed with Miss Woodmore's suggestion that she and Bradington spend their time walking in the garden. But Dimitri hadn't thought any further than the benefit of getting them out of the parlor, which was too near his study for vampiric ears, and hadn't considered the fact that the garden was, in fact, just outside the windows of his study.

He simply wouldn't be able to endure listening to the slushy, sloppy romantic prattle of the reunited lovers.

And it was only partly because, to his great mortification, he had once endowed his own sloppy, romantic prattle upon the lovely, if not improper, Meg. Many, many decades ago. When he was young and foolish and in love.

He'd been so in love, in fact, that he'd traded his soul in order to live with her forever.

Or so he'd thought.

Bitterness twisted inside him, and Dimitri settled on that unpleasant emotion. It was much better than thinking on feminine inkwells, which had the infuriating result of his belly softening and his veins swelling.

He glanced out the window of the carriage and saw that they'd turned onto Bond and were making their way along a street filled with shops and ladies patronizing them. Their maids and footmen followed along, carrying packages and navigating around dogs, street vendors, dirty-faced urchins and well-dressed gentlemen.

When he'd climbed into his vehicle, Dimitri had no particular destination in mind. He'd simply needed to leave. And Tren, smart man that he was, knew better than to ask if he wasn't given a direction…and also better than to allow his master to sit in the drive, waiting for the journey to commence. So he'd clucked to the horses and started off.

Dimitri had considered visiting Rubey's, which was, to put it bluntly, a brothel that catered specifically to the needs of the Dracule. Its eponymously named proprietress, one in a long line of women who'd taken on the name of the original madam, was a particular friend of Giordan Cale—and Voss, as well. She was also exceedingly astute for a mortal woman, as well as attractive, sensual and maternal—all at once.

However, Dimitri had no use for one of Rubey's women. Certainly there'd been times—rare times—over the last century when he had taken his pleasure, and usually given some in return…but that was always after he'd fed, when the bloodthirst wasn't on him… though there'd been the one incident when his body had gotten ahead of him. He still had the scars on his arm where he'd ended up driving his fangs, instead of into the heaving, writhing woman beneath him.

Dimitri closed his eyes momentarily. The last thing he needed to think about was a heaving, writhing woman beneath him, since he'd had just that this morning. Only with clothing between them, thank the Fates.

He lifted his hand to pinch the bridge of his nose in frustration, and Maia's scent came with it. This after he'd washed his hands thrice.

Was he now branded with her?

And he simply must *not* think of her as anything other than Miss Woodmore.

When he next looked out the window again, he noted that Tren had taken the opportunity to drive along Fleet and east toward Ludgate. The dome of the new St. Paul's Cathedral rose over the tightly packed houses clustering around it, visible even through London's constant filter of fog. At least, to Dimitri the church was new. To everyone else in London, it was the same cathedral that had always been there since its completion a hundred years ago.

But Dimitri clearly recalled the previous structure, whose spire had been destroyed by lightning in 1561, and then almost exactly a hundred years later, the rest of the cathedral had gone up in flames with eighty-eight other churches and thirteen thousand houses in London. The Great Fire of 1666 had melted St. Paul's lead roof, sending the molten metal pouring onto the streets, making rivers of glowing red heat.

He would never forget the sounds of houses collapsing and towers falling, combined with the shrieks of women and men shouting. The streets were so hot that neither man nor horse could bear to walk on them. He and Meg had earlier taken a room at one of the public houses on Cheapside and were awakened in the dead of night by the shouts and bells clanging. By then the fire already turned the sky golden-red, and smoke filled the air, enveloping the citizens in soot and choking them with smoke.

They stumbled out of the public house as the fire danced on the rooftop next to it, flames leaping like curling devils. Dimitri heard a cry behind him and saw a woman screaming at the small, flaming house, and realized her husband was trapped inside. He didn't hesitate but dashed around, trying to find an opening in the lashing tongues of fire. Only the front was burning, and Dimitri tore the door from the rear of the building and ducked into a dark, smoky hell.

It was his good fortune that the man was collapsed near the door, and Dimitri was able to pull him free. But by the time he reemerged, Meg had gone missing.

Even now, Dimitri remembered the terror of losing her. The paralysis, empty and cold amid all the hot chaos.

She'd become everything to him, to the man of thirty who'd spent most of his life buried with books and studies and had had little time or experience with the feminine gender. His Romanian mother, in adopting her new homeland of England, had embraced the Puritan tenet that affection toward children led them away from godliness. Thus she'd been remote and cool throughout all of his youth.

His father the earl, a Royalist who'd remained in England during the Cromwell years, took care to stay below the notice of the new government and taught his five sons to do the same by also seeming to adopt the simple, rigid Cromwellian ways. They had little social engagement and spent much of the time during the Lord Protector's reign away from London.

Thus, the sensual, earthy Meg—who was several years older than he—had changed Dimitri's world, bringing in a breath of life to an otherwise staid and bland one. She told him about her exciting, dangerous life as an actress in Southwark's stealth theaters during the time when the public stages were shuttered under Cromwell. Filled with enthusiasm and smiles, she was a bold woman who exuded sensual promise.

Meg had become his life. She lured him, the proper and staid fifth son of an earl, into her bed, and in doing so, wholly snared his heart and mind.

In retrospect, Dimitri had come to realize that she wasn't nearly as in love with him as he had been with her. Meg was enamoured by the thought of him being a peer and of a wealthy family, and what that might mean if they were attached, but she was not of his class, nor, more importantly, of his moral makeup. She lived for the moment and was scandalously loose while the genteel Dimitri lived only for the future.

Yet, that hot, red night when he emerged from saving the man from a house afire and found Meg missing, Dimitri's life stopped. He simply couldn't imagine his world without the sloe-eyed, coy-smiling, curvy redhead, and he stood in the burning street, frantic.

Then, somehow, above all of the chaos around them, he heard her voice.

There, up in the window of the room they'd let at the small inn, next to the flaming house. He saw her leaning out the window, screaming for him. She'd gone back inside? Why? Then he saw the ruby necklace dangling from her fingers.

She'd gone back in to retrieve the most recent gift he'd given her.

His mind blank and terrified, Dimitri thought of nothing but saving her. He bolted through the door of the inn, which had just begun to catch fire. Inside it was already filled with choking ash and the heat radiated from the buildings around it.

But he could save her. There was time.

He ran up the stairs, already narrow and steep, but now darker and clogged with hot smoke. Stumbling, staggering, he went two flights until he found the room they'd used, blind and hot, barely able to breathe. The roar of fire filled his ears, the sounds of timber shuddering and heaving as it crackled into debris, the walls warm and rough beneath his fingers.

Somehow, he found her, his hands filled with the soft, familiar warmth of Meg, who'd collapsed on the floor near the door. He gathered her up and fell more than ran down the stairs, his eyes stinging with smoke, gritty and blind. The roof above was now ablaze, and falling pieces from the rafters scattered in front of him, tumbling down the steps and catching against his legs and trousers.

Down, down, down he went, staggering against the walls, at last reaching the bottom. Just then, a loud rumble filled his ears, followed by a horrible crash.

The next thing he knew, there was pain and heat bearing him to the ground, and everything was light… tinged with red and orange leaping everywhere. He coughed, tasted smoke, choking out her name, and tried to crawl toward what he thought was the door.

Dimitri dragged them to the opening, his body weak and burning, his lover boneless and unmoving, the ruby still clutched in her hand, the chain wound around her wrist.

Save her. I'll do anything. Save her. Save us. Anything to live.

The thoughts ran over and over in his mind as he crawled with superhuman strength, over rubble and coals, burying his face in the ground to keep from breathing the smoke.

It was a miracle that he made it from the smoking, blazing building, and even more of a miracle that he was able to pick Meg up and carry her down the burning streets, staggering west and away from the rage of fire.

At last, he collapsed, coughing, his eyes gritty, his hair and back singed and his body screaming with pain.

He couldn't catch his breath. All he could smell was smoke. Her body was warm and comforting next to him.

And Dimitri collapsed there, curling with his lover under a bridge as the fire raged in the distance. The sun had begun to rise in the distance, but the sky was already an arc of red over London.

He closed his eyes, feeling the strength sap from him. Meg hadn't moved, even when he shook her, tried to listen to her breathing. But his ears were deafened from the great noise, and he couldn't tell if her chest moved with breath.

Anything. Save us. Let us live.

He fell into sleep, or a faint, or something…and that was when the dark, fallen angel Lucifer visited him. Offered him precisely what he wanted.

I can give you what you want, Dimitri. I can save her for you. Both of you. Live forever. With the woman you love. Will you agree to it? Both of you. Forever. Will you save her?

Even now, Dimitri felt the rush of cold over him when he remembered that moment. The clear blue eyes and the handsome face of the visage in his dreams.

What must I do?

Lucifer smiled. *You need do nothing but live. Forever. Enjoy life. You'll save hers by doing so, and ensure your long life with her.*

Dimitri remembered the vague feeling of evil, the cold skittering deep inside him. He opened his mouth— or perhaps only the mouth in his dream—to say no, to ask more, to question, perhaps even to pray…but Luce continued: *Do you not love her enough, then? Not enough to save her?*

Meg shuddered at that moment, and Dimitri felt her body as it gasped for breath. She was dying. He was losing her. *No.* He looked at his nocturnal visitor. *We'll live forever? Together.*

You'll live forever. Lucifer's hand reached out in the dream, settling on Dimitri's left shoulder. *Do you love her enough? Do you truly? Will you agree?*

Yes. I'll save her.

The devil's hand rested on his skin and a blaze of pain seared through him, from beneath his hair, radiating over his left shoulder and scapula. *And so it will be.*

When Dimitri opened his eyes, the first thing he saw was the ruby, dangling around Meg's neck. She was sitting up, her eyes bright and happy, her hair tumbling down over her shoulders. Not a hint of ash or soot marred her lovely face, nor were her clothes torn or singed.

Dimitri sat up and realized he, too, was intact. Except for a soft throb over his shoulder, right where the devil had touched him.

The city blazed behind them, a few miles away. They smelled the smoke, which choked out the sun and cast a pall over them even here. But they were alive. Uninjured. And together.

London burned savagely for three days.

Meg remained with Dimitri for three months. And then, fully realizing her power as an immortal, she left for greener pastures: younger men, an immortal career onstage and exotic travels.

It took years for the city to rebuild itself, disdaining lumber and using only brick and mortar.

Just as Dimitri rebuilt his own walls, stronger and more solid than they had ever been. Brick by brick.

"You look lovely, Miss Woodmore. Maia," Alexander said, smiling.

She had her fingers curled lightly around his arm and they were, as planned, strolling through the gardens at Blackmont Hall. The roses still bloomed, but the spring flowers that cast such heady scents—lilac, lily of the valley, tulip—were all gone.

Pink coneflower and Russian sage marked the paths, along with thick green moss and neatly clipped boxwood. Lovely gardens. It was too bad that their owner couldn't enjoy them…at least, in full sunlight.

"Thank you, Mr. Bradington," she replied.

They were alone. Her heart should be light. It *was* light. It was, and she was happy and calm, and—dare she think it?—relieved.

"I do believe you should use my Christian name as you have done in the past," he said, looking over at her. "After all, we are to be wed. Sooner, rather than later, I hope."

Maia smiled back and ignored the odd sinking feeling in her middle. "I hope so, as well, Alexander."

I could not hypnotize you.

You were never enthralled.

Maia blocked the words from her mind, along with the horrible feeling of mortification. It couldn't be true.

"I'm so glad you've returned," she told Alexander.

She spied an ivy-covered pergola and changed direction so that they walked toward it. Maia wasn't certain what she had in mind, but the fact that it was shaded and out of sight from the back windows of the house could be a benefit.

"When shall we?"

Angelica. She couldn't even think of a wedding until Angelica was safely home. And Chas had to walk her down the aisle. And Sonia must come from Scotland. "As soon as you can file for the license," she replied.

She hadn't told Alexander about her sister's abduction, and certainly not about Chas's occupation. How could she explain something like that? If she could stall for a bit until they got word about Angelica, at least...

"Will it be enough time for you? I can obtain the license easily within a fortnight. Will you be ready in two weeks? I know there is a dress to be made, but also flowers and invitations and announcements, and the food...and where would you like to have the ceremony?"

Maia's insides warred between delight and misery. Here was a man who cared what she thought, who listened to her, who understood what she had to do. But she certainly could do nothing until her family was back in place. And safe.

And she couldn't tell him. At least, not yet.

They'd reached the pergola. The shade from the clematis-entwined ivy covered a small area on the footpath, and, as if reading her mind, Alexander paused there, turning her to face him.

"As soon as possible," she said, knowing that she would delay it if she had to. But perhaps something else to focus on now would be good. There were so many other things she didn't want to be thinking about. "And I was hoping we could wed at St. Dunstan's. It's such a lovely little church." Her heart was ramming in her chest as she looked up at her fiancé.

He was watching her with his gray-blue eyes. They always seemed so warm and affectionate, unlike those dark, flashing ones belonging to…other people. And he wasn't quite so tall, nor as stiff and forbidding. He never spoke rudely. He never seemed as if her mere conversation was keeping him from something more important.

"St. Dunstan's would be the perfect place. I shall make a generous donation and speak with the rector tomorrow. If that is what you wish, Maia."

She swallowed, noticing the way his eyes changed. His hands closed around her arms and he drew her closer. Her heart was in her throat now, pounding. Her knees were shaky and her insides fluttered nervously. He was going to kiss her.

She was afraid of what it would tell her.

11

IN WHICH OUR HERO FACES
IMPOSSIBLE QUESTIONS

Two weeks later, Dimitri stared at the door of his study, rancid bitterness burning through him. His fingers curled into two fists that he ground into the desk in front of him—it was either that, or put them through the wall. Or window.

Or somewhere equally painful.

Impossible.

Impossible!

Voss had just left, and was about to walk out of Blackmont Hall. Into the blazing sunshine with no protection.

It was impossible.

Voss had broken the covenant with Lucifer.

Voss.

The most self-centered, selfish, manipulative person Dimitri had ever known aside of Cezar Moldavi had somehow released himself from the unholy contract with the devil. A man who'd lived a life of debauchery and hedonism without a hint of remorse, without a care for anyone other than himself—even before he'd been turned Dracule.

While Dimitri still bore Lucifer's Mark. And it burned and writhed and seared him daily as he denied himself, studied and contemplated…and nothing.

Nothing.

He glared at the stack of books, the curling, browned manuscripts and crinkling scrolls. His notes. His drawings. His hopes.

From somewhere deep in the house he heard the sounds of feminine squeals. Giggles, and a soft shriek. He knew what it was, and the sound infuriated him even more. He snatched up his heaviest cloak and stalked out of his den, calling for a groom and his carriage.

Damn the sunshine, he must get away from them.

Angelica had returned safely two weeks ago. Voss had rescued her from Moldavi as planned. But Chas, refusing to allow a demonic vampire—particularly such a rapacious one—near his sister, had intercepted them in Paris and brought Angelica back to London, where wedding plans for her elder sister had commenced with great alacrity.

Now, as of his meeting with Voss, Dimitri knew he would be subjected to twice the excitement, for Voss had announced his intention to wed the younger Woodmore sister. Now that he was no longer bound to Lucifer, there was no real reason Chas could deny such a marriage. The viscount was wealthy and a peer. And he was a mortal.

Voss had actually removed his shirt whilst in Dimitri's study in order to show him that the Mark was gone from the back of his shoulder.

When asked how he'd done it—how he'd shorn himself of the devil's Mark—Voss had said simply that he'd *changed*.

Changed.

Dimitri climbed quickly into the carriage, taking little care to protect himself from the sun's rays despite the cloak he carried. The flash of a burn skimmed his face and ungloved hand and wrist, and he fairly welcomed the pain.

The antiquarian bookshop seemed even less noticeable than usual, with the alcove entrance of Lenning's Tannery next door fairly dwarfing the small, dark entryway.

Once inside, Dimitri paused and waited for the strains of serenity to slide over him. When he'd drawn in a steadying breath of old books and worn leather, he stepped into the dark shadows of the rows of shelves and waited.

It didn't take long for Wayren to appear. This time, she wasn't holding a book, although she had her spectacles on.

"Dimitri of Corvindale. I was suspecting you might return." She looked at him closely, and all at once, he wondered what madness had brought him here. She knew nothing that could help him.

He found himself momentarily at a loss for words, anger and confusion churning like sludge in his gut.

Wayren cocked her head, watching him like an interested sparrow. "I've acquired something I think you might find interesting, and I've been saving it for you." She turned toward a shelf next to her and plucked out a bound pamphlet from between two other much thicker books and handed it to him.

Dimitri took the slender packet, which could be no more than a hundred pages, and didn't attempt to hide his distaste. "*La Belle et la Bête*? What is this—a fairy tale?"

She smiled benevolently. "Indeed. Gabrielle-Suzanne Barbot de Villeneuve is quite an entertaining writer."

He frowned. "I don't see how a fairy tale will be of assistance to me."

"And yet you study Faustian legend?" she said delicately. "You must see something of yourself in Doktor Faust's character. Perhaps you will find something different to relate to in Madame de Villeneuve's tale about the beauty and her beast."

Dimitri took the pamphlet and tucked it in his inside coat pocket, unwilling to offend the woman. "Very well. Bill my account for whatever it's worth."

From behind her spectacles, she watched him with a considering gaze. "Is there aught else I can do for you?"

She waited patiently.

"There is a way," he said at last, a hint of desperation making its way into his voice, "to break the covenant."

Why was he telling this colorless, quiet woman? What did he think she could do for him? Did he truly think she had some writ that would spell it out neatly and clearly; one that she'd kept from him during his previous visits?

"You must find a way yourself, Dimitri," she said, in an echo of his unspoken question. "Just as Voss did."

Dully he realized he wasn't surprised that she knew of Voss, and what had happened to him. That was what had drawn Dimitri here. Some deep-seated reason had brought him to this librarian of sorts.

"I don't know how he did it," he said, his voice thick. "He's neither pious nor has he ever denied himself anything. How could…"

"How could he have done it when you've spent so much of your life denying yourself everything in an effort to do the same?"

"Yes," he exploded. But his voice didn't shake the rafters. It merely settled there, a pained affirmation that hardly stirred the dust. "I always do what is right. I always have." He remembered those years of study, of Puritan starkness, of maintaining his honor even in the face of difficulty, when Royalists were hated during Cromwell's reign. Of rushing into a burning house to save the man.

Anger rushed through him. *I did. Perhaps not so well now, but I did then. Before.*

"But that is why he chose you, Dimitri. Do you not understand that? To have turned such a man to him—a man who sees in black-and-white, and who lived in the light and the right—was the greatest of successes for the Fiend. It's much easier to tempt and lure one who exists in the gray. Someone, perhaps, like Voss. Like Giordan. But you…you were different. You tried to live in the light."

"And the one time someone meant something to me…" His voice trailed off, for he simply couldn't put the disconcerting thought into words. *Meg.*

"Aye. The one time you allowed yourself to open and love, when you were desperate, he used that very power against you. You were very vulnerable and that was how he convinced you." She was nodding, her eyes serene pools of fog-laced blue. "He found your soft underbelly. That is the way he works."

"I accepted it. And he branded me for eternity," Dimitri said bitterly. So bitterly. He pinched the upper part of his nose, just above his eye sockets, as hard as he could. He wanted to make it go away.

Wayren was nodding. "Because of that, he'll not release you easily."

"But it's possible?" For the first time, he felt a real glimmer of hope.

"Anything is indeed possible. But it's not without trial and tribulation. You, too, have to change."

Dimitri looked at her, frustration simmering. "Change? I don't know what you mean. Change how? I'm honest. I give to those in need. I don't take, I don't feed. I've taken in Mirabella when she had no one. I've—"

"Certainly. You've done that…but have you given anything of yourself, Dimitri? Any care, any affection or love or even any *time?* Or has your generosity been only that of material things? Those things which remain behind in this world?"

Terror seized him. "I can't." His response came out in a heartfelt groan. "I cannot."

Wayren looked at him for a long moment, sadness lingering in her eyes. "Then you still aren't ready, Dimitri."

What precisely did one do?

"Turn, please, miss."

Maia turned obediently, feeling the tug of her skirt

as the seamstress's assistant folded it just-so and pinned it. Behind her, another assistant adjusted her bodice, carefully inserting another pin along the seam in the back.

What did one do when one's fiancé's kiss had lost its attraction?

When one would rather be removing a splinter than meeting his lips?

Maia opened her eyes and found herself staring at the image of a lovely bride. Golden-coppery-brown hair shone in a shaft of light from the window, and the beam filtered over the pale pink silk of her gown. Over it lay an icy-lemon layer of lace, which gave the frock a shiny, pearlescent appearance.

"You look beautiful, miss. He will be unable to take his eyes off you," said the seamstress. Satisfaction colored her voice, and she stepped forward to adjust the short puff of a sleeve. It was made from twisted swatches of pale pink, lemon and blue silk, loosely braided and sewn stuffed with padding to hold their shapes.

Maia scanned herself. She did indeed look beautiful—mostly due to the dress, she conceded. Though the bodice was low, and in a new neckline called a sweetheart shape, the little scratch on the top of her breast was no longer visible. It had healed weeks ago.

Since Angelica's escape from Cezar Moldavi and her return from Paris, both Chas and Corvindale had agreed that the danger from Moldavi had eased. The villain was now aware of Corvindale's far-reaching protection of the Woodmore sisters, and in light of his recent failure to use Angelica to bring her brother to heel, it was deemed unlikely that Moldavi would make another attempt so soon after.

Thus, the earl had eased his restrictions on the Woodmore sisters, although Chas assured Maia that they were still being protected, even if they weren't aware of it. Maia had, of course, noticed the extra footmen that always accompanied or followed their carriage, and the unusual number of shadows hulking about on the street from sundown to sunrise. She assumed that most of them were what Corvindale would term "good vampires," since they were obviously in his employ.

Meanwhile, Chas, to Maia's immense frustration and concern, had disappeared shortly after Angelica's return, leaving them once again in Corvindale's care.

Yet…since she'd fled Corvindale's study the morning after the incident in the carriage, his mocking words ringing in her ears—*you were never enthralled*—she hadn't seen more than the flutter of his coat hem around a corner. It had been more than a month and they'd managed to avoid each other.

Or at least, she'd avoided him. Whether he was doing the same, Maia wasn't certain. And since Angelica had returned with nary a scratch, and had announced her intention to wed Viscount Dewhurst, Corvindale hadn't been seen at all.

She'd heard the deep rumble of his voice, and noticed the closed door to his study. And, fortunately, she'd had no reason to disturb the earl.

But Alexander had been to Blackmont Hall often.

And he always seemed to want to walk in the garden, and to stop in that shady pergola.

But kissing him had become as interesting as kissing her own hand. Maia knew—for she'd tried it.

And what had once been a tingling anticipation for his arrival was now a heavy leaden ball in her middle.

She didn't love him.

One doesn't marry for love. One marries for money or prestige or position. Or even for good family, as long as it is a good match.

She'd often given such a lecture to Angelica, who, for a time, had thought herself in love with the very untenable Mr. Ferring-Dulles. *Love doesn't factor into it. It might come later if one is compatible with one's husband. Or if one is very lucky, it might also be there from the beginning.*

But one doesn't expect or seek love in marriage.

Maia knew better, for there was a time when she thought she'd loved Mr. Virgil. She'd thought they were eloping to marry on that night when she dressed in men's breeches and sneaked out of the house.

But instead, the night had turned out to be a horror, the details of which she'd long forgotten. Or otherwise suppressed. She shivered now, as a wisp of memory flitted through her mind. Corvindale. In the carriage. She in her breeches, hair tucked beneath a sagging cap.

Why could she not remember?

She sighed. No, love definitely could not and should not factor into one's choice of husband.

And that was why, in three days, Maia would be marrying Alexander Bradington. In the very lovely dress she was now wearing.

* * *

Dimitri looked down at the note, glad for the distraction.

The house was filled with energy and activity. Miss Woodmore was to wed Bradington in three days, and for some reason unbeknownst to him, everyone related to the nuptials seemed to be coming and going from Blackmont Hall today. It was as if the walls were swollen to bursting.

Angelica Woodmore's wedding plans were also progressing, if one were to judge by the number of appointments with flower-keepers and seamstresses and other entities, not to mention the swatches of material, scraps of notes and drawings, that had littered the parlor table yesterday. Couldn't the blasted chits wait until their brother was back to attend to these things?

Naturally that could take weeks. Or months. Or longer. He knew that Woodmore meant to find a way to kill Cezar Moldavi, for until he did so, Narcise would never be safe. But his continued absence was making things even more inconvenient for Dimitri. And the sisters seemed to have confidence that their brother would be in attendance for their weddings, regardless of whatever else he was attending to.

Dimitri hadn't had a good day's sleep in weeks, so there was no sense in attempting it today. Perhaps he would respond to the message.

Lord Corvindale,

I should like to invite you to examine a new collection of works that I have recently procured. I am hopeful that one of them might contain the information you seek. Please advise soonest, for I have other interested clients.

G. Reginald.

Gellis Reginald was another antiquarian bookseller that Dimitri had patronized, although not for months since he'd found Wayren's shop. Perhaps the man had heard that his most influential customer had gone elsewhere and wished to lure him back, or perhaps he truly did have something of interest.

Regardless, it was an opportunity to leave the house.

Dimitri put aside his other papers—contracts and balance sheets, bank drafts and bills that he'd taken a moment to peruse and sign merely in order to get Beckett, his man of business, to stop nagging him—and rang for the carriage.

The day was a normal gloomy one, with thick rolling fog and gray everywhere. Nevertheless, Dimitri needed his cloak. An abnormal wave of bitterness flooded him as he scooped it up and stalked out, leaving a house filled with squeals and giggles behind him.

When they arrived at Reginald's dingy shop front, Dimitri climbed out and bade Tren to return for him at the public house on the end of the block.

"I don't expect to be long," he said. "Two hours at the outside."

"Miss Woodmore asked that I—"

Dimitri flapped an impatient hand and walked into the shop, letting the door slam behind him. Immediately he was accosted by the smells of age and mold, as well as dust and even mouse dung.

He didn't want to hear a thing about Miss Woodmore. Likely she'd asked Mrs. Hunburgh to have one of the servants pick up some package or other for her, and Tren had been given the task. He didn't care. Soon she would be out of his house, and out of his thoughts.

And, pray God, out of his dreams.

"Reginald," he called in his peremptory voice when he saw that the shop was empty. "It's Corvindale."

Blast it. Why wasn't the man waiting for him? He'd sent the message, after all.

Dimitri had no interest in examining the old watches and ratty-cornered Bibles and poetry books that the shopkeeper attempted to foist off as valuable antiquities. That was part of the reason he had ceased patronizing the man after a while—his offerings were nigh worthless when one sought words from the ancients, and in their own languages. Too many things were lost in the translation of others, so Dimitri had learned to do his own.

"Reginald!" he called again in a voice that made the glass cases shudder. He sniffed the air, suddenly realizing the faint strain of blood that he'd just noticed was too strong to be something as innocent as a nosebleed.

Dimitri was behind the counter in a moment, pushing through the sagging door that led to the back room of the shop. Once through there, the smell of blood was stronger and richer, causing him to hesitate for a moment to determine the direction of its origin. The room was cluttered in what could have been its normal state, or the scene of an altercation. A single door in the back wall presumably led to the alley behind, and the one window was, thankfully, covered in grime, making the chamber dim and shadowy. On the floor was a half-dried pool of blood.

As he turned, another smell reached his nose. A familiar one that made him frown in shock and confusion.

And then all at once, the back door burst open and three figures vaulted through, into the room.

Dimitri reacted automatically as they lunged toward him, grabbing one by the arm and slinging him into the wall, then turning to meet the others. He ducked and easily sent a second one flying, then swung around to slam a fist into the gut of another. The dull flare of fire in their eyes identified them as makes, relatively weak ones, by his estimation.

He reached for a wooden stool, breaking off one of the legs into a jagged stake as he heard a noise behind him. The scent came with it, the familiar one, and it had him whirling just in time to see her stepping from the door at the front of the shop.

Impossible. She was dead.

Something red glittered on her hand and as Dimitri stumbled, his chest tightening and slowing, he saw that she wore ropes of them. Rubies. Dangling from her ears and around her throat and two robin's-egg-size gems on her fingers. Tiny ones glittered in her dark hair. So many… His body lumbered, limbs clumsy and heavy.

His attackers came behind him, pushing him forward when he would have spun away, shoving him toward her, and just before something black and heavy wafted down over his face and shoulders, he managed to gasp, "Lerina. How?"

Her laughter curled around his ears and into his consciousness as he fought to breathe. He saw the flash of red in her eyes and the gleam of fangs. Weakness deadened his limbs and the heavy cloth tightened around him. The rubies came closer; he could feel them through the fabric. Binding, burning.

And then everything went dark.

12

HELL HATH NO FURY

"I'm sorry, I am, my lady," said the groom as he opened the door for Maia.

"Is everything all right?" she asked, pausing when she noticed the stricken look on his face. He was more than thirty minutes late picking her up from her fitting at the seamstress's shop, and Tren had always been on time in the past.

"I wouldn'a been so late but my lordship...well, I but waited for him and he ain't never come."

"Well, I am certain he'll find his own way back to Blackmont Hall," Maia replied, settling in her seat. After all, as he was fond of reminding her, he *was* Corvindale. "Or perhaps we should make one more stop at where you were to meet him, in the event he was detained?"

"Oh, my lady, if you would permit the delay, I would do that."

"Of course," she replied, thinking mostly of the tongue-lashing poor Tren would get from his master if he weren't there when Corvindale expected him to be. Even if the earl was late, the fault would lie with his servant.

Maia frowned as Tren closed the door and retracted the unpleasant thought. Despite his impatience with her, Maia had never witnessed the earl being unaccountably rude to his servants. Firm and directive, certainly, but never overbearingly rude.

And then her thoughts wandered to the next logical step: that if they did succeed in meeting up with Corvindale, she would be forced to ride alone in the carriage with him again. Aunt Iliana and Angelica had gone on home earlier, for the latter had had an appointment with a flower-seller and Maia's fitting had gone on too long, for one of the seams had to be redone.

Maia's heart stuttered as she imagined him sitting across from her on the seat, filling the space and making it smaller.

Perhaps she ought to have Tren take her back to Blackmont Hall first.

No. Maia wasn't a coward. She'd face him if she had to. Nevertheless, her throat was dry as a bone and her belly swirled with nerves as Tren drove them along Picadilly and past Bond. The calls of flower-sellers and metal-workers clashed with the constant rattle of wagons and open carriages over the cobblestones. Dogs barked, children shouted, messengers dashed nimbly along the edge of the streets, weaving in and around shoppers and shopkeepers alike. Nothing ever seemed to slow or to quiet in London, she reflected, trying to keep her mind on something other than the possibility of riding home with the earl. Even the storefronts and houses seemed loud and overbearing, packed together as they were, built up against each other like uneven, brick teeth.

At last, the carriage came to a halt. Maia waited as Tren climbed down and went into a little pub called the Fiery Grate. As she sat there, she noticed the sign for G. Reginald, Antiquarian Books and Curiosities.

It was only a block from the public house, and she wondered…would Corvindale have gone in there? It seemed a place that would interest him.

That little prickling of instinct bothered her along her forearms, and when Tren returned moments later, she opened the carriage door and made the suggestion.

"Indeed, my lady, that is the place I took him first," the groom told her. "But he gave orders to meet at the Fiery Grate and he isn't there. No'ne has seen him."

Maia gathered up her skirts. "Perhaps he's in the shop and has lost track of time. If you like, I'll go in and look."

The poor groom's face was so relieved Maia smiled. She could imagine his reluctance to enter a shop dressed as plainly as he was, and in an unfamiliar place. Aside of that, she thought there might be items of interest in Mr. Reginald's place.

Inside she found the place strangely quiet and deserted. It wasn't all that uncommon to enter a shop and need to wait for the proprietor to come from the back, but the place was so silent that Maia sensed immediately that something was wrong.

"Hello? Mr. Reginald?" she called, leaning on the counter to see if she could peer into the back room. The door was ajar and she smelled something that wafted over the commonplace aromas of dust and age that often accompanied antiques.

Something was amiss. The smell on the air...it boded no well.

Maia started toward the back of the shop, then hesitated. She should ask Tren to come with her. What kind of fool would she be, walking into somewhere alone?

Yet, he'd have to find a place to tie the horses....

"Hello?" she called again, skirting carefully around the counter, looking for something that she might use as a weapon. Settling on a long, heavy cane in one of the display cases, she pulled it out and tiptoed toward the ajar door. Heart pounding in her throat, she raised the cane up in front of her shoulder, and stepped into the back room.

The first thing she noticed was the dark pool on the floor, and immediately attributed the strange scent she'd smelled to it. Blood. Lots of it.

But the space was silent, and she stepped in farther, lifting her skirt out of the way. The place was a mess, and appeared as if some sort of battle had accompanied the puddle of blood. Something gleamed on the floor and Maia glanced around nervously before stooping to pick it up.

Her heart gave an odd little kick when she recognized it. Corvindale's button; unmistakeable because it was stamped with the earl's crest.

So he had been here. That odd feeling settled into something less pleasant and Maia glanced toward the window, which was dark with dirt. If she had more light, she could see...

"Miss?" came a voice from the front.

Tren. Maia turned and hurried back to the half-open door. "Call the constable," she said. "I think something's gone wrong." She came back, snatching up a lamp, and crouched on the floor, searching for something else that might prove that the earl had been there.

When she saw the hairpin, Maia's heart kicked up again as she reached for it. This was no ordinary hairpin, but one studded with tiny...rubies.

Rubies.

Corvindale hated rubies. They infuriated him.

Maia shook her head. No. Something was wrong. She remembered how he'd been so odd in the carriage when Angelica had been abducted, when they both had been wearing ruby earbobs. It wasn't that he simply hated them...it was that they had some sort of ill effect on him.

The prickling of certainty, her instinct, lifted the fine hairs on her arms.

With a flash, she recalled the night of the masquerade, and Mirabella's description of the fight. *There was a necklace of rubies on him.*

A hairpin with rubies on it. Corvindale's button. Blood, and signs of struggle.

Maia went cold. It was no coincidence. Something had happened to the earl.

She looked down at the hairpin, recognition tickling the back of her mind. She'd seen this accessory somewhere before. Someone had been wearing it, or something like it. She frowned, concentrating, trying to pull up a picture of her in her mind.

Someone she'd seen recently.

Someone she didn't know.

But someone she was going to find.

* * *

Dimitri smelled, listened, felt…then opened his eyes.

He was in a chair, a large, upholstered one, sprawled as if dumped therein.

His body was still heavy—his arms, legs, nothing moved properly—yet he wasn't restrained. So to speak.

She was standing over him, wearing rubies, looking down with satisfaction. She appeared exactly the same as she had that night in Vienna. Tall and slender, thick dark hair, lush red lips and cheekbones that cut like right angles. Still lovely, but now there was a flash of permanent anger in her eyes.

"Lerina," he managed to say, looking around the chamber. It appeared to be some sort of parlor. Not particularly well-kept; it was dusty and some of the furnishings were covered with sheets. The windows were draped and the light was dim. Her scent filled his nostrils, along with other ones: blood, old fabric, dust, worn leather, water. Salt water. Fish. They were near the Thames, possibly the wharf.

"Have you missed me, darling?" she asked, lunging closer to pat him on the cheek. The rubies swung and shifted toward him. "We have so much to catch up on."

He closed his eyes as a wave of pain swept him, then ebbed slightly as she pulled back. "Moldavi, I presume?"

Lerina smiled, showing her fangs. "You are a smart one, Dimitri."

"Whose body did I find? Wearing…your gown?" he asked, trying to control his unsteady breathing. Now he knew how the secret of his Asthenia had become known. Being his mistress, Lerina must somehow have figured it out; for he certainly had never told her. Or she and Moldavi together had done so.

She shrugged and the rubies danced. "I haven't any idea. Cezar took care of that. Some mortal, most likely. The whole point was to make you believe I'd died in the fire."

Dimitri pulled himself upright in the chair. Every movement felt as if he were weighted down with leaden pipes while slogging upriver through a heavy current. The pain from his Mark had melded with that from the rubies, stealing his breath and burning his skin. Yet, when he could lift himself above the physical discomfort, his mind worked like an oiled machine. And it was working now.

"Aren't you going to ask me what I want?" Lerina said, leaning close again.

Her scent filled his nose, along with a renewed rush of pain from the rubies. Dimitri didn't flinch or blink, holding her gaze steady with his own. "You'll tell me. Although I'm also…quite certain I already know."

"Is that so?" Lerina grinned and ran her tongue over the points of her incisors. "I've waited more than a century for this, Dimitri, darling."

"An entire century," he managed to say. "Did you have nothing better to do?"

Her hand whipped out and caught the side of his face, one of her ruby rings slicing his skin. The blow left his ears ringing, but he didn't move. Warm blood trickled down his cheek.

Her nostrils flared as she drew in the scent, her attention focused on his cut. Then she seemed to refocus, shaking her head a bit and stepping back with an odd smile.

He was certain he was in no imminent danger of anything more than Lerina's nonstop chatter and further displays of temper. Moldavi had to be behind this, and Dimitri presumed the man would want to have a moment of glory in front of his victim before otherwise dispatching him—or whatever his plan was.

"Since you won't ask me, I'll tell you all," Lerina announced.

"Just the basics, please. No need to…embroider the details." He was finding it more difficult to remain easy and keep his voice strong.

Annoyance flared in her eyes, a bright glow ringing blue irises. "Very well," she said, mercifully stepping back. Her hand fluttered as she posed for what promised to be a dramatic soliloquy.

"Cezar ensured that I was made Dracule," she said, as if it were some great pronouncement. When he gave no discernable reaction—he would have rolled his eyes if he'd had the energy—her mouth tightened and then she continued, "I wanted *you* to sire me, Dimitri. We would have lived very happily together for eternity. But you refused."

"Thank the Fates," he muttered.

Her face darkened again. "You always were a testy, cutting person," she said. "Attractive as you are in… other ways. It's no wonder Meg left you after she got what she wanted. But I would have stayed. All you needed was to make me immortal, and I would have loved you forever."

Dimitri ignored the stab of surprise and pain at her

easy mention of Meg. More than a hundred thirty years and the memory of his foolish love could still twist his belly. Because of the foolishness, not so much the love.

"Cezar heard it from Meg, and then he told me the entire story. About how you pulled her out of the fire and as you both were lying there, dying, you asked for help. You'd give anything for you both to survive. Such a romantic sentiment, Dimitri, darling."

He resisted the urge to close his eyes against the image.

But the memory, though vague, hadn't fully left him. What he'd believed to be his deepest desire had been answered that night, in the midst of pain-filled, swirling half dreams, by a visit from Lucifer. He'd hardly known what he'd agreed to. He hadn't realized until later that the miracle was not a miracle at all.

"Did you try to pull *me* out of the fire in Vienna, Dimitri?" she asked with exaggerated coyness. "Or did you not love me enough?"

He declined to answer, allowing a blaze in his eyes to give her his response. As if he would have stood by watching anyone perish. Especially since fire was merely uncomfortable to a Dracule, and not at all life-threatening.

"You probably would have…and then dropped me like a hot potato, no?" She was wandering in front of him, pacing back and forth. "Did you think I hadn't seen the signs? Why do you think I went with Cezar that night? I knew it would either make you realize how much you loved me—pah!—or I would have found a new protector. And we both know how that ended."

Again, he remained silent.

"So you saved Meg's life, helped her to become a Dracule...and then she left you. Once she realized the power of her immortality and the liaison with Lucifer, she *left* you."

Dimitri concentrated very hard and managed a negligent shrug. "And you wonder why...I wouldn't make the same mistake...twice."

"Your poor broken heart. Has she ruined you for every other woman? It would seem so." She smoothed her hands over the generous bodice of her gown as if to remind him of what she offered. He grimaced.

"Meg's dead, Dimitri. Did you know that?" Lerina leaned toward him again, bringing those shimmering, lethal rubies along with a scent of bitterness. "Cezar killed her himself."

The rumor he'd long believed was true, then. A rush of relief surged through him, overshadowing a surprising dearth of pain, and was followed by a flicker of sorrow. He supposed he had loved her, in a youthful, clumsy way, even if she hadn't loved him. Or at least, loved him enough. Now, she was with Luce in hell. Never to leave.

Thanks, in part, to him. He closed his eyes.

"Poor darling," Lerina said, her voice bringing him back.

Her eyes shifted, focusing on the wound on his face. Before he could brace himself, she bent forward, rubies and all, and, grabbing his shoulders, pressed her lips to the oozing cut. The necklaces swung against him and Dimitri jolted as they slammed into his chest and throat, burning through his shirt like a dozen white-hot pokers. He gasped in spite of himself, in spite of the hot, wet mouth covering his cheek.

She sucked and licked the blood from his skin, her tongue making sensual circles over his flesh as he tried to keep his breath even. Then Lerina slid her blood-soaked lips to his, covering his mouth with her own, breathing his own bloodscent into him.

He used every effort to wade through the pain and tear his face away from her, but Lerina's hands held him tightly, and the rubies were potent. Her fingers dug into the back of his skull, pulling his hair, her incisors sharp and sleek as she mauled his lips.

When she pulled back, her red lips glistened with blood and saliva and her eyes glowed like coals. He met her eyes defiantly, cold and filled with disgust, and when she saw his loathing, she drew back sharply. And then she slapped him again, on the other cheek this time.

"And you wonder why I wouldn't sire you," he managed to growl.

"That was your chance," she said, stepping back and taking the evil, glittering rubies with her. "I was willing to give you an opportunity to see your error. Foolish, Dimitri. You've learned nothing about women in the last hundred years."

She walked away, and he was able to draw a relatively easy breath for a moment. Then she turned, contemplating him. Her eyes burned with loathing…and something else. His skin prickled.

"Moldavi is in Paris?" he asked in an effort to distract her and to confirm his suspicions.

"Yes. He's waiting for word from me that you've become cooperative." She fondled one of the strands of rubies. There were perhaps a dozen of them, each the size of his thumbnail, set in a gold chain. She wore three necklaces like that, each of different length, and each finished off with a large pendant ruby. "I've learned so much from him. So much about how to get what I want."

"You're taking me to Paris," Dimitri said, sniffing and again smelling the river. "To Moldavi."

"Oh, no." She shook her head, smiling. "No, you aren't of interest to him. Not any longer anyway. Not since we agreed that you belonged to me, and that I would take care of you."

She was close to him again, leaning forward, roped in gemstones. That hungry look was back in her eyes and as she caught his gaze, Lerina lifted one of the ropes of rubies from her neck.

Dimitri's breathing shifted and he struggled to move…but they were too close, too many of them. Too powerful. He could do nothing as she wrapped the chain around one of his arms, binding it to the arm of the chair. Rolling pain undulated along his arm to his shoulder, battling with that of Lucifer's Mark.

The room was turning red, his vision colored with struggle. She came closer and he was dimly aware of her busy fingers tugging at the ties of his shirt, warm and quick. He marshaled all his waning strength and gave a sudden heave. He managed to jolt her, but Lerina was quick and she whipped off a second necklace and bound his other arm. Her knee wedged onto the chair next to his thigh as he struggled against this new onslaught of pain. Sweat, warm and thick, trickled from his temple to mingle with the blood on his cheeks.

"You see, Moldavi is more interested in getting his

sister back. And destroying Chas Woodmore for taking her," Lerina continued. Her voice was almost singsong, but her eyes blazed hot and furious. She was very close now, nearly sitting on his lap. "Once you were out of the way, and otherwise occupied, he could obtain the prize he truly wanted."

Dimitri was vaguely aware of his shirt opening, the cooler air brushing his hot skin. Her hands, once familiar, now spread over his shoulders like spidery fingers, pulling the shirt wide. She grasped the opening and yanked. The sound of the linen tearing was like thunder in his waterlogged ears.

"Prize?" he managed to gasp, despite the fact that he had a sudden horrible feeling he knew what. No, *who*. *No.*

Lerina smiled. Her fangs were fully extended. Her breath smelled like his blood. Her fingers curled up into the hair that clung to his damp neck, lifting it so she could blow on his hot skin.

"I've dreamed of this moment," she said. Her voice penetrated the black and red clouds filling his vision and clogging his nostrils. "Since the first time you fed on me."

"Prize?" he demanded with his last bit of breath.

"The girls, of course," she whispered near his ear. "The sisters. The only way to get to Chas."

Maia.

He gathered all of his strength and tugged, groaning deep in his throat with the effort. But the paralysis was complete.

She slammed her fangs into his shoulder. He gasped, his body shuddering even as it remained horribly immobile. The release of the pressure in his veins, the surge of blood flowing into her warm mouth had him trembling. His fingers couldn't grasp the arm of the chair and he could no longer keep his eyes open.

The little tugs of pleasure as she sucked were lost in the vortex of pain. He didn't have even the energy to pull at his bindings, to kick or twist away. *Maia.*

And so he closed his eyes and screamed inside his mind: *Help me. Wayren, damn it, I'm ready.*

IN WHICH OUR HEROINE
PROVES HERSELF WORTHY
OF THE APPELLATION

Maia stared at the ruby-studded hairpin all the way
back to Blackmont Hall, trying to recall where she'd
seen it.

The design was distinctive: elegant curlicues of metal
twining along the pin, decorated with five small rubies. Of course, identifying the owner didn't necessarily
mean she, or—one couldn't eliminate any possibilities
at this time—he, was involved in Corvindale's disappearance. But the fact that it was rubies, combined with
Maia's very acute sense that something *wrong* had happened in the back room at that shop, certainly led to the
logical conclusion that if she found the owner, she'd find
information about Corvindale.

The constable had listened to her concerns, and
seemed willing to do something since a peer of the
realm was missing. But at the same time, he'd looked
at her sidewise as if to question why she was involved.
And even, why an earl must need to answer to the likes
of her in regards to his actions.

And on top of all of this, Maia realized she had no way to contact Chas to let him know what had happened. But Angelica would tell Dewhurst, and perhaps the other vampire, Mr. Cale, could be notified, and then they would start the search.

Maia shook her head. By that time, impossible as it seemed, Corvindale could be dead.

The thought was like a cold hand seizing her heart and she swallowed, looking at the hairpin with even more determination. She couldn't do much herself but try to find the owner. That was one thing Dewhurst and Mr. Cale couldn't assist with. But it was something that Maia could put her attention to. It obviously belonged to a woman, and there were two ways to go about identifying her.

Once back at Blackmont Hall, Maia sent Tren to notify Crewston and Mrs. Hunburgh about the apparent disappearance of the earl. Someone had to take charge, and Maia was so used to doing it that she didn't consider letting anyone else do so—including Aunt Iliana.

Then she sent for Angelica and Mirabella, only to find out that Dewhurst had taken them for a drive in the park. So she set Tren after them to bring them back.

Next, she called for the ladies' maid she and Angelica shared. Showing Betty the hairpin, she told her nothing other than that she wanted to return it to its owner, and that she was certain she'd met her at one of the recent events. Knowing how tightly knit the belowstairs community was, how servants gossiped from one house in the *ton* to another, and that of all people, the ladies' maidservants would be the ones to know of the person who wore such a hairpin, Maia felt this avenue was her best chance to identify the woman. Thus, she sent Betty off to the market and to do some shopping, where she was most likely to encounter other loose-tongued servants.

After that, she sent for Aunt Iliana and while she waited, began to peruse through the stack of calling cards and invitations that had arrived for her and Angelica, as well as for Corvindale himself. Normally he ignored such things, leaving it to his man of business to respond if necessary, or to Crewston to handle callers.

She thought that by reviewing these items, her memory might be jolted as to where and when she'd seen the woman with the hairpin. Maia knew it wasn't someone she'd known from the *ton*. It was either a newcomer—someone who'd married into the peerage from another country or area—or someone who hadn't been out in Society for some years, or some distant relative. Or even, she thought suddenly, someone of the demimonde. Those women who were neither fully accepted into Society, but who nevertheless interacted with the men as their mistresses. Perhaps she'd seen such a lady wearing this sort of decoration while shopping or at the theater.

"Maia, whatever is wrong?" Aunt Iliana appeared in the doorway of the parlor. A handsome woman of perhaps forty or forty-five, she was built nearly as tall and sturdily as a man, although she was by no means masculine in appearance. Her skin was nearly as dark as the earl's, and her eyes the color of strong tea.

Maia was more than a bit shocked to see her dressed in loose trousers and a manlike shirt, along with soft slippers. The older woman's dark hair was pulled straight back into a braid and her cheeks were damp and flushed. She looked as if she'd just been doing something with great exertion.

"I apologize for my appearance," Iliana said ruefully. "But Hunburgh said it was urgent, that it had to do with D—the earl."

"He's disappeared," Maia said, and explained. She ended by showing her the hairpin.

Iliana took one look and said a very unladylike thing under her breath. "Rubies. Someone knows about his Asthenia." Then she looked at Maia as if she'd been caught with her hand in the biscuit box.

"What is it about rubies?" Maia asked. "Do they affect all the Dracule that way?"

Iliana seemed to measure her for a moment. Then, obviously finding her not wanting, said, "It's called an Asthenia. Each Dracule has his own specific weakness. The effects are like paralysis, and when whatever it is is touched directly to them, it can cause great, excruciating pain. Your instinct is correct. Someone used the gems to weaken him enough to take him away. Dimitri would never have been caught otherwise."

Maia had known that without being told. Although she'd never had cause to see him in jeopardy or otherwise in a physical altercation, his presence suggested a man very much in control at all times. A flash of memory, of that bare, chiseled chest, broad shoulders and the long, sleek curve of his muscular arms had her insides fluttering again. No, indeed. He would not have been caught unless taken unawares.

She explained to Iliana the steps she'd taken to identify the hairpin's owner, and the other woman nodded in satisfaction. "Very good. When Angelica and Voss arrive, we can send word to Giordan and Chas."

Maia wondered about this woman, and certainly not for the first time. She spoke of the vampires and their world with such familiarity. "Who are you?" Maia asked. "You aren't really Corvindale's aunt, are you?"

Iliana laughed. "No, of course not. That would make me more than a hundred twenty years old, and a crone— or a Dracule—at that. No, indeed. I'm merely one who understands the threats of his world, and an old friend of Dimitri's. I helped to raise Mirabella after he found her. She needed protection from the earl's enemies, and I needed a place to live away from—well, that's another story for a time when we have time. Suffice to say," she said, "I've learned to protect myself to some extent from the beastly ones. Even your brother admitted that I'm quite capable."

Maia looked at her. "Could you teach me something?"

The older woman opened her mouth, likely to decline, but Maia pushed on. "If I'm to live in this world where my sister is to wed a former vampire, my brother hunts them and my so-named guardian *is* one, I think it only proper that I know something about protecting myself. Especially since there are vampires who are coming after us. My father taught me how to shoot a pistol when I was twelve," she added when Iliana began to shake her head.

"Your brother would never allow it."

"He doesn't have to know," Maia said firmly. "No one has to know."

Iliana frowned and then threw up her hands. "Very well. But don't tell the earl."

Maia awoke with a start, sitting bolt upright.

Her heart was pounding and her body slick with perspiration.

That had not been a pleasant dream. The darkness still lingered, wrapping the frightening images through her mind. Not of a warm, red world with sensual lips and tongue, the easy and welcome slide of fangs, but one of tearing flesh and screaming pain. Violence and violation.

She couldn't catch her breath, and Maia threw back the covers of her bed, trying to jolt the last vestiges away with sharp movement. It didn't work instantly, but slowly the ugly feelings eased.

Moonlight shimmered over her empty bed and the table next to it. Maia's attention fell on the two new additions to her bedside table: the ruby hairpin and a slender wooden stake.

True to her word, Iliana had taken Maia to an empty chamber in the servants' wing of Blackmont Hall. The room had no furnishings to speak of, and was windowless. There, she'd shown Maia how to hold a stake the proper way and where to aim when stabbing at a vampire.

"In the heart," she said, "and they die instantly."

A little shudder ran through Maia when she recalled how Chas had launched himself across the room at White's and thrust his stake into Dewhurst's torso. If he hadn't been wearing armor, he would have been dead.

Maia and Iliana had practiced awhile, with Maia

surprised by the other woman's speed and agility, and learned that she did quite a bit of training for this skill. Maia realized that her own days spent with merely a bit of walking, some riding and much sitting, had left her much less fluent in body movement. And although she was uncomfortably warm and damp after her session with Iliana, Maia also realized she felt energized. And now, however, her own body was a little sore.

She decided then that she would practice every day, with Iliana if possible. But now, Maia was unsettled and felt the need to get out of her bedchamber.

She left the stake on her table and padded down the hall to the stairs. Perhaps a book. Or a cup of milk or even a slice of cheese and an apple might help to distract her mind.

As she reached the bottom of the stairs, she heard voices. Her heart leaped and she hurried down and along the hall, her nightgown flowing around her ankles. A light poured from beneath the door of Corvindale's study, so, without much thought in regards to her attire and the mortification of the last time she'd seen him, Maia flung the door open.

"Oh," she said, freezing in the entrance. Not Corvindale.

It was Dewhurst…and Angelica. They were standing in the middle of the chamber, in an embrace whose image immediately replaced the last bit of horror from Maia's dream.

"Maia," said Angelica, pulling away from what looked like a very passionate kiss…among other things. Her lips were swollen and her cheeks a lovely dusky rose. Dewhurst didn't release her, and she didn't seem to be interested in putting space between them, either. "Is everything all right?"

Maia swallowed, trying to ignore the heat that had rushed to her face and surely made it bright red. "I heard voices and thought perhaps the earl had returned, or been found."

Dewhurst shook his head, and Maia couldn't tear her eyes from the way his elegant hand curled comfortably around her sister's neck, a finger sliding up into the loose braid at her nape. It was such a simple gesture, yet very intimate. So casual, bespeaking of a deep and comfortable connection.

A rush of envy shuttled through her and she was instantly ashamed. Alexander was a good man and he cared for her. He might not make her insides billow and burn when he kissed her, but he was financially comfortable and unfailingly polite and rather boring. She stopped any further thoughts right there.

"I've spoken with Cale, and have sent word to Chas—" Dewhurst was saying.

"How do you do that? Do you know where he is?"

He looked uncomfortable. "There are ways we do it with blood pigeons and private messengers and other techniques. But that's beside the point. I just came here to...er..." He looked at Angelica and the heat that passed between them with a mere glance was enough to make Maia's knees weak.

"He came to report that there isn't any news about Corvindale," Angelica said. At last she stepped away from her fiancé, and for the first time, Maia noticed that her sister was garbed in no more than a night rail, as well. "And to let me know that he was safe."

"We're doing everything we can to find him. When Woodmore returns, I'm certain he'll have other ideas about where to look and how to track him. One would expect Moldavi to be involved somehow, and since Dim—Corvindale isn't one to…uh…spend time around women, whoever was there and dropped the hairpin is likely in Moldavi's employ. And now that I can move about in the day, it gives me more freedom."

Angelica looked at him. "But you are no longer Dracule. Which makes you more vulnerable."

Dewhurst waved this off in the way men did when a woman raised an issue they preferred to ignore. "But I'm smart and fast and I no longer have an Asthenia."

"Your Asthenia now is a bullet," Angelica reminded him flatly. "As well as a sword, a stake and many other implements. Not to mention fire, and…" Her voice trailed off. "Please take care." These last words were little more than a heartfelt sigh, leaving Maia to feel like more of an intruder than ever.

"And you, as well," he said, looking at both of them. "That's the other reason I've come. Cale and I have arranged for more guards to keep watch over you now that Corvindale is missing. Both day and night. I suspect Moldavi has had him removed so he can more easily get to one of you. So don't go anywhere without an escort—particularly at night."

"But vampires cannot move about during the day," Angelica argued. "We're safe enough shopping and visiting the park."

"Corvindale was taken during the day," Dewhurst reminded her flatly. "Do as I say, Ange."

"I suppose I should return to my bed," Maia said,

turning toward the door. Why she felt so bereft was one thing, but the other thought that followed her as she climbed the stairs was the realization that she, the very proper Miss Woodmore, had just left her sister and a man alone in the study with hardly a second thought. At night.

What had changed her?

Maia slept fitfully for the rest of the night, and in the morning the first thing she did was send a message to Alexander that the wedding would need to be postponed until her guardian returned.

And then she sat down at the breakfast table. Alone.

Maia couldn't remember ever feeling so...alone. Angelica was clearly deeply in love with her viscount and didn't have time for sisterly talks—although it appeared that they might have much to talk about, if the position of Dewhurst's hands on her last night was any indication.

Even the thought of where they'd been made Maia blush.

She sat down with another batch of invitations and calling cards, determined to remind herself where she'd seen the hairpin. Only partway through her first piece of toast and cup of tea, the dining room door opened to reveal Betty.

"I've got some news for you, miss," she said. Betty was a plump, cheery woman old enough to be Maia's mother—or at least a much older sister. Her eyes were glinting with pleasure as she approached. "Tracy Mayes, who works for the Gallingways—easy way to remember with a bit of rhyme—says that Rosie over to the

Yarmouths' knows she's seen that same type of hairpin before. It didn't have no rubies, but sapphires, though."

Maia felt a spark of excitement. "It was the same, just different gems? It must be made by the same jeweler. Who had the hairpin?"

"That's what I thought, too, miss. I could send over to one of the servants at her house. It was a Mrs. Rina Throckmullins, and Rosie said as she met her and her maid at the milliner's last week. She remembered it because it was such a rainy day, and they shared an umbrella when they left the shop, so she had a good look at the pins in her hair, huddled as they were under it. Mrs. Throckmullins is a…well, miss, I'm not one to speak out of line. But she's a single woman who ain't looking for a husband, if you know what I mean."

Which meant she was a woman who interacted with men outside of wedlock. Likely of the demimonde, or perhaps even a widow who didn't move about in the *ton*. Which would have made it fairly impossible for Maia to have met her at a Society function. So she must have caught a glimpse of it somewhere else, as she'd previously surmised.

Giving a mental shrug, Maia finished her toast, contemplating this new information. Perhaps Mrs. Throckmullins wasn't the owner of the ruby hairpin, but at least knew the designer. It was the best lead she had so far, and Maia decided it was worth investigating. She'd have to wait until the afternoon when social calls were made.

Thus, later in the day, after a brief practice session in the special, empty room (this time without Iliana) and a bit of lunch, Maia called for Tren and the carriage. Angelica was otherwise engaged with a dress fitting for her wedding, and Mirabella wanted to look for some new lace and so they declined to go with her.

Mindful of Dewhurst's warning not to go anywhere by herself, she advised Crewston, who arranged for two other footmen to accompany them. Her plan was to call on Mrs. Throckmullins under the guise of returning the hairpin, which would allow her to find out whether it belonged to the woman or whether she merely had one similar. If the latter were true, then she could find out where it had come from and follow on that lead.

And she'd be home in time to get ready for tonight's dinner party at the Werthingtons'.

Maia opened her eyes.

Where am I?

Confusion and a dark, unfamiliar room made her mind groggy. She tried to sit up and realized her limbs wouldn't move. An ominous clink indicated the reason why.

What in the world?

Panic trammeled through her and she drew in a deep breath, closing her eyes, ordering herself into calmness. What had happened?

She flipped back in her mind…she remembered riding in the carriage to Mrs. Throckmullins's home, a room she'd let in a boardinghouse in a respectable area of the city, not far from Bond.

Mrs. Throckmullins was pleased to meet her in the parlor of the house, and Maia introduced herself and explained the purpose of her visit. She remembered giving her the hairpin, and Mrs. Throckmullins pressing her to stay for tea so they could talk about the jewelry.

The next thing she knew, the room was wavering and spinning…

And now she was here.

Wherever "here" was.

Maia tried again to move and realized that her wrists were bound to some object and that she was lying on a bed or sofa. It was difficult to tell, for the room was dim. Whatever was beneath her was soft, however, and the object to which she was tied moved beneath her when she pulled on it. Curtains covered the windows, and a faint gray outline told her that it was late in the evening, but not yet dark. So she'd been here for several hours.

The panic that could have spiraled out of control settled again. If she'd been missing for that long, someone would be looking for her. Angelica and Dewhurst and perhaps even her wayward brother.

Tren and the other footmen would have returned to Blackmont Hall when she didn't come out of Mrs. Throckmullins's boardinghouse…if they hadn't besieged it in the first place, looking for her. And if not, they knew where to search for her.

But Maia became aware of the pungent scent of fish filtering through the air; something she hadn't noticed in the parlor. So either Mrs. Throckmullins—who was clearly the villain or at least in cahoots with the villain, as Mrs. Radcliffe would describe it—had moved her to a new location, or someone else had.

Either way, that would make it even more difficult for the others to find her.

But on the bright side, perhaps Corvindale was here, as well.

Maia lay there, waiting for her vision to become used

to the dim light, listening to every sound around her that might give her more information. She'd read enough Gothic novels to know what a heroine who was in a dangerous situation *shouldn't* do, and she was determined to be intelligent about her predicament.

After listening for quite some time—she heard a clock tolling the quarter hour in the distance, and then a second toll—Maia concluded that she was either alone in the house, or whoever was there was either sleeping or very quiet. She also took stock of the room she was in, half pulling herself up on her side with her elbows. Sheets covered chairs and tables, making the chamber appear ghostly.

Her wrists were bound with a chain of large links that were looped around the leg of the chaise on which she reclined. Her bonds were loose and shifted up and down her arm, and Maia tried for some time to slip them over her hands. But her thumbs were in the way, and try as she might, she couldn't curl them flat enough into her palm to slide free.

Her next effort was to carefully climb off the chaise, taking care to make as little noise as possible in case she was wrong and the building wasn't deserted, to see if there was a way to unhook the chain.

Excitement bolted through her when she saw that it might be possible. The way the chains were looped and if she could lift the chaise and pull them free…

It took countless efforts, most of them aborted when the chains slid the wrong way as she struggled to lift the chaise with bound wrists and a short length with which to work…but finally, she worked it loose and at last pulled away from the chaise.

Her wrists were still bound, but she was free.

Moments later, she had figured out how to unravel herself and left the chains in a heap on the floor. Maia's first instinct was to start out of the chamber, but she forced herself to wait and listen for another quarter of an hour.

Her patience was rewarded when the house remained quiet and the gray outline around the windows had disappeared into black. The last thing she did before leaving the chamber was to take up the poker from the fireplace, and also to search for something that could be used as a wooden stake. The only possible article was an umbrella in a corner stand, and she used her foot to break its handle.

Thus armed, she tiptoed to the door and eased it open.

Through the glaze of pain, Dimitri saw the door in front of him ease open.

He closed his eyes, his head tilting back against the chair. *Again? So bloody soon?*

She'd visited him more than three times in however many hours and days he'd been here. His only measurement had been the light filtering through the curtains, and even that was inaccurate as he went in and out of consciousness. Lerina had opened one of the sets of drapes so that a slice of sun cut over the headrest of his chair close enough to sizzle his hair. And as a parting gift, she'd taken off her last ruby necklace and hung it around his neck so that it settled against his bare torso.

The pain…

It had finally dulled to something merely excruciating.

How long had he been like this?

He dared not move during the day for fear the sun
would fry his skin, keeping his head at an impossible angle, hardly able to breathe in the wake of pain
and paralysis. All the while, he was left with only his
thoughts, his fears. Dark and ugly, swirling over and
over in his mind.

It was because of that mad vortex of fear and anger
that he didn't just allow the sun to burn him. He remained intact, fueled by the desperate knowledge that
he must, somehow, escape. He must get to Maia before
Moldavi did.

A figure that was not Lerina had moved through the
doorway and into the chamber. Dimitri's labored breath
caught. This was new. This was—

Maia.

Was he dreaming it? Hallucinating now, his brain
turned to mush? He was too weak to even discern her
scent.

But no, the glance of moonlight over that amazing
bronze-gold hair and elegant nose confirmed his worst
fears.

*No, no, no! What are you doing here, foolish blasted
woman?*

He struggled violently, but nothing moved but for
the intent, deep inside.

She didn't see him at first; the room was dim and he
was too weak to make a sound. But then she did, for
she cried out and rushed to his side, dropping whatever
she'd had in her hands.

"My God," she whispered, suddenly there in front of him, close enough that he could smell her at last.

Such a clean, welcoming perfume after hours of his own blood and sweat mingled with the desperate essence of Lerina. His eyes hooded as he drank in the pure, fresh pleasure.

"What has she— Oh, *God.*" Her hands were everywhere, peeling away the blood-soaked shirt that hung from his shoulders, tugging at the rubies that bound him to the chair. When she lifted the necklace that had settled against him he was at last able to draw in a complete breath.

Even once he was loosened from the ruby manacles, Dimitri found he couldn't move. He sagged in the chair, at once infuriated by his weakness and focusing on gathering up strength again. Trying to lift even a finger was impossible.

She'd taken much blood from him. Much. Too much, and the hours encapsulated in his Asthenia had drained him to little more than a loose pile of skin and bones.

Dimitri tried to speak, and managed only to say, "A…way."

He was trying to tell her to take the rubies that she'd tossed to the floor away, far away, but Maia misunderstood. "I'm not going anywhere, you idiot man. Look at you." There were tears in her voice, and fear, as well. "You need water. Something."

Water was not what he needed.

No indeed.

Dimitri closed his eyes. Now that the incessant pain had ebbed a bit, his body was reawakening in a different way. Warmth stirred deep inside him, flowering into need. Soon, once he recovered his strength, it would be uncontrollable. *No. Not now.*

Maia—there was no use forcing himself to think of her as Miss Woodmore any longer; that shield was gone—had moved into the shadows and he dimly heard a dull clink. The next thing he knew, she was back, holding a pitcher.

It was a wonder there was any water left in it, after Lerina had dumped it on his head or splashed it in his face numerous times in an effort to awaken him. Perhaps she'd replenished it. Regardless, the cool water had been the highlight of his experience here, and now Maia applied it in a much gentler fashion that made his skin heat and leap.

She'd torn off a piece of sheet that covered a chair and used the wet cloth to mop up the grime and blood from his face. Dimitri closed his eyes, allowing the cool rivulets to trickle down his jaw and neck, concentrating on gathering what little energy he still possessed.

The room wavered and tilted, still tinged a dull red, due to his great loss of blood as well as the proximity of the rubies. He attempted to lift his head, but his best effort ended with him merely rolling from one side to the other.

How the hell am I going to get her out of here?

"My God," Maia said again when she got to the top of his shoulder, where Lerina had bit. And then her breathing changed into another unsteady rhythm when she saw the other shoulder, the bite at its corner, and then down to his left biceps. Also wounded and oozing blood from Lerina's pleasure.

He tried to snatch the rag from her hands, to clean

himself up, but Maia was too quick and strong and she batted his hands away as if they were gnats. And so he was reluctantly complicit, so aware of every brush from her fingers, every waft of flower and spice from her sagging hair…the warmth of her body as she bent toward him, the dark shadow down between her breasts. The sensual arch of her neck.

"Corvindale," she said suddenly, sharply, and he opened his eyes, realizing he'd started to tumble back into the depths of darkness…but this time, the depths had been warm heat, filled with her scent and silky skin. "What do you need? What can I do?" she asked, tugging uselessly at him, obviously trying to get him up out of the chair.

He looked at her, his veins surging with hope and heat, his fangs swelling inside his gums. His breathing was ragged and he could hardly focus the words. "Ru… bies…away," he managed to say.

She stumbled back, chagrin on her face. "Oh," she said, anger in her voice. "I'm sorry. I didn't realize…" Her voice faded and he heard the soft sounds of the gems being gathered up. She hesitated, looking around the room as if uncertain what to do with them, but before he could gather up the strength to tell her, she rushed toward the door and went through it.

When she came back, her hands were empty and by then, Dimitri was actually breathing. His fingers had moved and the pain had centered back on his Mark, where he was used to it.

"Is that better?" she asked, coming closer to him. Too close.

His nose twitched as he inhaled her and a shudder

rumbled through him. He wasn't strong enough to push himself out of the chair, to stand…he needed blood. He needed sustenance.

Dimitri managed to nod and tried to tell her to stay back, but she kept moving closer.

"Let me look at you," she said, right in front of him. She was examining the cuts on his cheeks. Her skirt brushed against the arm of the chair, where his ineffectual hand rested. "And I see that you can't even stand."

He tried to growl a warning and an argument, nothing but a dull groan escaped. She touched his face where the ruby had sliced his cheek. Dimitri closed his eyes, breathing deeply. He couldn't remember the last time someone had touched him with such gentleness.

Never, never had a woman affected him so.

A little shudder raced through his limbs, turning into something hot and powerful and needy. When he opened his eyes, she was very close. Her cheek, smooth and white, a breath away. That intriguing scent filled his space and a lock of hair hung just in front of his gaze.

"Maia," he whispered, turning his face away. "Get… away."

(14)

IN WHICH INTRODUCTIONS
PROVE UNNECESSARY

Maia heard the note in his voice when he said her name, and the tone made her insides plummet. It was a horrible combination of loathing and desperation. His eyes were hooded and shadowed, and she could see little but the dark shapes of them and the wounds on his face.

"Are you mad?" she said, trying to keep her own voice steady. "I'm not going to leave you here."

She could hardly fathom that a man who was as large and dark and powerful as the earl had become little more than a rag doll, sagging in the chair. At the same time, she wanted to touch him again, but without the protection of the damp cloth. She knew he was injured, practically dead as much as a vampire could die, but she couldn't stop looking at him. The curtains on one window were open enough that light from outside—moon, stars, streetlamps—gave the chamber layers of gray color, and she could see the details of the man in front of her.

The wide breadth of his shoulders, marred as they

were by small dark circles from what were clearly vampire bites, had felt so solid and warm beneath her hands. She'd seen his darkly haired chest from the door of his chamber, but now she'd touched the square curve of his shoulders and the sleek bulge of biceps, the skin smooth and firm. He had a strong, corded neck, the ragged edges of his dark hair plastered there and to his temples and cheeks.

"Get away...from me," he said again, this time more fiercely. His muscular hand moved as if to shove her away, but it flopped loosely onto his lap, barely brushing her arm. "Get Cale."

"Don't be a fool. I'm not leaving you," she said. "I went through a lot of trouble to find you and I'm not going without you. Aside of that, it could take me hours or days to find Mr. Cale. And I don't know when *she'll* be back."

He closed his eyes again. "Just...go. Please. Maia."

This was the second time he'd called her by her name, and the sound of it, so low and rough, made her knees weak. She couldn't leave him. She didn't know where she was or how long it would take to get a hack—and it was nighttime, as well. She didn't know when Mrs. Throckmullins was going to return—or whoever she was working with—and she certainly couldn't manage to drag the earl from the room. He'd crush her if he put even half his weight on her.

Maia's heart started pounding hard as she realized what she had to do. She licked her lips, trying to subdue a flash of nerves and titillation. It wasn't just the rubies. He had four or perhaps five wounds, bites, plus the cuts on his face. He'd lost blood. Lots of it.

"You need to…drink. You need blood," she said.

He jolted in the chair and growled. "No."

But she saw the sudden catch of his breath, then the rough rise and fall of his chest. The pulse pounded in his throat and his eyes fastened on her, dark in emotion, fiery in hue.

Her mouth dried and her stomach fluttered as she remembered her dreams. Even the room tipped a little at the flash of temptation that rushed through her.

"Corvindale, you must." She settled herself on the arm of his chair.

He'd turned away again and his jaw, dark with shadow, shifted. *"Go."*

She drew in a deep breath and thrust her arm in front of his face. "Please."

"I…can't." He was so close to her, her arm brushing against his bare one, his male scent and the warmth radiating from his skin filling her being.

"My lord, please," she begged, somehow generating a ripple of angst from him. "I can't get you away from here if you're so weak. And I'm absolutely not leaving without you. If she comes back…" She let the threat hang there, for, if she knew one thing about the earl, it was that he took his responsibilities gravely.

Surely he wouldn't want his ward to be here if Mrs. Throckmullins came back.

He remained mute and stoic, and Maia realized she was going to have to force the stubborn fool into it. She remembered the night in the carriage when he'd scratched her with his fang; the arrested look on his face when he'd noticed the blood.

She was just about to get up to search for something

to cut herself with—for she simply couldn't stomach using her own fingernails—when he made a low sound. Deep, like a struggle, rumbling from his throat.

Maia turned toward him just as he moved, curling his fingers around her arm. She looked down and met his eyes.

"Get...rubies," he said. "Quickly."

"What? Have you gone mad? Isn't that how you got—"

"Get...rubies," he said between tight jaws. "Argue. Always."

"Corvindale..." But she saw the fury in his eyes and she decided that he was probably right—this wasn't the time to argue. She'd known the man was mad since the night he bundled her up in the curtains and tossed her on the patio.

But he'd saved her then, hadn't he?

She rushed out of the room to get one of the necklaces from where she'd tossed them in a pile far down the corridor. When she returned to the chamber, she saw that he'd shifted in the chair and was sitting more upright than he'd been.

His eyes fell on the dangling chain of red gems, then lifted to hers as she approached slowly. Whatever expression might have been there was unfathomable in the dim light.

"What do you want me to do with them?" she asked, already noticing the change in his breathing and the stiffening in his limbs. From the mere presence of the jewels. She found it fascinating and frightening at the same time.

He glanced to the side, made a very faint gesture to the table next to his chair. "There."

Maia thought she was beginning to understand. He wanted them nearby so that…he'd remain weak? Her heart lunged into her throat and suddenly the prickle of anticipation turned into prickles in her belly. What was he afraid he'd *do?*

She laid the necklace on the far edge of the small piecrust table and then faced him, looking down at his dark hair and stony face. His eyes were closed again, brows furrowed, his hands clenched into fists down at his sides. The rise and fall of his chest matched her own. The bright white of his tattered shirt shone next to his dark skin and trousers.

"Corvindale," she said, and then, holding her breath, sat down on the arm of his chair again.

"Use them," he said, and she knew he meant the rubies. "If you…need."

Heart in her throat, she swallowed hard and offered him her wrist.

At first, she thought he would refuse again, but then he grasped her with surprisingly strong fingers. A bolt of fear shot through her and then, as he lifted her wrist to his mouth, she saw his fangs clearly for the first time.

She closed her eyes as she felt his breath on her flesh, and then, to her shock and surprise…not the bite of pain, but the brush of lips. Soft, moist, followed by the gentle touch of his tongue.

Maia shuddered as warmth blossomed through her, her skin prickling at the sensation. Her heartbeat seemed to have changed, and it thrummed in her ears, reverberating through her entire being. She hardly realized what she was doing as her free hand moved around to the back of the chair, propping herself up just next to his hair. He slid his lips gently along the inside of her wrist and then paused, suddenly looking up at her.

His eyes were clearly illuminated and the expression there was so dark and hungry, yet filled with loathing, that she jolted.

"I don't…want to…do this," he breathed over her damp skin, and then suddenly he went rigid and the points of his teeth were there.

The slide of his fangs into the tender part of her wrist brought a surge of pleasure and pain. He made a low keening sound like a wild animal being freed—or tortured—and Maia felt the burst of blood as it flooded from her veins. He vibrated against her as if something suddenly released from deep inside him.

His mouth was warm, covering her, and his fingers tight on her wrist as if to keep it in place. The heat flowed out of her, leaving her light-headed and aware of every movement of his mouth and tongue as he sucked, licked, sucked…drawing from her in a base, undulating rhythm.

She looked down, watching in fascination as his dark head bent over her white arm. She smelled the blood, heard the soft whistling as he fed, the quiet gulps as he drank. And as life drained from her, it was replaced by rolling heat, building and surging as if her veins sang.

Maia's fingers filtered into his dark hair, finding it warm and soft, damp from the water, and she sagged against him. Her breasts felt tight and sensitive and she realized she was breathing in little gasps with her lips parted. There was something more…she needed something more.

He shifted on the chair, suddenly releasing his fangs from her arm and then slipping his warm tongue over the wounds in sensual little circles. She sighed and arched, a painful little tingle of pleasure starting deep inside her belly and moving down.

His hand slid up behind her neck and grasped her skull as he pulled her down onto his lap. She closed her eyes, her hands planted on the solid planes of his bare shoulders and then she jolted when he bit into the soft part of her shoulder.

Maia cried out in surprise and pain, then arched toward him as hot blood surged from that delicate skin into his mouth. His tongue slid, flat and sleek, over her shoulder, then retreated as he drew rhythmically from her. Strong hands held her immobile, close, and she felt his body tight and hard against hers, lurching a little with the effort.

His big hands cupped her, his mouth took, the heat from his body burned into her hands and through her clothing.

Maia's world spiraled into a red blaze that was nothing like her dreams, but just as sensual and compelling. Blood coursed through her veins and she felt it swelling and surging, pouring forth. She couldn't catch her breath. Everything became *him*.

She wanted *him*.

Then all at once, he froze. Some guttural curse erupted from his throat as he whipped his face from her shoulder, his fingers tight as he shoved her back, his movements violent and sharp, his breathing loud and labored in the room.

"You blasted fool," he snapped, pushing her from his lap as if she were an unwanted cat. His eyes blazed like coals and his lips were full and slick, the very tip of a fang caught against one.

Maia, startled from the lull, stumbled as she tried to catch her balance. A hand whipped out and grabbed her arm just in time, but with the force of it, she knocked into the table and tipped it over. Her knees buckled and she sagged in his grip, weak and confused, her eyes rolling back into her head.

"Maia," he said, urgent now, furious. "Look at me, blast it."

She opened her eyes with great effort and tried to focus on the dark figure looming over her.

"Damned bones of Satan, I told you to use the damned rubies." He was fairly shouting, yet his hands were gentle as he eased her into the chair he had just vacated. "Why didn't you use the rubies?"

She noted vaguely that he seemed to have fully recovered, although when he bumped gracelessly against her chair and nearly fell on top of her, she was forced to revise that conclusion.

Other than that, she could hardly capture her whirl-wind of thoughts and emotions. The fluttering heat still swirled in her belly and she felt the slow ooze of blood from her shoulder. Warm. The wound on her wrist seemed to have stopped; all that was left were four dainty red marks.

She forced herself to focus now, and she let her head tilt against the back of the chair, looking up at him. He leaned over her, bracing himself with a hand on each side, his muscular arms bracketing her in.

"Maia," he said, a bit more gently now—which was to say, at a lower volume, though no less tense—and there was an odd note in his tone. "You…" His voice trailed off and their eyes locked.

Everything stopped. Maia could hardly draw a breath. Inside, everything exploded into hot fluttering. "Are you going to kiss me now?" she whispered.

His lips formed a silent "Can't. No."

But then he did.

She met his mouth as it crashed down on hers, hungry and warm with the residual of her own rich blood. His lips were hard and demanding, forcing her mouth open as he thrust his tongue deep. A powerful thigh wedged into the seat next to her and Maia found that she couldn't move; she was pinned down into the chair by his hands and mouth, his dark, powerful body rising over her.

Grasping at the tails of his shirt, she pulled, tugging him closer, her hands sliding over the planes of his chest. His muscles shifted and trembled beneath her palms, the hair soft and prickly, skin hot and smooth.

At last, at last… was all she could think.

He had her face cupped in his big hands, fingers curling behind, thumbs pressing into her jaw as he drank from her mouth now, then pulled away with a soft, deep groan to cover the wound on her shoulder again.

This time, he didn't penetrate, but instead, slicked his tongue over the curve of her shoulder, down into the little soft hollow of skin. Maia shivered and tried to shrug him away, for the sensation was intense, but he delved deeper, his tongue dipping and sliding, sipping from the last bit of her blood, his lashes tickling her neck. She felt her pulse coursing against his mouth, pounding against his lips, her heartbeat matching his as her hands found it through his chest.

"Please," she whispered, not quite certain what she needed, rolling her head against the back of the chair as she tried to find it, shifting her hips. She was hot and damp everywhere, tight and tingling and she wanted his hands and mouth in places they had no business going.

All at once, he went still and then pulled away. Before she could even gasp in surprise or disappointment, he clapped a hand over her mouth. His chest moved rapidly as he cocked his head and sniffed the air.

"Satan's bones," he muttered and vaulted off the chair, half stumbling yet silent. He yanked her up with him, his hand still over her mouth, his eyes suddenly blazing darkly into hers. "Don't make a sound. Don't say a word. Don't argue," he hissed into her face.

Maia managed a brief nod of acknowledgment, her brain still foggy from the sudden change of sensual assault to this frightening intensity.

And then she heard them: voices. The sounds of people below.

Corvindale said something vile under his breath, looking around the room. The rubies had fallen to the floor when she knocked over the table, still contributing to his sluggish movements. Their proximity was likely the only reason she was able to pull out of his grip, but she did, darting toward the pile of bloodred stones glittering amid gold.

Without a word or even a glance at him, she scooped

them up and dashed to the window, then flung a thousand pounds of jewelry out into the night. When she turned, she saw a flash of approval on his face, and then he gestured sharply toward the door.

But Maia knew that there were more gems just beyond, a larger cache, and if they met up with whoever was downstairs when he was in the proximity, they could be in trouble.

"Stay here," she hissed in the same way he'd done. "Don't argue. Don't say a word. Trust me." Despite her weak knees, she made it to the door before he did and slipped out as he lunged for her.

In the dark corridor, she heard voices below and recognized that of Mrs. Throckmullins and two masculine ones. They were moving through what Maia had realized was an abandoned or closed-up house, and one would assume that they would soon be coming to check on their prisoners.

The rubies that she'd dumped there earlier still rested in a little pile, and Maia picked them up, started back toward the room she'd just vacated and saw Corvindale coming out after her, his face ablaze with fury. So much for listening.

She hesitated, then spun and went light-footed down the hall to the room in which she'd been imprisoned, the rubies dangling from her hand. She couldn't stomach throwing them out the window, as well, but at least she could hide them far from the earl.

By the time she found a place deep in a drawer, far from the door, after stubbing her toe in the dim light, the voices were rising in volume. Corvindale had whipped the chamber door open silently. His face was black with fury, but Maia ignored it and dashed over to him. "Out of here," she mouthed, pointing toward the chest where she'd put the jewels.

They went out into the hall just as the tops of several heads appeared, coming up the shadowy stairs. Corvindale shoved her behind him and backed her roughly into a different chamber from the one in which he'd been imprisoned. But by that time, Mrs. Throckmullins had appeared at the top of the stairs and her furious shrieks filled the air.

Inside this new chamber, Corvindale grabbed Maia and pushed her behind him, then reached for a chair. It splintered on the floor just as the door slammed open to show a red-eyed, fanged Mrs. Throckmullins.

Oh. Maia realized she should already have figured out the woman was a vampire, but then, there'd been other things on her mind. Then all of her thoughts evaporated as she realized Corvindale had a broken chair leg in his hand and he was facing their abductor.

"Back so soon, Lerina?" Corvindale said. His voice was calm and cold, but Maia, who was held in place behind him, felt the tension rippling through his muscles.

The broken chair next to their feet reminded her of the stake that she'd dropped when she found Corvindale, along with the metal poker, which, of course, would be of little use now. She needed a weapon of her own, but knew better than to dodge down and snatch one up, distracting the man in front of her.

Mrs. Throckmullins—or Lerina, for, apparently, they knew each other—was speechless with fury. But Maia noticed that she wore several ruby rings, and that more hairpins glinted like blood in her dark hair. She felt the shimmering in Corvindale's body as their effect slowed him. And she was not certain how much feeding from her had restored him.

And then behind Lerina emerged another figure with burning red eyes and fangs, pushing past her into the room.

"I don't think I'm quite ready for you to leave yet, Dimitri darling," Lerina said. "Especially until you properly introduce me to your companion."

The tone in her voice, the way her eyes settled on Corvindale with a mixture of heat and fury, told Maia all she needed to know about their relationship. And who had put the marks on the earl's shoulders and arm.

Maia eased away from Corvindale, despite his blind attempt to keep her in place while watching the two at the door. She kept a hand on his back so that he knew where she was, and, using him as a shield to block her movements from sight, crouched slowly to the floor.

"I believe you two have already met," he replied to Lerina.

As Maia picked up a piece of wood, the second vampire edged into the room and started to move along the perimeter. Corvindale tensed and shifted his body so that he could watch both Lerina and the man as they separated. Maia stood, and he immediately curved his hand around to hold her behind him, giving her a hard, angry squeeze that clearly said, *Don't move.*

A noise behind them had Maia spinning to see a third vampire, climbing through the window.

He was holding a glittering red necklace.

Maia felt Corvindale's involuntary shudder and she

thought if there was ever a time for a lady to curse, this would be it.

In lieu of that, she realized whatever she did now would have to be careful and smart. The earl didn't think she was capable of thinking for herself, obviously, but she hadn't escaped from her chains *and* saved him by being a dunderhead.

Any further thoughts were interrupted by Lerina, as she made a sudden, furious sound that was almost like a shout. She was staring at Maia, her eyes narrowed.

"You," she said, and at first Maia thought she'd suddenly and unaccountably recognized her. But that was ridiculous—of course she'd recognized her—and that thought was dismissed as Lerina continued, now speaking to Corvindale in a voice that sounded both happy and taunting at the same time. "I see that you've been busy, Dimitri."

Her eyes turned back to focus on Maia, and they were evil. Their very weight seemed to make the blood course in her veins, and her bites throb as if responding to some siren's call. Maia gripped the wooden stick, trying to keep it hidden within the folds of her skirt, trying to keep her mind clear in the face of such animosity, and realized that the vampire was attempting to enthrall her. And if the shimmer in her vision was any indication, Lerina was succeeding.

As if realizing this, Corvindale moved abruptly, shifting so that he blocked their connection and severed the thrall. Maia touched him briefly in gratitude and realized she mustn't make eye contact with any of the Dracule. At least, the ones who meant her harm.

The third vampire with the rubies had moved some

distance from the window while the second one had continued to edge farther from Lerina. It was clear Lerina meant to distract her opponent while setting up her mode of attack. Now, the three vampires were spread out at the edge of the room, leaving Maia and Corvindale in the middle.

The earl continued to scan back and forth between the three, and Maia felt him easing her back as if trying to get to the wall where at least one side would be protected. He made no bones about hiding his stake, and despite the presence of the rubies, his muscles bunched and his breathing seemed relatively steady.

"You left me no choice, Lerina," he replied coolly.

"Whatever do you mean?" she asked, but her hands fluttered, belying her innocence. "Unless I'm mistaken, the last time you deigned to feed on a mortal, it was me. I hate to think that I'd ruined you for a century, darling."

Corvindale gave a disgusted snort. "As you wish. But, I confess, in a hundred years, I've met no one like you."

The other woman seemed oblivious to the sarcasm in his voice; or perhaps she was just used to it. "We could share, Dimitri, and then we wouldn't have to go through all of this mess. She does seem rather lovely. She's light and I'm dark…wouldn't we make a pretty picture? Together? We don't have to send her on to Cezar. I'll just tell him she…didn't make it and he can find another way to get to Chas Woodmore." Lerina smiled and her fangs showed, long and wicked. She looked over at the vampire with the necklace. He'd moved farther from the window.

"What do you suggest?" Corvindale replied, his stake arm relaxing. He sounded almost inviting.

Suddenly the vampire who'd been at the window raised his arm and slung the necklace through the air toward Lerina. Corvindale reacted instantly, and, with a groan of exertion in a great moment of pain, raised his stake to intercept the jewels midair. They caught on the wooden spike and in a sharp movement, he whipped them to the ground.

Maia didn't hesitate. She dropped to the floor and snatched them up, staggering a bit with the unexpected activity. Better that they were in her hands than their enemies'. But then, before anyone could react, she ran a few steps toward the window and winged the necklace toward the opening.

The vampire near it leaped but missed, and the lethal gems sparkled as they tumbled into the moonlit night.

Lerina gave a muffled shriek of anger just as the nearest vampire lunged for Maia. She tried to spin away, still gripping her stake, but he was fast as a breath and he caught her by the arm. His yank was hard enough that she fairly flew through the air, slamming up against him. She flailed out with her stake, stabbing as Iliana had taught her to do; but she was no match for the vampire and couldn't get him in the right place.

He laughed and shifted, twisting her around roughly, grabbing up a handful of her hair and baring her neck. He spoke for the first time. "Did you say something about sharing, mistress?"

Maia swallowed and risked a glance at Corvindale, expecting to see him apprehensive—or at least furious—but he wasn't even looking at her. He was watching Lerina, whose eyes had turned red and whose fangs were showing once again.

"Lovely thought," Lerina said.

Maia's heart was pounding and she couldn't get a good angle with her stake, which had been immobilized by the vampire holding her anyway. Then, everything happened at once...but it was as if the world slowed, underwater, and the events unfolded like a bolt of cloth.

As Corvindale turned, he made a sharp movement. Something spun madly through the air and slammed into the torso of Maia's captor. A stake. The vampire cried out and released her, tumbling to the floor, but by that time, Corvindale was there, slinging Maia up around the waist. She lost her breath and before she caught it again, he'd lunged toward the window. He caught the edge with his hand and pivoted them through the opening.

She heard someone scream as they went out, weightless, into the night, nothing but air around them.

(15)

An Interminable Carriage Ride
and a Preemptive Apology

"Do stop screaming," Dimitri said, his ears ringing, his feet flat on the ground. He hadn't even staggered when he landed. He adjusted his hold on the squirming woman in his arms, for now that they were on the ground safely, she was bound and determined to get free.

"You're mad," she was gasping. "Mad!"

This was no time to talk; Lerina and her make would be out and after them in a moment—either through the window or down the stairs. And though Dimitri had managed a perfectly executed escape, he was still more than a bit wobbly in the knees and trembly in the muscles. Yet, the rush of energy from real, fresh, human blood had restored him more quickly than he'd thought possible.

But he wasn't going to think about the consequences of that now.

Definitely not now. Much, much later.

Perhaps even never.

Ignoring Maia's contortions, Dimitri ducked into shadows and dodged around the close-knit warehouses. They were, as he'd surmised, near the wharf, and even at this time of night, sailors were unloading and loading cargo, drinking, gaming and whoring. An easy environment in which to get lost.

If someone would keep her mouth closed.

"Hush, blasted woman," he ordered. "They'll hear you." The last thing he wanted was to attract attention from anyone at the wharf and have to deal with that delay, as well.

It wasn't until he flagged down a hack and she disappeared within, disdaining his assistance, that Dimitri was able to take a deep breath. And suddenly everything halted.

The driver waited for him to climb in, his hand on the door, an impatient look on his face. Certainly Dimitri knew he looked beyond disreputable, with blood streaking him everywhere, and what had been left of his shirt lost somewhere along the way.

But he was Corvindale, and he wasn't about to be rushed into anything, particularly by the likes of a hackney driver. He glanced into the shadows of the carriage, easily able to make out Maia's figure even in the dark. The prickling over the back of his shoulders and the upheaval in his gut bordered on unpleasant.

If he climbed into that carriage with her, he knew what was going to happen.

"My lord," the hack driver said, allowing the barest hint of impatience in his voice as he looked around. "Shall I—er—transport the lady, and return for you?"

"No," Dimitri said at last, stepping onto the stair.

Then he paused and looked at the driver and, making a quick, probably foolish, decision, gave him Rubey's direction.

He couldn't take Maia home looking as she was, and himself the same. If anyone saw them in their respective conditions, let alone together, Maia would be ruined. At least they could get a change of clothing and washed up at Rubey's, and perhaps something that would even hide the mauling marks he'd left on her skin. *Damn it all. Damn me.*

He snatched the morbid thoughts away and continued on logically. Aside of getting cleaned up, going to Rubey's would be the easiest way to get word to Giordan and Voss that he and Maia were safe. Despite Voss's change back to mortality, the establishment remained a central location through which those familiar with the Dracule communicated and socialized. They knew Rubey could be counted on for confidentiality and secrecy even if she and her ladies weren't providing services.

It was the most expedient, prudent thing to do. Just like intercepting her before she waltzed at the masquerade ball.

With uncustomary care, he climbed into what he now perceived as his own personal hell and settled onto the bench seat across from his own personal tormentor. As the door closed behind him, its latch clicking into place with finality, Dimitri looked across at Maia.

She was not, as one might expect after such a harrowing experience, huddled in the corner, wide-eyed and meek.

Not Maia.

He steered his thoughts around. Perhaps it would be best if he went back to thinking of her as Miss Woodmore.

"You could have killed me" were her first words. Not shouted at the pitch or volume that set his ears to ringing, but in a low, hushed tone.

That was the first sign that something was truly wrong.

"Which time?" he replied, hiding behind a bored tone. *Not* thinking about how right she was. How close he'd come to doing just that.

He could, of course, see quite clearly in the dark. Everything was tinged bottle-green, and all shades of that hue and black, but he could easily discern the enticing curves of her collarbones, the sagging bodice of the simple dress she was wearing, the fact that her hair hung in a messy knot at the left side of the back of her neck, and that her mouth was a hard, flat line. He was not looking at the tiny marks on her shoulder. Definitely *not* remembering the taste of her…skin, lifeblood, scent, mouth—

"That's a very good question," Miss Woodmore replied, shifting a bit in her seat. Her very movement sent a shimmer of her essence toward him and he had to turn away, trying not to allow the scent to reach him. "Both times, in fact. The time when you threw a stake at me and hit the vampire and the time you jumped out of a window and dragged me with you."

Dimitri opened his mouth to correct her—after all, he'd thrown the stake at the vampire, not at her—but thought better of it. Perhaps if he simply didn't talk, he could get through this carriage ride with nothing more than having to listen to her reprimand him.

And that was much preferable to other things that could happen herein.

Things that he simply was not going to allow himself to think about. Or remember.

Like the moment when he really had nearly killed her, when he was so filled with her essence…her life-blood flooding his mouth, coppery and sweet, her skin beneath his hands as he forgot where he was…who she was…what he was doing. He took, and *took,* molding her with his hands, tasting, sipping, drawing on her, *from* her…

He closed his eyes, his fingers trembling, and tried not to smell her. He rested his head against the side of the carriage and pushed it all away.

Had he lost the chance to free himself from Lucifer? Black despair started to build inside him and he squeezed his eyes closed. And yet, he would do it again.

Oh, he would do it again.

Don't think about it now.

"How are you feeling?" She broke the silence with a voice that was soft, perhaps a bit husky with…worry.

Dimitri opened his eyes. No, that would not be a good direction for the conversation to go. It would be better to fight with her, keep her hackles up and therefore her at a distance.

The cold, hard ball in his gut had begun to grow and swell, despite the fact that he wasn't going to allow himself to think about what he'd done. What, after decades of control, of sacrifice, he'd given in to. And how good it made him feel. About how she moaned and writhed against him, pleading for something she didn't understand.

Lucifer's dark soul, he'd nearly killed her.

It was only a miracle that had brought him out of the maelstrom of need and pleasure. A miracle.

He examined her in the green-gray light. Even now, he could see how drawn her skin was. The ghostly pallor, evident to his sharp eyes.

He should ask her how she was feeling. But he couldn't speak for fear of what might come out. And so he pulled his cloak of cold, hard emotion around him and looked over at her with deliberately steady eyes. "Other than a rather nasty experience, I couldn't be better," he said, deliberately leaving the "experience" unspecified.

She bit her lower lip and lifted her chin in a gesture that he'd come to recognize as one of stubbornness.

Just then, the carriage stopped and it was all Dimitri could do to keep from leaping out with alacrity.

Instead he lifted one eyebrow and said, "We've arrived at Rubey's. It's not a place frequented by ladies of your esteem, and I'll preempt your complaints and criticism by offering my apologies now. I suspect we'll find not only Dewhurst but Cale here, as well, and perhaps even your brother. As well, Rubey will allow you to put yourself to rights before returning to Blackmont Hall."

She opened her mouth to speak, but, right on cue, the carriage door opened. Dimitri fairly lunged out, drawing in the refuse and smoke-scented air of London.

It was infinitely better than the essence inside the carriage.

* * *

Rubey, Maia learned, was the proprietress, or more accurately, the brothel owner. The moment it became clear to Maia that Corvindale had brought her to a *brothel,* she turned to glare at him and found him watching her with that condescending look as if to remind her that he'd already apologized.

She looked away and instead allowed herself to be brought into a luxuriously decorated residence that smelled faintly of flowers and tobacco. Although she had no idea what a house of ill repute looked like, it certainly wasn't this tastefully and elegantly appointed place.

The woman named Rubey, who looked comfortably like her name—for she had strawberry-blond hair and intelligent blue eyes, and spoke with a bit of an Irish lilt—took one look at Maia, then at the bare-chested earl, and immediately clamped her lips closed.

Corvindale, of course, was lavish with commands and directions, and Rubey was efficient and yet less than obeisant in her response. But her eyes were wide and shocked, if not speculative, and she said nothing as she rang for a maid. Apparently, despite Corvindale's certainty, neither Dewhurst nor Mr. Cale were currently present.

Not long after, Maia found herself in the deepest, warmest, most fragrant bath she could ever recall having. Tears gathered at the corners of her eyes as she rested back against its edge, as pleasure washed over her, followed by confusion and anger and a variety of other emotions.

She'd sent the maid away as soon as she slid into the

bath, telling her to return only when she rang for her. Maia needed time alone.

She could scarcely account for everything that had happened since yesterday afternoon—for the sun was just rising and it was a new day. Come to think of it, she could scarcely comprehend everything that had happened, and that she'd experienced, since Corvindale became her reluctant guardian. Everything from the existence of vampires, to being attacked, fed upon and kidnapped by them…along with her sister becoming engaged to one of them, who had become mortal once again.

In her exhausted and confused state, she could no longer ignore the loneliness that she often forced herself to disregard, that sense of having no one with whom she could truly talk and share the things that worried her. She let it all pour out in tears, silent and furious recriminations punctuated by violent splashes, and even a rash of prayerful words directed to Above.

Maia was grateful for the steamy water, for she used it to wash away the tears of frustration and anger and confusion, and when she was finished, she rang for the maid.

Determined to be as strong and resilient as she always was—for if she weren't, no one else would be—Maia allowed the maid to wash her hair and to thoroughly bathe her before helping her out of the tub.

Her dress, shift and corset were replaced by ones from Rubey, and despite Maia's suspicion that they'd be scandalous, she was pleased to find the garments tasteful and stylish.

Shortly after, her damp hair pinned in a loose braid

over one side of her neck, strategically placed to hide the marks there, Maia found herself in a parlorlike chamber, waiting for she wasn't certain what.

Rubey came in, looking fresh and elegant in a light green dress of muslin. She was carrying a tray and that was when Maia realized how hungry she was.

"I've met your sister," Rubey said, offering Maia a short glass filled with amber liquid. "Here, a bit of the Irish gold for you, as my papa called it," she explained when Maia hesitated. "After what you've been through, you should have twice as much."

Maia took it and sipped the burning liquid as her hostess arranged cheese and bread on a small plate and offered it to her.

"You've met Angelica?" Maia asked, sipping more of what she presumed was whiskey. Rubey was right, it made her feel better. Warmer and a bit looser.

"She was here some time ago with Voss," Rubey explained as Maia nibbled on the cheese. "The night of the masquerade ball where the vampires attacked. By the by, Dimitri has sent word to her that you're found and safe."

"I appreciate knowing that. Thank you. You seem more than a bit familiar with the Dracule," Maia said, and noticed for the first time that Rubey had bite marks on her neck, just below the ear. The sight reminded her of her own experience, and her stomach did a little flutter. "Are you one of them?"

"Stars, no, and I wouldn't if they asked me. In fact, they have," Rubey added with a wave of her hand. "I've been offered more than once to turn Dracule, and I've declined every time. Why would I want to live forever, and then be damned at the end of time?"

Maia flinched at the woman's use of the blunt word, but found herself fascinated nevertheless. Here was someone who might actually answer her questions without prevarication. "Is that truly how it is?"

Rubey nodded gravely. "It's unnatural, is what I say to Giordan. He's kind enough to me, and visits frequently when he's in London, but I'm merely a replacement for—someone else. And who'd want to live forever anyway? The same, day after day after day? Everyone you know and love, dying without you, while you're staying the same? Everything dies, everything has a season and a cycle—that's the way God made it. I don't mind a few gray hairs, either. But the sagging I can do without." She flashed a bit of a smile as she made a subtle gesture to her bosom.

Maia nearly blushed, but the woman was perhaps a decade or more older than she, and perhaps sagging was a concern. "Do you mean to say that Corvindale has made a pact with the devil? And that's how he's become a vampire?"

"They all have, for one reason or another, made such an agreement. But Dimitri has been trying to break the covenant for over a hundred years. That's why he studies so much, and why he refuses to drink or feed from mortals. Although—" her eyes glinted "—that appears to have changed."

Maia's cheeks warmed. "He certainly didn't want to, but it was the only way I could think to get him out of there. He was too weak to stand."

Rubey's eyes widened. "Do you mean to say, you saved Dimitri? Oh, how he must have loved that!"

Maia blushed more. "I can't say that's the whole of it, but—"

She stopped as the parlor door opened.

"Speak of the devil," Rubey said slyly, garnering her a sharp, annoyed glance from Corvindale.

He strode in as if he owned the place and helped himself to a glass of the same whiskey Maia had tasted. His serving was much more generous than hers. After a brief survey of the chamber—which was furnished with a sofa, where Maia sat facing two armchairs, one of which was occupied by their hostess, he disdained all of the seating possibilities and remained standing near a tall, narrow table to her left.

The expression on his face was haughty and removed, as always. But Maia found herself unable to keep anticipation from fluttering in her middle as she looked at him. His very presence changed the energy in the room, shrinking it, making it warmer. More interesting.

He'd obviously bathed, as well, for his hair was damp and spiked in sharp points around the collar of his pristine white shirt. He stood holding his drink, sleeves rolled up to his elbows to display darkly haired skin the color of suntanned leather. Elegant wrists connected strong, wide hands to muscular forearms, and Maia knew fully well the shape and girth of his upper arms and shoulders. She swallowed and averted her gaze from the loose ties at the throat of his shirt where just a hint of dark hair showed.

"Enlightening your guest with the darkest secrets of

my race, are you, Rubey?" His words might have been light if it weren't for the way his eyes bored into the titian-haired woman.

She didn't seem to mind. "She was just telling me how it all happened. Quite a story."

"I'm certain she was," he replied without glancing at Maia. "But it was beyond foolish of her to become involved in the matter. Things would have worked out much better if she'd simply stayed home."

Maia went rigid. "If it weren't for me, Lord Corvindale," she said in her iciest voice, "no one would have known about the ruby hairpin. Which is what led me to investigate Mrs. Throckmullins."

"And there's where you went wrong, Miss Woodmore. You should never have been investigating anyone. Dewhurst and Cale had things well in hand. They would have found me soon enough."

Maia could not hold back an improper snort. "I merely went for an afternoon call—"

"Nor should you have gone alone."

"I didn't go alone, you dratted man. Do you think I have feathers for brains? I had three footmen with me. How was I to know that Mrs. Throckmullins was your former mistress, and that she would have invited me into tea and then poisoned me? I certainly couldn't have brought three footmen into her parlor, now, could I?"

He raised the whiskey. "Very well. I stand corrected. You could have done nothing to prevent Lerina from drugging and abducting you."

Maia drew herself up even more, ignoring the avid interest on Rubey's face. "Just as you could have done nothing to prevent her from abducting *you*. Because of course, being the Earl of Corvindale, you know all and see all and could clearly foresee every possible circumstance. Which is precisely why you ended up in the condition in which I found you."

Rubey drew in a sharp intake of breath that sounded suspiciously like a stifled laugh.

"Furthermore," Maia continued, unable to stop herself, "if I hadn't managed not only to free myself from being chained to a chaise lounge and then gone in search of you, you would probably be dead by now from loss of blood."

"Dracule don't die from loss of blood," he sneered.

"Even when tied up by ruby necklaces?"

"You were tied up by rubies, Dimitri?" Their hostess looked much too intrigued by such a concept, her eyes narrowing contemplatively. "Now there's a fascinating idea."

"Is my carriage here yet?" Corvindale snarled at her. "Perhaps you ought to go check."

"Oh, but I find this conversation very stimulating."

"Go." He didn't roar, but the room vibrated as if he had. Rubey rose reluctantly and started toward the door, not at all cowed.

But Maia wasn't finished; no indeed. She had so much to say to the arrogant, impossible, infuriating man in front of her, she didn't know if she'd be done in a week. "And then you *throw a stake* at me—"

"I threw it at the vampire who was holding you—"

"You could have stabbed me!"

"Of course I wouldn't have, you addled woman. Do you think I'm completely incompetent? I knew precisely what I was doing, as is evident by the fact that you are here, intact, and so am I."

"And then you jump through a second-story window," Maia continued, her mind blazing with fury, the words tumbling out, "and take me with you! We could have been killed!"

"Dracule don't die from a fall—"

"But people like me do!" she shrieked, leaping to her feet. Maia drew in a deep breath and realized she'd truly gone mad. Perhaps he was right. Perhaps she was addled. She reached down for her glass, taking the last swallow of her whiskey while managing not to cough or choke. She heard the faint click of the door closing behind Rubey.

Corvindale didn't seem to notice; for he was watching Maia from over the rim of his own glass, his eyes dark and steady. Wary. "The fact is," he said in his chilly voice, "that you were perfectly safe once the rubies were out of my proximity."

"And how," she said sweetly, but with a steely edge, "did it happen that those blasted rubies *got out of your proximity?*" Her hands planted on her hips, she glowered up at him.

"Speaking of rubies," he said, setting his glass on the table with a definite clunk, "why in the goddamned *bloody* hell did you not use them?"

She closed her mouth, for she truly had no idea what he meant. "I—"

"I could have killed you, Maia," he said, his face terrible. Darker and more frightening than she'd ever seen. "I *nearly killed you.*"

She was shaking her head, anger dissolving into confusion. "You didn't hurt me, Corvindale," she said, at last understanding. "You needed to feed. It was the only way."

He made a disgusted sound and reached for her. "Look at this," he said, yanking her arm out to display the bite marks there. "And here," he said, shoving her braid away from her shoulder. "You would have let me go on and on until there was nothing left."

"But—"

"I've done it before," he said, his voice dropping into an awful pitch. It made her nauseated, the loathing and malevolence therein. His dark eyes glittered, holding hers like magnets. "I've torn a woman to shreds, left nothing but mutilated flesh behind. *I could have done that to you.*" His voice had dropped to an agonized whisper.

"But you didn't. You stopped. I didn't realize—"

He gave a bitter laugh, still holding on to her wrist. "Only by the grace of—something, some miracle—did I stop. It had been one hundred thirteen years, Maia." He drew in an unsteady breath, his thumb sliding over her skin. "And even now…"

He dropped her arm abruptly and turned away. "Where the bloody hell is my carriage?"

"Corvindale," she said, her voice quiet. She stepped toward him, reaching for his arm. It was in her nature to comfort, to set all right, to take care of things, and for the first time, she sensed the deep pain rolling off him like fog from the sea. It had been hidden beneath that brittle, dark exterior all this time.

When she touched him, he froze, the muscles of his

forearm tightening like bowstrings. "Miss Woodmore," he said coldly. "You are out of line."

"Look at me and say that," she said, noting that he didn't pull away from her grip. He needed something. Something perhaps he didn't even understand.

He turned. "You have no idea what you're doing, Miss Woodmore," he said tightly. "Don't be a fool. Release me."

She looked up at him, finding no humor in that ludicrous command, and silently, fearlessly, she met his eyes. Her heart pounded in her throat, echoing through her entire body as she lifted her other hand and placed it on the warm expanse of his chest. Flat, there over one of the solid planes of muscle covered by crisp white linen.

Time stopped. The room shrunk, and she was caught up in a moment of…something. Something potent.

When he moved, it wasn't to spin away, but to pull her toward him. Hard and quick, with strong arms enfolding her, he brought her up against his tall frame as he bent his head. Maia met his lips with hers, hungry for what they had begun so many times earlier.

Their mouths clashed and fought, his tongue strong and sleek, battling with hers in an erotic melee. She had him under her hands, her fingers against the warm skin of his neck, the damp fringe of his hair, pulling at the strings of his shirt.

Corvindale lifted her onto the table next to him, clinking glasses, raising her to a height that brought her eye level with him. His hands pulled at her hair, loosening it from its braid, his fingers sliding down her neck and along her shoulders, drawing the edges of her dress's neckline with them. The fresh air felt cool on her warm skin, and the rough pads of his fingers made gentle texture on her.

When he pulled out of the kiss, she made a sound of negation and frustration, but he was merely moving to the side of her jaw, in front of her ear. She shivered a little when he got there and she felt his warm breath deep inside her ear, then his hot mouth covered the wounds on her bare shoulder. Maia sighed and tipped her head to the side, opening her neck and throat, pressing up against his mouth, but he didn't bite. Instead she felt the little shudder of his torso where it pressed against hers and his tongue sliding over and around the marks, his lips sucking gently on the rise of her shoulder, his hands strong and busy over the rest of her, cupping her breasts, sliding down over the swell of her hips.

The ties at the back of her dress loosened, and the bodice gapped before she knew it, his hands drawing the neckline down over her shoulders, completely baring them and the top of her shift. When he realized she couldn't recline any farther on the narrow table, Corvindale made a sound of frustration and scooped her up.

Maia clung to his shoulders, dazed and already aroused, as he pivoted around and deposited her on the sofa, easing down next to her. She caught a glimpse of his face, dark and intense, his eyes hooded, and the very image of that desirous countenance sent deep waves of pleasure in her belly.

His weight pressed her gently into the upholstery, leaving her breathless but not frightened or overwhelmed. She started to say something—she didn't even know what; perhaps to order him to remove his dratted shirt—when he gave a sharp yank and pulled the top of her corset away. He'd already loosened it, and her breast slipped free, round and ivory with a swollen pink tip.

He made a little sound, then ducked his head and flicked out his tongue just over the tip of her nipple. Maia watched, jolting at the light sensation that spiraled through her, and when he covered her with his mouth, the undulating waves of heat trammeled through her, down past her belly and to her core. His tongue sleek and warm, swirling around as he drew her hard and fast in his mouth, made her lose her breath. The pang of pleasure stabbed her belly again, and she felt herself opening, flowering and swelling down at the juncture of her thighs.

Pulling away, he looked up at her. Their eyes caught and Maia could hardly catch her breath at the dark heat there. She could see the tips of his upper fangs just below his upper lip, and she wanted them…inside her.

Instead of asking that, she whispered, "Your shirt, Corvindale. Make it go away."

His eyes darkened and he eased back, whipping the linen up and over his head with a sharp snap. She had to touch his broad shoulders and the ridges of his belly, the slabs of his chest, slide her fingers through the thick patch of hair and over flat, oval nipples. She moved her hands up to cover the marks on his arm and raised her face to touch them with her mouth, wondering if she might taste more of him there, too.

He was solid and smooth, his skin damp and hot, and she felt something deep beneath leaping and trembling as she scored him gently with her teeth. His head tipped to the side, leaning against the sofa, his eyes closed, his beautiful lips—the mouth she'd so admired at the masquerade ball—parted as he drew in steadying breaths. Maia shifted, and his heavy arm came around as if to keep her from slipping away, but she had no intention of doing so.

She planted her hands flat on the warm slabs of his chest and curled her fingers around his shoulders to pull herself up. She had to taste that strong, corded neck, and it was warm and soft and she felt him groaning deep in his throat as she nibbled along the tendons there. When she closed her teeth over him, giving a sharp nip, he shuddered, his arm tightening around her.

"Maia," he murmured. "Take care."

She shook her head in the warmth of his neck, smelling his particular smell, now fresh with bergamot. "You won't hurt me."

He gave a short laugh, and she shifted, realizing she was now pressed against him all the full length of their torsos and legs. She could feel the outline of his powerful thighs, fairly twice as thick as her own, her skirt and shift tangled in with them and the hard rise from behind the buttons of his trousers. The very feel of it made her belly ache and her center tingle with sharp pleasure.

Before she could slide her hand down over the gentle ripples of his stomach, he moved, easing all along the length of her until his knees were on the floor. Before she could sit up, he had his hands up and under her skirt, sliding the layers up and baring her legs. When he bent to kiss the inside of her thigh, Maia felt uncontrollable shivers starting up along her.

What if he bit her…*there?*

His tongue moved sleek and strong along the sensitive skin inside her leg, and Maia watched his dark head moving against her ivory thigh. She caught a glimpse of his teeth, white and sharp, against her flesh, her breathing coming faster and harder as he moved higher up. A flash of a fang had her veins surging and pounding, and when he spread her legs, burying his face down in the heat of her there, Maia nearly arched off the sofa.

His fingers were clever and gentle, baring that most sensitive, most private part of her, and somewhere in the back of her mind, Maia realized she shouldn't be doing this. Not her, not Miss Woodmore, not the woman who was going to marry someone…else….

But she didn't care. This was it, this was *him,* this was what she wanted…and his mouth was hot and fervent, and she quivered, swollen and wet, and when his tongue slid over her quim, she knew she couldn't stop this. She didn't want to, especially when he did something that made her insides gather up and explode into deep trembling waves.

Nothing…she'd never felt anything like that before.

"Oh…" she whispered, her hand closing over his head, still settled between her legs, her fingers buried in his warm hair. But she knew there was more, and she wanted it.

"Please," she murmured as she'd done before, not knowing precisely what she wanted or needed, but knowing that he—only he—could give it to her.

He shook his head against her, down by her knee, giving her a quick slip of tongue in the curve there.

"More," she whispered.

"No." His breath and lips were hot against her. "Don't be a fool." He slipped his tongue down around in the heat of her and she gave a little squeak of pleasure, a shot of fire rippling through her. "You can't," he said.

"Yes...*please*. I want...all of it."

And when, suddenly, he pulled away, his face hot and eyes burning, she almost wailed in distress. She throbbed, ready again for more. For the rest of it.

But then he was tearing at the buttons on the fall of his trousers, and she was helping him, and he gave a short, sharp shake of his head as he muttered, "Always interfering, Miss Woodmore," and then he was there, against her again, this time his bare chest warm, printing on her skin.

She didn't see him, that hard bulge she'd felt earlier, and for a moment, she was bereft, feeling lost...but then his fingers moved between them, and found the very hard, tight core of her being, and before she knew it, they'd slipped and slid around so that she was even more full and hot and throbbing, and then he paused.

"Maia," he breathed, withdrawing his hand. She knew it was a question. "This is—"

"No," she said, shifting against him, in distress. "Please."

He made a soft, strangled sound, and the next thing she knew, he shifted and fitted himself to her. Maia sighed: this was it. *Yes*.

Then he moved and she felt a snap of pain deep inside. Maia froze for a moment, her eyes opening, the pleasure filtering away...but before she could think, he began to move. And her mouth gaped, her body heated, and everything in her world became focused on the sleek slide, in and out. It was long and beautiful, this feeling of *right*, the tingle of desire centering there between them.

He muttered something deep and low near her ear, but she couldn't understand. She didn't care. There was the heat and the rhythm and the growing blossoming, and she cried out when he sank his teeth into her shoulder, her body seeming to explode deep inside.

Pleasure undulated through her in little echoing ripples as he groaned into her skin, his body hot and damp against her. And then he moved one last time, hard and deep, with a soft cry of exertion. He pulled his face away, burying his forehead into her neck, the scent of blood in her nose as he shuddered against her.

16

OF APOLOGIES AND RECOMPENSE
AND INFLATED DOWRIES

No sooner did the blaze of pleasure and fulfillment begin to fade than a cold, hard stone settled in Dimitri's middle.

By Fate, what have I done?

A chill washed over him and he drew in a deep breath, his mind shooting off in many different directions.

He halted it with cold control. *No.* There'd be time for recriminations and regrets later. Now he must keep his thoughts clear and extricate himself—literally and figuratively—from…*this.*

This…moment of quiet fulfillment, of delight, of something that had shaken him deep in his core. Something that made his insides move, like a heated flower opening and sending its warmth through him. But that quickly turned bleak.

He forced himself to open his eyes, pulling up gently from her shoulder. He'd already retracted his fangs, but the essence of blood still lingered on his tongue, filtering into his nostrils. *Beautiful.* Her eyes were closed, her face slack with satiation. He'd never seen anything that made his heart ache like this. Though he must, he couldn't look away.

Her lips, full and moist, rosy and inviting, were half-parted. The damp braid that had confined all of the strands of blond, bronze, copper, auburn and walnut was a distant memory, and her long, thick hair clung in places to her skin, and his, as well. Bare throat and shoulders, with an uncovered breast that couldn't have been more perfect. The mere sight of it, the memory of its smooth, sweet texture, the hard, sensitive nipple beneath his tongue and lips, made his body begin to tighten all over again.

What have I done to you? To me?

Even as he pulled away, Dimitri struggled with how to undo what could not be undone. He pulled down the cold wall behind which he could be safe, and watched as Maia—*Miss Woodmore, she must be Miss Woodmore again*—opened her eyes with a flutter.

So wrong.

He wanted to poke at her, to cut with his words and send her reeling away. If he did that, then she could continue to loathe the Earl of Corvindale. She could wed Bradington with perhaps a twinge of conscience, but at least she would still wed him.

Instead of demanding that Dimitri come up to snuff. Tempting him.

That would…could…never happen.

"Corvindale."

Even the way she said his name, still used his title in all formality, sounded husky and intimate.

He'd sat up and was putting himself to rights, rebuttoning his trousers and then locating his shirt in a crumpled wad on the floor. *Your shirt, Corvindale. Make it go away.*

You won't hurt me.

Please.

He closed his eyes. *Lucifer's bloody hell.*

She was sitting up now, and he dared not look at her and see those wide, questioning eyes. Hurt. Or perhaps they would be filled with anger and recrimination—as they rightly should be.

"Corvindale," she said again, more firmly. "Look at me."

He hesitated, then did as she asked. Thank the Fates she'd pulled up her bodice and righted the rest of her clothing. The only sign of their activities was the new bite on her shoulder. He slid his gaze up to her face. What he saw there was not question nor confusion, neither was it anger or recrimination. There was a hint of softness, the heavy-liddedness of pleasure, and something else. Acceptance?

"I suppose this wasn't what Chas had in mind when he named you guardian," she said, pulling all of that thick bundle of hair forward over one shoulder. She began to plait it in a fat braid.

He swallowed a derisive sound. "You do realize, Miss Woodmore, that, while I cannot begin to make things right in regards to this, nothing will change."

She lifted an eyebrow, her green-brown eyes fastened on him with a bland expression. She was silent for a moment before replying, "What precisely do you mean, that nothing will change?"

He noticed that her busy fingers were either very quick, or they were trembling a bit. Sorrow pitted his insides. "I mean that we need never speak of or acknowledge this…er…event to anyone. No one need ever know, and you will go on to wed Bradington without even a whiff of scandal."

Maia—blast it, Miss Woodmore—continued to watch him steadily. She'd finished with the braid and now her fingers settled in her lap, within the folds of her gown so that he couldn't tell if they were shaking.

"The way you put it, it's really rather simple then, isn't it, my lord? We both go on as if nothing has happened. But in fact, Corvindale, you clearly realize that a great deal has happened." Her voice became more strident, rising a bit at the end. She wasn't shouting, or even furious. But simply strong. Knowing.

"I realize that you can never—nor should you—forgive me for my behavior today. It was beyond inexcusable. I shall settle an additional dowry on you for a wedding gift as an apology and a clumsy attempt to comfort you. I'm quite certain, as well, that your brother will remove you from my guardianship immediately."

"I thought," she said from between unmoving lips, "you just said no one need ever know. I presumed Chas was included in that statement. Or," she continued, a new flash of fire in her eyes, "was this all a great ruse to entice him to remove me and my sisters from your custody?"

"Certainly *not*," he snapped. "I had no intention of ever coming near you, Miss Woodmore. Let alone—*this*."

She nodded. "That is what I thought. I'm relieved to

know that my impressions were correct." Standing, she continued, "So I am to understand that, firstly, you are apologetic for today's events. Secondly, you wish for no one to know what has transpired. And third, that you intend to bestow a great deal of money upon my nuptial union in order to assuage yourself from any lingering guilt you might have. Do I have that right?"

Dimitri managed to nod. This was so…odd.

"A *great* deal of money," she repeated, spearing him with her eyes. "Correct?"

He nodded again.

"Because of your behavior."

He nodded a bit more slowly this time. Was this some sort of snare?

"Then I have one further question for you, Corvindale." Again, those syllables took on a bit of a note of intimacy merely because they came from her mouth.

"And what is that?" He glanced toward the door of the parlor, for he'd heard the sounds of someone approaching. Or, more likely, Rubey listening at the door.

"What sort of recompense do you expect me to offer for *my* behavior?"

He stilled, staring at her. "Er…"

"After all," she continued even as the parlor door rattled, "I was a fully participatory member in what occurred here. In fact," she added, spearing him with her eyes, "I do believe I was rather instrumental in them. I did say please, did I not?"

The door opened and Rubey stood there. "Dimitri, your carriage has arrived."

What the hell had taken so long?

* * *

Dimitri didn't join Miss Woodmore in the carriage. He wasn't that much of a fool.

Instead he sent her back to Blackmont Hall with a relieved Tren handling the reins. Then he glared at the far-too-fascinated Rubey and induced her to loan him her vehicle.

He had a particular visit to make.

The fact that it was yet another gray, foggy day in London only added to the ease with which he alighted from the carriage in front of Lenning's Tannery and ducked under the wooden awning that stretched in front of the antiquarian bookstore.

For a moment he hesitated, peering through the window, aware of the sun's rays filtering through the fog and teasing the back of his neck between hat and collar. The shop seemed dark and empty, and he was suddenly terrified that Wayren had gone.

But when he pushed on the door, it opened and he stepped in.

Drawing in a deep breath of peaceful, musty air, Dimitri closed the door behind him. The place was silent and the only illumination came from a distant corner of the shop. It was a soft, orange-yellow glow that displayed the dust motes he'd just stirred with his entrance.

For some reason, he felt odd about disturbing the silence and calling for the shopkeeper. Or perhaps he feared that she wasn't there, and that he would have to continue to face his confusion and frustration on his own.

When he heard the soft scuff of a foot on the floor,

followed by the whisper of fabric over the ground, Dimitri's heart leaped and he turned.

Wayren appeared from around a corner. Interestingly enough, she didn't emerge from the area with the light, but from one of the more shadowy ones. Today, she was empty-handed and without her spectacles.

"And so here you are," she said, eyeing him steadily.

Dimitri nodded. His mouth didn't seem able to move, nor his brain to form the words he needed to speak. He didn't know what to say—how to ask.

She waited. Peace and serenity emanated from her, along with the indefinable scent of something warm and comforting.

"You were there," he said at last. "You...stopped me."

She continued to watch him with those peaceful eyes. "You stopped yourself, Dimitri of Corvindale."

He shook his head, the black bubble of uncertainty spreading like tar inside him. "If you hadn't appeared in my mind...I would have killed her. I would have taken and taken, I would have drained her to death." It had been the flash of a vision, clear as if she'd been standing in front of him, that had erupted in his mind as he fed on Maia. That peaceful face with the serene blue-gray eyes had broken through the red-tinged world of need and pleasure, easing the desperation. Giving him a reprieve.

"As I said, you stopped yourself. I did nothing."

"But you did show yourself to me."

She raised her brows with a noncommittal expression, and he realized that he would get no confirmation from her. She seemed to know whereof he spoke, but that was the most she would give. "I can do nothing for you," she'd said once.

She had done something.

But it hadn't been enough. Where had she been when he was first faced with the choice from Lucifer? Why hadn't she stopped him then?

Wayren was looking at him, almost as if she could read what was in his mind. "You had the choice then, Dimitri. You made the decision of your own free will."

"I was weak. He took advantage of my weakness," Dimitri replied. But even to him, the words sounded hollow. Even then, he'd known there was something wrong. Something evil. He'd hesitated, yes, but then he'd allowed himself to be tricked, manipulated in a moment of desperation. For all he knew, Meg might have lived anyway. For all he knew, Luce had known it then, as well.

"Aye, Dimitri. He did. That is what the Fiend does." Despite her words, Wayren watched him with a calm, peaceful expression. "He makes it easy to see his way. He takes advantage."

Just as I did.

The image of Maia's face, slack with pleasure, filled with her own sort of peace, slid into Dimitri's mind. He shoved it away.

It was too late. He'd lied when he told Maia nothing had changed.

Everything had changed.

"And so now all of my years of self-denial are for naught," he said. "It's over."

She looked at him searchingly. "Is that so?"

"Of course it's so," he replied, more angrily than he'd

ever spoken to her. "How can I expect to break the covenant, to distance myself from the devil, if I act like the demon he turned me into? If I take from people, feed on them, pull their very life from them, how can I ever become human again?"

"So you've fed on a mortal, for the first time in decades, and you believe that action has destroyed your chance to be released from the Fiend? Oh, yes, I can see that a century of self-denial has already gotten you so very close to your desire."

He glared at her mutely. She was looking at him with a sort of arch expression that he'd never seen before. "You don't understand," he said tightly. "I *fed* from a person. I drank her blood. I…" His voice trailed off as saliva filled his mouth. Even now, he could hardly control the physical reaction of his long-denied body. He could still taste it. Feel the energy, the *life* flowing through him. "It's a violation. A sin."

"But has denying yourself done anything but make you a cold, hard, empty shell? Hardly a person at all."

To his shock and eternal mortification, Dimitri felt a stinging in his eyes. He pinched the bridge of his nose fiercely before any tears could form. "My…dislike of social engagement has nothing to do with the problem at hand. I've never been…particularly social."

"Have you read the story I gave you?" Wayren asked.

Dimitri frowned, blinking hard. "The fairy tale about the beast? A bit of it. I found nothing of relevance."

"Indeed?"

Impatience flooded him, and he made a sharp, frustrated gesture with his hand. "I'm sorry to have bothered you. I thought..." He shook his head sharply, pressing his lips together.

"Dimitri of Corvindale," Wayren said. Her voice had gentled. "If you want to become truly human again—no longer bound to the Fiend—first you must allow yourself to live again. To feel again."

"I *feel*," he snarled.

"Do you? Or do you snarl and growl—as you've done here, today—and then run in the opposite direction whenever something begins to soften your heart?"

"Earls don't run," he snapped, but something shifted deep inside him.

She smiled at him. "No, not this one. Instead you lock yourself away within a barricade of stone walls so that none can touch you, so that you can keep yourself from feeling anything."

It was safer that way. Easier. Less complicated. "I lock myself away so I can study," he said. But even to him, the words sounded false. "I don't like to be bothered."

Wayren gave him a sad, soft smile. "But that's why men are here. To *be* bothered. To feel. To live. To *love*. And...to be loved. That is what makes you different from every other creature. And that is what makes man ultimately more powerful than the Fiend. Do you not see? He's taken your soul, and with it, he's taken your very humanity. The very part that could save you."

His belly twisted tightly and his head throbbed. Maia's face filtered into his memory, then was supplanted by Meg. And Lerina. He shook his head, but at the same time, something small and warm moved in his chest. Something he hadn't felt in a long time.

Wayren was watching him. "Very well, then. Dimitri of Corvindale, I wish you all of the best."

During the ride back to Corvindale's residence from that of the sharp-eyed Rubey, Maia tried to keep her mind blank. She had so much to think about, so many emotions to sift through and to determine which ones to focus on, that she dared not begin it until she was in the privacy of her own chamber.

Preferably during another bath, where she might wash away the remnants of the interlude in Rubey's parlor.

She shivered, a little flutter of heat streaking through her. That episode alone was enough to send her thoughts spiraling into confusion. But she dared not let herself think about it now. About: *Nothing need change. We need tell no one.*

Her lips tightened. Corvindale was addled if he thought nothing had changed.

When the carriage pulled up in front of Blackmont Hall, the first thing Maia noticed was another familiar vehicle parked there. Her stomach became a mass of fluttering bird wings.

Alexander.

As if she didn't have enough to contend with. Biting her lip, she opened the little door behind the driver and asked him to take her around to the servants' entrance.

It simply wasn't done, of course, for a lady of the peerage to come through the rear entrance. But that would be preferable to trying to explain to Alexander why her hair was a mess and why there were four delicate marks on her neck. And shoulder. And on her gloveless wrist.

Thus, she slipped into the rear entrance and through the warm kitchen, down into the hallways that weren't quite as gloomy as they had been when she and Angelica had arrived here. At least some of the windows were unsheathed from drapes now, so many weeks after their arrival.

Maia sent a message down to Alexander that she'd arrived and was safe, asking him to come back later in the afternoon, for she needed time to rest.

No sooner had she sent off her maid with that task, and to order a bath, than the door to her chamber was assaulted by an insistent knock. Before Maia had the chance to bolt the door—for she well knew her sister—said sister burst into the room.

"Maia! Oh, thank heavens you're back!" She threw herself into Maia's arms, and nearly bowled her over onto the bed, for not only was she enthusiastic, but Angelica was also a bit taller and heavier than her elder sister. "Are you hurt? What happened?"

"I'm not hurt at all," Maia replied, "except for the fact that you are squeezing the life out of me."

Her sister released her and stepped back. "Is that better?" she asked. And then her face froze with shock. "Is that what I think it is? On your neck?"

Maia touched the bite marks, which were what had caught her sister's eye. "If you think they are vampire bites," she said in a much lower volume than Angelica, "you would be correct."

"One of Moldavi's vampires?" Angelica asked, sitting next to her on the bed. "Were you terrified? Did they kidnap you? All I heard from Corvindale's message was that you'd been found safely."

"Yes, I'm safe, and uninjured. Have you heard anything from Chas?" she asked in an effort to avoid Angelica's question about the bites.

"Chas has not been in contact, but we've sent a message. He'll be here soon. Alexander is below."

"I know that, but I sent word that I would see him this afternoon. I need…to freshen up."

"He's refused to leave. He says he'll wait here until you're ready to come down."

Maia closed her eyes. Noble. So noble. "It will be some time before I come down. Perhaps you can tell him for me, that I am well, but I must freshen up."

"I shall do my best, but he's as stubborn as you." Angelica looked at her sharply. "What happened to you, Maia? Where did you get the bites?"

"I don't wish to discuss it," she replied firmly. "But I do wish for a bath."

Despite Angelica's protests and questions, Maia managed to send her from the room with direction to talk to Alexander. Then she indulged in her second bath of the day, along with her second bout of confused tears.

Whatever was she going to do about Alexander? How could she marry him after what had happened with Corvindale? How could she marry him when she was in love with another man?

In love with another man.

Those words jumped up out of her mental whirlwind of thoughts, freezing in her mind. Maia paused, water and tears mingling and dripping from her face.

In love with another man who happened to be a *vampire*.

How *could* she be in love with him? The thought was absurd. He was rude and arrogant and he raised his voice to her and he argued about everything. He condescended. He insulted.

He kissed her. Oh, how he kissed her.

He argued with her, but for all that, he didn't ignore her. For all his annoyed comments, he nevertheless seemed to listen to her. He was honorable. Intelligent.

He could never picnic with her, under the sun. He could never ride or accompany her anywhere during the day.

But the way he looked at her…with something in his eyes. Something…needy. Something lost. Something lurked there.

She let her hands fall into the warm, vanilla-and-lily-scented water, causing it to splash over the rim.

What a fanciful notion. That she was in love with a vampire. With the earl. With a man who could hardly stand her presence.

And if she *were* in love with him—truly in love, although how could she be, *truly?*—what difference did it make? He certainly couldn't love her. And…

She was to wed Alexander. A good man. Who possibly loved her, and who at least held her in high regard. Even if his kisses were boring and his conversation not nearly as interesting, if not as explosive, as Corvindale's.

The wedding was to have been…dear heaven…*tomorrow!*

In the blur of Corvindale's disappearance and Maia's own abduction and return…she'd lost track of time. She was supposed to have wed Alexander *tomorrow*. No wonder he wouldn't leave.

Maia bit her lip again, noticing that it was tender from all of the worried gnawing she'd done on it…and perhaps from the rough kisses of earlier today. She closed her eyes, a flush of memory warming her. Pleasure stabbed her belly.

What was she going to do? She'd already postponed the wedding when Corvindale disappeared, but now that he was back and so was she…they must decide on another date.

What am I going to do?

Cold truth settled over her. She had to marry Alexander. She was ruined now, thanks to the earl. She could even be carrying his child.

That thought turned her alternately hot and then cold again. It was followed by rage that Corvindale meant to pay her off by settling a dowry on her for her wedding, after he'd ruined her. To pay for the child, if there was one.

A child that would be passed off as Alexander's.

Nothing need change.

How dare he say such a thing? Perhaps for him nothing had changed, but for her? Everything. Everything had changed.

She'd done something outside of foolish, but…she'd do it again. There'd been no way she could have stopped, pulled back. She wanted him, needed him in that way.

What they'd shared had been… She shivered, heat unfurling in her again. It had been like her dreams. But better. Real.

Maia's thoughts sharpened, settled, stopped. Her

heart paused, her breathing stilled. Her dreams. Of making love to a vampire.

It had been him. Corvindale.

In her dreams, all along, it had been *Corvindale.*

She'd been dreaming about him, ever since she moved into his house. And that last dream, the one that had frightened her, that had been filled with darkness and pain and *red*...that had been while he'd been captured by Lerina.

Was she somehow connected to him? Through their dreams? Had she dreamed what he experienced? Or what he...dreamed?

She shook her head, shivering. *The Sight works in mysterious ways.*

Maia wished suddenly that Granny Grapes was still here, so she could ask her about dreams and connections. She closed her eyes and pursed her lips. There were other problems at hand.

Like what she'd done today, with Corvindale, was foolish. She could ruin herself, ruin her family. Hurt Alexander.

But...despite the way he'd handled it, the abhorrent, cold, *earlish* way...she would have done it again. She would do it again. It had been *right* despite the fact that everything about it seemed wrong.

The water had turned cold, and her hands and feet wrinkled like a silk gown left on the ground. And still Maia didn't know what to do.

Logic, propriety, everything she'd ever learned told her she must marry Alexander. There was truly no good reason not to, and every reason to do so.

A broken engagement would cause a great scandal,

particularly so close to the wedding. One of them must take the blame for it, and it would either be Maia—who would be ruined—or Alexander, who would be made a fool. She didn't wish either consequence, but certainly she didn't wish to make Alexander a cuckold nor a scapegoat, for that would be the result if she broke the engagement.

And if he made the announcement, which would be his right in this instance, Maia would be branded a loose woman. Her reputation would be ruined and she would never marry, and quite likely never be admitted into polite society again.

If she were with child, it would be even worse.

Nausea flooded her. How could something that had been so beautiful, that had felt so deeply *right* have such dreadful consequences?

She shook her head. Marrying Alexander wouldn't be so bad.

It would be good, in fact. It would be nice and it would be the right thing to do.

She rose from the tub. It was time to go down and see him.

Dimitri opened his eyes to find the point of a stake resting upon his chest.

"Do it," he said, looking up into the dark, furious face of Chas Woodmore. He closed his eyes against the dimly lit, spinning room and waited. Hoped. *Put me out of this misery.*

The pressure moved away from his torso. "Open your bloody eyes, Dimitri. I want to hear it from you."

He forced his eyes open again, and the room tilted

violently. He closed them, tasting the blood whiskey still clinging to his lips and tongue, smelling it on his hands and from the empty bottle on the desk in front of him. A bleary glance told him dawn threatened, but that the world was still silent with night. He was in his study, which was good, because that was the last thing he remembered. Settling into place with two—perhaps three—bottles of the stuff. Just as the sun went down. Tuning out the sounds, the scents, the memories, the darkness.

It was two days after the Incident at Rubey's.

Two days after everything had changed.

"What did you do to my sister?" Chas said. His voice was slick with anger and dark with loathing. He stood across the desk from Dimitri, a mere arm's length away. "I trusted you."

"There is no explanation for what occurred. You have every right to finish things now." Dimitri pulled his waistcoat helpfully away from his shirt. "I won't fight you, Chas. I won't even ask you to make it quick. Just bloody well do it. It's a long time coming."

"Devil take it, have you had the whole bottle tonight?" There was a clink as Woodmore picked it up as if to check its contents.

"No," Dimitri drawled. "Two." His eyes sank closed. Oblivion was lovely.

More clinking and the rustle of books and papers. "What in the devil are you doing, Corvindale?" Chas demanded.

"Waiting. What the damned hell is taking you so long? You're never this slow." His eyes remained closed.

"What did you do to Maia?"

Dimitri purposely picked the most vulgar of words. "I fucked her. I violated her. I bloody fed on her." He tried to focus. "But she's going to marry Bradington. No one will know. And you're going to stake me. Anytime now."

"And if she's with child?"

"I pray she is not. It's highly unlikely." But, oh, the Fates, it was possible.

"But if she is…then Lucifer could claim him."

A wave of nausea surged and Dimitri swallowed hard. As if the thought hadn't been swirling around and around in his whiskey-fogged brain, sloshing along in his upset belly. Threatening him for days, threading through his dreams.

Silence.

Dimitri opened his eyes and found Chas looking at him. Pity seemed to have replaced pure loathing, although the hard, dark fury was still there. What the hell was he waiting for? Dimitri wouldn't have waited. He'd have driven the stake home long before now. "It was Rubey who told me," Woodmore said, answering a question Dimitri hadn't cared to ask. "Not Maia. She's said nothing. To anyone."

Dimitri adjusted his position in the chair and blinked. Apparently they were going to have a civil conversation before the man killed him. "There isn't a damned thing I can do to change it," he said. "It's done. I've settled a dowry on her—"

"She doesn't need a bloody damned dowry from you," Chas said. "And there certainly isn't anything you can do. If you were a mortal, I'd have you at the altar tomorrow because I know at least you'd never hurt her. At any rate, I don't want you to touch her again."

Dimitri gave a bitter laugh. "There is no chance of that."

"Very well. The sad thing is, I believe you, Dimitri." Chas shoved the stake back into his inside pocket. "I came for another reason, besides to kill you."

"But you haven't killed me," Dimitri said flatly. "Damn you."

"No, and I don't think I will. It's clear killing's too easy a way out for you, Corvindale. Aside of that, I might be in need of you in the future. You'll owe me."

"Why are you here?"

"I'm going to visit Sonia, in Scotland. I'm going to see if she'll use her Sight to tell me about Moldavi so we can stop him for good. Narcise won't be free until he's dead."

Dimitri felt a stirring of interest. "Sonia has a different skill than Angelica. She might do it. She might be of help."

"But she won't use it," Chas said. "I'm hoping to convince her that it's worthwhile."

Dimitri sat up, gave his head a little shake to rid himself of the fogginess. "Narcise is going with you?"

"Yes." Woodmore looked at him, seemed ready to say something, then stopped. "We leave in the morning. I might not be back for Maia's wedding."

Maia's wedding. He'd been afraid, initially, that something would have happened to cancel it altogether, but Dimitri knew it had been rescheduled for two weeks from now. Not soon enough. But at least it was going forward. At least soon she would be out of his hands. Out of his reach.

"Does she know this?"

"No. That's part of what you owe me, Corvindale. You can deliver the news…and take my place, walking her down the aisle. Giving her away."

"I'll go to blasted Scotland, you stay here," Dimitri suggested.

Chas's response was a laugh as bitter as Dimitri's. "No, you'll stay here and make certain my sister is wed without a bloody damned hint of scandal. If you have to force Bradington down the aisle, if you have to enthrall all of the *ton,* you make certain it happens. That it's the happiest day of her life, damn you. You owe me, Corvindale. You broke my trust, you put your damned *vampire* hands on my sister when she was under your care. And your fangs. You're worse than Voss. You damned well owe me. If we didn't have a history, if I didn't owe *you,* you would be dead by now."

No one had ever spoken to Dimitri in that way and lived to tell about it. But this time, he allowed it. Because Chas had the right.

"I'll see to it. Gladly," he added. He couldn't wait to wash his hands of Maia Woodmore.

17

THE LION IS BEARDED
IN HIS DEN

Maia sat up, suddenly wide-awake.

She'd been dreaming. Or perhaps she hadn't.

The world was dark, for there was a new moon tonight and the stars were cloaked in clouds and fog. She could barely discern the shapes of her dressing table and the chair in the corner.

Lingering in her mind was a memory…a dream or reality, she wasn't certain… She was in a chamber furnished with great luxury. There were men there, and a woman who was tall and broad and sported a bit of a mustache. Although the place was richly appointed, Maia felt *wrong*. It was wrong. Horrible and evil.

She shook her head, trying to clear her mind, trying to focus. Hands grabbing at her, lascivious smiles, the clink of glasses as drinks were poured…Mr. Virgil was there. Smiling. Laughing heartily.

Her heart stopped. Mr. Virgil.

Maia got out of bed as if to escape the images, her heart pounding. She didn't like this. She didn't like this at all, the feelings crawling over her. The ugliness, dark memories that began to pour into her mind.

And then something changed in the memory…there was a burst of energy, something dark and fast. Glowing red eyes. Lashing out, violence, and suddenly she was caught up in it…

And then she was safe. Away from it. In a carriage. With Corvindale.

Maia stood there in her dark chamber, breathing hard. Her stomach hurt, her hair plastered to her neck and throat. Her face was stark, and as white as her night rail, reflecting back from the mirror in the dim light.

She needed answers.

"My lord, there is an individual without who wishes to speak with you."

Dimitri looked up from the bloody damned book Wayren had foisted upon him. Anything for an excuse to leave off reading about the beauty and her beastly host in a conveniently Gothic castle.

The fact that it was past midnight and someone had come calling bothered him not one bit, nor would it be a surprise to his butler Crewston. There was just as much activity at Blackmont Hall once the sun set as there was during the daylight hours.

Such was the lifestyle of a Dracule.

"Who is it?" he asked, rising from his desk.

"It is a female individual," Crewston explained. "She waits in a carriage. She asked that I give you this." He offered a handkerchief.

But Dimitri didn't need to take the scrap of fabric; he could scent her the moment his butler waved it. Lerina.

His flash of rage was instantly banked. She wouldn't trick him again, and he had no desire to waste any thought or energy on her. Yet, he was curious as to why she would chance encountering him again.

Instead of responding to Crewston, he pulled on his coat and slipped a slender wooden stake into the pocket. He suspected she was here on a peacemaking visit, but naturally there was no trusting the woman.

Outside in the late-summer heat, Dimitri sniffed the air as he walked down the three steps. Her carriage had been drawn up in the half-circle drive, only a few paces from the stairs. The air was humid and heavy with the perfume of mature roses and lilies, underscored by London's constant tinge of waste and garbage. The vehicle's door opened as he stepped down to the ground, but he went no farther.

"It's safe, my dear Dimitri," she said, peering out from the opening. "Not a ruby in sight."

"Pardon me if I don't trust your word on that," Dimitri replied. "I cannot imagine what you think you might have to talk to me about, but you must come out if you wish to do so."

"It was a misunderstanding, Dimitri darling," Lerina said as she emerged gracefully from the carriage, her hair and skirts tumbling prettily about her.

He paused, waiting to see if he sensed the proximity of a ruby or two. Or a dozen. He didn't, and he hadn't expected to. Nor did he scent anyone else in the area, other than her driver.

Lerina might not be the brightest of people, but she apparently had a great sense of self-preservation. And she knew him well—that, unless provoked, he wouldn't harm her.

"If that episode was a misunderstanding, I cannot imagine what you think the incident in Vienna was. A picnic? Let's not play games, Lerina. You tried to abduct me, you failed and now you are here…for what reason, precisely? You must know you won't have the advantage of tricking me again."

She pouted. "But I'm still in love with you, Dimitri."

"You have a unique way of showing it."

"I was a fool. I always have been."

"How gratifying to know that nothing has changed."

Her face tightened, losing that flirtatious expression for the first time since she'd arrived. "I had to take the chance to see you alone. The others who were with me are Cezar's makes. If they realized I was here…"

Dimitri was shaking his head. "No. Try again."

"Damn you, Dimitri."

He shrugged. "I'm afraid you're a bit late on that, too. Now what do you wa—"

A noise behind him had him turning. *Bloody damned Lucifer's soul.*

"Miss Woodmore," he said, with what he deemed great control. Great, immense, precise control.

She ducked her head and shoulders back inside the open window, where she quite probably had been eavesdropping, and seconds later the front door opened. There she stood, the proper Miss Woodmore, wearing nothing but a flimsy night rail. Her thick hair poured over her shoulders in dark waves, glinting gold in the weak circle of illumination from the streetlamp.

Dimitri paused for a moment to thank the Fates there

was no moonlight tonight to shine through the fabric as he struggled to keep his expression blank. "What are you doing?"

She'd stepped onto the top step and he noticed a slender implement in her hand, half hidden behind her and by the folds of her skirt. A stake? Did she mean to protect him? A wave of annoyance and fury battled with some other emotion that he dared not define. Addled woman.

"Mrs. Throckmullins," Miss Woodmore said as easily as if she'd just arrived for tea. "I should not have expected a social call from you, after our last meeting."

"Get back into the house, Miss Woodmore," Dimitri told her, glancing at Lerina. To his dismay, her face was rapt with attention.

"I was just leaving," Lerina said to the new arrival. Her eyes narrowed and her smile seemed forced. It was a cunning expression that didn't bode well, along with a spark of something dark. "I have everything that I came for."

Dimitri turned back toward Miss Woodmore, turning his furious glare on her. She ignored him and he stepped onto the lower stair in an effort to draw her attention to him, and away from Lerina. If the chit would see how angry he was, she'd listen and go back inside. "Miss Woodmore, you will catch your death of cold out here. Dressed in *that*," he added flatly, studiously ignoring the way one side of her bodice had slipped, revealing the curve of a delicious collarbone.

"There's not the least bit of a chill out here," she replied. The fact that her nipples were outlined by the light fabric put her statement into question.

"Miss Woodmore," he said in a low voice, his teeth clenched. "I don't know what you think you're doing with that, but your interference is unnecessary. And—"

He heard rustling behind him, then a faint creak. When he turned, it was to see Lerina's carriage door closing behind her. The vehicle lurched into motion and he watched it drive away, an unpleasant prickle running down his spine mingling with the throb from his Mark.

"In the house," he said, brushing past Miss Woodmore to open the door, wondering where in the damned bloody hell Crewston was, and what he was thinking, allowing her to come out dressed as she was.

He was only slightly mollified when his ward stepped into the house without further argument. Just then Iliana came rushing around the corner, long braid flying, stake in hand. Her bare feet slapped to a halt and she looked at Dimitri.

At once he realized what had happened and it was all he could do to keep from shouting at Miss Woodmore that he *didn't need to be bloody damn protected*. Lucifer's black soul, what had possessed her to think so?

Iliana took one look at his face and pivoted away, prudently heading back from whence she'd come.

This left Dimitri alone with his ward, for apparently, Crewston had other things to do. Or, more likely, he was lurking somewhere, had seen the fury on his master's face and decided to remain out of eyesight.

"I need to speak with you, Corvindale," Miss Woodmore said coolly. She was still holding the stake.

Here, inside the house, he wasn't quite as fortunate. For the lamps lighting the front hall and the small sconce on the corridor provided a spill of soft, warm illumination around, and through, her night rail.

Before he could respond, she turned and flounced down the corridor to his sanctuary. His study. Dimitri looked away, grinding his teeth as he followed her— *he* followed *her*—into *his* den. He had a few things he should say to her, as well.

But when he came into the chamber and closed the door behind him, Dimitri had a sudden attack of wariness. His palms actually began to dampen. For the bloody Fates, he hadn't had sweaty palms since he was standing for his first Latin exam at Cambridge.

What was it about this woman who needled him to no end?

"Incidentally, you were wrong, Corvindale," she was saying. She'd positioned herself at the far end of the room, where two chairs faced the center with a small table between them. The window whose curtains she had the temerity to open every bloody time she came in was next to one of the seats. The chamber was suffused with her scent, that of slumber and spice and fresh cotton and whatever she used to clean her hair.

He forced himself to wander casually to the cabinet where he kept his French brandy and Scotch whiskey. Since the night last week when he'd downed two full bottles of blood whiskey, he hadn't indulged. But tonight he thought he might be able to justify at least a finger or two of the best vintage, especially since he'd made certain he hadn't been face-to-face with her since the events at Rubey's. He hadn't seen more than the flutter of her hem around a corner since he'd tucked her into the carriage for the ride home.

"I? Wrong?" He sipped the golden liquid and realized his heart was slamming in his chest. His insides were tight. What in the bloody damned hell was wrong with him?

"You said she'd tried to abduct you and failed. That isn't precisely true, is it? Mrs. Throckmullins—Lerina—did succeed in abducting you. And if I hadn't shown up, who knows what would have happened?"

His fingers tightened over the glass. What did she want, honors and an audience at court in appreciation? "As I understand it, you didn't exactly show up. You were abducted, as well."

"That is quite true," she replied. "But I managed to free myself. Although I do understand there were extenuating circumstances on your part."

Dimitri struggled to keep his voice steady. "Indeed. I suppose I have been remiss in expressing my gratitude for your...assistance."

Surprisingly, forcing those words out didn't have the debilitating affect he'd expected for himself. Instead, when he saw the flash of surprise and the hint of rose flushing her cheeks, he felt rather...pleased. He took another generous taste of whiskey.

"Thank you," she said, her voice soft and without that edge so often there. "We were... We worked together."

He looked aside, trying to regain the annoyance and frustration that had begun to slip away. "What did you think you were doing tonight, Miss Woodmore? Did you really believe you and that little stake would have had a chance against Lerina if she had been a threat?"

She'd begun to straighten a pile of books on one of the tables. "In my mind," she said, pulling out a French translation of *The Iliad* and placing it atop its counter-part, *The Odyssey,* "it never hurts to be prepared. One never knows when one might be caught unawares."

"I'm never—" He stopped abruptly.

She looked up at him and their eyes met. And held. Something hurt, in his chest, something sharp and hot as if he'd been stabbed. Or staked. Yet, while unexpected, it wasn't wholly unpleasant.

Her lips twitched, that full, luscious upper one curving into a hint of a smile. "Is it possible you're learning, Corvindale? That you aren't always right?"

"What do you want, Maia?" He forced steel into his voice, forced his expression into stone. His heart rammed hard inside.

Her face changed, the affection fleeing. "That night with Mr. Virgil," she said, "the Incident…I had a dream about it tonight. About things I don't remember happening. The whole night, almost, is blank in my mind."

Dimitri raised a brow. "That's not unusual for a traumatic situation, Miss Woodmore. People often forget what happened to them."

"Yes, and sometimes with a bit of help from a vampire and his thrall. Is that what happened? Did you alter my memory?"

"What makes you think I'm capable of such a thing?" he prevaricated. His glass was empty and he put it on the cabinet. He had a feeling he was going to need all of his faculties. "And if so, why would I do that?"

"Don't be absurd. You know you are. You've attempted it. You said I've *become* immune to your thrall. Did you manage to do it that night?"

"It was best that way."

"What happened?"

What didn't happen? Dimitri drew in a deep breath. "Your Mr. Virgil wasn't taking you to Gretna Green for your elopement. He was taking you to an establishment in Haymarket that…well, Miss Woodmore, if you found yourself offended by Rubey's place, you would have been beyond frightened at this place. A marketplace of sorts for young, virginal women. You wouldn't have been able to leave."

He watched the disbelief and then horror filter over her delicate features. She'd stopped rearranging his books and now stood as if frozen. "And then what happened?"

"I followed you when I recognized you. Of course, your brother had pointed you and your sister out to me in the past." And the impression she'd made on Dimitri had been strong and unforgettable, even then. Even from a distance. Especially when he passed by and breathed in the perfume that was her. "I was able to extricate you from the woman who owned the…establishment…with little fanfare. Then I saw that you were taken safely home in a hack."

"Did she have a mustache?" she whispered, and he nodded in response. "I dreamed of her."

The hypnotism was weakening; which was no surprise, as he'd been unable to inflict it upon her recently. Something had happened since that night in Haymarket that made her immune to his thrall. *His* thrall. He felt a little uncomfortable niggle in the back of his mind when he recalled Voss telling him that he couldn't enthrall Angelica, either. Was it something about the Woodmore sisters that made them indifferent to a Draculian thrall?

But no, for Lerina had managed to ensnare Maia when they were trapped. He didn't understand it.

Maia was talking slowly, pulling things out of her memory. "I have a recollection…in the hack. We… You were there. You had a cut on your cheek, and one on your hand—I remember now. You weren't wearing gloves."

He held back a snort. "Even in the midst of such a harrowing experience, whilst you were clothed in boy breeches and a cap, you commented on my lack of gloves with your nose in the air. And a little sniff of disdain."

"I did not." She gave that same little sniff, lifting her pert nose.

He found himself hardly able to keep a smile in check and raised his brow instead.

"I… We were discussing herbal poultices for your cuts," she said slowly, as if unraveling the memory like a thread. "You were promoting the benefits of dried woad."

"You were under the impression that Dioscorides's recipe for slippery elm and comfrey was the best treatment. I confess, I was amazed to learn that you were not only familiar with his writings, but that you'd read them in their native Greek. And so I commenced with a discussion to see if it was possible."

"You," she said, the corners of her mouth tipping up a bit again, "were singing the praises of John Gerard, simply because he was a native Englishman."

"Aside of the fact that he was a friend of my father's, the benefit of having a medicinal written only about plants native to the local soil, my dear Miss Woodmore, is much more efficacious than one written by an ancient. There is always the problem of translation."

"Not if one does the translation oneself," she reminded him. "As I did."

"That was precisely what you said that evening."

Their eyes met and he saw the clarity back in hers. She remembered it all now.

He'd never forgotten it.

He'd almost kissed her that night. Secure in the fact that he could mottle her mind and twist her memory, he'd nearly given in to the sudden, inexplicable urge. And now he was thankful, so very thankful, that he hadn't done so.

Because he would never be able to explain that.

All at once, a rush of desire flooded him. He stood halfway across the long chamber from her, and all he could think about was what was beneath that loose, flimsy night rail.

Dimitri turned away, his fingers trembling, his gums suddenly tight and swelling. There was an odd ache in his middle.

"Has it occurred to you," she said suddenly, "that I might be with child?"

Had it occurred to him? Oh, yes, oh, yes, indeed. By the Fates, by God, by Luce's black heart, it had occurred to him.

"I pray you are not," he managed to say. He'd been so careful over the years, for any child he sired could also be bound to Lucifer because of the agreement Vlad Tepes had made with the devil. It was inconceivable that he would visit such a burden on his child. It was a good thing he'd never had a great sexual appetite.

He looked away from Maia. Until now.

"I'm not," she said softly.

Relief rushed over him so strongly he nearly sighed aloud. *Thank God, thank God.* "Thank you for telling me."

"I couldn't marry Alexander until I knew for certain."

"I'm certain he'll appreciate that." The words came from between stiff lips. "Are you finished, Miss Woodmore? I have things to attend to." He gestured vaguely to his desk.

She straightened, pulling her shoulders back and outlining her breasts even more readily. Dimitri studied his hand. His fingers weren't quite steady.

"Yes. Thank you for your time," she said. There was more than a bit of sarcasm in her tone, but he ignored it.

He must ignore her as she walked past him toward the door, taking with her that thick, sweet-smelling hair, those delicate feet and slender wrists, those full, erotic lips.

"La Belle et la Bête?" she asked, pausing at his desk.

Leave. By all that is holy, by all that is damned, please leave.

"It's a French fairy tale," he said, forcing boredom into his voice.

"I'm familiar with it. This version, in fact." She glanced at him. "How do you find it?"

"I haven't finished it yet," he growled. "Which I might perhaps be able to do if you'd leave me be."

She looked up at him, quite close now as she skirted the desk, and he could hardly meet her eyes. He struggled to keep his breathing steady, to keep the pounding of his heart inaudible as it reverberated his torso. His fangs threatened and he pressed his lips together because all he could think of was how close she was. How much he wanted to touch her. And of course, how he could not. Ever. Again.

To slide his hands over that ivory skin, to gather her against him and bury his face in her hair, to cover that impudent mouth that alternately argued and smiled and lectured and challenged.

He turned his attention to the ever-present throbbing on his shoulder, focusing on the pain there. It didn't seem to be as harsh as it used to be…or perhaps he was becoming even more inured to it.

"Is everything all right, Corvindale?" she asked. Her night rail billowed out enough that it nearly brushed the tops of his boots. Her essence filled his nose.

"Other than the fact that you're disturbing my studies, yes, of course," he replied and managed to step back without appearing to retreat.

"Very well, then," she said. "Good night."

She left.

Maia fled to her chamber.

Her stomach was in an upheaval, swirling and pitching like a ship in a storm.

She'd thought for a moment that he was going to… do something. Reach for her. Touch her. Ask her to stay.

Tell her not to marry Alexander.

But he'd been the same cold, harsh Corvindale.

She sat on her bed. Perhaps not quite the same. There had been those moments of softness. She hadn't imagined them.

Had she?

Flopping back onto her bed, she looked up into the darkness, misery welling up inside her. Emptiness filled her chest, making it hollow and cold.

She closed her eyes at the sting of tears. Foolish, addled woman.

That was she. Foolish. Addled. In love with a cold, hard man. The wrong man.

Foolish...

Maia must have slept, for she dreamed.

He was there in her dreams again, but this time she recognized him. The wide, strong hands, the dark hair, the smooth sensual brush of lips, the flash of fangs as they slid easily into her shoulder.

For the second time that night, she woke suddenly, heart pounding, breathless.

Her dreams were so *real*. Her body was damp and alive, throbbing and tight...but she was alone.

Maia sat up. All at once she remembered the dream she'd had when Corvindale was gone, the dark, frightening one. The dream that must have been...could it have been...what he was experiencing? At the hands of Mrs. Throckmullins?

Did that mean that...

She swallowed hard, heat rushing through her. Could that mean that, just now, he was dreaming the same thing that she had been?

Heart thumping madly, hardly realizing what she was doing, Maia slid off the high bed to the floor. She glanced at the window to see a faint glow in the distance, out over the rooftops. Dawn was near. Her feet made no noise on the wood planks as she went to the door and opened it.

If he were dreaming what she was dreaming...

Her fingers closed around the doorknob and she hesitated. Her knees trembled. She knew what she wanted to do. What she was about to do...but would it make any difference? Would it not only cause deeper problems?

But as she stood there in the shadows, half in the corridor, half in her chamber, she realized that she stood on a different threshold.

If she went back to bed, she would remain Maia Woodmore, soon to be Mrs. Bradington, peer of the *ton,* the epitome of propriety and gentility. She'd marry Alexander and they would be happy together, they would have children, God willing, and she would have a very even, calm, *proper* life. And she would never forget the Earl of Corvindale.

And if she didn't go back to bed... Her insides filled with butterflies, and for a moment she almost swooned with fear and apprehension...and hope.

If she didn't go back to bed...anything could happen.

Good or bad.

Loving or hurtful.

Maia closed her eyes, struggled and made her decision, closing the door softly.

18

WHEREIN ALL IS LAID BARE

Dimitri woke to find himself hard, hot, damp and tangled in the bedcovers. His fangs were fully extended, his body swollen with need. The Mark on his shoulder shuttled pain through his limbs, but even that deep agony wasn't enough to chase the potent dreams from his thoughts.

All at once, he realized his chamber door was ajar. *Opening.* That was what had awakened him from the dream.

He smelled her.

Satan's stones. Dimitri froze, holding his breath, pulling himself out of the sleek, hot dream with great effort.

He dared not move. He could hardly think as she slipped into the chamber and closed the door behind her. His heart pounded, filling his ears, and in his mind he kept thinking, *no, no, no, no.*

Yet his body raged and beckoned.

If it had been anyone else disturbing him, he could

have bellowed and ordered them out. Or even leaped
from the bed to show them the door.

But he was paralyzed.

She stopped next to the bed, and he looked up at her
in the dark, able to see the details of her face, even the
curl of a lock of hair over the white night rail.

"Maia," he managed to say. "What are you doing
here?" *Get out.*

Her eyes found his in the dim light. He saw her draw
in a deep breath and bite her lower lip. "I'm not certain," she replied.

"Then leave. Now." His breathing had become unsteady and he gripped the bedcoverings, curling his
fingers into them, forcing his body to remain still. Like
stone.

"I'm going to call off the wedding." She was close
enough that her gown brushed the side of his bed. His
hand, wrapped in a sheet, rested on the edge right next
to it.

He forced himself to remain rigid. Tight.

"That would be outside of foolish," he said, his voice
harsh and grating even to his own ears. "Maia. What
are you doing?"

"I'm here," she said, shifting. The warm cotton gown
brushed the back of his wrist and Dimitri's fingers released the crumpled bedcoverings all on their own.

"Here?" He forced an edge of disdain into his tone.
"Whatever for?"

She shook her head as if to clear it, her eyes steady
on him, as if to somehow read the lie there, even in
the dark.

And then she touched him. Her fingers, settling gently on his bare wrist next to the edge of the mattress, released him from his paralysis. He was done.

His arm lurched, moving before his conscious thought, and his hand whipped out, dragging her onto the bed. His other hand moved around to slide fingers into her hair, guiding her lush warmth down onto him. *Yes.*

Maia didn't pull back, didn't resist. If she had, he'd have released her immediately. But, foolishly, she came willingly, sliding onto the bed, her knees pinning her blousy night rail to the mattress before she collapsed next to him, tangled in the soft cotton.

Dimitri was aware of a rushing sound in his ears, of a warning voice in his head, but it was too late. He had her. In his arms, wrapping Maia in the warmth of his body and the tangled bedclothes, their flesh separated only by a flimsy gown. Wild need surged through him, and he ignored all of the reasons he should send her away.

Taking care not to cut her with his fangs, he covered her mouth with his, drinking desperately from the corners of her lips, sliding over and across them, nibbling and sucking as she shifted against him, her mouth hot and teasing in a slick, sensual kiss, her breasts rounding against his chest.

He gathered her close, imprinting her body against his, capturing her against him with one bent leg and his hands, sliding along her slender back, pulling her onto him, into him, close. She burned him.

His breathing was out of control, his body tight and throbbing, his fangs jutting so far that his mouth hurt.

"Maia," he managed to say, focusing on the sudden

sharp pain from his Mark. Ah, that was it. If the pain became worse, then Luce was unhappy with his actions. And right now, now that he'd stopped, now that he was set to do the right thing, to send her away, the pain was white-hot, blasting and searing down his side and around by his left hip. An incentive for him to change his mind. "This is your last chance. Leave now."

Perhaps her eyes had adjusted to the dim light, for she focused on him, met his gaze. "I'm not going to leave," she said. "Unless you truly do not want me."

Even then, he couldn't do it. He couldn't send her away.

"Very well," he said in a harsh voice, horribly aware that his Mark eased. That Lucifer approved. "I will give you nothing, Maia. Do you understand? This is nothing more than me, taking what you offer."

"Is that not how it's always been?" she replied.

"You must wed Bradington," he said, grasping the front of her gown as he twisted around, shoving her back onto the bed, curving over her, pinning her down with the weight of his hips. "I can give you nothing else," he said again. "Nothing. And wedding him will save you."

"I make no promises," she replied.

"Nor do I." And, his patience gone, his goodwill trampled, he shoved his conscience away. She'd come to him. He'd warned her off. He grabbed her gown with his other hand and yanked, renting it down the middle with a loud, violent tear that made her slender body jerk.

With a little more care, but no lesser intent, he whipped the cloth away and bent to her again, covering her mouth with his. She reached up and slid her arms around him, pulling him down so that they were skin to skin, her soft, pale and silky curves rising up into his hard, hirsute body. So warm. Her long hair caught beneath them, and he tugged it away, threading his fingers in and around it.

He buried his face in her neck, tasting the hot, sensitive skin there, his lips tracing the curve of her shoulder as he struggled to keep from sinking his fangs deep. The need pounded in him, in his swollen gums and thrusting teeth, through his veins, in his cock, tight and raging against her thigh. Maia shuddered and sighed as he sucked hard on the delicate rise of her shoulder, still fighting to keep from sinking deep and drinking of her.

Dimitri moved to her breast, covering the taut rise of nipple with his mouth, sliding his tongue around the sensitive little tip. She dug her fingers into his hair, arching closer as he licked and gently sucked, his fangs gently surrounding the areola, brushing her skin with their tips. One little nick... She exuded heat, and the musky, sweet scent of desire filled his nostrils as she writhed and moaned against him.

He slid his hand down between her legs, finding her slick and swollen. She shifted against him, lifting up into his palm, and he pressed down into her, trembling a little at her passionate response. Sliding a finger inside, into the tight heat, Dimitri shifted as he teased and slid in and out and around, releasing her lush musky scent, turning his vision red and cloudy. Desire pounded in him and his gums throbbed, his cock shifting insistently next to her. Maia gasped something, reaching out blindly, her hands pulling at his shoulder, drawing him close.

He could wait no longer. Dimitri moved quickly and

decisively, rising back up to rear over her slender white body and sliding his leg between hers. She curled her fingers around his shoulders, pulling him down as he fitted himself inside her. Maia's gasp was swallowed by the roaring in his ears as he slid in, deep, filling. His muscles shuddered with the effort of control…she was sleek and tight and he found his face buried once again in her throat as he moved rhythmically: away, then closer, away…closer. Hot, damp, smelling of her, that sensitive, erotic spot…

It was too much to resist. His fangs brushed her skin and as he slammed deep between her legs, he bit into the warm, silky skin at the juncture of neck and shoulder, the points of his teeth sliding in with ease. She jolted and gave a soft cry, shuddering, but he was too intent, and he held her steady as the warm flow of lifeblood rushed into his mouth. The pleasure was heavy, the taste of rich, lush earth and life laced with Maia's own particular essence, filling his senses, over his tongue, down into his body.

There was no holding back, no waiting. His world turned into a frenzy of pleasure, rising uncontrollably. His veins sang, swelled, his body slid against hers. Dimitri was vaguely aware of her nails scoring into his back, her head twisting and rolling on the pillow as he drank, as he thrust in and out, driving closer and longer until he could no longer think.

The explosion, when it came, was white-hot and red, draining him of awareness. He barely remembered to pull free of that hot, sleek place just before his seed spilled, twisting his hips away as he released her neck. Heavy, warm blood still in his mouth, he gave a soft groan of release as he pulsed and throbbed, damp and warm. He swallowed the last bit and closed his eyes.

Maia gave a soft whimper next to him, bringing him back from the easy slide into darkness, and he rose up to look over her. Her eyes were dark in a pale face, her lips parted, her breathing unsteady. She didn't seem frightened or overset by his roughness. She beckoned.

Dimitri bent to her shoulder and tasted the leaking blood with his lips and tongue, gently licking it away, swirling the last bit into his mouth to stop the bleeding. At the same time, he reached down between them to slide over her quim, full and damp and still ready for him.

With a little nibble of apology along the tendon in her neck, he found the tiny core and as he shifted to cover her mouth, he slipped and stroked, luring her over into the same vortex of pleasure he'd recently enjoyed. His mouth stifled her soft cry of release and he felt her shudder against him.

Dimitri finished the kiss with a soft little nibble on that top, full lip, then collapsed onto his back, still wrapped in sheets and legs and her long hair.

He didn't know how long they lay there, tangled and close, for he slipped into something between sleep and wakefulness, comforted by the slight, warm figure next to him, the sensuous smells of their coupling and her.

Something distant must have awakened Dimitri, for it drew him from that half slumber and into the wakefulness of reality. The first thing he saw was a blood streak on the sheets, and then the small marks on her slender, ivory neck. The scent of coitus stained his fingers and the bedcoverings, the little flutter behind her eyelids told him she was dreaming.

Maia was curled up amid white sheets and his dark body, her hair cascading over the bedsheets and pillows. A soft, delicate snore was coming from her parted lips. Something started to turn inside him, rolling and opening, and he stopped it.

He stopped it cold, pulling that brick wall back around to bar those soft feelings.

Oh, what he'd done. Dimitri closed his eyes as uncertainty and anger flooded him. After so many years of denial, he'd succumbed easily and thoroughly in the past weeks. Bitterness tinged his mouth as his heart thumped an erratic, accusatory beat. He'd warned her, yes, he'd told her to leave, but he knew better.

It was never that easy with a woman. Never that simple. And the tender, unfurling feelings in his belly were guilt and pleasure wrapped into one. Emotions that he must learn to do without.

He heard rapid footfalls coming down the corridor, and then there was an urgent knocking at the chamber door.

"My lord!" The knock became more urgent.

"One minute," he growled at the door.

"Please, my lord, it's an urgent matter!"

Dimitri glanced down at Maia, who was now stirring. He clapped a hand over her mouth just as her eyes bolted open in shock and dismay.

He put a finger to his lips and then yanked the bedclothes up to cover her. "What is it?" he bellowed. "Come in."

"It's the elder Miss Woodmore," said Crewston, poking his head around the open door. A single shaft of day-light spilled into the dark chamber from behind him. "She's gone missing!"

Dimitri felt her go rigid beneath the sheets. He pressed his hand down on top of her to keep her still, glad that Crewston was mortal and unable to scent the strong essence of coitus that lingered in the chamber. "Nonsense. She's likely gone for a walk or shopping this early in the day."

"I don't know about that, my lord, but her Mr. Bradington is below, claiming she agreed to walk with him this morning. Surely she wouldn't have left before he arrived."

"Tell Bradington—" Dimitri barely managed to keep a snarl from his voice "—that she had an emergency with her wedding frock and had to visit the seamstress this morning, and that she will return shortly. And send him on his way, if you please."

"But my—"

"Crewston."

"Very well, my lord. But the younger Miss Woodmore is beside herself with fear that Miss Woodmore has been abducted again."

"Advise Angelica that I am confident her elder sister will return shortly. And I don't wish to be bothered for any reason until she returns, or until after dinner. Whichever occurs first."

"Yes, my lord." Crewston withdrew, his disbelief and annoyance barely masked.

No sooner had the door clicked closed than Maia erupted from beneath the sheets, holding them to the front of her torso. She opened her mouth, likely to begin barraging him with questions or recriminations, and Dimitri decided to take the bull by the horns, so to speak, and launch his own attack first.

"Are you aware that you snore, Miss Woodmore?" he asked in a mild voice.

She drew back, a glint of fierceness in her eyes, and closed her mouth. The sheets were a bunch against her chest, revealing only the barest curve of one shoulder. "Why, I—"

"It didn't bother me, but if you decide to share a bed-chamber with Bradington, it might become a concern."

Her lips tightened and she replied in a low-pitched voice, "Don't be a fool, Corvindale. Do you think I don't know what you're doing? Trying to divert me, trying to anger me? Or hurt me so that I go running off to Alexander?"

He closed his mouth and blinked. Her intelligence and foresight never failed to surprise him.

"I know better than that, Corvindale. I know you better than you realize," she said, lowering her voice still further, watching him steadily. "And you've lost the power to hurt me like you might wish to, because I know why you do it."

He'd become very still. "Is that so?" was all he trusted himself to say.

"You're just like the beast from that fairy tale, locked away, cold and angry and afraid to allow anyone close to you, or to divert you from your research. But you've missed everything that's important. And this," she said, spreading her hand to encompass the events of the last night, "is…was…a bit too close for you. I'm sorry for that."

"Miss Woodmore," he said, barely holding on to the fury he managed to dredge up, just able to keep the truth of her words from penetrating, "you have no idea of what you speak. The only thing I care about," he said, his lips and jaw tight, "is freeing myself of this."

He turned sharply so that she could see the back of his left shoulder.

Maia's sudden intake of breath was audible and he felt her body still next to him. "My God."

Dimitri knew what she saw: the horrible Marking of the devil spreading down like black roots over his shoulder. When he'd first awakened to find himself signed thus, the lines had been narrow, like fine cracks in shattered glass. But over the years of his abstinence, his disregard for Lucifer's will, the lines had grown thicker and darker as they welled with pain. Now they rose from his skin like slender black-red veins, writhing and twisting with agony, pounding and pulsing with his every defiance of the devil.

"This is the Mark of my covenant with Lucifer," he said, keeping his voice steely. "I'm damned, Maia, damned and tied to him, and because of that, I cannot— I don't *want*—anything or anyone in my life. I want to be left alone. I want to be *free*."

She hadn't taken her eyes from his shoulder, and when she reached to touch him, Dimitri moved away.

"Now," he said, taking control of his voice, changing it from the desperate tones of a moment ago to one matter-of-fact and calm, "this is what will happen. You're going to leave here, Maia, you're going to go to your chamber and dress and pretend you were on a walk and forgot your appointment with Bradington.

And you're going to marry him as planned. And you're going to forget about all of this."

"I can't do that, my lord," she said, surprising him with the formal use of address.

"You must. There is nothing I can do for you, nor that I want to do. I've allowed you to invade my house, my den and now my bedchamber—" she tensed at that comment, and, gratified that it had hit the mark, he went on "—but I'm finished now. Lerina's visit last night has me concerned that she has some other plans. And I've done everything I can to ensure that you wed Bradington without a hint of scandal. That is all I can do for you."

Her mouth had tightened. "I cannot do that, Corvindale. Did you not hear me?"

"Yes, you—"

"I cannot, Corvindale," she interrupted in a stiff voice, "because, much as I desire to leave your vile presence, I cannot walk from one end of your house to my chamber in the other dressed like *this*." She flung the bedcoverings away from her naked torso.

Lord. He caught his breath before he realized it, then looked away. But the image was burned into his brain, the delicate shape of her body, the shadow of her collarbones, the high handfuls of breasts tipped with tight pink nipples, the hollow of her waist and curve of hips, and the peek of a slender white thigh. *Remember it.*

"Very well," he said in a strangled voice. "I'll arrange it for you, Miss Woodmore."

She was shaking her head, her full lips flat and mutinous. "I will return to my chamber, but I don't see how I can marry Alexander when I'm in love with you."

He stilled as something sharp darted through his gut.

"You're even more foolish than I thought if you believe that, Miss Woodmore."

"That is one thing I believe we must agree on, my lord. I am foolish."

"And regardless of what you might think you feel, Miss Woodmore," he said, "love has nothing to do with whether you wed Bradington or not. Is it not all about the match? The income, the family, the title? Whatever you might think you feel has no bearing on your reputation or your marriage."

Something glinted in her eyes and he thought for a startled moment that his feisty Miss Woodmore might be tearing up. But she blinked and the shininess was gone.

"Nevertheless," she said, "I will tell him the truth. And either he'll wish to go forward with the wedding, knowing that not only do I not love him, but I don't come to him untouched, or he'll drop me and our engagement will be broken."

"There will be a scandal," he said, despite the fact that he would *ensure* that Bradington didn't drop her. "Your reputation will be ruined."

"Please refrain from stating the obvious, Lord Corvindale," she said in a parody of an admonishment he'd once given her. "I'm willing to risk it. I will not live a lie with Alexander. He needs to know the truth. And that is why I felt compelled to tell you the truth of how I feel, even though I knew precisely how you would react."

"You don't understand, Maia," he said, keeping his voice cold so that it wouldn't break. "I'm immortal. I live forever. And when I die...I belong to the devil. I belong to him even now. I have nothing to give. That," he added nastily, thinking of Wayren and her stories, "is what makes me different from the fairy-tale beast. I own nothing of myself. I have *nothing to give.*"

19

OF IRONY, UMBRELLAS
AND INFERNOS

After his icy pronouncement, Corvindale swept out of the chamber into his adjoining dressing and bathing room, leaving Maia sitting alone on the bed. Numb.

Moments later, she heard the door open onto the hall from that room, and then shortly after that, he returned, stalking into the bedchamber, his hands filled with garments. He was dressed simply in an untucked shirt and trousers.

"I suppose you'll need assistance dressing," he said, placing the clothing on the bed with surprising gentleness. She'd expected him to throw them.

"No," she said, snatching up a chemise. She refused to ask how he'd obtained the garments. It was impossible to imagine that the earl would have gone into her chamber and dug through her wardrobe and drawers. "I don't need your assistance."

The chemise floated down over her shoulders and hips. Maia disdained the corset and drawers and pulled on the simple day dress he'd provided. Fortunately the empire-waist style allowed for her to go temporarily without the corset. She would thus be able to return to her chamber and then get properly dressed with Betty's help, appearing as if she had just returned from a walk if anyone encountered her in the meanwhile.

Then she could go down and have a difficult conversation with Alexander.

After she found a way to cover her vampire bites.

Once his grudging assistance was refused, Corvindale turned away and stood in front of a curtained window, his back to her, while she finished dressing.

As she did so, Maia reflected on the amazing fact that she was in the earl's bedchamber, alone with him and dressing after spending several hours wrapped in his arms. Naked. And now he would hardly acknowledge her presence. They'd talked so coolly and calmly about everything that had happened, as if it were a story that had unfolded on the pages of a book instead of *to* them. In real life.

Looking at the bedraggled mattress, she gave a little shudder of remembered pleasure tinged with regret. She would never forget the feeling, tumbling onto his nude body, warm and hard, rough with wiry hair and firm with planes of muscle, his arms closing around her. His mouth taking from hers.

She belonged there.

"The only time I loved a woman," he said suddenly, still turned away, "I gave everything for her. My heart. My life. And, quite literally, my soul."

Maia's movements were arrested as she bent to pick up the unused bundle of clothing. Her heart thumped. She had so many questions. "Lerina?"

"God and the Fates, no. Do you think I'm completely mad? Her name was Meg. It was because of her that I… that I am what I am today."

"You made a pact with the devil for her?"

He nodded, fingering the heavy drapes that still cloaked the window. "I thought I was saving her life. Our lives."

"What happened?" Maia asked, imagining that she'd died of old age in his arms as he remained forever young.

"She left."

Oh. "I'm sorry."

"I was, too."

Something soft swelled in her chest and it was all Maia could do not to reach for him. Even with his back to her, she could see the tension in his shoulders. She imagined she could make out the black lines of the horrible marking on his skin, the writhing black veins as thick as rose stems, through the cotton of his shirt.

"Did you love Lerina, too?"

"I've loved no one since."

Maia swallowed. *Including me.* "I'm sorry for that, too, Corvindale." She held the bundle of clothing to her chest and paused.

He shifted as if he meant to turn, then stopped suddenly and remained with his back to her, his fingers curling around the edge of the curtains. "You're aware that my given name is Dimitri."

"Yes. I see no reason to use that appellation," she said stiffly. Lerina had, calling him "darling Dimitri" with such a false, sugary tone that Maia had felt ill. Aside of that, they weren't intimates. Not any longer.

"I wasn't suggesting that you do, Miss Woodmore." His voice softened a bit as he continued. "My mother was a Romanian princess who married my father the earl, and she named me Dimitri Gavril. She called me Gavril."

Maia's lips twisted, for she understood why he'd told her. "Gavril, or the Greek, Gabriel. I believe it translates as 'man of God.'"

As she looked at his dark head, held high, his shoulders broad and straight, and the hint of the black markings of the devil beneath his white shirt, she knew the irony must be that much more bitter to him.

"If you please, advise Mr. Bradington that Miss Woodmore is here to speak with him," Maia said to Alexander's butler, Driggs, as he took her umbrella.

"The master has been indisposed since last evening, miss," Driggs told her gravely. "I shall attempt to rouse him."

She swallowed her nervousness as Driggs gestured for her to wait in the small, private parlor. Alexander had left Blackmont Hall the morning after the "mix-up" with their appointment to go for a walk. And he hadn't returned that afternoon, nor the day after.

The fact that he hadn't done so left an uncomfortable feeling in the pit of Maia's being, and now today, when she finished dressing, eating as much dinner as she could stomach—which was to say, not very much at all—she decided to take matters into her own hands and call on him directly.

Calling on a gentleman wasn't done, unless one were chaperoned, but in the case of one's fiancé, it was much more permissible. Still, Maia didn't particularly want to be noticed and so she was grateful for the heavy rain and dark clouds that gave her an excuse to hide under an obstructing umbrella as she hurried up the short walk to his front door. For that same reason, she'd ordered a hackney instead of taking one of Corvindale's carriages. And, conscious of the warnings of both Dewhurst and Corvindale, she'd left Blackmont Hall through the back, servants' entrance, well-cloaked and hidden under a hood. Anyone waiting for an opportunity to abduct her not only wouldn't see her leave, but if they did, she would be assumed to be a maid or other servant.

Now inside, listening to the pouring rain, she adjusted her skirts neatly across her knees. They were weighted by their damp hem, which just skimmed the tops of her water-speckled slippers. They'd be ruined, but the state of her shoes was the least of her worries.

How was she going to tell Alexander? *What* was she going to tell him?

Did he suspect something, and that was why he was indisposed? No, certainly not. How could he suspect anything?

He must simply be unwell, which explained why he wouldn't have come to call. Poor Alexander, always the gentleman. Likely attempting to keep her from getting his sickness. Perhaps… She hoped he wasn't ill over worry for her. That would be simply too much for her to bear.

The parlor door opened suddenly, and Maia jumped at the unexpected noise.

"Alexander," she said, calming her nervous heart and

rising promptly to her feet. She scanned him closely, looking for signs that he had been ill or sleepless.

"Maia," he replied, smiling at her. He didn't appear to be unwell, his Scottish heritage showing in a handsome face shaven and faintly ruddy as it always was. His gray-blue eyes scanned her with appreciation and his chestnut-colored hair and sideburns were combed and pomaded as if he'd dressed for her. "I am so delighted to see you. I meant to call on you today, but I'm afraid I must keep an appointment this afternoon. Perhaps you would join me, and we could talk in the carriage? I believe we have much to catch up on."

"Yes," she replied, feeling a bit off center, as if nothing had happened. Perhaps, in his mind, nothing had.

In his mind. A very cold feeling settled over her. *Corvindale.* Had he come and persuaded Alexander that nothing was amiss? Had he enthralled her fiancé to force him into marrying her, regardless of what she told him?

Could he even do that?

Maia firmed her lips. She would have to have a word with the earl. Again.

"Very well, then, my dear," he said, offering her his arm as he opened a large umbrella. "I promise our appointment won't take long at all."

He held the covering up and over as they fairly ran through the downpour to his waiting carriage. The rain came down so hard that it splashed up and under the umbrella, soaking the bottom third of her frock.

"There's something I must tell you," Maia said, gathering up her bravery as well as her heavy skirts as she settled into the carriage across from him. She was breathing heavily from the short dash. "There's something we must talk about."

Even if Corvindale had been here, or somehow talked to Alexander, she would still tell him what she needed to tell him, and deal with the earl later.

"I have things to talk with you about, too," Alexander said as he latched the door and knocked on the roof of the vehicle. "Things have changed."

That was when she realized something was wrong. It was the way he said it, the way he was looking at her. There was an odd note in his voice, a strange inflection that sent a prickling along the backs of her arms.

"What do you mean?" she managed to say as the carriage lurched off speedily.

He smiled at her, displaying a gleaming white set of fangs.

Maia barely stifled a shriek. "Are those real?" she asked, trying to keep her voice—and her mind—steady. Impossible. Her mind tried to scatter, but she forced herself to focus. This was not the time to panic.

In response, he settled eyes on her that glowed red. "Why do you not come here and find out?" He leered, patting the seat next to him.

"Alexander! How did this occur? What happened?" Her heart was a runaway in her chest, her palms damp beneath her gloves, but she remembered to keep her gaze averted.

"I had a visitor on the day you forgot about our engagement to take a morning walk. It was all very odd, for she asked me to come for a drive in her carriage, that you wanted to meet clandestinely."

"Mrs. Throckmullins. Lerina," Maia said, her heart sinking.

Alexander nodded, a funny smile twitching the corners of his mouth. "Yes, indeed. It didn't take me long to realize that she wasn't taking me to meet you, but that she had another plan in mind. She's quite annoyed with Corvindale, and as it turned out, I wasn't at all averse to her suggestion that I join her race. It was either that, or she was to kill me. When confronted with immortality or death, I didn't find it a difficult choice."

"But you...you've given your soul to the devil," she said. "You chose the certainty of being damned for eternity."

"But I shall live forever," he said. "And in the care of Lucifer. Thus that event will never come."

Maia shook her head. "Alexander, no, you—"

"Enough of that." He moved, suddenly shifting to the other side of the carriage next to her. "I see that you've already been introduced to the particular pleasures of my new race," he said, grasping her arm with one hand to keep her next to him. With the other, he lifted the thick choker she wore to hide the nearly healed scars from Corvindale's bites.

"Release me," she said, trying to keep her head. The carriage door was on the other side of Alexander, and it was latched. She'd have to get past him, and get it unhooked in order to jump out—and the carriage was going at a very rapid pace. Her insides heaved unpleasantly as a chill blanketed her. "My brother will have your heart on a stake if you harm me. If Corvindale doesn't get to you first, which I assure you, he—"

"Ah, yes. I've heard about your attachment to Corvindale." His smile had been relatively benign, but now it hardened. "I presume that is how you obtained these marks."

Before she could react, he turned, his weight shoving her into the corner of the seat as he lunged onto her. Maia drew in a breath to scream, but he clapped a hand over her mouth and plunged his fangs into her shoulder.

She jerked at the pain, arching up, clawing with gloved fingers and fighting at him, trying to twist away from his smothering hand. She felt the release of blood from her veins, the feel of his lips over her skin, the heavy, hard weight of his body pressing her down, down into the dark corner of the carriage as the wheels rumbled beneath them.

He groaned, his chest heaving against her as he gulped the blood from her flesh, his hand tight, pressed roughly into her mouth and cheeks. One of her arms was trapped between them and the back of the seat, but the other one she whipped free, flailing desperately at him, pulling at his hair, scratching ineffectively at his arm.

Alexander pulled away after she managed a particularly loud cuff against the side of his head, over his ear. Eyes blazing red, blood gathering at the corners of his mouth and staining his teeth, he shifted, releasing her mouth and grabbing both of her arms. He captured her wrists with one strong hand, forcing them down between them, where his weight held her arms captive between their torsos.

"Alexander," she gasped, trying, hoping that she might somehow penetrate whatever frenzy had seized his mind, "Corvindale and Chas will kill you. Let me go."

"I can't do that, my dear Maia," he said, his tongue swiping around the corners of his mouth to get the last bit of blood. "I have my orders. But there isn't any reason why I cannot sample you. I never expected it to be this pleasurable." He bent again, and she tensed, expecting him to shove his fangs into her once more, but this time, he covered her mouth roughly with his.

Tainted with blood, he tasted like copper, and something dark and ugly. He was hard and brutal, his fangs scraping against her mouth and cutting her lips as his tongue thrust and stroked. She twisted and fought more, tears of frustration and fear leaking from the corners of her eyes.

Corvindale. Chas. Hurry.

She felt the warmth draining from her body from the wound on her shoulder as he moved to the side of her neck, then the slice of pain as he drove his fangs in once more. They weren't going to get to her in time. He was going to drain her. Kill her.

Maia closed her eyes, trying to focus, trying to push away the horror blinding her. In the background of her fear, she heard the drumming of rain on the roof and the vibration of the vehicle as it rolled along. She must remove herself from this moment of terror and think. *Think.* Was there something she could do to stop him? He hadn't begun to tear her clothes away, but she felt the hard bulge that indicated his arousal, and she suspected with a deep, terrible fear, that he soon would move on to other violations.

But the heat and life flowed from her, along with her consciousness, and she found herself floating somewhere in a plane of fear and pain, hands rough on her, the incessant rumbling of the carriage beneath her.

And then it stopped.

He pulled away and sat back, looking at her. A drop of blood colored the corner of his mouth and his eyes, glazed with desire, burned down at her. "Alas," he said, "we've arrived."

Maia tried to pull herself up, but the interior spun and she fell back weakly onto the seat. Blood trickled down her shoulder and neck, over her upper chest and seeped into the neckline of her dress.

She heard a click and the carriage door opened. The rush of cool, damp air did a bit to revive her, but when she saw Mrs. Throckmullins standing there, Maia felt a rush of fear.

"Hello there again, my dear Miss Woodmore," she said, rain drumming frantically on her umbrella. "I see that you've taken a bit of a sample of our friend here, darling Alexander. But what a mess you've made of it. Fool." Her voice hardened. "She cannot bleed to death."

With a sharp movement, Lerina flung the umbrella to someone behind her, and Maia caught a glimpse of a brick wall looming beyond in the low light. Then all other thoughts fled as the woman surged into the small space and pulled the door closed behind her.

"Now let's see to this," she said, settling on the seat across from her and Alexander. "Hold her," she said as Maia began to struggle, trying to slip up and out of the small vehicle.

Alexander grabbed her shoulders and then her wrists, holding Maia still as Lerina moved closer. "She smells delightful," the other woman said, sniffing delicately.

"I thought as much the first time we met." She traced a finger down into the blood still oozing freely from the bites on her neck, then brought it to her lips. With a vigorous swipe, she tasted the red drop and smiled.

"Now, now, you needn't fear, Miss Woodmore," she told her, seeing Maia's eyes grow wide. She grasped her chin, holding it with strong, sharp fingers. "It won't hurt a bit, and then I'll see to stopping the bleeding. We don't want you to die until Dimitri gets here. Just close your eyes now and enjoy."

Maia would have screamed, but the woman slapped a flat hand over her mouth. "I don't need your cries ringing in my ears," she said angrily. "It ruins the experience."

Maia couldn't move, for Alexander's weight and hands kept her body in place and her arms pinned between them while Lerina held her head immobile. The woman bared her fangs, a dark glint in her eyes, and drove her sharp teeth into the top of Maia's shoulder.

Maia's vision fluttered dark and light, her stomach pitched and rolled as she gagged behind the fingers clamped over her mouth. The rhythmic tug and suction from the woman's lips echoed through her body, dragging up from deep inside. A little flutter of unwanted pleasure uncurled in the pit of her belly, just a quiet tingle within the dark world of fear and pain and Maia felt tears rolling from her eyes again.

After a long moment, it was over. Lerina pulled away, her lips full, her eyes bright red. She made a soft humming sound of pleasure, bloodscent filtering from her heavy breaths. Maia kept her eyes closed, focusing on the fact that they weren't going to kill her. At least until Corvindale arrived.

A trap for him. Of course it was a trap, but he was smart. And strong and powerful. Too smart to be tricked, especially again. And he had Mr. Cale and Chas and even Dewhurst and Iliana to help him. Surely he wouldn't be hurt. Surely—

Lerina leaned forward again, and Maia tensed, feeling the tightening grip of Alexander's hands on her shoulders. She twisted, but she was powerless, and this time, instead of biting her, Lerina swiped her tongue out. Worse than having the fangs penetrating her flesh was the feel of the woman licking her shoulder, licking and gently sucking away the last bit of blood from the fresh wounds.

Maia trembled low and deep as they held her down, both of them now lapping at the marks on her neck and shoulders, one on each side. Her skin crawled beneath the sleek whorls of tongue and lips and she tried to faint, tried to fall into some black unconsciousness so she didn't have to feel the sensations on her sensitive skin.

She didn't have long to wait. Mercifully, weakness overcame her, and darkness flooded her vision. Maia slipped into it gladly.

Dimitri stared down at the note. His body had gone cold and then numb, then his mind shattered into terrified pieces. Now it was working its way into blazing fury.

He couldn't allow terror into his mind, so he focused on the fury.

I have something you desire.

That was all the missive said, but he needed no other information. Lerina's scent, along with that of Maia's *blood* permeated the paper.

Dimitri stopped his thoughts as soon as he smelled it. *No.* Going down that avenue would turn him mad. Focus on the facts, on what he knew.

Maia had left early that afternoon, many hours ago, to call on Bradington. She'd taken a hack instead of one of his carriages, a fact which he didn't learn until supper when Angelica pounded on his study door to inform him that her sister hadn't returned.

Even then, he hadn't allowed himself to be too concerned, instead torturing himself with the image of two lovers reuniting and forgetting the passage of time.

But now…

He forced his mind to remain calm and empty. To go through a list of steps with logic and objectivity. Obviously Lerina wanted him to come. Obviously she had something planned.

Obviously Maia wouldn't be killed, at least until he got there. He hoped. Lerina wasn't Cezar Moldavi.

He'd need assistance, someone to have his back. He wasn't that foolish. Giordan. Chas was still in Scotland, blast. Iliana. Even Voss. Eddersley. Gehrington. Perhaps Eustacia, the woman who sometimes practiced fighting with Iliana, if she was back from Rome.

Not that he would wait for any of them to arrive. But at least they'd be coming behind him.

Thus Dimitri kept his thoughts cold and steady as he barked orders to Crewston to send messages to Rubey's, to the back rooms at White's and to Dewhurst. He called for Tren and Iliana, giving Hunburgh direction on how to secure the house and whom to contact in the event the worst happened.

He wouldn't think on that.

Where would they be? She'd given no direction, no indication…they had to be at the same place they'd escaped before. Or, at least, he had to start there and track them if necessary. He wished he had his dogs, but he never brought them to Town.

These thoughts, these cold, steely thoughts, kept him calm as he removed his waistcoat and changed into clothing meant more for a tradesman than an earl. Loose trousers with pockets and a shirt, sturdy shoes. And a coat with more pockets, where he put stakes. He picked up his saber that masqueraded as a walking stick and walked out of the house as prepared as he could be.

He disdained the carriage that was waiting, for a saddled horse was much faster, and Tren, quick as he was, had prepared both. The carriage would follow once the others arrived.

If they did.

Dimitri galloped through the streets, grateful for the full moon that lit the world nearly as brightly as the sun. It was well into the night, and dawn would be only hours away.

When he got near the abandoned, shrouded house near the fishermen's wharf where he and Maia had been imprisoned, Dimitri slid from the horse before he even stopped. He landed on the ground and gathered up the reins, looking for somewhere to tie the beast, or some urchin to pay to watch him. The house was several blocks away, and he wanted to approach it as secretly as possible.

Despite the fact that it was long past midnight, the docks were by no means deserted. Fishermen and sailors walked, talked, fought, loaded and unloaded. The air was filled with noises of altercation and jollity. The smells of fish and seawater mingled with something burning nearby and the ever-present odor of garbage.

Still calm, icily so, he looked around. And then he saw them.

Lerina stood in the center, in the narrow street. She was flanked by two men—likely vampire makes—and she watched Dimitri as he approached. Her eyes glowed faintly and she stood regally, as if she were a queen and he a subject approaching for obeisance.

"Where is she?" Dimitri demanded, his control slipping when he scented Maia on Lerina…and on the man standing next to her. Bradington. Whose eyes glowed mockingly.

Alarm rising inside him, Dimitri fought it back. So that was how Lerina had managed to get to Maia. He allowed his eyes to glow just a bit, to show the very tip of a fang. They were no match for him in strength or speed, and Lerina must know it. Even she, without the use of rubies, was no threat to him. And he sensed no rubies on her or her companions.

That fact filled him with unease.

"I wasn't certain you would still want her. Now that we've finished with the little chit," she replied. "Although I can see now why you've enjoyed her. She's a tasty piece." A lift in the breeze brought a stronger waft of fish accompanied by the smell of flame and burning wood.

"Where is she?"

"I wasn't certain about your feelings for her the first time," Lerina was saying conversationally. "After all, you were under duress. But you did feed from her—your control and abstinence are legendary, you know, and it was a shock to find that something had caused you to give it up. And then there was the way you looked at her... Well, I had my suspicions. So of course I had to see for myself. It was rather amusing the way she came to your assistance, that night at—"

Dimitri moved sharply and had Lerina in his hands, a stake poised over her generous bosom before she could finish. "Where is Maia?"

Her eyes widened in blatant admiration and she arched a bit toward him, her hips bumping his. "Luce's cock, you can still set my heart fluttering, Dimitri. All that power and rage rumbling beneath." She shrugged in his arms, her breasts pressing beneath them as she tipped her head back as if to give him a better target. "Go ahead, do what you will. But if you kill me, you won't know where to find Miss Woodmore. And time is running thin."

Frustrated, fighting rising alarm, he released her, trying to keep his thoughts from scattering into wildness. "Tell me where she is." He glanced at Bradington, who'd taken a step back and looked a bit less confident than he had a moment ago.

"Ah, feel free, Dimitri. I'd love to watch you, and he was merely a tool to get to...here. Right here, right where I wanted you."

"And so I'm here." He glanced behind her when another blast of smoke reached his nostrils and noticed a low glow in the distance. All at once, his senses went dead. The house, the very house in which they'd been imprisoned, was in flames.

"Yes, Dimitri. She's in there," Lerina said.

But he was already pushing past her, flying toward the house. His heart in his throat, he tore through the night, knowing there had to be some sort of trick…some sort of surprise waiting for him.

She could be dead. She could be *made*. She might not even be in there, it might be some sort of ruse… Even Cezar could be waiting inside.

Tongues of flame snarled through the windows, smoke poured from the roof. The house was wholly ablaze. If she was inside, how could she be alive?

For a moment, Dimitri was propelled back in time to the Great Fire, and he slowed for a moment. A mere moment, and then he went on, as strong and fast as before.

For this was different. This was Maia, this was *now*, and he was a Dracule. Fire didn't harm him; it merely lashed around in a reminder of what hell would be like. Hot, searing, but without actually eating into him. If he could find Maia, he would be fast enough to pull her out, to cover her and streak safely through the flames with her.

If he could find her. If she was still alive.

His mind was three steps ahead of his feet, and he tore off his shirt, plunging it into a rain barrel. Wet and damp, it would help to protect Maia if—*when*—he found her and brought her out.

This time, as he approached the building, he didn't have to find an opening that wasn't burning. He crashed through a flaming door and found himself in a dark, hot place, filled with smoke that blinded him though he could normally see through the dark.

"Maia!" he bellowed, inhaling a lungful of the hot smoke and ash as he tore through the lower level, looking for a place that wasn't aflame. He tried to smell her, to find her scent amid the soot and burning wood, and he caught it at last as he came to the stairs.

She was here. She was here.

Or she *had* been here.

"Maia!" he shouted again, ducking as a flaming beam tumbled from the ceiling. The entire place was in shambles, the sheets that had covered furnishings gone up in flames. Fire snarled through spots in the walls, and the roar like a powerful windstorm filled his ears.

He called her name over and over as he dashed up crumbling stairs, down the hall to where they'd been imprisoned—he could tell by scent more than sight— and back. There was no one there.

Tears stung his eyes, and they burned with the grit from hot ash and the heat. He used the dripping shirt to wipe it away. She had to be here. She must—

And then he heard something. Faintly.

"Maia!" he shouted, stumbling over a half wall as he turned toward the sound. He wasn't certain where he was any longer in this building, he just listened, smelled, and then...

No.

He realized the trap before he even got there, for the weakness took hold.

He found her, coming into the very deepest part of the house, and stumbled into the chamber.

There she was, sitting in the center of the room with

flames licking the edges, smoke swirling above. Maia was slumped in the chair to which she was tied.

Bound by ropes and ropes of rubies.

(20)

HELL

A great roar started deep inside and Dimitri fought it
back. He would do it. He had to do it.

Dimitri started toward her, panting, sweaty and hot,
but his limbs wouldn't work. They weakened, slogging
him to a slow halt as if he were fighting to run upstream
a violent river. He released the shirt clutched in his fingers and grasped at the ground, trying to pull himself
along using his fingers between old rotting floorboards.
But they were weak. He was weak. His lungs tight, his
limbs like lead.

Maia. Please.

He couldn't get to her. *He couldn't get to her.*

"Maia," he managed to groan. Was she even alive?

He could see little in the dark room, but when she
shifted, lifting her head, hope rose in him. She was
alive.

"Maia," he called again, coughing a bit and when
she tried to respond, nothing came from her mouth but

a choking cough. "I'm here," he said. "I'm coming for you."

The flames roared closer, and a large beam tumbled from the ceiling, clattering to the floor next to him. It appeared that the fire had started from the perimeter of the building and was working its way in and up, crawling along the walls and across the roof. He knew Maia couldn't last much longer with the thick, clogging smoke. While he...he could stay forever in this hell on earth.

Dimitri took another step and his knees wavered, then gave out. He tumbled to the floor and felt a wave of paralysis roll through him, constricting his lungs, leadening his muscles. *No.* He'd fight through it.

He had to get to her. He couldn't—

There was a movement behind him, and he twisted his head to look up and behind. Lerina stood there, as unaffected by the fire as he was.

"I see you've found her," she said over the roar.

Rage sliced through him and he tried to lunge to his feet, but the rubies did their work and made him clumsy and slow.

"Why," he managed to gasp, curling his slow, fat fingers into the hem of her gown and dragging her down as he tried to pull himself up. But the rubies...they weighted him down.

Lerina pulled away and he tumbled to the floor, his hand landing on a piece of loose wood. "Because," she said, pitching her voice to be heard over the roar in his ears, "I wanted you to watch her die. I wanted you to see what it's like to lose what you love. And to live with that image for eternity."

He closed his fingers around the wood, feeling its slender length, and felt the rage surge through him. Gathering up all of his strength, what little remained, he launched himself toward her ankles and captured them in the crook of his arm. He'd pull her down to the ground and use his weight to hold her until he could slam the thing into her black heart.

"You've…spent…" he gasped, trying again to get his muscles to cooperate, to upset her balance, "too…long… with…Cezar." His grip was weakening as she fought to free herself, the desperation evident in her flailing movements and wild kicking. He was never going to let her go. She would die along with Maia. Even slow as he was, she was no match for him.

But then a noise, a great crash behind him, had his rage disintegrating into blind fear. His grip lessened and Lerina pulled away as Dimitri turned back around with a weak lurch. A large flaming chunk of building had fallen between Maia and him, bouncing to the side. The fire leaped and danced, and he couldn't see past it.

"Maia!" he shouted, forgetting Lerina, dragging himself closer to the blazing piece of wood and to the side. "Maia!" he cried again, desperate to hear her respond.

But he knew the closer he got to his goal, the weaker he'd become. Her hands were bound and she had no way to loosen herself from the rubies. There were too many of them.

It was an impossible task. Impossible.

Impossible for a vampire whose Asthenia was rubies.

A labored twisting on the floor to look behind told him that Lerina had gone, perhaps fearful that if he gave up on saving Maia he'd come after her.

He collapsed on the floor, his face and bare torso grinding into the grit even as he used his toes, his fingers, to try to propel himself closer. Just a little closer. The length of a fingernail. The distance of a flea jump. He dragged, writhed, heaved, trying to make himself move.

The power from the gems emanated from Maia more strongly than the flames and smoke, but at last he moved himself to where he could see her again.

"Maia," he gasped.

"Corvindale," she said, then coughed. She seemed to be more awake now, more lucid. She'd regained her strength, only to die?

"I…can't…" he choked out, his throat closing with emotion. "I *can't*." His fingers dug between two wooden planks, but they were so weak that he could barely fit them into the groove. It was too much. Something stung his vision, gritty and bitter.

"I know," she said, somehow mustering the strength to speak over the choking smoke in her lungs. "I know it." Her beautiful face was streaked with black, her hair messy and sagging, her gown filthy and the malevolent rubies shining like dancing red beacons in the roaring flames.

"Maia. God, Maia…I'm…sorry," he groaned, tears stinging his eyes. "I'm sorry."

"I know," she said, holding his gaze somehow through the smoke and darkness. "I love you…Gavril."

I love you. The emotion flashed into his own mind, burning there like some great revelation. Truth.

At the same time as that self-realization, that long-denied truth, a sharp slice arced through him. For a moment he thought something had fallen, landing on his naked back. Or that a stake had stabbed him, piercing his heart. But it wasn't that, it wasn't external. It was something inside, cracking, splitting. Pain blazed through him and his muscles collapsed at last, his face slamming into the dirt. He couldn't lift his finger. Could barely blink. His breath was short and restricted, his mouth filled with dirt and ash.

Dimitri squeezed his eyes closed, the pain overtaking him. With one last breath, he heaved himself up, lifted his face to look at her once more. He had to tell her. He couldn't let her die without knowing the truth.

He couldn't even speak the words, but he *thought* them, sent them to her with his gaze. *I love you. Maia, I love you. I have always loved you.*

The pain snapped and sizzled, centered at his Mark and raging through his flesh, his muscles and organs, and down through his limbs, radiating torture like never before. He cried out in agony, seizing and shuddering, trying to throw it off, to escape.

Never. Never anything like it.

It burned like a thousand fiery whips laying into his skin until he thought he would explode, go mad, scream until his throat was raw. And then, impossibly, he saw Wayren…nodding, with a quiet smile.

Then…nothing.

Black. Darkness.

21

IN WHICH MIRACLES
BECOME CURSES

Dimitri opened his eyes to darkness and a roaring that filled his ears. *Heat. Roiling heat.* His thoughts were confused, sluggish, and as he lifted his head, he remembered.

Pain. But it was gone now.

Maia. Oh, God.

Emptiness and fear stilled him for a moment, then he dragged his eyes back open and looked around. Golden and red flames swirled and danced, heat seared him. His lungs burned, his eyes were raw. Beyond the flames, darkness loomed.

He'd died. He was in hell.

Where is Lucifer?

He'd seen Wayren for that one, odd moment…but nothing of the fallen angel.

Dimitri found that he could move, and he rolled over, his body weak and aching, but mobile. And then he saw her. Maia, impossibly, still there, still in the same place.

On the chair, still bound in rubies, the flickering light illuminating her face.

How could she still be there? How could the fire not have swallowed her up, choked the life from her?

She was watching him with a horrified expression that, as he staggered to his feet, changed into one of bewilderment. And then wonder.

The same shock and strength rushed through Dimitri, even as he coughed and choked, the black smoke swirling around him. The heat raged and he felt it on his skin as if it sat there, branding him.

But he was moving. Toward her. The rubies seemed to have no effect on him any longer.

Yet, Dimitri stumbled, clumsy, coughing and choking so hard that he doubled over, clutching at his middle. *What's happening to me?*

And then, suddenly, he realized *he felt no pain.* No pain. Not even from the Mark of Lucifer.

Just the blazing burn of flames roaring around him. The gritty heat of smoke and soot.

With a sudden burst of clarity, he touched the back of his left shoulder. Although covered with grit and sweat, it was otherwise smooth. Unblemished.

The Mark was gone. The shock stunned him, paralyzing him as he stood there, doubled over, panting. He realized all at once the blessing…and the curse… of his realization.

Wayren. That was why she'd been there.

His covenant with Lucifer had been broken.

He was mortal again.

Mortal.

He kept on, and then he was there, gathering Maia

to him, that sweet, smoky, soft bundle. Tearing at the ropes of rubies, he flung them away and pulled her completely into his arms as the dark smoke choked and enveloped them.

"Maia," he said in a rough, smoky voice, then his breath was cut off by the smothering roil of smoke.

She coughed, sagging against him, and he bore them both to the floor where the smoke wasn't quite as thick, wrapping her close to his body, wishing he still had his damp shirt to put over her face. She was kissing him, kissing his jaw and along his bare throat, and he found her lips, sooty and salty, covering them with a desperate hunger. His face was damp with sweat and tears, relief and warmth. And something good unfurled inside him. It was going to be all right. He had her now.

He was mortal again. Human again. He loved.

Maia. Thank God I found you.

She was saying something, and at first he couldn't understand it. But then he heard it, felt the shape of his name on her lips: "Gavril."

I love you.

He felt, rather than heard her say the words. Her lips formed them against his mouth, and he bowed his head into the floor, trying to escape the smoke. "I love you," he said into her hair. *How could I have been so foolish?*

An ominous cracking brought him back to reality. "We have to…get out of here," he said, then was overtaken by a fit of rough coughing.

When he looked up, he saw the wall of flames in front of them. Everywhere he turned, there was fire, raging and snarling. The smoke rose and filled the room, thinner but no less potent near the floor.

He looked again, twisting his body around on the floor while protecting her from the flames and smoke. A chill began, deep in his belly, and began to roll through his body, leaving him numb.

There was no way out.

The fire burned too tall, too hot, too encompassing. There was no way to get through.

Impossible.

Impossible for a mortal.

Fury and impotence raged through him, replacing the cold fear, and he looked down at her. Their eyes met and he felt the acceptance in her limbs as she relaxed into him, closing her eyes. Resting her smudged cheek on his arm. Preparing to die.

She knew it. She'd probably always known it.

No. There had to be some way.

He looked around again, seeking some break in the flames, some low rise that he could jump over, carrying her. But there was nothing.

Bitterness, oh, such bitterness.

If he weren't holding Maia, Dimitri would have raged and thrown himself into the flames, wild with fury and frustration. He didn't care about dying. He'd been ready for decades. It was Maia…it was all Maia.

He gathered her up, felt her arms curling around him as she shuddered a cough, trying to speak but unable to because of the heavy smoke. Closing his eyes, he huddled around her, positioning his large body to protect her from the falling beams and dancing flames.

Please.

The irony, the horror of the situation—that he'd obtained his deepest desire, that he'd finally freed himself from Lucifer but was now useless to save the woman he loved—brought harsh, stinging tears to his eyes. They fell into her hair, burning his dry eyes, salty as they trickled down his cheeks.

Damn you. Damn you.

Help me. Someone.

He thought of Wayren, her slight, elegant figure appearing in his mind, and her platitudes. Her meaningless platitudes that had come too late: *But that's why men are here. To be bothered. To feel. To live. To love. And…to be loved. That is what makes you different from every other creature. And that is what makes man ultimately more powerful than the Fiend.*

Yes, he'd found love. He'd opened himself to it, just in time to lose it. Her. To lose life. The miracle had turned to a curse, and now she would die.

Maia would die, just as Meg would have.

If he had stayed immortal…kept the covenant…

The chill was back, the horrible knowledge that he had the choice. That he could save her, just as he'd saved Meg. It washed over him, dark and evil, even more potent than the fire raging against his mortal body.

He hadn't known what it meant, before. When Lucifer came to him the first time. But now he knew. He fully knew the hell, the horror, the blackness of what that covenant meant.

He didn't want to live it again. But he could.

Something snapped inside him, something widening into cold, then hot…and then deep, deep calm. An oasis, an island, in the fiery, terrible vortex of the fear and horror that battled within him, and without.

He could do it. He could save Maia.

"I take it back," he shouted into the darkness, his voice rusty and barely audible. Tears streamed from his eyes as he made the decision. "Lucifer! Attend me!"

The flames roared and curled, heat surging in incessant waves. It was getting close. Soon, he wouldn't be able to breathe. It was a miracle they hadn't already been engulfed, for the fire seemed to lick and devour, but its speed had slowed. Something seemed to keep it at bay.

"Lucifer!" he bellowed again.

And then there he was, the Fiend, the devil, there in his mind. "You have the temerity to call me back after breaking our contract?"

"You asked me once if I loved Meg enough to save her," he said…or, more likely, *thought,* for this was a dream just as the other had been. "I didn't know, but now I understand. Once again, I give you *my* soul, but this time, I do *not* give you hers. You have me, but she is untouched. Do it now, you bastard. Do it *now.*"

Luce smiled that warm, tempting smile and his eyes narrowed. "It is always gratifying when the most God-fearing turn to me. I'll have you back, Dimitri. I'll have you back." He stretched out his hand to replace his Mark, and searing pain, a shock of white light, blazed in the darkness. Dimitri caught a glimpse of Wayren and thought, *Too late…*

And then he was falling.

OUR HEROES IN DARKNESS

Maia felt rather than saw the flash of white light from behind closed eyes, and heard a loud crashing splinter. Corvindale's arms were around her, and suddenly they were falling, tumbling into nothing.

They landed on hard, cold ground with hardly a jolt. Coughing, wiping her gritty eyes, Maia struggled out of Corvindale's grip and realized she could breathe.

It took her only a moment to ascertain that they'd fallen through the floor of the burning building, and were now in some sort of cellar. The fire raged above them, and would soon burn through the rest of the floor, but for now they were safe from smoke and flame. It didn't surprise her that a strong stench of refuse was mixed with smoke and burning wood, and she suspected that there was a cesspool close by, for that was the purpose of cellars such as this. But perhaps, pray God, there was also a way out. Even if it were through the waste.

Regardless, they were out of the fire. Miraculously, safely. At least, for now.

Except that Corvindale wasn't moving.

Maia crawled up next to him, tugging at his soot-streaked arm and touching his sweaty, filthy face. The light was dim, but the fire cast a yellow glow from above and when his eyes fluttered and his head moved, she could have cried with relief.

"Corvindale," she said, shaking him urgently. "We have to get out of here."

He groaned and she saw in the dim light that he'd opened his eyes. "Maia," he murmured in a smoke-roughened voice. "I'm sorry."

"Apologies later," she said, wincing as an ominous rumble sounded above. Something fell from the wooden slats that formed their ceiling, landing nearby and making the hole above larger. "We have to find a way out of here. Now."

"Safe," he said, struggling to his feet, his eyes never leaving her. "You're safe. Thank God."

He was too tall to stand upright in the small space, but, crouching, he gathered her up to him, touched a quick, tender kiss to her mouth, and then pulled her against him in a tight embrace. She felt the tremors in his arms and torso and breathed in the scent of his salty, sooty, masculine skin, burying her face in the coarse hairs of his chest.

After a moment, he released her and, still holding her arm, began to look around. But Maia had already noticed the way the tendrils of smoke seemed to be drawn toward a particular corner.

"There," she told him, just as he pointed in the same direction and said, "This way."

His hand steadying her, they picked their way, leaving the small glow of light and stepping into the dark. It was like ink, black everywhere, close and damp and small. Maia didn't like it. Something furry scuttled near her foot, and once, she stepped on something that squished and moved, but she stifled the little shrieks that threatened and soldiered on, clutching Corvindale's arm.

Her thoughts were spinning, filled with so much to comprehend and absorb that she couldn't allow her mind to focus on anything except getting out. When they were safe, she'd sort it all out and be with the man she loved.

Who loved her, too.

That thought she couldn't keep submerged, and a flowering warmth started through her limbs, strengthening her wobbly legs and aching body. She'd get out. Because Corvindale—Dimitri Gavril, the Earl of Corvindale—*loved* her.

At last, there was a shift in the air and the faintest buffet of cooler breeze. They were close. The impossible darkness eased into dark gray shapes that grew more and more defined as they went on.

A little splash told her they'd found water, and at first she was concerned it was one of the sewage channels. But there was no accompanying stench, and as it grew deeper, rising to her ankles, she realized it was a relatively clean stream running from the nearby wharf.

They slogged through water now nearly to her waist, drawn by the light, navigating blindly through the river along uneven rocks, slippery with algae. One of the rocks moved suddenly, scudding against another, and the uneven surface sent them slipping and plunging into the water, which was suddenly up to her shoulders.

Maia knew how to swim, and she didn't regret the

sudden dunking. When she came up, her hair dripping in her face, she felt cooler and cleaner. She ducked back under again, glad to rinse away the remains of blood and smoke, and the sensation of violating lips and fangs. Relief rushed through her when Corvindale emerged, as well, whipping his wet hair back with a sharp toss of his head.

"Are you hurt?" he asked, reaching for her hand as she found a stable rock or brick to stand on. The light was growing stronger by the moment. The sun must be rising above.

"It feels good," she said, her voice still rusty from the smoke. "The water was refreshing."

"That is one thing even I cannot argue with," he replied, and his hands were on her shoulders as he looked down at her. "Maia, I'm sorry. For all of this."

She was now able to see the water dripping from his brows and hair, and the odd set to his face. "What is it? What's wrong?"

She couldn't understand it, didn't understand why he looked so stricken. They'd escaped the fire, they were nearly free, he'd admitted his feelings for her and he certainly knew how she felt about him. Why did he look as if something terrible had occurred?

Beyond that, she was certain that something miraculous had happened there, during the fire. She knew that Voss had become mortal after some horrible incident involving Angelica, and part of her believed—and hoped—the same had just happened to Corvindale.

How else could he have approached her, as she sat wrapped in rubies?

Only moments before he came to her, she'd seen him,

seizing and fighting what must have been unimaginable pain, screaming in tortured agony…and then collapsing on the ground in the midst of the fire. She'd seen a blast of darkness, a shock of light, a sort of searing, sizzling explosion as he lay there, unmoving.

She'd thought he was dead.

And then he'd awakened and come to her.

"Maia," he said again, as if he couldn't get enough of saying her name. "I love you. But I can't…" He cut himself off, pulling her against his warm, wet body and covering her mouth with his. She met him eagerly, tasting cool, fresh water and feeling it dripping between them, seeping through their clothing as his heat flowed into her. Her hands planted on the sleek planes of his chest, sliding through the dark hair and over the tops of his shoulders.

His lips were soft and needy, fitting to hers, nibbling and caressing with tenderness and an underlying desperation. The arrogance and confidence from previous kisses was gone…this felt like the apology he'd been trying to make. And a severing, a farewell.

It wasn't him. This wasn't the earl who took what he wanted on his own terms. Who begrudged every bit of softness.

"Corvindale," she said, pulling away to look up at him. "Gavril. What is it?"

His face was damp, his eyes hooded. "Something happened in there, Maia. Something…terrible." He glanced toward the light, which had become even stronger.

She could see the faint outline of a stone jutting out, and realized that the tunnel and the river turned just ahead, and that there was safety. Escape. And it was daylight. There would be no vampires waiting for them. She could find covering for Gavril…if she needed to.

He drew her to the edge of the underground stream where the water was only just to her knees and settled her on a stable rock. He stood next to her, water trailing in rivulets down his face, plopping steadily to the ground.

"I couldn't get to you. She—Lerina—knew that, she knew I couldn't, once I got through the fire. That's something perhaps even you don't know, Maia, my love," he said, the hint of an affectionate smile curving his lips. But only for a moment, then it was gone and the harsh, stone-faced earl was back. "The Dracule are impervious to fire. So she knew I could find you… and then she knew I could do nothing when I came upon the rubies. She meant for me to watch you die. She knew it, even before I admitted it to myself, that I love you."

"But you came to me," she said, reaching to touch his cheek, certain. She remembered the calm presence that had wrapped itself around her during that entire event, once she awakened in the chair to see him struggling toward her. *All will be well,* had said a voice in her mind. The force seemed to swirl around the chamber, whisking in the air to keep the fire at bay, and the smoke from becoming too thick. It had been pale and golden and peaceful.

"You got past the rubies," she said. "Something happened…I saw it. There was a flash of light, like an explosion, or a shock of lightning."

A grimace tightened his face and he closed his eyes

briefly. When he opened them again, she saw that they were flat and dark. Empty. "I broke the covenant. I separated myself from Lucifer and became mortal."

Joy rushed through her...then stopped. Why was he still stricken, upset? "Is that not what you've wanted? Is there something else?"

What if, by leaving Lucifer's covenant, he had to do something else? Like...die? What if there was some sort of punishment?

"Yes, that's what I wanted. Until I realized that I couldn't...I couldn't save you. I'd saved my soul, but I couldn't save *you*. We were trapped in there, and the only way I could get you out was to become immortal again. To bind myself to him again."

Maia's breath stopped and her heart thudded. "You..." She couldn't form the words, she could hardly comprehend it. "You went back to him...to save *me?*" Horror and shock had her clutching his shoulders, her fingers digging into the muscles there as she stared up at him, disbelieving. "No, no, you wouldn't have done that.... You *couldn't* have done that. You know what it meant."

His face had become stone, his countenance devoid of emotion. "Maia. I had to. I couldn't let you die."

"We all die, Corvindale. We *all die*. How could you give up your *soul* for...me?"

He shrugged, his broad shoulders moving beneath her hands, his face placid. But his eyes were now well-illuminated by the sun streaming from around the bend in the tunnel, and she saw how they burned with emotion. "When one finds real love, one does anything to protect it."

She was shaking her head, tears filling her eyes. The last bit of relief and joy had sagged away, now a heavy burden settled over her shoulders.

"And so," he said, his voice flat and earlish once again, "I won't be going out there with you." He gestured toward the light.

"Corvindale," she began, but he held up a hand to stop her.

"Please," he said. "For once, please don't argue with me, Maia."

She nodded and then pulled him down for another kiss. Her fingers slid over his chest, up along the strong cords of his neck as he pushed her against the damp stone wall with his body. That sharp flutter of pleasure started in her belly and spread down, flushing out, but was tempered by sorrow.

Her fingers dug into his wet hair, sliding up along his neck and shoulders…and then she stopped. Pulled away, her heart pounding.

"Turn around," she said, pushing at him. "Turn around, Corvindale."

He frowned, his face darkening, but then it eased as he turned, one of his hands going up to touch the back of his shoulder.

"It's gone," she said, smoothing her hand over his back. "The marking is gone."

"Impossible," he said, his face stunned. "It can't be. I gave myself…I called him back to me. He raised his hand to touch me—" Then he halted. "She stopped him." He was looking into the distance, his eyes focused on something Maia couldn't see. His breathing changed, roughened and hurried. "She wasn't too late," he whispered. "She stopped him."

And then, for the first time Maia could ever remember, the Earl of Corvindale *smiled*.

LENNING'S TANNERY EXPANDS

Nearly a month later...

"I simply don't understand how you can be so calm about it all," Maia said, planting her hands on her hips. She was looking up at Corvindale, who'd become Gavril to her in both mind and heart. "They're cutting holes in your house. *Big* holes."

"Yes, indeed, they are, Miss Woodmore," he replied. But now, when he called her by her formal name, there was a layer of intimacy, of verbal caressing over the syllables. "Blackmont Hall is so dark and dim, most particularly my study, that I want more windows. Larger ones."

"But there is dust everywhere. And flies are coming in. And the noise!"

"I suppose we could have waited to have it done while we were on our honeymoon," said the Earl of Corvindale, looking down at the future Lady Corvindale, "but I have lived in darkness for so long, I didn't want to wait any longer. And God knows when your brother will return from Scotland to attend the festivities."

Maia's heart shifted as it always did when she realized just what he'd been through, and what he'd given for her. "Of course," she said, blinking sharply at a sudden sting of tears. "How foolish of me to complain." What man could give more for the woman he loved?

She smiled and returned to the stack of books she'd been sifting through in hopes of organizing his bookshelves now that the room was being renovated. Perhaps her propensity for easy tears and sensitivity to dust and noise had to do with the fact that she'd just missed her monthly flux. And like everything else in her life, it was normally ordered and regular.

"Wait a moment," Gavril said, curving his strong fingers around her arm and turning her back to face him. "Is there something wrong, Miss Woodmore?"

She looked back at him in surprise. "No, indeed. I couldn't be happier. Truly."

A little quirk touched the corners of his beautiful lips. "But you aren't arguing with me. You've agreed with me. Are you quite certain nothing is wrong?"

Maia laughed. She pulled her arm away and patted him on the cheek. "I'm certain nothing is wrong." She wasn't going to tell him until she was certain. "But if you prefer that I argue with you, perhaps I ought to take you to task on this disaster." She gestured to the pile of books that reached from her hip to her shoulder. "Did you realize you have five copies of the same volume of Shakespeare's tragedies, but none of his comedies?"

He frowned and ran his elegant fingers over one of the spines. "But that was purposeful, my dear. I was in no mood to read the likes of *Two Gentlemen from Verona* or *As You Like It* for the last century."

"So instead you buried yourself with *Hamlet* and *Macbeth*." She gave a little sniff, but a smile lingered around her mouth. Then, suddenly, she found her eyes getting a bit damp again. "It's fortunate you weren't following in the footsteps of poor, tragic *Romeo and Juliet*," she said, looking at the dog-eared pages of that play.

"There never were two more foolish lovers," he said arrogantly. "If they'd merely used a bit of sense, both of them would have been alive."

"You weren't so different, you know," she said. "Selling your soul back again to the devil. Then where would we have been? You shackled to him after trying to rid yourself for over a century."

He shrugged, his face settling into that flat, stubborn expression. "I did what I had to do to save you, Maia. I'd do it again, even if it hadn't worked out as well as it has. And it has all worked out quite well, has it not?"

"I'm not quite clear on how it did, precisely, work out," she said, the dratted tears hovering in the corners of her eyes again. He really was the most amazing, loving man.

But how had it happened? Was it because he'd known the hell and torture he was taking on again when he made the sacrifice for her, calling Lucifer back to him? Because he knew precisely what he was giving up this time? That had made the sacrifice all the more meaningful…giving up what he'd wanted more than anything in the world to take the burden back again. That must have been how Wayren had been able to stop him from making the covenant a second time.

She couldn't know for certain, but it made sense, in its own strange way.

And Lerina was dead, thanks to Lord Eddersley, who'd taken it upon himself to skewer the horrible woman when he arrived on the scene. Alexander Bradington had scuttled off into the night like the snake he was—athough Maia hadn't said that aloud, for surely Gavril would remind her that snakes didn't scuttle. They slithered.

Nevertheless, he'd assured her that Alexander was long gone to the Continent, and probably beyond, where he was safe from Chas's vengeful stake (at least for the time being) and Gavril's own fury.

"Are you truly free of Lucifer, even though you called him to you and offered yourself?" she asked, blinking hard.

Gavril nodded and took the book from her hand. "I am. I'm free and mortal and my soul is my own again. Thanks to you, my dear Miss Woodmore. For nagging me into loving you."

She looked at him archly, heaving up the heavy stack of books. "I didn't nag you into loving me. You already did. I merely nagged you into admitting it."

He chuckled, a low, deep sound that sent a delicious little tingle deep in her belly. "That might be the case. But," he continued, taking the books firmly from her hands, "I think it's your turn for an admission. That you shouldn't be carrying such a heavy burden." He gestured with the stack of books.

Maia looked up at him, her cheeks warming a bit. "Whatever do you mean, Lord Corvindale?"

"I mean," he said, "that you've got another burden

to carry, and a much more important one, being a future earl."

The blush went full-blown and she smiled. "Well, it's possible," she said. "We have been a bit busy since you sold your soul for me."

The light that came into his face was like nothing she'd ever seen before: a bit of wonder, a bit of surprise, a lot of love and a twinge of chagrin. "I do love you, Miss Woodmore," he said, his voice rough. "And I couldn't be happier that I got my soul back to share it with you. So please don't lift anything heavy for the next nine months, my darling. Promise me that."

"I shall endeavor to do my best," she said, not meaning a word of it. "Particularly since you used the very unearlish word *please*."

Then, as was his way, even now, the softness in his face ebbed a bit. "And now that we have that settled, I find that I am overdue in a trip to my favorite antiquarian bookstore."

Maia knew the one he spoke of, of course. "No more trips to buy Faustian legend, I presume?"

"No indeed," he said, a little bit of a smile twitching his mouth again. "But I find I am missing several volumes of Shakespeare. In fact, I'm particularly interested in one comedy in particular." His eyes danced.

"And which one is that?" she asked, although she was already laughing, for she knew the answer.

"The Taming of the Shrew."

The little antiquarian bookshop was gone.

Gavril wasn't surprised.

In the place where Wayren's narrow little establishment had once been was a window that showed nothing but the interior of the tannery.

After a moment of wry contemplation, and peering into the dusty window to see the tanner stropping a piece of leather, Gavril turned away. Instead of climbing back into his carriage, ducking under the fanlike awning, he walked down the street in the sun.

Smiling.

★ ★ ★ ★ ★

ACKNOWLEDGMENTS

The process of writing, publishing, promoting and distributing a book is always one that involves a multitude of people—and when the book is one of a trilogy with overlapping scenes and characters, it's that much more difficult and intense.

Because of this, I'm especially grateful to Emily Ohanjanians, as well as the entire team at MIRA Books, for their dedication and support for the Regency Draculia books. I only hope you're as proud of them as I am!

Thanks, too, to Holli and Tammy for reading the early versions of *Dimitri* and for their thoughtful feedback. And also to Erin, Danita and Jen for being beta readers on this second-in-a-series book.

I owe my firefighter brother Sean a big round of thanks for his information about fires, fighting them and what it's like to be engulfed in flames.

Thanks to my mom for her support, always, and for her early reads of this and all of my books. Even if no one else likes it, I know I can always count on you!

I'd also like to thank all of my Italian fans for their

enthusiasm and support—especially those whom I met in Ravenna and Venice. I hope to return to your beautiful country someday!

And finally, much love and affection to my husband and children, who consistently allow me to get a little frazzled near the end of a book, and who are always willing to eat carryout or pizza—and who still love me anyway! I love you all!